The Highwayman's Folly

DARIA VERNON

BOOK ONE of *THE REWARDS OF RUIN*

The Highwayman's Folly: Book One of The Rewards of Ruin
Copyright © 2020 by Daria Vernon

Print ISBN: 978-1-7359814-0-6
Digital ISBN: 978-1-7359814-2-0

www.dariavernon.com

This book is dedicated to a girl that spent many days playing make believe in the backyard.

I owe you this.

1

Beth Clarke scrubbed the frostiness away from a windowpane with the side of her fist and looked out. There it was. Happiness, frosted over.

A whole childhood's worth of bright summer memories stretched out across the lawns of Ashecote House. There was the stream that soaked every petticoat Beth owned—at least once. There were the slate steppingstones that scraped each of her knees—at least twice. And there was Aunt Dahlia leaping from the hedgerows to startle her when she was not yet as tall as her pony's shoulder, scaring the fear right out of her from the start.

Aunt Dahlia.

Beth had lost her mother too young to feel motherless, but now, the notion held a sudden pang of familiarity and the emptiness of the bed behind her was keenly felt.

In lieu of a mother, it was Dahlia who had educated her on

womanhood. She'd provided such a spirited model of it that her father might not have endured it had it not been delivered by his own dear sister.

Tree climbing, pond swimming, and sword fights with the statuary were all encouraged. At the end of those summer days, Beth and her aunt would trudge back to the house so that Uncle James could deliver a half-hearted chiding about the state of their clothing before they changed for dinner.

Most antics fetched barely a raised eyebrow from Beth's father, Barnaby. The only time he'd attempted to draw the line, it was in regard to riding. Dahlia had told him: *The best way to protect Beth from an accident like the one that befell her mother is to give her an excellent seat on a horse.* The argument must have been compelling because Beth started learning to ride at her earliest memory. By her last teenaged summer at Ashecote, she was the most skilled equestrian in the family.

Now those memories were covered in snow—not the sort of snow that leaves the expanse looking downy and festive, but the sort that freezes hard to the dead grass and soon makes mud. In nearly three decades of visits to Ashecote House, she'd never once seen a January there. Looking outside now, she could understand why her father had avoided it.

A sigh made the glass fog up again, and Beth remembered the embroidery hoop in her hand. A needle still dangled from the fabric on rosy floss, leaving a beautiful amaryllis a few petals shy of a bloom. She held it up to the gray light of the window and examined it.

She had enough skill to serviceably finish the piece where her Aunt Dahlia had left off, but did she have any desire? She looked back up as if she could still see through the glass, as if she could see everything as it once was, green and blooming. The girl she was back then would have left embroidery in the sewing basket. The girl she was back then would have sifted through her aunt and uncle's library for tomes that had maps of faraway places. The girl she was back then might have batted her eyelashes at a stable boy.

Now she looked at the embroidery hoop and felt it calling her dutifully. She was thirty years of age and had not been that girl for more than a decade. She turned around to face her aunt's empty bed. She was this girl now. This *woman*. Now and for the rest of her life.

She wrapped the fabric reverently around the hoop and placed it into a trunk atop the last of Dahlia's things. Her eyes skimmed the room for any other items of importance.

She caught a glimpse of herself in the dressing table's mirror and paused. How glum she looked, how tired. Her pallid face and the white stock at her neck struck a puritan contrast against the dark navy of her traveling habit. She tucked a strand of brown hair behind her ear and tried to smile for the benefit of the reflection but could not.

Most of her aunt's things had been loaded onto a cart the day before and sent ahead, but Beth had first rescued one of her aunt's cloaks from a chest. It was a black woolen thing, long and hooded, and quite out of fashion. Dahlia had worn it in mourning for her husband, and now Beth would wear it in mourning for her.

She was adjusting it on her shoulders when its massive heft suddenly lightened. Knuckles, cool and clammy, brushed against the back of Beth's neck.

"Desmarais." Beth pulled away sharply, putting space between herself and Dahlia's rangy land steward. "I'm almost ready."

"You look . . ."

Beth pulled the front edges of the cloak together before his hollow eyes had time to peruse her body.

"... just like an angel in her clothing. She would have approved."

Beth sidestepped the knobby hand that seemed to be moving fast toward a caress of her cheek. "I'm almost done here," she said. "I'll join you outside momentarily."

Desmarais' hand opened up and a pendant dropped between his pale fingers, caught by a black ribbon. "Don't forget this. She wished for you to have it."

I know. Beth suppressed a frown as she reached for the familiar necklace. Dahlia had promised it to her explicitly. The enamel pendant depicted Ashecote House in a ring of flowers. Dahlia had worn it daily, even in the sick bed. Noticing it missing during funeral preparations, Beth had immediately suspected Desmarais.

The soft velvet ribbon pooled in her hand. "Thank you," she said curtly, snapping her fingers shut around it.

Beth closed the lid of the large trunk beside her. "Tell them that this one is ready to be loaded onto the boot."

"Of course, and I assure you that this, and everything we sent ahead this week, will make it safely to Greenthorne." He moved to take her hand, but she didn't allow it. He continued with his slithering, servile tone just the same. "It is my duty, after all, to take care of the whole affair. Her things will arrive safely, and so will you, my dear."

"Of course. Thank you."

"Which is why I shall accompany you."

Beth's blood seemed suddenly taken by the winter frost. "You'll what?"

"I'll come along, of course. There's much to discuss with your father and his solicitor regarding the will and the estate. With the Halliwells having had no children, it's all very complicated."

"It isn't, though. It's already been read. The estate was

bequeathed in fee simple. To me. Ashecote belongs to me now."

Desmarais cocked his head and pushed out his thin lip—a pitying expression that she'd come to know too well.

"Of course, dear—"

"Miss Clarke."

"Yes . . . of course, Miss Clarke. And we want all of that to go smoothly. So don't worry your lovely brow about it, because the men will see that it's all settled back at Greenthorne. We'll deal with the bankers, the deeds, the drafts . . . You won't have to lift a finger."

Trapped in an overnight carriage with an utter worm. And who does he mean by we? She was too mad to think.

"You may leave." Beth folded her hands in front of her like a proper lady of the house and leveled a glare at him that commanded obeisance. At last, he bowed and left her.

To Beth, he was the archetypal snake. He did all the right things so that no one could be angry that he did them with the glitter of ambition in his ghoulish eyes. He'd been expertly picking his way through the estate's ranks for decades. Upon James' death, Desmarais devoured so many responsibilities as to render him utterly indispensable to the widow's household.

Soon his social ladder would be cut down. Beth had been looking forward to signing his termination letter once she was far away, but now that small joy had been taken from her. It was clear from his own, patronizing opinion of the will that he would not accept her as his superior if she tried to dispatch him now.

Desmarais was now some fifty-odd years of age, but anyone might be fooled into thinking him older. Grayness defined him, be it his skin, his eyes, or the stringy queue of hair that trailed down his neck and right into the gray velveteen collar of a frock coat too fine for him.

His disconcerting nearness to her had only intensified the sicker her aunt became. Although Beth recruited many of the servants to look out for her, the snake still seemed an expert at catching her off guard. He'd made her months of caregiving into a nightmare. He insisted so much on chaperoning her outside of the home that she simply stopped going anywhere and kept to the gardens instead. The poor weather had robbed her even of that. Now she was trapped inside a home that seemed more infected by his grayness with each day that passed.

It had been easier for Beth to force Desmarais to the back of her mind when Dahlia still needed her. In Dahlia's final week, the man grew reviled by the sickbed, only stopping in to mutter insipidly into his kerchief about the odor that the bedchamber was taking on. A blessing. It had kept him out of the room when Beth sat down to read aloud the final letter that arrived from her father, who had been informed the end was coming:

Dear Sister,

It distresses me to be so far from you as you ail and as you prepare to leave this world behind. The doctor, as you know, recommended that I myself should not travel so far in the winter. But I take heart that you are receiving my love through the love of my daughter. I am glad to remember you as my vibrant, creative, full-spirited and—sometimes foolish, but mostly clever—sister, who taught me much, and with whom I spent a most blessed childhood. I know I cannot hold your hand, but I am there. I promise, I am there.

All my love,
Your family for eternity,
Barnaby

Beth's tears had dripped onto her aunt's wrist as she squeezed her hand. A hand that, shortly thereafter, ceased to be warm. Dahlia's passing seemed a release from both their sufferings.

Beth could finally escape the heat of Desmarais' breath. She'd grown ever more dismissive of him, imagining that by tonight, her freedom would be complete. Evidently, she'd been wrong.

Beth tied the necklace's ribbon over her neck stock and cast a final look to Dahlia's mirror. Her eyes widened in the reflection as a jolt of memory struck her, and her attention turned to a tiny drawer at the mirror's base. From it, she took the smallest leather notebook, with a little pencil tied to it. Almost forgotten. She opened it and examined a fragmentary passage.

> *The courage of the flower to open*
> *When pummeled down by storm*

Her chilled fingers fumbled the tiny pencil into their grip and wrote:

> *The strength to push the earth up*
> *As the new'st growth is being borne*

Beth fished through her petticoats for the pocket that she'd tied over her shift and thrust the notebook inside for safekeeping.

The frosty window drew her eyes. A stripe of dull gold cut through the obscured landscape. *Sunset.* Though, one might have been forgiven for concluding from the gloominess that it were perpetually night.

The plan was to drive through the night, stop for breakfast and a rest, and then arrive at Greenthorne by evening next—the final step before she would be home. By the time she ran into her father's arms, what would it matter who she'd shared her carriage with?

Beth crossed the threshold into the sharp January air. Her heart was as heavy as the oak door that closed behind her as she bade farewell to what had been a second home. Someday she would see it again, but it would never be the same without Dahlia.

Beth looked up. Mist clung to the house's decorative pinnacles, making the home's once familiar facade as uncertain as its future.

Turning herself toward the waiting berline carriage, everything loomed gray and cold. The melting snow along the stone path had been muddied by the boots of footmen loading things up. Large droplets fell from the trees overhead, and Beth couldn't tell if it was rain or snowmelt. The elegant conveyance seemed cut from a single piece of obsidian. Two black hackney horses were hitched, and two men in dark greatcoats and tricorns sat on the driver's bench. Beth didn't recognize them, and they both stared down at her as she neared. Desmarais stepped ahead, opening the carriage door and pulling out the step for Beth.

Taking her hand, Desmarais acknowledged the men staring at them from above. "This is Tom." The short young man with the reins and whip tipped his hat at her without changing his scowl. "And this is Mr. Shelby, your aunt's solicitor."

Strange. Beth didn't recognize him from the reading of the will. The roughened man looked briefly at Desmarais, then back to Beth before tipping his own hat. Neither said a word.

Something wasn't right. *Why wasn't the solicitor riding inside with them? Where was Dahlia's coachman?* Beth's heart began to pound, but Desmarais had already led her up into the carriage, as if in a trance, and before she could snap out of it, a footman clapped the door shut behind them both.

Desmarais fell heavily into the back-facing seat. Beth perched lightly on the bench across from him and reached for the door. "I believe I forgot something," she uttered breathlessly. But she'd hardly moved before Desmarais rapped on the wall twice, signaling the driver to go. The hard lurch knocked Beth back into her seat.

Desmarais shook his head gently. "You didn't forget anything. And if you did, they can always send it after you."

"It was a book," she said and hoped that the fear in her voice was less evident than the menace in his. "I forgot my book and will be quite bored without it. It would be so easy to get, while we're still right here."

Desmarais simply shook his head again, in a slower, more sinister manner. "It will be far too dark for reading." The sound of the horses' hooves changed as they left the gravel of the drive and hit the muddy lane.

Something terrible, something tight and poisonous was welling inside her . . .

Beth lunged for the latch.

But Desmarais' hand intercepted her wrist like the talons of a hawk, and her eyes followed his other hand to where it reached into his coat. He withdrew a pistol and pointed it at her heart.

She went for the door again anyway, kicking out at him and screaming for help, but her voice was trapped inside the box—her muffled banging and screams carried away on the winter wind.

Desmarais moved fast to pin her to the carriage's cramped floor. She couldn't bear the feeling of him—those awful bones jabbing at her, the strength of his stringy limbs. Her hands flew out at him with claws bared. She caught him straight across his sallow cheek, and it tore like crepe beneath her nails.

He reared back.

Where had he dropped the bloody pistol?

Beth's fingers stretched upward, searching his seat.

Her wrist was perfectly vulnerable when he swooped on it

again. This time, his grip was a shackle. He pulled a long length of fabric from his coat pocket and tied her wrists together in front of her. Within seconds he had wrested her back into a seated position across from him.

There was a long silence as he situated himself in a pistol-drawn position of calm. Beth took the opportunity to regain her own dignity. She used her bound hands, rather gracelessly, to drag the hood of her cape back over her head. Retaking her composure, she demanded, "Why?" Though she was certain she knew.

Desmarais smiled.

"You are soon to be a wealthy woman."

She'd smelled the thirst for such wealth emanating from this man since she was just a little girl. Her nose scrunched as though a foul odor had consumed the space. She'd asked an obvious question, and she'd received an obvious answer.

She turned her attention to gazing out the foggy window. She would not give him the pleasure of her attention. Desmarais reached across her to close the velvet curtain and cut off her view.

"Not to mention your beauty."

Beth tried not to look at him, but heat rose to her cheeks—the shame of not having seen this element coming.

"Big brown eyes, a lovely, if somewhat narrow, figure . . . who is near too old to wed." The hairs on the back of Beth's neck stood on end.

His painful soliloquizing went on.

"I could get the money in the gentlest way possible, through marrying the lady I've been in love with for over ten years."

Beth might have retched. Her face shot up to deliver such a look of fiery disdain that she hoped it might cut through the darkness.

"In love? What do you know about that? You're not going to

convince me to marry you, and you're not going to convince my father when we get there either. What game are you at?"

"I wasn't really thinking *convince* so much as *threaten*. And would it not be a charity? Your father might be quite thrilled to marry you off at this ripened age."

Beth stayed quiet.

"You see, I'm not taking you straight home. I'm going to keep you in a safe location. Tom will watch after you, and Shelby and I will go make an offer to your father. If he wants to see you and your reputation safe, then he'll have to freely give his blessing. He'll cooperate as Ashecote is signed over to you, at which point I will absorb the estate as your husband and protector."

Beth snorted at that and turned away as the delusional man continued.

"Come now, it won't be so bad for you. You adore your aunt's home. We can live out our days in that sanctuary as husband and wife."

Husband and wife. What a disgustingly permanent phrase to hear on his serpent's tongue. Beth tested her wrists against the fabric. The initial rush of alarm that flooded her—that had fed her energies as she'd struck out at him—was now waning. She didn't know what to do. Her heart continued at a sickening pace even as her breath steadied. His words were coiling around her, poisoning her courage with despair.

"Get some rest, my dear. Long road ahead." Desmarais said it in a jolly, clipped tone, clearly pleased with himself.

So this is what he sounds like when he's not busy licking boots. She stared into the gray shadow, where a sliver of teeth flashed against the dark like a crescent moon. His true smile was much less toothy than the ingratiating grin he'd manipulated her family with for years.

The length of the journey stretched out before them. Each passing hour would be an opportunity to plan, an opportunity to run. Beth wouldn't squander any chances.

"Yes. I think I'll try to sleep now." *And dream up ways to cook a hatchet-faced snake.*

The fall of night was complete.

In the total darkness, Beth felt the relief of no longer having to rest her eyes on the twisted face of her kidnapper. It was safest to assume that he remained awake. Every now and again, a sliver of light from the carriage lanterns would slip through the curtains and sparkle off the barrel of his flintlock, still trained on her.

Her feet were freezing. Desmarais had thrown a dark wool blanket over her, but the cold kept creeping in. She clung tightly to the blanket's rough edge with her bound hands, trying to wriggle it upward toward her nose.

Desmarais didn't squirm as she did. He was but a shadow in a much darker shadow.

Beth shivered from her thoughts as much as from the cold. Desmarais couldn't kill her. The outline of his ideal future hinged upon her becoming his—

No, best not to revisit that.

If he ever set his weapon down, she likely wouldn't notice, not in the darkness, and not over the din of their conveyance shuddering down what sounded like a poorly kept road.

What could she do anyway? Jump from a moving carriage? How much do the men up top have invested in her? Surely they're paid, but how handsomely? Would they let her go? Would they fire at her? *What good is she dead?* The last question stuck in the flow of her thoughts like a boulder dropped into a stream. *What good is she . . .* There indeed seemed no way for Desmarais to get what he wanted if she—

Her chest rose, swelling with hope.

But—

Her thoughts returned to the men up top. Surely they weren't willing to be hanged if something went wrong.

There it was. *That* was what her abductors held over her.

If she escaped, she had a story that would put them all in jeopardy. They would prefer her dead then. Desmarais would spin a yarn as fine as a spider's silk. He'd tell the authorities and her father of some terrible disaster on the road. Accidents, highwaymen, illness—there were so many believable falsehoods to choose from when traveling dark roads on winter nights.

And such a winter night it was. She couldn't move for fear of losing the warmest position she'd achieved yet. She couldn't survive out there if she ran. Every avenue of ideas led to a different, more distressing end.

The alternating waves of hope and despair were wearing her thin. Perhaps opportunity would improve with the daylight once she was left at some mysterious location with this Tom fellow. She frowned. The thought of waiting to act sat with her about as well as soured milk.

She took a deep breath. *Patience.* She repeated the reminder over and over. *Patience.*

Her thoughts turned to Dahlia: Days in the garden. Refreshments by the stream. Acting out Greek plays in the library. The awe of looking up to this woman who seemed so unlike any other . . .

Beth's eyelids flickered with exhaustion.

Dahlia who never once abandoned her. Dahlia who embraced

her missteps in a way society never could . . .

Beth closed her eyes.

Dahlia would have found a way to save herself.

Beth could find a way too.

Patience.

Beth's dreams were warm. Lovely. Far away from the present.

But then her beautiful visions were snapped apart like a wishbone—

Her heart surged to alertness before her eyelids even fluttered.

Something was different.

The rumbling vibrations of the carriage that had lulled her to sleep were gone.

Her ears rang in silence.

2

The dull glow of the driver's side lantern lit the gap at the curtain's edge. It was enough light to illuminate Beth's careful breaths as they suspended in the cold air before her.

A wheezing inhale broke the silence. *Desmarais.* Was he awake? Or was this some pathetic sound of slumber?

Something glittered across from her, catching just enough light—

His pistol.

More silence. She didn't know what had stopped the carriage, but the little star of light that gleamed off the firearm was luring her in, tempting her to gamble for an opportunity.

She lowered the blanket from her face. Held her breath. Leaned forward—

Another gentle wheeze.

Asleep.

The blanket fell to her lap, and she reached her arm carefully across the space, keeping her eyes locked on that sterling barrel—

"There are four of us! Do not move!"

She lurched back against the squabs as though struck by a blow and scrambled to rearrange her blanket.

The shouting outside continued. "Do not even try to move!" Hooves beat the road around them chaotically. The cabin shook gently as the driving horses spooked and stirred.

Each of Beth's senses rose to a full, overwhelming alertness. She blinked over and over, as though she could blink the darkness away. Surely Desmarais was awake now.

Another strange voice, much closer than the first, spoke more calmly. "Set your weapons slowly on the edge of the seat and step down." She heard the bench outside squeak with the shuffling of Tom and Mr. Shelby. One of them grumbled a swear.

Perhaps someone at Dahlia's household had suspected something, perhaps—

Might these be rescuers?

Beth didn't dare to move without being certain. Not until the loaded weapon across from her had been dealt with.

She pressed an ear up to the wall. More horses kicked gravel onto the road. There were thuds as men dismounted. Footsteps.

"Kneel here and wait." The voice was coarser than the others. "Harry, check 'em fer coin."

Beth's racing hopes capsized.

Highwaymen.

Beth pulled the blanket all the way up past her lips, which moved silently with prayers she'd not uttered since she was a little girl kneeling at the bedside.

Heavy bootsteps neared. Beth pressed herself deeply against the squabs. The thumbs of her bound hands tightened on the blanket, as though it could shield her from whatever transpired next.

The door to her left swung open with a great clack and—

CRACK

Smoke filled the small space as a shot rang out.

"Curse it all, ya bastard!" The coarse voice outside went shrill with complaints as the spent flintlock fell to the floor.

Beth had barely settled her eyes on Desmarais in the moonlight before an arm reached inside the compartment to brutally drag him out by the ankle. She clung to the shadows, opposite where the door hung ajar on its hinges. Lost in the commotion and protected by the darkness, she escaped notice.

Outside, the man with the ugly voice didn't let up.

"You fish-boned cull!" There was a blunt sound of impact, followed by a brutal expulsion from Desmarais' lungs. "I ought'a show you the pit o' the fine Bristol Newgate for try'na murder me." The scuffing sounds of the kicks were interrupted, between impacts, by Desmarais' gasps and pleas.

"Enough of it, Lionel!"

"He shot at me, Captain! What am I supposed to do?"

"Search him, for one thing. Bring him there with the other two. Tie him up. Harry, see what's on the back of the carriage."

Beth leaned her ear toward the open door to better listen as Desmarais was seemingly dragged to someplace beyond.

She stiffened as the carriage suddenly creaked and moved—as this "Harry" began to fiddle with the straps on her trunk, outside.

"I'm bleedin'," moaned the whining accomplice, from farther off.

"Bleedin' stupid," mumbled the youthful voice of the man unloading the boot.

"The ball barely tore your sleeve." It was the same voice that the sniveler had referred to as Captain. The voice was commanding and calm, yet . . . weary.

There was no more shouting. From the sound of it, most of the men had moved a little ways down the road to conduct their business.

The younger voice mumbled from behind her again. "Can't see a cursed thing." Beth held her breath as light footsteps crossed the closed side of the carriage. One of the lanterns was taken from its hook and the dim light swung wildly, casting orange flickers through the cracks in the curtains as the lad passed by with it. Moments later, the compartment swayed again as the trunk was lugged from the boot and dragged away.

The open door creaked on its hinges, casting light on the opposite bench. How fortunate Beth was to be in the forward-facing seat, where the interloper hadn't spotted her first.

Her mourning attire cloaked her like a bat, and for the moment, she felt safe. Desmarais himself wouldn't give up her position, would he? That would be like giving up the gold. But the thieves would surely search the compartment before absconding.

She kicked off the blanket and tested the fabric that wrapped roughly around her wrists. *Too tight.* Nothing she could do about that now.

Outside, the coarse one was swearing again in his gravely tongue.

Beth twisted herself to kneel on the bench seat and peeked beneath the curtain of the carriage's small back window. There they were. Six figures, some ten yards beyond. Tom, Shelby, and Desmarais all knelt, their hands tied behind them.

See how well you all like it. Beth couldn't suppress the thought as her wrists tensed against her fabric binds. At least *her* hands were bound in front.

Tom was spitting a slew of nasty words, and the coarse one was giving as well as he got. Desmarais sat still while being searched by a lumbering man. Was that the one whose voice she'd heard before? The Captain?

The lad, Harry, was rifling through her luggage on the ground. He appeared grown, yet his voice had a youthful smoothness to it.

Beth's shoulders jumped as another man joined the group, seemingly out of nowhere. A cape falling to his shins gave him the appearance of a mast hung with a black sail. A rather *tall* mast. If not for the blue glow of moonlight at his back, he'd be invisible. The menacing shadow was crowned by the shape of a tricorn, pulled low. Only the flash of his eyes could be seen over his high collar and muffler. Before he even spoke, she knew she was wrong about the other man. *This* was the one they called Captain.

"Hush!"

His words brought on obedient silence, even from Tom. He sauntered up to Desmarais and reached down to pinch the lapel of his frock coat.

"You all seem the sort that I'd expect to see on a crowded stage-coach, not in a fine berline."

Mr. Shelby chimed in. "We're solicitors. Riding on someone else's business."

"Hmm." The stranger didn't sound convinced. "Does your client often trust you to ride around in their fine carriage on danger-ous, lightly traveled roads at night?"

"There's a purse in the bottom of that trunk, if your man keeps digging there."

Beth had never heard such shaky discomfort in Desmarais'

voice. She'd always imagined she might enjoy hearing such a thing, but now it only made her heart beat faster with the fear of her own circumstance.

The captain called out to his man. "Harry?"

"It's just a bunch of ladies' dresses so far," said Harry, with a mix of disdain and amusement as he pulled up one of Beth's gowns.

"The plot thickens." The captain's voice was so strong and clear that Beth could make it out easily, even from behind the scarf bundled around his lower face.

The sight of the man tearing through her things made Beth's nails dig like claws into the wooden trim above the seat. She knew that the discovery of the dresses would stir curiosity. She needed to act soon, if ever she was going to.

She slid, liquid-like, from the bench, her skirt and cloak pooling around her. *Where was that bloody pistol?* She groped about with her bound hands, sifting through the volumes of fabric that nearly filled the small floor. She wondered if it might have been dragged out with Desmarais.

She almost didn't notice when she touched it beneath his bench. Her icy fingertips could hardly register the feel of cold silver.

Gripping it by its muzzle, she raised it overhead.

Anxious shivers ran up her arms. Her heart skipped and thudded as she thought back to her childhood friend, Dyckson, who had teased her for her poor aim of snowballs. She hoped this went better.

Before the shivers could rattle the damn thing from her hands, she flung it as hard as she could through the gaping door.

It clacked and skidded across the gravel at the road's edge.

At first, she thought no one had heard it, yet all had gone quiet outside. She chanced to take a peek. The captain pointed in the direction of the sound. His men looked to the forest's edge.

Desmarais and his men did not look to the woods, but instead, looked surreptitiously to one another.

Beth watched as Shelby wound himself up to strike the lumbering man who guarded him. An elbow to the back of the big man's knees saw him felled like an oak, and all three captives staggered to their feet.

After that, it was chaos. Scattering, grunting, cursing, stumbling—like animals, all of them.

"Stop them!" The captain's order did nothing to curtail the anarchy.

Tom, Shelby, and Desmarais had all beaten different paths into the trees, and a brief confusion as to who should chase whom doomed Captain's men to failure.

It was more disorder than Beth ever could have hoped for. She slithered out of the carriage.

As best she could, with two hands acting as one, she gathered up her skirts and hurried toward the two hackney horses. The icy mist dug its sharp teeth into her ankles, but she had to take her chance and run, as the others had.

Then, in the scant light of the remaining lantern, she saw it— the reason they had stopped. A tree was fallen across the narrow road. A clever trap set by the highwaymen.

She went alongside it, investigating it with her hands. She wondered how quietly she could unhitch a driving horse, or if she could even manage it at all in such low light. She heard the captain call back his men.

Every heartbeat felt like a grain of sand falling through the smallest timeglass. No time to take a horse. She just had to get past the tree and run. But even as she thought it, the fallen tree reached out a branch in the dark to trip her.

She kept a sharp inhale from becoming a shriek as she caught herself, but her tied hands had reached out to the nearest thing for balance—

The horse she fell into reared against its harness, sending her down. The other horse joined its mate in distress, creating a horrible cascade of striking hooves and jangling tug chains.

The timeglass in Beth's chest shattered apart.

Rhys Bowen chewed on his lip and waited for his men to reemerge from the tree line. No other night on the road had gone so truly fuck't as this.

The cry of a horse drew his eyes back to the carriage. *What now?*

An out-of-breath Harry returned to his side. "I'm sorry, Captain. They're gone."

Rhys could hardly peel his thoughts away from the ominous stir of the driving team. It didn't sit well.

"Were they all searched?"

"They were."

"Then it's no matter. We should pack what we've found and leave."

"I agree," huffed Harry.

Rhys put a hand on the lad's shoulder without turning to him.

"What do you make of that?" he asked.

"Of what?"

Rhys squinted, as if trying to shake off a trick of the darkness. *No, it was real.* He was certain he saw a figure struggling between the horses and the felled tree. Shapeless as an inkblot. A cloak, a large one, was draped on a figure that twisted and writhed within it—trying to detangle from something.

"There." Rhys pointed.

Harry sucked in his breath when he saw it. "Is it . . . is that a *lady?*"

Rhys turned Harry by his shoulders and gave him a gentle shove.

"Go see about it."

Rhys lifted his hat just high enough to drag a gloved wrist across the sweat of his brow. Despite the cold, the excitement of this mess had made the insides of his greatcoat feel downright Mediterranean.

He fiddled with his cuffs, trying to ignore the ball of regret that dropped into his stomach like a stone as soon as he'd sent Harry to investigate. They should just get out of there. Just leave. The uncommon coldness. The unexpected shot fired. The runaways. And now *this*. He should have let it be. But he couldn't do that, could he? This was who he was. This sort of thing was the way he damned himself and all those around him.

A voice rose up near the carriage, spewing vigorous objections—a *woman's* voice.

The staggering footfalls of his cronies grew louder behind him.

"Captain, they're—"

"Lionel, did you actually *look* inside the compartment before you got a ball through your sleeve?" asked Rhys.

"I didn't—how's that my fault?!"

Rhys stepped away from Lionel and Solomon. As useful as billy goats, the both of them. Crossing his hands in front of him, he waited for the delivery of the remaining traveler.

"What are we waiting for?" asked the typically silent Solomon.

What indeed. The curiosity that was already making a stew of his thoughts began to boil as he saw Harry emerge from beyond the carriage, guiding a woman at the elbow and holding his lantern aloft with the other hand.

"Holy mother o'——"

"Be quiet." Among other vile qualities, Lionel could be a lech. Rhys had no intention of letting him talk to her.

A grim-faced Harry deposited the lady in front of him. The boy withdrew his hand from her as though she burned him.

Her hood had fallen, and the blue moonlight made her face glisten like a pearl as she set her stern, dark eyes on Rhys. Tendrils of brown hair flopped down into her face, lending her a feral look. It belied what she really was—just another pretty toff.

Rhys took her in, curiosity tightening on his temples like a vise.

Unmoving eyes. A nose, pink from the cold. A white stock at the top of her dark traveling habit. A cape, askew from her shoulder. Chest heaving with exertion and possibly—fear, he realized. Then her hands, which were—

"Harry, was it necessary to tie her?"

"I didn't, Captain. I found her as such."

Rhys lifted her hands to investigate, and she did not so much as flinch. He ran a finger along the strips of fraying fabric, sloppily tied. A small shiver charged through his wrists. Her hands were so cold that he could feel it through the leather of his gloves. He took her hands between his.

Her eyes darted up, even more piercing than before. As she breathed in and out against the hair fallen in her face, he resisted the urge to clear it away. She slid her hands from his.

"You meanin' to tell me that *she* was in there the whole time? Not possib——" Rhys put up a hand and gave a warning look to Lionel, who miraculously held the rest of his opinion.

"What's your name?"

"Need we be acquainted for you to rob me sufficiently?"

And here he'd thought her afraid. A rueful smile tugged at his lip, behind the scarf that concealed him.

"Not typically." He shrugged. "But then, I don't often come across marks who are already tied up, and it makes me wonder why."

She broke her gaze and scoffed before turning back.

"I just thought I'd make myself as convenient as possible. Now, are you going to liberate me of my belongings, or shall I call for tea while I wait?"

A coarse and ugly "Ha!" pierced into the pause between them. "I agree with the lady," said Lionel. "Let's get on wit'it."

"This explains all the pretty things in the chest," said Harry.

A shiver racked the poor girl but she didn't break her straight-backed posture.

"What was found on the men?" asked Rhys.

"Several shillin', a couple o' middlin' time pieces, nothin' o' note." As Lionel listed his report, Solomon calmly passed something forward.

The moment the crisp packet crinkled in Rhys' hands, a change passed over the woman's face. Her eyes followed the document as he unfolded it.

"*The Last Will and Testament of Dahlia Kathryn Halliwell.*"

His insides froze as he read the header aloud. The cold sensation was familiar to him.

"Are *you* a Halliwell?" he asked carefully.

Lionel pushed forward. "That's a fat set o' papers. Just how much're you worth?"

Rhys pushed the foul man back into his place.

"No," she said. "I am *not* a Halliwell."

He believed her, but the answer didn't stop his thoughts from congealing around a theory. He passed the papers to Harry. "Tell me what you make of these." Then he turned his attention back to her.

"Those men you were with didn't seem very nice."

"Neither do you."

"Tonight—" Rhys looked up to the stars as if they could help him. Why on earth was he about to explain himself? "Tonight isn't how things usually go. It's typically a more polite affair, where smart traveling parties hand over their decoy purses and everyone moves along peaceably."

To his astonishment, the woman took a step forward, craning her neck upward at him.

"Oh? You fancy yourself a gentleman highwayman? The moral descendent of John Nevison, perhaps? Sir, you are *no* Swift Nick."

"John Nevison had bad nights too."

"Bad nights that saw him hanged at York Tyburn."

Rhys' shoulders went slack. If only she knew just how close he'd been to the gallows. How close they all had, because of wealthy people like her protecting one another.

Over her shoulder, Harry held the will close to his nose, reading it by the lantern. If she was worth three thousand, one thousand, anything *at all*, it could buy them out of this life.

Harry nervously broke the silence. "Pardon, Captain?"

"Yes?"

Harry pointed to a spot on the document. "Perhaps she's a Clarke?"

Rhys looked to her. She had no response to that. But her eyes took on a deadened look—her fire, extinguished.

"Are you a married woman?" asked Rhys.

"No." A denial spat with surprising venom.

"Was that pallid weasel in the carriage hoping to change that?"

Her cold silence answered him.

"I see," he said, taking the will back from Harry.

Folding the document, he noticed something on it—dark streaks that weren't there before. He looked closer, realizing, before looking back to Harry—

"Harry, are you bleeding?"

Harry shifted on his feet. "Sorry, Captain. She got me good on the hand back there, and it won't stop."

"What do you mean *got* you?"

The young man lowered his head. "She bit me."

Rhys stepped back, reassessing her.

Lionel let fly another one of his choked cackles before slapping a filthy palm onto Rhys' sleeve. "Oh, she's rich, isn't she, Captain? But 'haps we should get off the road soon, aye?" Rhys was too stunned to shake Lionel off right away.

Solomon pulled off his knit cap to rub his bald head and parroted Lionel with a more serious tone, "Aye. She *is* rich."

Rhys' eyes fixated on the woman's clenched jaw. The temptation to laugh at Harry's little misfortune was quelled by some recognition of her ferocity. He could admit he'd miscalculated her.

He should leave her.

He should rob her and leave her, as was their routine.

Yet, fierce though she was, something clamped down on his gut at the thought of riding away from her. She was alone. What would become of her cold hands? What did those other men have planned for her? He imagined himself lying awake at night, wondering forever how her story ended and whether he'd left her for dead.

Another shiver jerked through her and she cast her eyes down. She curled into herself the way a blossom closes for the night.

She's just another pretty toff. He swallowed the words like a tonic, but suddenly they didn't go down so easy.

Lionel slapped his arm again. "So, what're we doin', Captain?"

He looked down at Lionel and that wretched grin. *This* was what he wanted to be freed from most of all. If he did this right, it could be their last night riding together. *Or* it could see them all marching to the gallows again and really deserving it this time.

"Captain?" Harry looked at him expectantly.

Captain, Captain, Captain. He'd be done with that too.

Rhys locked eyes with the stranger and took her wrists in his hands.

"For now, you come with us, until we see what you're worth."

"No!"

Rhys looked away from her to direct his men—anything but to see her distress. "Harry, go check the carriage for anything else. Sol, Lionel, go unhitch the driving team."

The men disappeared, leaving him alone with her in the moonlight.

"Just leave me, please. You have the option to leave me."

Rhys regarded the foreboding tree line. He wasn't sure he *did* have that option. "Do you plan to sleep alone in a broken carriage on the coldest night of the year? Don't forget, stranger, your kidnappers are unlikely to have gotten very far on foot. There's little around for miles. They'll come back."

She shrank visibly before another inspiration struck.

"Let me take one of the driving horses. I could—"

"Why are you even trying me? Why do you think that I—"

"Because—" she said but stopped herself.

Because? He wanted to know what she was about to say but couldn't make himself ask it. He was accustomed to being the one to uncover another's secrets. Yet here was this stranger, making him feel like he'd somehow just tipped his hand.

He pushed the cloak back from her shoulders. The sudden

touch made her go rigid.

"Well, I won't keep you waiting any longer. This is the part where I *liberate you of your belongings,* as you so finely put it. Do you have any weapons?"

"Wouldn't I have used one by now?"

"It's not unusual for a traveling lady to carry a dirk."

"Be careful, I'm very deft with one when my hands are tied."

The temptation to engage with her sarcasm was difficult to resist, but Rhys held his tongue.

He took off his right glove and patted the side of her traveling habit. "Are you wearing pockets?" With no response forthcoming, he lifted the edge of her caraco and felt around her waistline for the gap in the side of her skirts. And felt around some more. *And—damn women's fashion, where was it?*

The exercise must have grown tiresome, because she contorted herself to grab his hand and guide it to its target.

"Thank you," he whispered.

His hand slipped past her wool skirt and quilted petticoat, until the backs of his knuckles brushed against fine linen. Her chemise. Warmth radiated from where he hovered near her hip. The hearth of her body—so different from everything cold and horrible outside. But no pocket hung there.

He caught her eyes and held them overlong. A nebulous panic seized him. The edges of the fabric felt suddenly like a fox trap around his wrist, about to clamp down and hold him there forever. He quickly withdrew.

The panic left him shaky under her persistent gaze, yet he succeeded in finding the other access without her pitying assistance. Here she wore a pocket. It jangled promisingly as he slipped his hand in.

From it, he withdrew a healthy handful of guineas, a pair of kidskin gloves, and a delicate gold watch, but most interesting to him was a tiny notebook with a short pencil wrapped up in its strap. Her eyes followed as it dropped into his pocket. Perhaps its pages would shed some light on who she was.

He unfolded the gloves, and she offered up her hands. Taking them in his ungloved hand, he felt her skin for the first time and realized that he too had grown cold. He tugged the gloves onto her narrow fingers, wondering if her soft knuckles always turned so pink in the cold.

She wore but one piece of jewelry—an enamel pendant at her neck. She'd seemed indifferent when first he'd reached for it, but the moment that its weight fell from her neck, she emitted the smallest, most pathetic sound, as though a pebble had struck her heart. It made him want to replace the thing immediately, but that would only leave it for Lionel to take later.

He wrapped her cape back around her and pulled up her hood. Without a thought, he pushed the hair from her eyes as he'd wished to do before. Beneath his fingers—cold and numb—her soft cheek felt like air.

Harry approached them, leading one of the driving horses and Rhys' chestnut gelding. "I tied the mare to yours, Captain."

"Well done, Harry."

"Ready?" Rhys asked her, not anticipating an answer. He lifted her to sit aside on the black hackney mare and guided her bound hands to one of the harness's rein terrets, where he secured the tail of her fabric manacles with a firm knot.

She studied the process from above him. "Hook my heel into the trace, would you? Or I think I'll not survive an accidental trot."

He did as he was bidden.

The other men were done loading their own horses and had ridden up to join him, leading the other hackney horse as part of their take.

"If our captive's ready, then let's not linger any more, eh?" said Lionel.

Captive. Rhys wanted to take Lionel to task for the word, but the ass was right. They were kidnapping her.

Rhys checked that her foot was secure and peered up at her from under the brim of his hat. She sat rod-straight, with all possible dignity as she rode practically bareback on the side of a driving horse.

"Yes," said Rhys, finding it hard to peel his eyes from her. "Let's go, mates."

3

Beth's tied hands clenched and unclenched, tightening the delicate kidskin against her knuckles. The purposeful movement helped to push the slurry of wintery blood back into her fingertips. Every time she unclenched, the brief flood of warmth reminded her of where her hands had been some hours before—blanketed by the heavy, hearth-like palms of her abductor. Her *second* abductor. She huffed out a gentle scoff of disbelief at her uncommon misfortune.

What a fool she'd been to imagine rescue—to *hope* for it. Her prayers had been heard and answered in terrible irony. Here she was, released from the burden of Desmarais' shadow . . .

And worse off than before.

Colder, and at the mercy of lesser known evils.

Not to mention the impenetrable ache going up her spine from her interesting seat on the hackney horse. She thought she'd ridden every way possible in the course of her life. When Beth was a little girl, Dahlia had even helped her stand up on her pony once or twice, the way they'd seen the acrobats do at Astley's Circus. But bareback *and* to the side? The combination was novel. And uncomfortable.

It was a strain to look forward without a pommel to hook a leg on, so she resigned herself to gazing aside and watching the landscape pass by. The sky had grown gray, and her eyes could drink up just enough moonlight to see the entire ghostly horizon.

They didn't ride on roads but cut through scattered woodlands and leas. Early morning rides were typically where Beth found her peace, but never had she ridden across a stretch of England so desolate at so quiet an hour. To lay her eyes on the country in so foreign a manner—as though she had it all to herself—was more satisfying than sticking her nose in her uncle's atlases. But for all the maps she'd once devoured, she now found herself completely untethered from any concept of their whereabouts. Adrift.

She flicked her thumb distractedly at the knot that tied her to the harness. Another futile exercise in keeping her hands warm and her fears tamped down.

A patch of trees became a forest. Denser and darker, until the ranks of tall timber sentries obscured almost anything beyond them. The void of darkness was broken only by the slow plod of their horses on damp ground and heavy drops of snowmelt sloughing from the tree branches.

The one they'd called Captain rode alongside her, but she gave him her back. Even when stealing quick glances forward, she didn't dare catch his eye.

But she felt him there.

The others lagged behind. They slumped in their saddles, looking more like grain sacks than men. It seemed that the late hour and the cold air were taking their tolls indiscriminately.

Back on the road, she'd stolen a good look at most of them as their faces had passed in and out of the lantern light.

The coarse one, Lionel, had an appearance as rough as his tongue. His lack of any obvious eyebrows led her to suspect that he was towheaded, but an abundance of filth made the true nature of his hair color anyone's guess. It sprung, haphazardly, at different lengths from all about his face and neck. What larval creatures must be thriving in that beard? When she'd picked up on a fetid smell back on the roadside, she had known it to be his breath.

The lumbering man still had no name. He was older, and the removal of his knit cap had revealed mostly baldness but for some close-shorn grays. He was the only one that rivaled the captain in height, but his proportions were different. A broad torso was sewn to lanky limbs, and a belly pressed at the lowest buttons of his jacket.

The young Harry had surprised her. He was a man of average height, but his boyish leanness lent him a taller appearance. He could not fill his greatcoat, which must have been lifted from a traveler nearly double his size. His hair—of a medium color, somewhat inscrutable in the dark—flopped loose and straight about his face. Like the captain, he wore a scarf to obscure himself, but the objective of concealment had been thwarted by their tussle near the carriage. Now his hairless chin was wrapped for warmth.

The one they called Captain was more . . . enigmatic.

Beth was well read on highwaymen and other rogues. The tales and songs of Swift Nick and Dick Turpin had enthralled her as a child. However, much like piracy, the crooked practice was being strangled by the modern times. Epping Forest was being bled of its thieves, and the country would soon be the better for it.

It was true that the man beside her struck her as no inheritor to the legacy of one such as Swift Nick, but she was bewildered by how easily he'd rankled at the accusation. The reaction was paradoxical to her first impression—that he was stoic, unmoved . . . dangerous. An impression gathered from his no-less-than-haunting appearance.

To be near to him was to feel him tower over her. Even up close, there were so few clues as to what lay beneath the cape and coat and hat. There were just those eyes, as dark as the rest of him. They gave away little.

His hands were more telling. Not once had they been rough with her. They were solid. Warm. Difficult to draw away from when her frigid fingers had sought to burrow themselves, out of instinct.

He had brushed the hair from her eyes. What had that been?

She'd thought, for one incautious moment, that he was going to let her go. *Because*—, she had said. *Because* she could have sworn that the idea had crossed his eyes. She'd thought that with that singular plea, she could grab on to that passing idea and hold it between them to take shape. She'd been wrong. She wasn't often wrong about people.

The tenderness of his hands, it seemed, had been no indication of a tenderness of heart.

Somewhere an owl began to *hoot*, and to Beth's ears it sounded an awful lot like

fool

fool

fool

Their horses walked along the ridge of an embankment. It was on her side of the overgrown trail that everything dropped off into oblivion. To be braced so precariously atop a tall animal at the very precipice of that abyss—it left her struck by a vision of tumbling down it to her death. She gulped at the thought and looked forward, trying to evade a shiver of fear. It overtook her anyway and jerked at her spine.

The sudden toss of her head displaced her hood. Before she'd time to swear at her frustration, she felt the cool side of a glove against her neck. Turning, she caught the captain leaning over, setting her hood to rights. His eyes focused carefully on the little chore before he returned them, indifferently, to the path ahead.

She stared at that swaddled face, at the dark eyes that now ignored her. How did anyone know where they were going? All she saw was a pattern of tree trunks, identical in every direction.

A muscle in her knee twitched painfully. For miles, her left foot had been braced on naught but a leather strap. Now the entire length of her leg was stiffened—throbbing to hold her upright. How could she be expected to ride in this fashion for so long? Her readjustments came at an ever-increasing pace.

"The place where you sleep strikes me as awfully far from the place where you hunt," said Beth.

"Does it?"

The captain pulled her own watch from his pocket as if to goad her. She pretended not to notice. He brought it close to his eyes in the low light.

"It's only been two hours. If not for taking so much—" He flicked his eyes up and down her before choosing his word, "*cargo,* we might be at a canter."

"Sorry to have inconvenienced you so much. As you know, I had every choice in the matter."

His face was unmovable in its glower. "It'll be a little over an hour 'til we arrive."

Beth experienced a twinge of surprise that he didn't engage with her sarcasm. Surprise and . . . disappointment? Light harassment was the only way she hoped to keep him talking, and it seemed vital that she did. Now his demeanor had gone as cold as the air around them. She had to attempt a question, whether they were in conversation or not.

"What will you do with me there?"

Every second that ticked by after she choked out the words seemed to buzz with a terrible energy. Her question was swallowed up by the silence of the pre-dawn hour. The captain's eyes did not so much as flinch in her direction.

She brought her focus back to flicking at the fabric knot with her thumb. A comforting habit to escape her deafening anxiety. It was because of that anxiety that she hardly knew what happened when her thumb suddenly flew upward.

The loop on her tie had given way.

Her heart sprang at the revelation. She stared, agog, at the little circle of frayed fabric. Panic and hope tangled together inside of her as she tried to sort out how best to seize on the small blessing. She looked up at the captain, who still looked ahead.

Her thumb hooked into the loop and eased it the rest of the way.

"A lot of it depends on you."

Beth's hands stilled. *What?*

The captain looked squarely at her, and she wondered just how many jumbled emotions she could possibly suppress with her one current expression.

He looked expectant, and at last she realized that he was answering her previous question.

"How?" she asked.

"Well," he said. "If that last will and testament has anything to do with you—and I very much suspect it does—we'll need to know how to secure our price. So, all of this depends squarely on your degree of cooperation."

Beth waited until she had his eye again. "I owe you no such thing as *cooperation.*" Beth's cheeks heated. She still didn't have her answer. "Regardless of my cooperation, will I be safe?"

The man sighed heavily. She didn't know what it meant. He lowered his voice. "It's to our benefit to keep you as safe as possible until you can be delivered."

The answer wasn't good enough.

"I can't let my—" Beth thought better of sharing a detail. "I can't let those close to me be hurt by this."

"Even just in the pocket?"

She didn't answer. How could she? She couldn't explain to him the whole life story of what she owed to her dear father.

He reached out and grabbed part of her horse's harness to draw it, and her, nearer. She tightened her grip where she pretended to still be securely tied.

"Tell me. Was I right? That the thin man was going to force you into marriage—at a profit?"

The stranger's eyes were almost pleading. The expression unnerved her. She averted her eyes from the penetrating glare, knowing that by doing so she was giving her answer.

"I thought so. A man like him couldn't have a woman like you any other way."

"I wouldn't have let him have me *that* way either."

"Oh? What would you have done, then? What if we hadn't come along?"

"Don't pretend to be my hero." She forgot her harsh whispering and spat out the words sharply. Loudly.

Sounds at their back—of a horse picking up pace—cowed her.

Lionel's horse trotted up alongside the captain, and Beth was nearly squeezed off the trail. She took in a sharp breath as she was pressed closer to the abyss.

"You talkin' of plans without me, Captain?"

"Yes, in fact."

"Don't I get a say in how we handle this?"

Beth stole a glance over her shoulder at the wretched man. He waggled the skin of his brow at her playfully. Her nostril ticked up in disgust.

"This isn't very complicated, Lionel. We'll find out where she's from and how much our price will be. Then we'll exchange her for it."

"And in the meantime?"

The captain looked to her, softening his eyes. "The *meantime* will not be prolonged."

"She's an awful pretty lady, so if the money don't work out—"

Beth's grip on the harness tightened with rage. It was a good thing because the captain kicked his horse, and suddenly, he and Beth were trotting ahead.

"I'm just sayin', Captain. 'Specially if we don't get our monies. She'll be good for somethin'." The shout faded behind them.

They slowed down, much farther ahead now than the others.

"Apologies for him."

She didn't acknowledge him. The slope they rode alongside was no longer as steep.

Lionel's horrible grin chewed at Beth's imagination. It dug into her in a gory, unshakeable way. Her hands were still bound together but successfully unmoored from the harness. Her knee still trembled to hold her upright. Staring down the embankment into the woods, her options suddenly looked quite different.

*   *   *

One moment, the woman had been right there beside him, the next, she had vanished from sight.

In an instant, Rhys was on foot, hurrying to the edge of the trail and calling out for his men. An acute cry of pain rang out from somewhere below, and there was a faint rustling as loose rocks and leaves cascaded gently down the embankment in her wake. At the trail's edge, a deep gash in the wet leaves marked where she had flung herself down the slope.

Lionel was, unsurprisingly, the first to speak up. "What the hell did you do? Where is she?"

Rhys pointed down the hill, daring Lionel with his eyes to say one more word.

Harry piped in with compensatory helpfulness. "I can go down and fetch her."

"I'll do it," said Rhys grimly. "It's my own wretched fault."

"Why are either of you goin' down there?" Lionel raked a hand through the tangles of his beard. "She's more trouble than she's worth. We got no guarantee with her. She's taken our time enough, hasn't she?"

Solomon didn't speak up but nodded in solidarity with the smaller man as he stared down into the gully.

Rhys hardly heard the argument. He couldn't peel his eyes from the shadows, from searching for movement. She would die down there. She was lost—injured from the sound of it—and there was no place she could get to before the cold and damp got her first.

He'd not been paying enough attention. He'd underestimated not only her desperation but her will.

Rhys wrinkled his face, having smelled Lionel's approach.

"Sellin' the hack horses will probably turn a better profit in the end."

"No." He put a hand on Lionel's chest, urging him to back off. "I think this will be worth it." He looked back down the slope. "I think *she* will be worth it."

The filthy man stepped back and grumbled before spitting on the ground. "She's probably dead."

She might be. But Rhys had to know.

Harry pulled a rope from his kit and tied it to a sturdy tree trunk nearby before handing the slack to Rhys. "This'll help."

"Thank you."

Harry turned to the others. "We haven't been taking much this winter. I think Captain is right. I think she's valuable."

Rhys thanked Harry again by way of a tragic nod. The poor lad thought he was helping. The young man's eyes brimmed with a steady respect for Rhys, in spite of all of his mistakes. If there was anything that Rhys could take back now, it would have been involving the boy in their original crime. He was educated. He could have had a real life, instead of—*this.*

Rhys went to the edge and tugged at the rope, testing it. Nothing else could be heard from below.

"Hullo!" called Harry from over Rhys' shoulder. Nothing. But why would there be, even if she were well?

Still, the lack of response reached into him and tightened on his gut. An uncomfortably familiar feeling. An instinct. The same one that had overtaken him when he first touched her hands and felt the coldness there. It was the same now but much, much stronger.

Raindrops began to fall. Large, but sparse.

Rhys undid his cape and threw it over the saddle. Scrambling down would be challenge enough with only his greatcoat in the way. "I'll be back up as quickly as possible. Stay nearby so I can call to you."

Harry nodded. The other two watched idly.

Rhys kicked the heel of a boot into the ground to test it. It gave way easily. There was no chance she'd slid down in any graceful manner, particularly if her hands remained tied. Gripping the rope in one hand, he began to guide himself down, sideways, into the wilderness.

$$4$$

Beth's eyesight reeled. The tree trunks still spun like wheel spokes, even though her body had come to rest. Her eyelashes fluttered, trying to trap a drunken reality in their tiny grasp and hold it upright for her.

As her blood stopped spinning, her mind cleared, and she began to take stock. She was resting on a landing in the slope, where the base of a tree had caught her—not very gently—from tumbling farther. Her left shoulder felt odd, swirling with a strange mix of heat and cold. She strained her chin down to have a look.

Her traveling habit was slashed open and a plume of her white cotton chemise erupted starkly from the damage. The air licked against her exposed neck and shoulder, pointedly cold and cruel. Just as she strained for a better look at the puff of chemise, it was pinched by a spot of crimson, which quickly became a web. She watched, entranced as the little billow of fabric deflated beneath the weight of her own blood.

The laceration itself was impossible to see. Her fingers fumbled around on her collarbone, searching, until one intrusive fingertip stabbed its mark too perfectly and made everything white with pain. She sucked in tightly. Bit her lip. Slammed her palm flatly against the wound. At least the bone beneath did not feel broken.

She wiggled the fingers on her left hand. Everything moved, but every tiny sinew sent ripples of pain up to her collarbone. Still, she brought it up to her neck to check for something else—Dahlia's cape. Instead of finding its ribbons, she found the chafed and tender skin where the tumble had violently torn it away from her.

It still rained. Large droplets, coming heavy and slow. They invaded her eyes, making her vision no better than the view through a crown glass window. Thoughtlessly, she removed her right hand from her wound and swiped the water from her eyes with a drag of her wrist.

Clearing her vision, she stared at that hand, red with her blood. The fall had ripped the palm from her fine glove—likely as she'd grappled for purchase on her whirling surroundings. Now it hung there, a limp flap of kidskin. Something else hung from her wrist too. Fabric. It finally sank in that her hands were moving independently, that—

Freedom.

While she had liberated her wrists from the harness, it was the tumble that had liberated them from one another.

She breathed in a new breath, full and hopeful, while she tested the use of her fingers, her ankles, her knees . . .

Everything seemed to be in working order, in spite of many pains.

She cast her gaze up the steep hill. Perhaps her cloak was not too far up? Perhaps she might get to it. Thoughts of such a retrieval were borderline delusional, she knew that, but she couldn't dismiss the fact that an extra layer was now essential to her survival. She tried to push herself up on her good side and failed. Steeling herself for another attempt, she suddenly heard the rustle of loose debris flowing down the embankment.

God. They were still coming after her.

She clawed her fingers into the wet ground and heaved, successful. The nearby tree that had bruised her was now her support as she used it to shimmy up into a kneeling position. She cast her eyes down the rest of the hill—the cliff, more like. It was her last avenue of escape. There was more undergrowth there to slow a descent—dead bramble and berry bushes—but she didn't know what lay beyond them or how much more of this her body could take. She was still surveying it keenly when she heard him behind her—

"Please don't," he said.

She whipped around, making the raw skin of her neck sing with anguish. She bit back her reaction. The captain was only a couple of yards away.

His own cape was gone, making him seem more the size of a mortal man, but his face was still bundled up against the cold and against recognition. A damp tendril of dark hair clung to his temple, a previously obscured detail that led her to look heavenward. The sky was a brightening gray, the hour now more early than late.

The man crouched low, stretching an arm between them—the posture of one trying to accustom a frightened animal to human touch. Something was draped over his arm in offering—her cape. His other hand lifted up in surrender.

Through her panting breaths, she took it all in. The large stranger, making himself smaller for her. The dark eyes beneath his dripping brim, unblinking. Puffs of hot breath escaping from behind his muffler. His shoulders heaved up and down, just as hers did. For a fleeting moment, their breaths fell into step.

She looked over her shoulder at escape below. The berry bushes promised her their clawing thorns but also their protection from broken bones—a difficult bargain.

"Please don't." The repetition was so near to how he'd said it the first time that she almost wondered if she'd imagined it. She looked back to him.

He got lower, taking a knee to be more level with her. She could swear he'd drawn nearer when her head was turned. He laid the cloak, looking tattered and useless, between them.

"I found this," he said. "I think you probably need it. You can take it if you want, and go down there, but I have to tell you that I don't think you'll make it."

She looked into his eyes and they held hers unwaveringly. His dark eyebrows drew up. The expression was uncomfortably earnest. Pleading, even. She'd been wrong about him once; could she not also be wrong about what she saw in his eyes now?

Without looking down the embankment again, the dark image of its abyss crossed her mind. She swayed with weakness, trying not to show it to him.

But her good shoulder slumped against the tree for support anyway. She leaned into it, allowed it to cradle her while her head swam with thought.

"I've learned some things about you in the last few hours," he said. "I underestimated you. You're resourceful. Educated. Smart enough to glean that it's an exceptionally cold and wet week of winter. It's a couple hours yet 'til the sun is up, and even when she rises, she will shine from behind a blanket of rain clouds. That frock of yours, which barely kept you warm under the best conditions, is now wet and ruined. You know that you're injured. You know that you're far from home. And you and I both know that you're lost. You probably know all of this and are considering it anyway because you think the alternative is worse. But it's not."

Beth slumped deeper into the tree's embrace, considering his words, knowing their cruel truth. She inhaled deeply, and the cold filled her lungs, foreshadowing the consequences of exposure. Still, how could she trust him? She scooted herself closer to the edge, where the hill ran steep again—

"Please!"

She looked to him, her eyes peeled wide by his note of alarm. Then she settled into his gaze.

"Captain, I need to know—"

"Please, you can't call me that."

"Then what do I call the thief who is bidding for my trust?!"

"I'm sorry. I'm sorry." He looked at the ground frantically, as though his eye contact might send her over the edge—quite literally.

Beth's chest collapsed from the brief exertion of outrage, and the wound at her collarbone reminded her of its needs with an evil stab.

There was a long silence before he looked up again. "Rhys. My name is Rhys."

She stared at him. She could tell that the extended silence caused him discomfort—he shifted and looked up into the trees—but it wasn't on her to make her captor comfortable. She had her own discomfort to consider.

Rhys. Had he just offered up his given name?

"Alright, Rhys. Where were you taking me?"

"It's an abandoned hunting lodge, utterly dilapidated. It's

neither clean nor comfortable. It's just a hideout, a lumber house, but there will be fire in the old hearths."

"Those badgers will put their hands on me."

She watched him digest her fear. A penitent lowering of his chin acknowledged that he knew who and what she meant.

"They won't. I promise. I won't let them. Trust me."

Trust me. She didn't move or answer him.

All her choices clashed noisily within her as images of different futures surged through her head. She saw herself dead and frozen at the bottom of the gorge but also saw herself on foot, spotting chimney smoke and running toward a friendly cottage. She saw herself coming home after many days, into her father's arms, but then saw her wound festering until it took her life. She saw her father being swindled by these bandits as she was handed over to him. What if they didn't just hand her over? What if they wanted more than just a purseful? What if they hurt somebody? It broke her heart to think of her father losing everything because of her.

Yet there again was that vision of herself frozen amid the bramble. Her father's heart would break much more were she to die.

Beth sniffed against the tears that she'd only just realized were in her eyes. She wouldn't let them spill.

Rhys inched closer to her, still extending his gloved hand. The rough leather gauntlet had seen better days. His palm collected raindrops as she stared at it . . . thinking . . . grappling . . .

Please, he'd said.

Trust me, he'd said.

She looked up again to the sky. Rainclouds made up the eerily glowing ceiling of the known world. Somewhere in the branches overhead, an early rising songbird began its call. But the hope of that song was strangled by the icy gusts that nipped against her shoulder's flesh.

Beth looked back at him, illuminated now by the misty morning light. His gaze glowed from beneath his cap as a wild animal's does from the shadows of its den.

So how was it that those piercing eyes could make her less afraid?

She reached across the space between them . . . and gave him her hand.

His fingers closed, ironclad, around their agreement. Sensing that she could not now pull away, her heart twitched, at this, the first small taste of consequence.

The leather of that rough glove was now against her skin. The beads of rain trapped between their palms felt far too cold to not be ice, yet some semblance of warmth still escaped him. She soothed herself with that, trying to relax into her decision. Trying to accept her instinct to believe in him. Trying to hope.

He moved over her with Dahlia's tattered cape, wrapping her up in its feeble protection. From his coat pocket, he pulled some of the fabric that had been around her wrists. It must have been left on the slope behind her. Trust and hope shattered in her chest at the sight of it.

Disbelief. Anger.

"How dare you restrain me, when I've just—"

She'd been right to assume she couldn't ever just pull away. Both her arms went up to stave him off, but his movements remained fluid and unbothered by her protesting pushes at his arms. His strength, though undirected at her, made her feel as little more than a horsefly to him as he moved for her. "You can't—"

Wordlessly, he wadded up the fabric and pressed it to her shoulder before guiding her good hand to it and holding her hand there. Her next biting words evaporated.

Sheepishly, Beth took over, applying a comforting pressure to the wound. Looking away, she allowed him to help her to her feet.

Their trip back to the top was tedious, even with the rope. Rhys helped her and caught her whenever she slipped, but she exerted almost all her remaining strength in the crawl.

"It's gettin' daylight up here. Can you move it?"

Beth knew the obnoxious voice was Lionel's. They could now see the rest of Rhys' band looking over the edge. As they got close, Harry slid down a distance to meet them and help. He took Beth's other side, and she was grateful that he was the one helping and not one of the other two. After staggering back onto the flat trail, she moved stoically toward her horse, trying to avoid the one called Lionel.

It didn't work. He came right for her.

"Yer goin' to learn a lot o' humblin' lessons while we're watchin' over you, let me tell you. Because you think you can get away or pull things like that, and yer mistakin'. We'll—"

Rhys interrupted him by pushing him out of the way. "You're so antsy to get back on the road, are you? So then, let's do it." The troll slunk back to his own horse.

Beth was surprised when Rhys guided her away from hers.

"I'm afraid you've lost that privilege," said Rhys, moving her around to his own horse. The real saddle, waiting there for her at eye level, looked so inviting to her weary haunches that she almost reached out and stroked it. Rhys started to put his hands at her waist, but she brushed him off, grabbing the saddle herself and bracing her left foot in the stirrup.

Two hops, then she launched herself upward, just as Dahlia had taught her years ago during surreptitious rides astride.

But she'd forgotten her shoulder.

Her arm buckled, and she slipped downward, feeling Rhys' palms catch her backside and elegantly assist. It happened so quickly that it was as though nothing had gone amiss. Lionel didn't growl with laughter at her folly, and the man who now stood at her heel said nothing derisive. Still, her cheeks flared from her stubbornness and a little, too, from the singed sensation that now ran up the backs of her thighs.

Rhys put a hand to her lower back, scarcely brushing the nap of her wool. "Move up a bit."

She did, until she was positioned on the less comfortable slope of the pommel.

She inhaled as he swung up, anticipating—

His great weight slid against her, displacing her even farther forward as he dropped into the saddle. Every part of him was against her. She held her breath, at an earnest loss for how to exist in such a situation. Then she began to feel it. His heat. It permeated through her from her spine, thawing her. She closed her eyes and pictured frost melting from the edges of a leaf as she molded herself to the source of the heat, without another thought.

The other riders passed by them as they got situated, and he didn't seem to mind. He'd thrown her torn cape over her legs, to defend her now exposed ankles from the cold, and he had his own cape back on. With an arm around her waist, he somehow pulled her even more tightly to him before closing his own broad cloak around them. She sleepily grabbed its edges, taking it as her duty to hold it shut in front of them both.

His large thighs tensed around hers as he gave the horse a gentle squeeze and he clicked his tongue to signal them forward.

His cape was like a little shelter. Within its protection, he crossed an arm against her chest, palming her shoulder to keep the pressure on it. The fabric against it now stayed there on its own, where the dried blood had clung it to her. Yet even though the bleeding had stopped, she wished for his hand to stay. There was a comfort in the weight of his arm as it rose and fell with her breath, holding her upright even as it lulled her.

Her cheek rested near his bundled neck. Scents of damp wool and pine emanated from his muffler. It drew her in, reminding her of days when nature was less cruel. Her eyes blinked against another drop of rain in her eye, and she retreated deeper beneath his chin. So near now that she could hear the gentle sound of his breath.

Her spine stiffened then, and her tired eyes protested as they were peeled wide. Her heart was alert. Racing. Like the heart of a rabbit who senses a predator that it cannot yet see. Yet the arm that held her seemed to detect none of this. It was forged in place to steady her, to comfort her, and she *was* the warmest and most comfortable she'd been since leaving Ashecote. Her alarm softened into a warm, tingling sensation that stretched through her slowly before disappearing through her fingers and toes. The most comfortable she'd been . . .

And all in a stranger's embrace.

Beth hadn't realized she was falling asleep until she was waking up. Her eyes blinked open in the brighter light, but it was the rain picking up that had roused her. Rhys curled himself over her as the rain steadily patted down on the shoulders of his wool cape. The tip of his tricorn hovering over her kept most of it off her face. She liked the sound that the drops made as they pummeled the forest.

Rhys shifted, and the movement brought to her attention that he'd rested a cheek against her hair. The arm that crossed her still held her firmly, but the hand with the reins now led the horse quite lazily from where it rested . . . in her lap.

She didn't have to look down to see it. She could feel it. The back of his large hand warming her skirts where they bunched up on the pommel. So many layers of fabric to separate them, and yet that hand—the hand of a man likely half dead with exhaustion—sent a crack of lightning through her as she let the heat of it seep into her, as she imagined . . .

Behind her stays, the muscles over her stomach spasmed, and she drew in a ragged breath. She knew the sensation well enough, but she flushed with shame to feel it here.

She shivered as though to shake off any other uncommon instincts.

"Are you still cold?" The sound came so close to her ear that it raised tiny hairs at the back of her jaw.

"No," she mumbled, "I'm lovely." Her eyes slammed shut. What an imbecilic response to give without any cut of sarcasm. Hopefully, she came across as a half-asleep fool who didn't know what she was saying.

"We're here," he said.

She looked ahead. The other men were riding into a clearing, and as they approached the break in the trees, she saw more and more of the strangest house rising out of the mist.

It was opulent and eccentric, looking much like an ornamental folly built for a lavish palace garden. The pretty windows—or what was left of them—exposed its true nature as a one-time residence. Ivy and other creeping things had consumed much of the creamy, marble facade. It was two stories but with a small footprint—likely only a few rooms top and bottom. It looked fairytale-like, almost too saccharine to exist.

"It looks French," Beth mumbled, not taking her eyes off it.

"It is." Rhys walked their horse to a crude hitching post. "It reminds me of follies I've seen in gardens on the Continent. So that's what I call it—*The Folly*."

She whipped around at him in disbelief. Had she not just thought that very thing?

His eyes crinkled, perhaps in concern, but then they changed. Was he smiling?

"What?" he asked.

She shook her head mutely, deciding to leave it.

He slid off from behind her, and the loss of him and his cape exposed her to the rain and, in a sense, to reality.

Hitting the ground, she found it to be a mix of slushed snow and the gravel of an old drive. All the men's boot-soles crunched in its iciness as they tied their horses to the shoddy hitch.

Rhys placed her hand on his arm and hurried them under the portico, out of the rain. Harry and Solomon rushed ahead of them to get the doors. Beth didn't understand why that was necessary until they began to pry at the ornate entry. The hinges were strangled by woody tendrils that tugged and cracked as the doors were fought open. Lionel came up to assist the other two, with an ugly looking knife drawn.

Beth looked down at her hand in Rhys' arm, while the others worked on their entry. He rested a hand on hers as if they were just a cheery couple sidling up to a grand house for a fete. With a final hack of Lionel's knife and a loud snap of protest from the ivy, the doors were opened.

Once inside, Beth could see just how much of nature had invited itself in. A great room to the left had been almost entirely consumed by things of the forest. Decorative paintings of leaves on the walls blended into the piles of real leaves on the floor—wet and rotting. One window had been pushed out entirely by an intrusive branch. The wall around it crumbled too, and a keystone lay on the floor, calling the stability of the entire place into question.

Small drifts of snow had blown into the room, leaving dark and soggy streaks on the herringbone floor. Some furniture was toppled and rotting, but other pieces were draped in white linens. Their ghostly silhouettes reminded her, with a pang, of what Ashecote had looked like when she'd closed the door on it the night before.

The odor of the place was fusty but inoffensive. Now she knew what Rhys had meant by *dilapidated*.

In front of them, the base of a grand staircase took up an exorbitant fraction of the ground floor. Unlike the rest of the place, it looked solid enough to hold up the sky. Beth drifted away from Rhys, taking it all in.

"Harry, bring in our things. You know what to do with the takings. Lion and Sol, see to the horses."

"And what's yer job, Captain?" asked Lionel.

"Her," he said, pointing to where he thought Beth was and then correcting to point to her by the stairs. Solomon wandered behind her like a watchdog. Clearly, she had no one's trust.

Lionel laughed at the captain. "You let our money run off again, and I'll have no part in gettin' it back." He deliberately bumped against Rhys' shoulder as he pushed past him to the door. "And I won't be happy."

Rhys approached her, and Solomon decided it was all right to drop his guard and head outside. Rhys and Beth were alone at the bottom of the staircase.

Beth kept her head down, observing the mundane routine of Rhys pulling off his gloves and rubbing his hands together. Before knowing what came over her, she reached up and tugged at the scarf on his face. He caught her wrist—fast as a viper—and pulled away from her. But the scarf now lay lopsided, and she could see the corner of a stubbled lip draw upward in a disarming way.

He released her much more gently than he'd caught her and calmly unwrapped the rest of the scarf for the benefit of her rapt attention.

Her idea of what he must look like had changed so many times over the course of the night, yet it was almost as if she had figured it out by dawn. So, while his face left her completely speechless, it wasn't from surprise. She reached up again to pull down his collar and he allowed it.

Instead of the pallor of winter, his skin was warm and vital. The tip of his nose was a little pink from the cold as hers likely was. A strong jaw was rough with short, dark hairs that threatened to become a beard. Strays of equally dark hair spilled out from under his hat to frame the penetrating brown eyes that she'd noticed before.

"Tell me your name?" he asked, breaking the hold his eyes had on her.

She swallowed hard. She wasn't sure how she felt about giving that up. It still felt far too cooperative.

He nodded, accepting her silence as answer.

"Shall we?" He gestured up the steps.

"Is the second floor even intact?"

"Much more so than the salon."

He proffered his arm again, and Beth took it as they ascended. She caught herself escaping once more to her previous thought—that they were just another pair at a party, in a grand house, arm in arm.

5

Rhys caught himself escaping into the moment as they ascended, savoring something . . .

Perhaps it was the banality of it, or perhaps it was the long-forgotten sensation of a woman's hand in the crook of his arm. His eyes drew upward to the dark hallway ahead. Whatever pleasant thing it was that he was feeling now, some grim realities were about to sweep down and break the spell.

The knob of his bedchamber door burned him with its cold, and a turn of it failed to open the rotten thing. Wordlessly, the woman at his elbow drew away to give him space. She backed herself into the shadows, leaving only her lips and chin in a crooked streak of light from a window at the hall's end. The sight was menacing, the obscuration making her look dangerous and occult-like. It struck him that he must have looked much the same to her before his face was shown. He smiled then, intending to reassure her, but she gasped when he slammed his shoulder into the old door to make its hinges give.

He held the door for her and, following her in, sagged at the sight of the place. It wasn't that it was any different than it had ever been. It was no uglier or worse for wear than the last time the crew had come, a month back. No, it was just that *she* was in the room, and it made him feel an uncompromising embarrassment to expose her to it. The endearment he felt toward the old ruins all but evaporated.

His room was furnished with naught but a basin in a stand and one small, ancient-looking bed. It was topped with a makeshift pallet that he'd once stuffed with a mix of every scavenged thing, soft and dry, that he could find on the property. The space was large, but the meager furnishings, and a few odd things on the floor, were all crowded near the fireplace.

The French windows were mostly hidden behind thick brocade drapery. They were kept closed to defend the room from drafts, rather than light. The only places they gaped were where the stitches on their tabs had turned to dust.

The woman wandered into the room, inspecting its yawning emptiness. Rhys watched her face curiously and frowned. His neutral mood was souring inexplicably.

There was a rap at the open door, and Rhys turned to see Harry standing there, burdened with two sacks and a bucket of snow.

"Thank you. You may set it down here."

Harry shuffled swiftly into the room to drop the things by the large hearth.

Errand complete, Harry nodded, not only to Rhys but to the delicate stranger, whose eyes went wide at the lad's courtesy. Then Harry scurried out, closing the fussy door repeatedly behind him until it finally latched shut with a slam. Rhys locked the door with a key withdrawn from his boot. When he turned back to the room, the woman stood at a gap in the curtains, staring out, as though she could see past the thick morning mists.

Rhys touched the meager stack of firewood against the wall. Still dry. The stand of wrought iron fire tools had toppled. Rhys set them upright and crouched before the hearth, getting to work. There was a creak of the bed behind him as the lady settled herself on its edge.

He looked over his shoulder often as he worked. He half expected to be shoved into the fire, knowing now what she was capable of. Catching glimpses of her though, that didn't seem to be on her mind. She didn't look like her daring self. All the challenge seemed to be drained from her eyes. Now they glowed stoically in the developing fire, concentrating on some distant inferno.

He ruminated on what seemed to be her sudden surrender, wondered at her quivering, sparrow-like perch on the lip of the bed, then realized—

She'd been locked into a room, a prisoner, with one strange man and one bed.

He gave the fire a frustrated stab with the poker.

What she must think of me.

The flames took hold, bathing her in golden light, declaring her heat and vitality to the cold room. Only her spark was missing. He had taken it.

The muscles of his abdomen clenched, struck by the fist of guilt. All he wanted was to be back on the horse with her, holding her, riding away from the folly, rather than toward it.

He shook off the vision. The truth was hard but very real. There were things to be seen to. Why be so worried about the discomfort of one gently bred woman when his own men had hardly seen bread for more than five days in a row for the last three months? He owed them. People like *her* owed them. They'd see it through until they saw their reward.

He stood up in time to see her drop the tattered cloak from her shoulders. *Her shoulder.* He'd almost forgotten because she'd been so calm.

The cloth he'd put against it had dried to the wound. He observed her as she prodded gently at it, investigating. She moved to pull the cloth away—

"Wait."

She froze at the abrupt command.

He pivoted to kneel before her and inspected the edges of the cloth, testing them with a gentle pull. "It'll start bleeding again when you remove it. Let me get some things first." Removing his greatcoat, he draped it over her lap. He turned away and heard the soft rustle as she gathered up the coat against her. The sound made the cold more tolerable as it penetrated his shirtsleeves.

With a healthy fire roaring, he put on the pot of snow that Harry had brought. He dragged one of his sacks over to himself on the floor, and he could feel the woman's eyes on him as he dug for tools. Ripping a flask from the side of his sack he thrust it toward her. She cocked a brow in suspicion.

"Gin or water?" she asked.

"Gin."

She took the flagon and threw back a heartier swig than he'd expected. He let her keep it as he continued his rifling. The kit had to be in there somewhere. At last, his hand withdrew a scroll of leather. Unrolling it, he scrutinized the condition of his kit. It hadn't been used since he was at sea. There were needles, waxed silk thread, some cheese cloth . . . It was a medical kit that had, in recent years, more oft been used to patch his shirts, but at least the needles had not gone rusty.

His stomach rumbled hollowly, and he realized that she must be hungry too. Sustenance would help them both if he were to tend to her shoulder. Dragging over the other satchel, he pulled out a fabric-wrapped bundle. He was breaking off a little chunk of hard cheese when—

"Damn."

Rhys looked up at the breathy exclamation. She still sat at the edge of the bed but held the crusty cloth away from her wound. It glistened with fresh red droplets. The look on her face—like that of a young child who was just caught making trouble—why, he might have laughed loudly at it had the consequence of her mischief not called for some urgency. Instead, it was *she* who laughed, wincing delicately as the chuckle, no doubt, brought on pain. Her brief sound of gaiety was so extraordinary to his ears that he hesitated before moving toward her.

"I'm afraid I'm not very patient. I was too curious to see how bad it was, which is ridiculous. I can hardly see it from my angle at all."

Rhys took her gently by the arm and fluffed a hopelessly flat cushion behind her before pushing her to lie down. Her eyes flared briefly with what he imagined was distrust, but then she softened and succumbed to the reclined position.

She swallowed and averted her eyes from him. "Impatience and curiosity—my flaws."

"Impatience, I suppose, is not often a virtue, but I might argue with you on curiosity." The words drew her eyes back to him. "Or perhaps I only say that because I'm too curious for my own good too." He knelt to scoop up the sewing kit from the floor.

"What are you *too* curious about?" she asked.

You.

He took a moment to craft a different answer before he turned back to her. "People," he said.

"People? It's possible to be *too* curious about people?"

Rhys tore off a generous piece of cheesecloth with his teeth and dipped it in the heating water before setting himself on the edge of the bed.

"A few years back, my curiosity about people got me in a lot of trouble."

"What happened?"

He raised an eyebrow—why the devil should she wonder? It seemed she spoke the truth about her penchant for curiosity. He hoped he might say something interesting enough to distract her while he cleaned the blood from the lesion.

"Well, I was once too curious about someone's actions and their motivations. Put more exactly, I was suspicious." He touched the cloth to her wound and her lungs swelled beneath his hand as she held her breath against the pain. He waited until she relaxed before he started to clean it. "You see, I was under an obligation to trust someone, but something didn't feel right about their actions. I nosed around in their affairs, and my suspicion only grew. I didn't have the courage to approach them alone, to make them answer for it *alone*. So I dragged others in with me." Rhys hadn't recounted it to anyone before, even in so vague a manner. He honed his focus on cleaning the wound, walling himself off to a lump forming in his throat. "It didn't end well for anybody."

There was silence between them. Her eyes were wide, not from pain, it seemed, but from her rapt anticipation of what came next. But he could give her no more.

He leaned over her as he worked, propping himself up on his other hand, which he now realized was next to her face. A night of misadventures had shaken her hair loose, and tangled brunette waves spilled around his fingers.

"I'm sorry," she said softly. "For whatever it was that didn't end well."

Her words felt like a warm hallucination, something he only ever heard in his dreams. *I'm sorry*. He'd always thought that he might flinch at pity, but her words caused him the very opposite of pain.

Her brown eyes didn't flee from his gaze. It was easy to transport himself to a different time and place, where she might have welcomed him to lean down and press his lips to her cheek. To thank her for the small kindness—*I'm sorry*—that seemed to slip out of her as easily as breath.

"How bad is it?" she asked. It took him a moment to shake loose his daydream, to catch up and realize that she spoke of her injury. He lifted the blood-encrusted bandage from her hands and displayed it for her. He pointed to a shadow in the middle, a bit wider than a guinea. "It's this bad."

She winced. "That seems very round—very, *open*."

"It is. I'm surprised you're not screaming."

"Maybe it would be best if you just . . . burned it shut."

The notion churned his stomach—just the mere thought of scarring her like that. Yet she stared up at him with a logical coolness as though it were the only clear solution.

"No. Absolutely not. I can stitch you up. I've done it plenty of times before. It's split right over your collarbone where the skin is very tight, and it likes to bleed, that's all. Perhaps three stitches should do it?" He unrolled the sewing kit next to her and she looked at it with some trepidation, but she lifted the flask that she still had in hand and sucked down another swash of gin.

"If you think it best."

Rhys didn't wait for her to change her mind. He drew the bucket of snow, now melted, over to the bedside and dunked a strip of clean gauze into it. He selected a hooked needle and wiped it off, concealing his work from her as much as possible, hoping to postpone any anxieties.

It was his own anxiety he should have been concerned for. The needle wobbled in his tight pinch, and it took a great deal of concentration to quell it.

No different from any sailor I've patched up before. But it *was* different, wasn't it? It wasn't a sailor's sun-leathered skin he'd be stabbing at. It was hers. It was ripped silk. And there she lay, looking placid as the waters of Blagdon Lake, in spite of it all.

He borrowed the flask of gin from her and took a dram for himself. Perhaps its warm bite might bring some calm to his nerves.

He passed it back. "You keep this. You'll need it."

Rhys sighed his relief as he threaded the needle in one go. *Ready.*

He stood up and leaned over her, quickly realizing that something wouldn't work. He needed both hands for the task but needed to support himself somehow too. If he bent over her, he'd block what little light they had from a sliver of one gloomy window and the fire's glow.

He crossed to the other side of the bed, thinking. Her eyes seemed to be working with the same deft inquisition, but he avoided them. He knew how to make it work.

"Please forgive this next bit."

He stretched out on his stomach along her injured side. She collected a deep gasp within her, but it was not audibly expelled. He draped his left arm across her bodice, feeling the rigid surface of her stays.

"Explain this."

Never before had Rhys heard such softly spoken words carry such dark threat.

"I regret that I'm not left-handed. I need to lean on you. We can try this sitting up if you like, but the wound loves to bleed, and I'd prefer if gravity were in our favor."

She nodded. He tested more of his weight on her. "Is that too much for you?"

She hesitated then shook her head. "You may lean on me."

He settled against her. No matter how they proceeded, it was going to put them at odd angles. Her strong lungs pushed his heavy elbow upward with every steady breath.

He pushed aside the frayed edges of her torn traveling habit and folded them under. As he did, his knuckles brushed against her skin. His calluses caught against her like splintered wood on satin. *Different.* They were so very different.

A flash of bone was visible beneath the split, a fact he kept to himself. Gently, he tested the skin, pinching it closed. She breathed in sharply, shuddering, before her breath steadied with purpose.

Just faint. It would make his task that much easier to see her unconscious of her pain. But of course, she didn't faint, and he knew it was best to move quickly. He pierced the needle into her, and her body gently quaked again.

Her fortitude was impressive. When he stabbed at her, he could feel those lungs working beneath his arm. He could feel her chase down every ragged breath and tame it before it became a scream. It was more than he could say for most sailors he'd stitched up. Though, he admitted, their wounds were often much, much graver.

He pulled the first corner together—so tight. It would be more than three stitches. Again, he kept the knowledge to himself.

On the fourth stitch, she cried out, and her whole body suddenly contracted around where he pinned her. Her hands flew to his shoulders, drawing him—the source of her pain—strangely nearer.

She bit her lip, sucking air through her teeth. She'd drawn him down so hard that Rhys stiffened to keep them from knocking heads. He hovered over her, watching her chase and tame the demon of pain—her pupils working rapidly beneath clamped-shut eyelids. The scent of gin swirled in the warm breath between them.

He waited. What else could he do? How could he get her through it? His thumb stroked idly at the soft skin adjacent to the wound. All he could feel was the rasp of his own skin, yet it seemed to soothe her. At last, the fingers that dug into his shoulders softened and slid tiredly back to the bed. It was an invitation for his own tension to depart, and his shoulders slumped as though a taut rope had been cut from between them.

Her chin was tucked protectively downward, instinctively guarding her injury.

"We're almost there." He coaxed her chin up with his palm, desperately hoping that his eyes ferried some reassurance. She turned her chin up, opening herself to the rest of the gruesome task.

In a few more minutes, it was over. Wiping off the sutures with the cloth, he looked down at his handiwork. It pained him to see the skin puckered by a glover's stitch, but it was significantly less grisly than leaving the wound to seep.

He returned to the fire's side of the bed and unraveled a fresh bandage, watching her. She hadn't fainted, but she was glassy-eyed and spent.

"It looks much better now," he told her.

"I'm sure it's very pretty." She gazed distantly toward the gloomy window.

He rattled the flask where it lay next to her hand. "You should have some more of this."

She rolled her head toward him with a sardonic half-smile.

"Is getting me deep cut on rag water some part of your plan?" She said it even as she brought the drink to her lips.

"You not being kept awake with pain is part of my plan. How do you know such language anyway? Have I accidentally nabbed a doxie instead of some daughter of the peerage?"

Her cheeks pricked up in amusement. "It would serve you right if you did."

"It really would, wouldn't it?" He wrested the flask from her hand just as she was about to drink again and set his own lips against it, smothering a grin. Her spirit had regained its edge.

He dropped himself to sit at her side and they drank together in silence for a spell. If she had any high complaints about sharing a bottle with a poor blackguard, she didn't make them known.

His own quip churned in his head. *A doxie or a peer's daughter.* Or neither? What if she *wasn't* a lady? What if that entire carriage had been up to some scheme, her included? His eyes glazed over, teasing out every possibility.

"Tell me Rhys, were you right?"

His eyebrows raised, both at the question and at her use of his given name. It was much better than hearing *Captain* on her lips but a jolt just the same.

"Right about what?"

"About the man you were suspicious of. You say that it didn't end well for anyone, but I have to know, were you right about him?"

The woman represented her claim to curiosity well.

"I was."

He took her hands and helped her upright. He began to wrap her shoulder.

"So then, you did the right thing, did you not?"

"I'll never be certain," he said.

His response seemed leaden with remorse, and while Beth wanted to keep pressing, she could sense his lurking frustration if the conversation were not immediately concluded.

The morning grew later, but the light that came in between the curtains didn't quite seem like the light of day. It felt like it might never be day again. She was so tired.

Rhys was bandaging her up, hovering around her with both arms as he spun gauze around her like a spider wrapping up his fly in silk. Was that what she was? An idiot fly seduced right into the web? Into trusting the spider himself? And she *did* trust him, to an extent. It seemed to her benefit to do so. To be alone among the thieves, without any indication of an ally? That would have served her far worse.

The scent of him—that of pine and damp earth—drifted to her every time he leaned near. She rocked gently under his care, letting him move her as he lifted her arm intermittently to twine his gauze. The movement deepened her introspection. A realization was surfacing, one that must be drowned.

Because she didn't just trust him coolly and logically, to a purpose. *No.* The burgeoning trust was innate.

She'd always been a swift and accurate judge of character. It was an instinct she took pride in. When the rest of the Ashecote household found Desmarais to be a simpering, but useful employee, her young gut had told her better. She waited decades for him to show his stripes, but she always knew that they were there.

Now, without his knowing it, Rhys had sat trial in her court. Her gavel had come down as he'd been pleading for her not to fling herself deeper into the wilderness. To her undying surprise, her judgment of him had not been so damning. Perhaps his character benefitted from being contrasted against that of the obvious scoundrel, Lionel. Perhaps—

Her thoughts bade her to look up and watch him as he worked.

The dark hair that had loosened from his queue moved against his temples. His lips parted in deep focus. The concentrated expression softened his edges, making him seem much like a schoolboy drawing his letters. Expression aside, nothing else about him was boyish. Unlike the young Harry, Rhys' shoulders were round with muscle. When he'd first removed his greatcoat, Beth had been astonished to find that his white shirt—if *white* one could call it—was all he wore beneath.

He lifted her arm again, so tenderly, and began to tie things off.

His scent, his nearness, his focus . . .

The fire was crackling, and Beth's fingertips were thawing. She was suddenly finding herself quite soothed. What did that make her? Was she *so* starved for something visceral after all the months cooped up at Dahlia's bedside?

Rhys finished his work and Beth, weary to her bones, reclined once more, rolling onto her good side to face the fire.

"I have some food if you're interested."

"I am *very* interested."

He sat on the floor beside the bed, pulling out bits from a small bundle and dividing up bread and cheese with his knife. "How does the shoulder feel?"

"Terrible, but shouldn't it?"

Rhys grinned shyly. "Truth be told, I hoped you'd faint."

"What? Why?"

"If you couldn't tell, I took no pleasure in the pain that I caused you." He gestured to her shoulder with his knife—his face stricken—as if reliving the ordeal.

"Here. Your *petit dejeuner, Mademoiselle.*" He spread a small napkin next to her on the bed, with a smattering of hard cheese, bread crumbles, and hazelnuts.

"A *very* petit dejeuner," she said.

"Is it enough?"

The concern in his voice prevailed over her little joke. She nodded in earnest reassurance. Soon he produced his own, similar little breakfast. Flicking her eyes between her portion and his, she realized that he was giving her half of his rations.

"Thank you."

She couldn't stop staring at the food though, at how little there was of it. She recognized the cheese as being that which her own party had carried in the carriage.

"Tell me," she said. "Is the profession of highwayman not so lucrative?"

He paused, a piece of bread halfway to his lips. He dropped it back to the cloth. "It's feast or famine. You see with your own eyes which one it is now."

"And other times you live like kings?"

"Not kings, quite. But when it's not the worst weather in a decade, we fare much better. Your carriage was the finest thing we've intercepted all winter. We could save more, but some of my men have a knack for squandering the earnings."

His words prompted a million new questions, but he spoke again, distracting her.

"This probably isn't what you're used to," he said, looking around at their shabby lodgings.

"Being kidnapped? Oh, as of last night I'm a professional. I gathered as much experience for my curriculum vitae in a few hours as most people don't in a lifetime."

He laughed. It was a deep, rolling sound that pushed over her in waves. It was contagious laughter, but a pang of something in her heart left her immune to it. She took a bite of bread.

He went on. "Perhaps you could write a book on all you've learned, to help the next generation of the kidnapped? You could teach at Oxford."

She cleared her throat delicately: "*How to Survive Two Kidnappings in One Winter's Night.*"

She let herself laugh with him then, but it expired quickly and artlessly beneath a fallen slab of shame. His died with the same pathetic whimper.

She waited until he dared to look up at her again. "And then I shall write a second volume," she said.

"Oh?"

"*How to Escape.*"

He held her eyes for such an excruciating period that she wondered who might break away first. At last, it was him. He stoked the fire idly with the poker and finished his breakfast with his back to her.

A chill traveled up Beth's legs. She found the edge of his greatcoat, still on the bed, and pulled it up. "Is my cape still down there?"

Rhys lifted it from the floor, shredded and wilting. "I'm afraid it's seen better days."

She took it from him. Dahlia's beautiful cloak was indeed

ruined. The small grief must have read on her face.

"Did it mean something to you?"

"It was my aunt's."

Rhys' expression lifted in a way that did not match their lighter banter. Beth went cold.

"It must be her will, then, that we found on your first kidnapper?"

Beth thrust the cape angrily against the bed. Tension tugged her fresh stitches taut, but she didn't care. "How dare you."

No, how dare *she*. How dare she forget for a second what this man was after. She'd let her guard down, and this was her own terrible fault.

Rhys looked momentarily stunned by her rage, but then she saw his jaw tighten. "Is that a yes?"

So many emotions washed over her at once—anger, regret, sorrow, shame—they were there like a line of soldiers ready to lash her, one by one. They seized on the exhaustion of the last twelve sleepless hours, shattering her.

"I'd like to sleep now." It was all she could muster. She wanted to roll to her side, to hide from him, but she couldn't turn away onto the bad shoulder, so she stared stoically at the ceiling instead.

"All right."

She listened as he moved across the floor to another pile of his things. Emotional and physical exhaustion drew her eyes closed. After a few minutes, she felt him working at something on her wrist.

"What are you at now?" she snapped, pulling her hand away to find it stopped by his. Looking down, she saw that he was tying a little string around her wrist. "What, exactly, is that supposed to do?" She yanked away again, realizing the other end of the string was around his own wrist.

"Just a little alarm system."

"Is this necessary?"

He shrugged. "You're going to write the treatise on escaping, so . . . *escape.*"

"I'll just untie myself again."

"I'm a very light sleeper. Besides, the door's locked, and you don't know where the key is."

He was right about the second part—she'd not been paying attention when they'd entered the room because she'd been too wrapped up in trusting this utter saint of the highways.

"I just want to have fair warning if you get up to anything while we rest."

"Like killing you?"

"Like killing me." He yawned, and she couldn't tell if it was real or if he just meant to goad her.

"Well, why on earth is it on your right hand if you intend to sleep on my good side?"

"I prefer to sleep on my stomach."

"So do I."

"You won't today—not with your shoulder like that. I'm sure you're tired enough to manage." That said, he stretched out on his chest alongside her, turning his head toward her arm.

She tried to pull the greatcoat up higher, but his hand was an anchor that would not cooperate.

"What do you need?"

"I'm cold."

He didn't open his eyes but grabbed the greatcoat and slid it up around her. It was tucked neatly around her shoulders before he rested his hand—with hers—on her stomach.

So perhaps she couldn't trust all of her instincts.

This man had patched her up effectively, tenderly even. Yet he was also the reason she needed the patching.

His breath was steady beside her. She resented that he was the warmest thing in the room besides the fire itself. Resented that she wanted to sneak her own hand beneath his fingers for a taste of that warmth.

She tested the stupid string more than once, and he stirred each time she did, often mumbling some incoherent admonishment.

Beth grew acquainted with the frescoed ceiling as she strained to stay awake. It was the most well-preserved part of the room. Above her, a tangle of bodies—some nude, some draped in sensuous fabric—all mingled. Pan observed the sensuous rites from his seat on a throne of grape vines.

Beth tried to imagine what sort of person had conjured up this gauche place and where they had vanished to. Catching a glint of gilt on the plaster above, she imagined debtor's prison was a fair guess.

She closed her eyes.

Pan offered her a bowl of wine. She reached out to take it—

Her eyes snapped open as her body jerked. Rhys moaned and resettled himself. She was so tired. She had to stay awake, had to think of a plan, had to wait for her moment of opportunity.

The maidens placed a laurel wreath upon her head and draped her in a purple cloth before pulling her into their ring of sin . . .

6

R hys opened his eyes to a scene that he'd more or less expected. The brave woman stood over him, steadying the tip of the fire iron over his throat. In an ingenious stroke, she'd decided to stick it in the fire first. Hadn't seen *that* coming.

"Where's the key?" she demanded.

Beads of sweat formed on his neck beneath the heat.

"It's on my person."

Her shoulders dropped as she rolled her eyes. "You're so tiresome."

But it was the truth.

The poker hovered steadily, but he could tell that it was heavy for her to hold outstretched, even in her good arm. "Just how are you going to search me with only one good arm?"

"Watch me." She put a knee on the bed to balance herself while her other hand lunged for his breeches, absent any thought of her injury. The iron was rapidly cooling. It posed less and less of a threat, but some deviant part of him wanted to see how this played out. She patted down one of his hip pockets—nothing. Then the other.

Her touch left him biting the inside of his lip.

"Perhaps I should steal whatever I find on you, just as you did with me."

He smiled ruefully. He'd spent much more of the day awake than she had. He'd risen earlier, had cut himself free of her to give himself a shave. He'd read her little notebook. He'd read the will.

Her hand brazenly explored the fall of his breeches and Rhys' heartbeat froze on a high note. He grabbed her wrist, instinctively preventing a sort of nearness that he didn't feel prepared for. "That is *not* where men keep their things."

"Oh, you mean you haven't any *thing* there? Pity for you."

The iron faltered and tapped his neck, pinching him with its remaining heat. He hissed.

"Where's the key?" She stared down at him, her hand still commandingly near to his member, yet stayed by his own grasp. If her hand lingered any longer, she would be made uncomfortably aware of his *thing*. With her hot eyes burning like coal above him, it suddenly felt dizzyingly unclear who the hostage was.

Grabbing the middle of the iron, he found it still hotter than expected but used his leverage to push her away. She staggered back before swinging at him with it. Rolling off the opposite side of the bed, he put some space between them, but she soon closed it with another swing for him to dodge. The momentum of the fire poker carried her too far around, and he grabbed her from behind. Clasping his hand over hers on the iron, he controlled it and held it aloft. The maneuver had no effect on her wrath.

Her small foot was suddenly hooked behind his leg, and

dropping her weight against his knee, she nearly took them both down to the floor. Rhys caught himself before they both went down, but she cried out in anguish and pulled away from him.

The noise she made stilled him. Had he hurt her?

She turned, holding her wounded shoulder. Then she regained herself, straightening up into a practiced, dignified posture. The posture of a fine woman. After reading Dahlia Halliwell's will, he now knew who this fine woman was. It was time to admit as much.

"You're Bethany Kathryn Clarke," he said.

She took a step back.

"How—"

"I wish I could claim premonitory powers, but alas, I'm just a mortal reader of legal documents." If any look of hers had been designed to make him feel guilty, the one she wore now was working.

"While I am a very light sleeper, Bethany, it turns out that you are a very heavy one. I woke up hours ago, snipped myself free of you, and read the will. Besides, didn't you notice my prettiness?" Rhys dragged the back of his hand across a freshly, if unevenly, shaven jaw. "I'd just rested my eyes again when I heard you get up to something."

"I could have killed you!"

He cocked his head, and a pitchy *"hmm"* escaped him. The sound of skepticism set her eyes ablaze.

He stepped toward her.

"You're the beloved niece of Dahlia and James Halliwell— Dahlia Halliwell, née Clarke. It says that Bethany Kathryn Clarke, an inheritor of the widow, was born in 1753, which would make you thirty. I thought—no, surely she's not *that* old, but then you do seem to have been around long enough to possess a certain wisdom. I grant you that."

He allowed the fire iron to clang to the floor between them.

She swayed on her heels as though in a stupor. He eyed her shoulder. Whatever strain their little struggle had put on her stitches, they thankfully hadn't started bleeding.

Her eyes searched around frantically, aimlessly. Her fine posture crumbled, and she curled inward as if struck by an invisible blow—*his* blow. She always seemed so unbreakable, so brazen. It made it so easy to push her. Yet there always seemed to come a moment where he found he'd twisted the knife too far. Moments like this one. And now he wanted either to reach out for her or to run away. But there was no place to retreat to except the dark cave of his regret.

He wanted this misery over with. He softened his tone. "Just tell me the rest. Tell me where Mr. Clarke lives—where this *Greenthorne* is—and we can deliver you and leave you alone, Bethany."

Dark, shining eyes lifted. "Beth."

"What?" He said it even though he'd heard her.

"Beth. No one calls me Bethany."

Beth. The intimacy of that one little syllable pricked at his heart.

She lifted her chin higher. "And as the inheritor, I'll negotiate for myself. Tell me how much you want."

Rhys shook off his thoughts and started high. "Ten thousand."

She snorted. "Ludicrous. My father doesn't have it."

"But I'm negotiating with *you*, didn't you just say? Do *you* have it? How much is this Ashecote place worth?"

"I don't have it *yet*, you fool. I was disrupted in the business of securing it, *remember*? First by one greedy man and then another."

Cold eyes snapped up and down his body, ensuring that her implication was received.

The door handle rattled loudly, followed by a polite knock.

Rhys ignored it and went nearer to her, to *Beth,* placing a hand on her arm. "You can go home—I *want* you to go home—but I can't let you leave without delivering on my promises to them." He nodded toward the door. "Yes, I'm one of these *greedy* men, but I must distinguish myself somewhat in the comparison to that Desmarais fellow. Because I would *never*—"

The knock at the door came again, more insistently, and Harry's voice called from beyond. "Everything all right, Captain?"

Rhys forgot what he'd been saying. Beth's eyes glittered expectantly. He squeezed her arm and whispered, "Just tell us where your father lives. You can go home. It's up to you."

With one eye kept on her, Rhys went to the door. Her expression tightened as he withdrew the key from his boot. With a displeased huff, she turned her back.

Rhys opened the door and Harry poked his head inside. "Sorry to bother you, Captain. Heard some ruckus, wasn't sure if you could use a hand?"

Before Rhys could respond, Lionel shoved past them both. "O' course he could use a hand!" He pointed accusingly toward Beth. "Because he keeps lettin' this cat loose."

"Better than leaving a filthy *Lion* loose to shit all over the place," she spat.

He swaggered over to her with an amused expression. "Oh, so you caught my name, did you? I didn't catch yers." He grabbed her chin roughly, but before Rhys could move to stop him, Beth took a clawing swipe at Lionel, making a harsh connection with the side of his head.

Rhys whirled her away from his horrid associate, not wanting to see how Lionel might retaliate if given the chance.

Lionel stretched his jaw in adjustment and cast a fiendish look at them both.

"I think it time we do this proper. Sol!" Lionel hollered over his shoulder to the hallway where Solomon had been lurking. The large man slipped into the room obediently. Lionel pointed a knobby finger at Beth. "Tie her up. Really, truly this time, and throw her in the other room."

Rhys blocked Sol with his body.

"That's not going to happen," said Rhys. Sol started to look over his shoulder at Lionel, but Rhys reached out and grabbed the man's face. "You take your orders from *me*."

"Take your orders from him, and I doubt you will see any coin at all."

All the men's heads swiveled at the sound of Beth's voice. Lionel spoke first. "Wha'dya mean, girl?"

Beth shifted in place. She had their attention. Now, what to do with it?

"I was baggage that none of you wanted to deal with, except for your captain here. So why would he give any of you a cut? He doesn't intend to."

She met Rhys' eyes and couldn't tell what she saw there. He turned to his men. "It'll be split the way it's always split."

Rhys walked away, leaving Beth in the shadow of the looming Solomon. The man smelled of burnt meat.

Rhys stopped at a spot near the window and struck a floorboard with his boot heel. The other end lifted, and he bent to pull a packet from the little alcove. Dahlia's will.

Harry had been standing with his back to the wall and a hand dutifully ready on his sword. Rhys crossed over to him with the document. "Harry, would you please take these half-wits downstairs and interpret the probate inventory for them?"

Lionel puffed up. "I just need the short version. What's she worth?"

"A lot," said Rhys.

"And how do we get it?"

"We'll decide that tonight. We'll convene downstairs at ten."

Lionel chewed on his chapped lip, clearly mulling something over. Beth knew what was coming.

"Sol, take her to the other room."

This time Sol looked to Rhys for permission first. Rhys spared a glance for her, and she felt utterly buried beneath the weight of his eyes as he drew near.

He leaned close to her ear. "I promised safety. Not comfort." Then he nodded to Sol, and it was done.

Beth was left on a pallet no thicker than two fingers, in the corner of what must have once been a very elegant bedchamber. She tried to imagine the comforts of its past life—a curtained daybed against the wall, candles in each of the half dozen sconces, and most importantly of all, a fire flickering in the small hearth across from her. What a lovely scene that would be. Instead, the old wallpaper sloughed off and fell about her like dusty rose petals each time that she shifted against it.

The place was crumbling down around her, much like her situation.

The older man named Sol had tied her up this time, and it hadn't gone unnoticed that he was rather more adept at it than Desmarais. Nothing was too tight, but it was firm, and her hands were now uselessly in back of her.

To look at him, one might think him over sixty, but it was hard to say. His peppered gray hair—what was left of it—was close-cropped as if shorn for a wig, but Beth could not imagine him in one. Thin arms dangled from broad shoulders and a thick neck, but their appearance belied their sinewy strength.

The tail of her binds had been leashed to the only remnant of the room's past, a toppled marble statue, near as tall as she. Beth had been left with enough slack to lie down but not enough to stand. She'd watched idly as Sol had tied the final knot—elaborate, purposeful . . . ironclad. A sailor's knot.

Was that what they all were? Sailors? She hadn't let go of the thought since the man departed.

She would have plenty of time to wonder now.

Her words had landed her here. Her *lie*. The suggestion that Rhys wouldn't pay his men.

It hadn't taken any elaborate divination to detect the discord between Rhys and Lionel. Beth wished to believe that this was all some great strategy of hers, that she was planting a seed to capitalize on their distrust and sow chaos and distraction. But that wasn't it, was it? That wasn't what drove her. No. Her venom had been spat in the primitive spirit of revenge. Simple and stupid. Retaliation for some imagined way that Rhys had broken her trust. He had never made any promise but to ensure her safety. Had never forfeited his original intent. And yet, at the sound of her full name on his lips, she had felt thoroughly betrayed.

Beth sighed. Such thoughts would be her main companion for—how long? Hours? Days? Weeks?

"What good fortune that I should be the reflective sort." Beth spoke to the marble woman who looked at her sideways.

The sculpture struck Beth as depicting a maenad—an ecstatic member of Dionysus' retinue. A pitcher of wine teetered on the reveler's shoulder as she danced, its contents spilling out in an organic swirl of stone. Grapevines, heavy with fruit, crawled up her legs in relief and tangled with a snake around her neck. *What is it about this place and the wild children of Greek myth? What sort of sensualist once lived here?*

Beth looked into the maenad's eyes.

"When do you think they'll realize that I need to relieve myself sometimes?" Her hollow-eyed companion didn't respond.

It must have been a half an hour or so before there was a knock at the door. *Why even bother knocking, you coward?* But it wasn't Rhys who entered. Young Harry timidly poked his face around the door as it opened.

"Miss Clarke?"

"Yes?" Clearly her name had made the rounds.

"I came to see to your needs—afore bed."

"I see no bed here, Harry."

He smiled but seemed to be unsure if it was all right to do so. "Are you hungry?" Helpfulness and effort strained his voice. "I also, uh . . ." She'd already spotted the chamber pot that was hid demurely behind his hip in one uneasy hand. He thrust the thing forward. "If you need it. I'll untie you and just wait around."

"Thank you. I think I will need it, *after* some food and water."

"Of course." The young man set the thing down and rubbed the sleeves of his threadbare jacket. "It's cold in here, isn't it? Let me make you a fire."

Beth's heart leapt so greatly at the idea of a fire that the stitches on her shoulder tightened. She brought a studied restraint to her response. "That would be very kind of you." She wasn't going to antagonize anyone until she was warm again.

Harry hastened off in search of food and firewood, leaving her to wait.

The young man had a lean but hale appearance. He couldn't

have been more than twenty. His face and some of the strands of his tawny hair seemed overly sun-kissed for the snowy season, but it was his sheer sincerity that most caught her attention. Feeling the loss of an ally in Rhys, perhaps she could turn to this young man instead.

The door creaked. *Speak of the devil himself.* Rhys was re-bundled in his full thief's regalia of a black hat and greatcoat. His frigid, awkward motions recalled automata she'd seen at the clockmaker's. He made a performance of inspecting the empty fireplace.

"You need a fire," he said.

"I know."

"I'll see to it." He whirled back to the door, where he almost ran over Harry and his armful of wood.

"Your man is on it," said Beth.

Rhys exchanged one more look with her before absconding. A look of—concern? Anguish? She couldn't finger it. It didn't matter.

Harry set himself on the floor beside her and began to work the knots at her wrists.

"Have you met my companion?" Beth nodded toward the maenad. Harry smiled, more certain of the humor this time. "She and I are going to get very deep in our cups tonight and have a wonderful time in this fine forest folly."

"Fine forest folly? You already sound deep in your cups, Miss Clarke."

She smiled warmly, but the warmth didn't quite reach her insides.

"I have to spend my time somehow. Why not with an imaginary intimate from Ancient Greece?"

"I don't know, Miss." He looked at the statue. "She looks like she could be a bad influence on a good woman such as yourself."

"What if I were to tell you that I'm more likely to be a bad influence on *her*?"

"I don't think I'd believe you."

"Not believe me?" She feigned astonishment and adjusted her voice to a higher pitch, all innocence. "Pray tell, young man, how'd you get that bite mark on your hand?"

He smiled and huffed out a small laugh. "*Touché*. Are all fine ladies such wits?"

"No."

Harry looked uncertain again.

He was right, she *was* acting a bit foxed, but her strange mood persisted. She pondered whether her next question was wise.

"Are all former sailors highwaymen?"

Harry dropped his hands from the knot that he worked, then tried to return to it, but the quivering hands against her back informed her that he'd been shaken. "What makes you think us sailors?"

"You all report to Rhys as *Captain*."

"That doesn't much mean anything. We just call him that. Like a name."

"It's not just that. There is also something of Lionel that strikes me as . . . *scurvy*." The word rolled off her tongue with savored contempt.

Harry lowered his voice, hopefully because he was about to dabble in gossip. "Sailor or not, he *is* the worst sort. Solomon too."

"And what of Rhys? Is he like them?"

"No, Miss Clarke. He's done good by all of us—or best he can. Even Lionel knows that, whether or not his pride lets him admit it." An apologetic veil dropped over his words. "Captain is as honorable as a man can be, given his past."

"What *was* his past?" The question came out with force. She took a deep breath and tried again, more gently. "Tell me, Harry. Was he once your captain, the captain of a ship?"

Harry looked her in the eye. "No. Never." There was no hesitation. His response matched the truthfulness that she'd read in him all along. So she was wrong again . . . just when she'd felt so certain.

Rhys had been beating the ground in circles for at least a few miles. But weaving through the trees while staring at his boots wasn't sufficient enough a tonic for his troubles. Even the bracing air couldn't clear the stench of Lionel's foulness from his nostrils.

The circuitous route brought him back to the folly once more, and he set himself on a fallen log at the clearing's edge. He craned his neck. Beth's window glowed and flickered above. *Good.* At the very least, he had promised her a fire. She'd be warm and Harry would dote on her. Concern flitted through him as he remembered again what she was capable of. *Would Harry be all right up there?* Rhys shook off the worry. The lad was kind, not incompetent.

He rubbed his hands together with a passing wish that he'd brought his gloves out with him. A gentle scoff escaped him. One doesn't think of little things like gloves when they're fleeing from something. He needed to be *away*. He needed to think. Yet what answers had his ruminations yielded? *Nothing.*

The questions persisted. When had he let Solomon come so under Lionel's spell? The winter had been hard, but how did he miss that Lion and Sol's confidence in him was sloughing away? In better times, Lion had been more than pleased with his take, bleeding his ill-gotten guineas in brothels and gambling houses and coming back to the crew to do it all over again.

Back on their ship, Lionel had been the most eager of the

mutineers. It was now becoming clear that his mutinous nature extended beyond that one life-altering event.

Rhys lifted his hands to his lips to puff warm breath into them. Then he thrust them into his greatcoat's pockets. He brushed the leather cover of something—Beth's little notebook. He couldn't escape her.

Resting his eyes, his memory lingered on how she had looked as she slept next to him on the little bed. A ratty halo of loam-colored hair. A dark navy redingote muddied and torn. Yet a look on her face of utter tranquility in the depths of slumber. His chest had tightened with a mix of awe and heartache that he couldn't detangle then. Now he recognized it as his own gratitude—that she wasn't lying broken at the bottom of a ravine.

A fine way he was showing that gratitude now, by letting her be tied up in another room. Her attack on his character in front of his men was deserved retaliation, even if it was an utter falsehood. Regrettably, it was also the death knell of his broader ability to help her. She'd called into question his faithfulness to his men, and he couldn't let it stand. Not when tensions among the crew were so precarious.

He'd read her aunt's last will. As contemptible as it had made him feel to look back and forth between the document and Beth sleeping at his side, he'd found what he needed in the pages. The probate inventory alone was as thick as a chapbook. She was set to inherit a manor house, land, and more wealth than he'd started his negotiations at. The only problem was that while she'd assured him she could negotiate with her own wealth, she didn't have it yet.

Whether she liked it or not, it would be Mr. Clarke who would have to pay. She'd protested that her father wouldn't have money like that, yet the will hinted at a deeper family pocket. With such means, Rhys could pay his men. He could leave the roads. He could send money to the quartermaster's widow—a fund that Lionel had stopped contributing to more than a year ago.

Rhys withdrew the little notebook from his pocket. He flipped through its pencil-scratched pages, looking for a fragment scribbled near the back. He'd committed it to memory that afternoon, but he had to see it again. *There—*

> *The sweetness of solitude*
> *Wearing thin as gauze*

His thumb brushed the page affectionately, meditatively.

A breeze nudged at his back and carried with it a rare sound—something he'd heard only once before at the folly—the bays of what he could swear were wolves.

But there were no wolves in England. Or at least there weren't supposed to be, not for a century now. But he knew the sound well from his travels. These were not the howls of dogs.

He looked over his shoulder with a wary eye on the forest. Whether he imagined things or not, perhaps it was best to take the horses inside.

7

Heading downstairs to their late-night conference, Rhys once again nearly ran Harry over.

"Sorry, Captain."

"Sorry of what?"

Harry shrugged. "I was worried you might be cross that I saw to the prisoner."

The two fell into step together as they descended the stairs. Rhys sighed. "Harry, it's your very initiative that I like you for."

Below them, one of the horses nickered from where it had been led into the nature-ravaged great room for the night. They'd all be waking up to the scent of manure tomorrow. Such a fine life it was.

A vicious, snorting laugh rose from the dining room that they were both walking toward.

Rhys assessed the young man at his side, seeing an ally, seeing someone he was proud of, seeing . . . the closest thing he had to family. He would trust Harry with his life, and he wanted to say as much—but it just didn't seem fair. Not when Lionel and Solomon were coming together as a separate entity. Sides were being chosen. It felt wrong to influence Harry, even with the sincerest of sentiments.

As they entered the room, Sol looked up from a game of cards, his chapped lips drawn tightly. "He's skinnin' me, Captain. Care to join and win my shillings back for me?" Before Rhys could decline, Lionel slammed his hands down with a hearty cackle.

"This bore won't join us in anything merry!" Lionel pushed a stool toward Rhys with his foot. "But we do need to talk, don't we?"

Solomon quietly scooped up the cards. Rhys and Harry took their seats at the crate which stood in for a table.

"You think me devoid of mirth when I bring such good news to us all?" Rhys strained for a confident ease that he did not feel.

"Good news?" asked Lionel. "Has the kitten given up her secrets then?"

Harry cut in. "I explained the estate documents to you. If there's not good news in that inventory, then you're just being an ass."

Lionel shrugged—unbothered at being accused of agitation for its own sake. "A plunder's no good without a fence, without some way to convert it into coin. So where do we take this nob's daughter to change her for guineas?"

"I don't know yet," said Rhys.

Lionel made a familiar and disgusting noise with his tongue out—his signature scoff. It left spittle all over his dirty beard every time.

"I'll not linger in this lumber house 'til the thief-takers find us." Lionel's already red face turned a plum hue.

Solomon nodded along with his usual dim deference.

"Unhitch us from this useless cart, or make it turn into some gold that we can carry. Either way, get rid of it." Lionel's vicious snarls were disrupted by a bout of hacking before he continued. "Or have you been taken in by the rosy-gilled girl upstairs?"

Rhys hated the perverse way Lionel raised his eyebrows when he spoke of Beth. But he couldn't let on. He leaned forward onto the table, lacing his fingers in a collected fashion.

"She won't tell us where this Greenthorne is. That much is clear."

"'Haps you're not tryin' hard enough," said Solomon. Lionel wagged his finger in enthusiastic agreement with his lackey.

Rhys went on. "Which is why tomorrow I'm going to the nearest village to ask around discretely about her family, putting only myself at risk of suspicion."

Lionel crossed his arms. "How can you inquire about some missin' lady's rich family without raisin' unwanted curiosities?"

"Don't worry your lousy head about it, Lion. I'll come up with enough pretense."

"Besides," added Harry, "there's a chance that she was multiple nights from her destination to start with. She may not yet be counted missing at all."

"Aye, what luck that'd be for us. How *convenient* if she lived at the other end of the isle." Lionel leaned across the crate to goad Harry, but Rhys grabbed his sleeve and yanked him back down into his seat. "Sod," mumbled Lionel.

A long silence was punctuated by the sound of a horse pissing in the next room.

"A husband should take it off her." Lionel took a gulp of whatever swill was in his mug. "Maybe that's the better way, and that slippery man on the road had the right idea all along."

Rhys tightened his fist where it rested on the rough crate.

"Who wants to volunteer for the couplin'?" Lionel looked around the group as he raised his own hand. He pushed his lip out into a mocking pout as his eyes fell on Rhys. "Why Captain, yer hand's not raised. I thought ye'd want to challenge me. Ah, pity." Lionel stood and adjusted his crotch with a grin before taking some long, cocky strides past Rhys.

Rhys had him down so fast that there were no intermediary steps. The other two stood to watch as Rhys pinned Lionel beneath him and gripped him by the collar. "You were nearly fed to the filthy hounds at Newgate, and I got you out."

"But first, ye got me *in*!" Lionel howled.

Rhys looked up at Solomon and Harry without letting go of the vile creature he sat on. "We've had poor luck this winter, through no fault of our own. But we've lived through it, and, until recently, we've lived quite well." Lionel groaned and Rhys looked back down at him, giving him a shake. "Lived well on takings that *I* secured for us. You all trusted me to do that. Now trust me to fix our bad luck. Let me get us out of this blasted winter and even—" He looked directly at Harry, "—out of this life, if we choose."

With one hard thrust, Rhys dropped Lionel's collar and dismounted him. Panting more from anger than exertion, Rhys pointed down at the pathetic Lion who was slowly sitting up. "Furthermore, we can do it respectably. We started this to survive, not to cause undue violence. Miss Clarke is an innocent in all this, and I'll have her remain so."

"She has to stay untouched anyway." All heads turned as Solomon contributed. "'Cause her innocence is our bargaining chip. Is it not?" He shrugged and took a drink.

No. No. There is no bargaining. There will be no threats. There can't be—God—

A horrible chaos was taking Rhys over—the realization that he had no plan—it was settling around him with the weight of a jailer's chains. That's where he still belonged, wasn't it? Suffering in the fetid bowels of Bristol Newgate? It's what he deserved for subjecting Beth to such a wretched lot. He should have made greater promises to her in the forest. And he should have *kept* them.

Lionel crept back to his feet and tossed his hands up in mock surrender.

"I'll not spoil her so long as Captain delivers." Lionel slumped back onto his stool, not daring to meet Rhys' eyes. *Good. He was cowed.*

Rhys raked a hand painfully through his tangled hair and retook his seat. "Can we now talk about how all of this will work?" His men nodded soberly, and their meeting passed an hour longer into the night.

Sunlight warmed Beth's eyelids, seducing them open. *Actual daylight.* It streamed through cracks around the drapes, highlighted by all the motes of dust in the thick, abandoned air. The night's fire had dwindled to faint embers and the room was chilled, but the sunshine that fell on Beth's face felt like springtime and hope. She basked in it with the ever-silent maenad reclining at her side, as though they were just two girls in a garden.

"I'm very glad to be away from my dreams, maenad. I dreamed of a villain." *Of Desmarais.* Memory of the dream was hazy, but it made her wonder . . . Where was the steward now? Had he survived the night? Had he found his way to her father's doorstep? Had he donned his liar's mask while he expressed the tragedy of their being accosted on the road?

She imagined her father, clasping his arthritic hands together so tightly that they went white. It was what he did when he was worried. An arrow of homesickness lanced through her heart.

As Rhys had said, it was up to her, wasn't it?

She could just tell them where Greenthorne was. She could ask that Lionel be kept out of any direct dealings with her father. Surely Rhys would be amenable to that. There would be a transaction and she'd be home.

Home. In her room at the upper corner that overlooked the rose arbors in spring. *Home.* Having breakfast with her father while Mrs. Brimble floated about. *Home.* If nothing else mattered, then why could she not just get on with it? *Just tell him.*

But she was nothing if not stubborn. She'd been told as much all her life. This wasn't the first time her life had been upended by an injustice and, just as before, she was left alone for long hours to reflect on it.

"Rhys does not know what he asks for."

The maenad just stared back at her, listening with her perpetual smile.

Rhys had mistaken Beth for someone of the aristocratic set. She was surrounded by such people certainly, with aunts on both sides marrying well, but her father? A gentleman. With ancestors in trade. Greenthorne was comfortable and cheery, but it was no Ashecote. It was Dahlia's inheritance that would ensure Beth never became a burden to her father—unwed as she was and unwed as she thought to remain.

Ten thousand. What was Rhys thinking? Only a handful of people in the entire realm had assets so liquid that they could quickly pay such a sum. But then—

Beth thought back to their breakfast of crumbs. Thought back to Rhys' absence of a waistcoat and his unusual pairing of a greatcoat and cape. The hints at a past gone horribly wrong. What would such a man know of the difference between one thousand and ten thousand pounds? What would comparing the distance to the moon and the distance to the sun mean if you could never reach either?

Beth stretched her fingers to get some blood into them. *Just negotiate.* They didn't have ten thousand, but might she offer two or three? Perhaps they could get by on credit until Ashecote was let?

Yet the notion still tugged at her heart. Her father had done so much to protect her in her life. Was it not her duty to protect him in turn?

She whispered once more to her stony friend. "What do I do?"

"'Haps Bedlam would have you. Since yer talkin' to yerself now."

Beth strained her neck to see the grubby creature that leaned against the doorjamb. Lion leered down at her. His hand stroked the hilt of his saber in an unsavory way.

Beth remained still. She didn't fancy pulling herself upright when doing so would demand squirming against her binds. She would not let him humiliate her.

There was a sound—a distant clanging—from below stairs. The lion briefly acknowledged it with a turn of his head.

"That'll be the lad fetchin' yer piss pot." Lion resumed stroking his hilt, and Beth did everything to avoid looking where he wished her to look.

Lionel's silence was somehow more distressing than his usual spittle-filled ranting.

Lazily, he turned his back on her. "All roads lead to Rome, Miss Clarke." And departed.

His words wormed into her. They bore their way through all

her strong-held hopes and reassurances. They poked pinholes in her courage, leaving her permeable to doubt. Never before had she heard the expression wielded as a threat.

All roads lead to Lion getting something he wants, he meant, *whether it's coin or—something else.*

Beth needed to speak to Rhys.

Unbidden, her shoulders began to shake. Tears surged to the backs of her eyes and began stabbing around, searching for their egress. Fighting them off, she finally struggled herself up into a seated position. But the sobs still sought to erupt.

Floorboards creaked in the hallway. A moment later, it was good, stable Harry who entered.

"Good morning, Miss Clarke." A chipper greeting, like that of an overfamiliar lady's maid on her first day of employment.

Beth inhaled sharply, as though she could extract a sense of calm from the air around her. And she flashed as brilliant a smile as she might muster.

"Miss Clarke, are you ill?" He swooped down to his knees beside her. His face of concern was much more theatrical than any of Rhys' expressions.

"I'm the picture of health, Harry." Her answer did nothing to wipe the worry from his brow. She sighed and felt a tear find its way to the corner of her eye. "Truthfully? I was indulging in some melancholy."

Harry deflated. "And here I come in, chirping like we're about to sit down to a holiday dinner." He bowed his head. "I'm sorry, Miss Clarke. I know that *this* . . ." He gestured around himself and said no more, but his final word was as heavy as lead.

"Why do you do it then, Harry? How did you end up here? You don't seem the sort."

He sat back on his haunches, taking her question seriously. "Indeed, I'm *not* the sort, but sometimes . . . sometimes dishonest people take others down with their lies . . . then the people they hurt have got to do some dishonest things to survive."

It was as poetic as it was simple. She understood it.

"You need the money, then?"

"We only needed the bits and bobs from your carriage to get us through the month, but more would let us retire from the roads."

"Which you want?"

He nodded. "Aye, and which Captain wants. Quite badly." Fiddling his thumbs in his lap absently, he inclined his head toward the door. "Can't you tell why?"

Beth nodded. "Yes." Apart from Lionel's prowl, she'd heard the shouts from the night before. The anger, boiling up from the ground floor, had kept her awake.

She'd not heard everything, but words like *her* and *innocent* and *respectable* had floated up from downstairs. Rhys' words. He'd fought for her.

But she'd heard Lionel's words too.

"I confess that the dynamics of your chosen family puzzle me."

Harry threw his head back in laughter. "Chosen? No. Not." He shook his head as his fit died down. "This was all fate. Dumb destiny. Not unlike your situation. No, it wasn't chosen."

Like her situation. Like being rescued from one kidnapper by another.

Harry moved to the nearly dead fire and knelt down to stoke it. "I'll fix this up, then get you some food."

Beth watched the young man's back as he turned over wood and tossed kindling on.

She tried to speak, but every thought she wished to verbalize was so different from the last that she couldn't land on any one thing. Harry's talk of fate had burdened her some, making every word feel heavy on the path to her future. But there was no better time than now.

"Harry?"

"Hmm?"

"Let me go."

He cast a tortured look over his shoulder. The *I can't* was plainly written in his blue eyes. She spared him by moving to a request more easily met.

"May I see Rhys?"

The relieved boy turned back to the fire and tried to be light in his voice as he delivered another disappointment.

"He isn't here."

Never had she considered that any of them might *leave.* Particularly Rhys.

"Where's he at?"

Even with his back turned, Beth could tell from the way he slumped that she would not like the answer.

"He went into town to discover where your Greenthorne is."

Beth's mouth fell open. All of this time, her secrets and information had been her leverage, her power. It had somehow never occurred to her that it might all be undercut by some light espionage. She didn't know where they were in the country, but a village could be nearby, and she'd have no idea.

"I thought I might go with him, but he suggested I remain to take care of you." He switched his voice to a whisper. "And after last night, I think that's wise."

She repeated his words in dazed agreement, while staring at the drawn curtains, narrowing her eyes at the sliver of sunlight that escaped them. An idea took her—

"At least there's some sunshine today. I've *missed* it terribly, Harry."

"Yes, I'm very glad for it too, Miss Clarke."

Harry fussed again with the fire. He'd not caught her meaning.

"Your captain will have a pleasant ride today. I wish I were out there, on horseback."

"Do you like to ride?"

She had to make him think it was his idea . . .

"I do, Harry. I *love* the outdoors. I get quite depressed when I cannot feel the sun." She looked wistfully at the darkened windows for effect. At last, Harry saw her and cocked his head sympathetically. He strode to the drapes and heroically cast one open. The sun cut through the cold room like a gleaming sword.

"Is that better, Miss Clarke?" Pleased to be useful, Harry smiled radiantly.

And so did Beth—because it worked.

Soon, the fire was glowing again, and Harry unleashed her from the maenad to repeat their routine of food and freedom. He stood by the door, pistol in one hand, apple in another, while they chatted, and she stretched her legs.

Beth took a turn about the room and paused at the tall window. The sun really did feel nice. She basked in its glow, as much for herself as for the benefit of her current warden. But her mind was moving like a mill's wheel as she reduced the beautiful view to sheer information gathering.

Do the woods seem to go forever?

They do.

Does smoke rise somewhere in the distance?

It does.

8

The unpaved parts of Cobton Dale were pure mud. Rhys' faith in the sale of a hackney horse on such a poor market day was feeble, and yet, he'd managed to offload the sturdy mare. A merchant without scruples had taken the beast off his hands for a mere four guineas. She'd been worth ten, but the purchaser, no doubt, recognized the elegantly bred creature for the stolen good that she was.

Rhys rattled the gold in his palm and pocketed it. His next errand would be far uglier. Cobton Dale wasn't a bustling place, but it was just small enough and dull enough to possess a healthy network of gossip. A few carefully placed questions might lead to the whereabouts of Greenthorne.

Rhys had dismissed Harry's idea that Beth could have come from very far away. That gray old snake that kidnapped her would have wanted to stop as little as possible. His plan wouldn't have worked very well if they'd had days of travel ahead of them—not with a woman so cunning in their midst. Besides, Rhys could catch the subtle Yorkshire accent in the undercurrent of Beth's low, sometimes breathy, lilt. It was there in the way she shaped her mouth when saying her *Os*. She was local enough.

And now he couldn't stop thinking of her mouth . . .

Rhys looked down the road toward an alehouse, wondering how else he might procrastinate. He pulled his muffler higher. He'd left his cape back at the folly, opting for a jaunty, if threadbare, knit green scarf. The idea had been to make himself less noticeable, less menacing by eschewing his highwayman's garb, but now here he was, surrounded by everyone else in layers of black with their hats pulled low. He pulled his own hat down and took not a full step toward the street when a man rounded the corner and slammed into him.

The hasty man—with a spray of brown, wiry hair coming out from beneath his Quaker hat—steadied himself against Rhys' arm and quickly gripped his brim in apology. Rhys returned the gesture, but the man was already scurrying away on his original path.

Rhys returned his eyes to the signs of the local establishments, trying to jog his memory of what he'd been about to do when his thoughts had been so startlingly knocked askew. Something wasn't right.

His thoughts swirled until they dropped into his stomach like an anchor. His pocket—it was lighter.

He whipped his head in the direction of the miscreant. *Gone.*

The length of Rhys' greatcoat trailed behind him as he sprinted around the corner to where the man had disappeared. Footprints deep in the mud led him quickly to another corner, where they disappeared onto the pavement.

Frustration swelled within him as his eyes snapped up to take in the street scene. Market stalls were more prevalent on the opposite side of the road, all the better to conceal someone's flight. Rhys crossed the street and put his back to a wall. His keen eyes hopped between the faces of shopkeeps and their patrons.

As he made his assessments, he absently felt around in his pockets for what was missing.

Sorrow grabbed his heart like a talon. Beth's necklace and little book were gone. The guineas from the sale of the horse were safe in his other pocket.

His eyes paused on the mobcap of a woman selling hot cider from a vat. She was ignoring her fragrant concoction and staring down the adjacent alleyway. She turned into Rhys' stare and the eye contact alarmed her so that she looked quickly away, pretending never to have seen it. Calculations were made in seconds—a thief knowing a thief—and soon Rhys was pounding through the mud of that little alley.

He slowed down at the end of the narrow corridor and peeked around the corner. The street behind the buildings was much more open and quiet, and down the avenue, in front of the chapel, he spotted a familiar mat of hair jutting from beneath a Quaker hat.

Rhys unbundled his distinctive muffler and tucked it beneath his coat. Lowering his head, he fell into a calm and distant pursuit. The ignorant man ahead walked with an almost happy rhythm, unaware that the necklace dancing around in his pocket was about to bring a monster's wrath upon him.

Rhys slipped behind a small building and briskly circled it, aiming to cut off the thief from the other direction. He reentered the road ahead of the man.

He angled himself into the pickpocket's path. As the two were about to brush shoulders, Rhys darted his hand out and caught the man's wrist just as it jumped in recognition. The crook tried to bolt, but in Rhys' iron grip, the scrawny man just twisted and slipped down to the mud, scrambling.

Rhys pinned him easily. "My things. Give me my things."

"What're you on about?"

Rhys dug a knee into the man's side to put a finer point on their conversation. In the periphery, Rhys could tell people were gathering, but his common sense was riding away from him on a current of rage. He needed Beth's things back.

The man groaned under him, unyielding. Rhys decided to relieve him of the contents of his pockets himself.

There were shillings mostly . . . lint . . . a tangle of ribbons . . . The other pocket contained two watches, one of them quite nice, and then he felt it—another ribbon weighted down by a pendant. He ripped it upward and watched it dangle from his fingers. That bucolic miniature. *Her necklace.*

"Where's the book?" he growled, grabbing the man's collar roughly.

"Why would I carry around a book for?"

Rhys frantically continued to pat the man down, but it wasn't on him.

"What's this about?" A voice rose above the small gathered crowd.

Rhys turned and straightened when he saw an older gentleman approaching. Regret sank into his gut as he realized what a scene he'd made. So much for blending in. He stayed as calm as possible while the thief under him growled and writhed.

"Get this wretch off me! He's robbin' me blind!"

"Hush, you," hissed Rhys, before flashing an innocent smile up at the man above him—who scowled deeply.

"Why are you assailing this man?"

"*This man* is the thief here." Rhys deftly returned his hand to the man's pocket to withdraw the two watches he'd discovered. He passed them up to the gentleman and stood.

No sooner had the thief been freed from Rhys' weight than he scuttled to his feet and began to run.

"Stop him." The older man pointed authoritatively, and several young lookers-on appeased the request. The bounder didn't get far.

Rhys observed the gentleman, who was weighing both watches in his small, thick palm. "Are either of these yours?"

"Might I plea for an introduction first, sir?"

The man lifted an auburn brow but not in insult.

"Mr. Crofty. I'm riding through with the district magistrate on business."

Rhys wished he hadn't asked. "I have no claim on the watches. I sought only to recover this." Rhys held up the necklace. "And a small book, which sadly seems not to be on him."

The gentleman assessed the necklace. "*Your* necklace?"

"It belongs to a dear friend," said Rhys. "I thought I'd get a new ribbon for it while I was in the village."

Crofty nodded, seemingly satisfied with the explanation. He seemed more preoccupied with the watches. He lifted the more ornate one and squinted to inspect its engraving.

"As it happens, this timepiece belongs to the magistrate himself." Mr. Crofty chuckled softly, eyeing the watch with glee. "Stolen just last night. He'll be very glad to have it back." He took Rhys' hand in an eager shake. "To whom shall I tell him to extend his gratitude?"

Rhys' mouth went strangely dry as he uttered his usual alias and pulled his hand away.

"Osbourne Booker."

"Tell me, Mr. Booker. What happened here? It will need to be recorded."

"The man bumped me while I stood outside the stables. It was a moment before I noticed things were missing. I tracked him through the market and on to Chapelgate. I went round that building there to head him off, and I grabbed him."

"You *tracked* him?"

Rhys shifted in his boots, trying to distract himself with the feel of the cobblestones. This Mr. Crofty was asking a lot of questions.

Rhys nodded. "Yes. I saw his footprints in the mud toward some of the market stalls. I suspected he would seek escape through the more cluttered side of the street. I noticed a cider girl looking up the little alley she was set up next to, as though someone had just gone past—"

The restrained thief spat at Rhys, but most of the pathetic spray just dribbled down his own chin.

"Aye, thief. You know her, don't you?"

Mr. Crofty drew Rhys' attention back. "Are you just passing through, Mr. Booker? Pity, if so." The short man was staring, looking Rhys up and down. "You've done something most decent constables can't. Take a watchman from any town, village, or hamlet in England, and he wouldn't know a thief if he looked him dead in the eye."

Rhys blinked, breaking the dead-in-the-eye gaze of Mr. Crofty. He tried not to let a smile of irony reach his lips as he spoke. "Surely they're not all so ridiculous."

Mr. Crofty was about to speak again when a slew of curses spewed forth from the thief. Mr. Crofty rolled his eyes and sighed.

"One moment, please." He turned to the young men holding on to the blabbering man and exchanged words with them. Doling out some coins, he pointed the men in a direction that they might drag the presumably arrested fellow.

"Now, where were we?" He took Rhys by the shoulder and began to walk with him. Here he was in conversation with a magistrate's colleague—his pockets full of stolen-horse gold and a ransomed woman's necklace . . .

Rhys' mind wandered away the very moment that he thought of Beth. He pictured himself taking the steps two-by-two as he ran up to see her. He wanted another night like the one they'd had but unsullied by his misdeeds. He wanted to see her smile. He wanted to get her out of there.

"Are you familiar with them, Mr. Booker?"

Rhys looked down at the man by his side and tried to pick out a word that he might have caught whilst he'd been daydreaming. *London. The Home Office. The Runners* . . .

"The Bow Street Runners, yes, I am. Vaguely."

"Something tells me that a man like you could be very beneficial. Another friend, Mr. Wright, is the chief magistrate, and he's putting together some exciting things down there. You should consider it. Do you have any experience in such things? As a thief-taker perhaps?"

Rhys laughed loudly before he could control it. He bit his lip and shook his head. "No, I'm afraid I don't."

"Here is my calling card. If you're ever in London seeking employment, you'll have my enthusiastic referral. Now, I had better go see about that thief's transportation. Thank you again for your services. Good day." Mr. Crofty slapped Rhys heartily on the arm.

"Same to you, sir."

And then he left. Rhys stood alone on the pavement. The last of the onlookers had already returned to their business. Beth's pendant was still in Rhys' left hand, where he'd been stroking a thumb along it through his entire conversation with Mr. Crofty. Now he noticed something that he hadn't previously. There were tiny stones encircling the setting of the enamel. It would be no surprise if they were little diamonds. The necklace could support his crew for a year or more . . . and all he wanted was to get it back to her.

Lionel wasn't going to take well to Rhys returning without information, but Lionel's needs were sinking further and further into the background.

The loss of Beth's poetry book left Rhys a grieving man. He pinched the bridge of his nose, straining to remember his favorite passages. He retraced the steps of the foot chase with his eyes cast to the ground. But the mud and pavement and straw offered no glimpse of the little leather-bound thing. He had lost not only Beth's voice and words but the ability to restore them to her.

He was toeing the mud with his boot, his mind ten miles away, when something blew into his face on the breeze. He looked up and drew his lips in annoyance as the tails of dozens of ribbons gently slapped at him. Evidently, he'd been doing his daydreaming right next to a haberdasher's storefront. The rainbow of trims danced on the wind from where they dangled on their hanging racks. He thought they might be the brightest things in the entire dreary town.

One blew off the rack and his reflexes responded, snatching it from the air, a flying snake caught by its tail. He dragged it through his pinched fingers, feeling the brush of the silky pile. It caught against his roughened skin. He sensed the shopgirl staring at him before he even looked up.

"How much?" he asked.

"Four shillin'."

He handed the emerald ribbon to her to be wrapped in paper, along with one of the guineas that weighed down his coat pocket.

She disappeared inside.

At the next building over, two women sat on their stoop, talking loudly while they watched a bundled-up child, rounded by layer upon layer of wool, struggle to take a few steps.

Rhys' racing thoughts had drowned out their gossip until the name *Clarke* stabbed through the noise in his head, like an arrow. He stiffened as the shopgirl dropped his purchase lightly into his hand, his ears sharply attuned to the conversation behind him.

". . . Mr. Clarke's daughter . . . seen in days . . . highway . . ."

The shopgirl looked ready to speak the praises of more ribbons, but Rhys' cold eyes must have told her to walk away. She dropped his change into his palm and departed.

Rhys' blood felt heavy, like he was willing it to be still. He inched nearer to the edge of the haberdashery. He stroked another ribbon idly between his fingers and listened to the woman.

"They should have arrived at Bartswell outside of Hull no later than yesterday. Harold knows Clarke's solicitor. Says the poor man is beside himself with—"

"It's just an elopement. They'll find that out in the end. They're always just elopements."

"I think she's dead."

"Oh, Ginnie, don't be so bleak," she begged. Just then, the toddling child toppled onto the pavement and began to wail.

Enough.

Rhys had been drawn to listen, yet he wished he had not heard. It was precisely what he came for, fed to him without having to lift a finger—and yet he wished to vomit it up and leave it behind in this gray village.

He cursed under his breath as he returned to the stables to leave the village and his filthy errands behind.

* * *

Beth's entire body jumped when the door to her room swung open. Her startled heart leapt into a racing beat. She must have dozed off. There was so little else to do with her day but sleep.

But her pulse took on another pace entirely when it registered that it wasn't Harry at the door, but Rhys. She straightened.

"What're you doing here?"

"I thought I'd come . . . check on . . . you." Why was he so out of breath?

She studied him. Snowflakes were freshly melting on his shoulders and his greatcoat was buttoned to the throat. He pushed his great presence into the room, backlit by an amber halo as he dropped his saddlebag with a thud before the fire.

"Harry is due to take care of me soon. He's very on top of his duties." She wished she hadn't said it. It didn't send Rhys away though. He dropped a knee to the floor and removed his gloves. She caught herself staring at his hands as he vigorously rubbed warmth back into them.

"I'm glad he's taken good care of you. I trust him very much." Rhys began to undo the buttons at his throat.

"How did your little errand go?"

His hands froze.

"Your secret is still safe." He looked her right in the eye as he said it, and there was something haunting in the delivery. Something almost . . . sad.

He crossed the floor on his hands and knees to where she sat, and he was suddenly so close to her that she leaned back against the wall.

He crouched in front of her.

"How does your shoulder feel?"

"It doesn't hurt me much. Doesn't throb."

"That's a good sign," he said, "May I?"

She nodded gently. He set about unwrapping the bandage before realizing it was to his advantage to untie her wrists first so that she could lift her arm as he worked.

"It feels more comfortable in here now," he said as his cool fingers worked at the knots. "It was nice to see a bit of sunshine today. Not as cold."

"Yes, the weather has broken a bit, hasn't it? I daresay it will be glorious tomorrow for a country ride. Shall we talk of trade next? I hear the brewing business is quite bustling. *Honestly.*"

He smiled. "Your point is taken. It's not really right to chat like we're at some dinner party."

"At a dinner party? That's your *dinner* conversation? The *weather?* I should have hoped you could do better than that."

"Forgive me. I have never been to a dinner party in all my life." He smiled at her as though to let her know it was all right to smile back—he wasn't wounded.

The fine hairs at the back of her neck raised in response to his breath as he tugged on the knots. He didn't seem so deft with them as Harry or Solomon.

Rhys glanced around the room. "But truly, Beth, what do you do all day in this prison of my design?"

At least his humor was frank in regard to culpability.

"I talk to her." Beth nodded toward the maenad.

"And is she good companionship?"

"She listens, yes. But she doesn't contribute much, and she spills good wine on the floor."

"That's a pity. You could probably use some wine after a couple of days in here."

"I would accept the flask of gin again."

His eyes sparkled playfully at her, and she felt very conscious of it as she mirrored his expression. With the toe of his boot, he hooked the strap of his bag and dragged it near. Digging with one hand, he withdrew the flask they'd used before and took a swig.

"That's not fair," she said. "I don't have my hands back yet."

He leveled his eyes at her. "Then I won't keep you waiting." Scooting up to her side, he leaned against her. Whether from the heat of his body or the suddenness of his proximity, Beth no longer felt chilled. The air around her now smelled of snow and of that piney scent she'd caught before. He lifted the flask toward her lips.

"You'll drown me in it." Laughter, nervous and breathy, fluttered up her throat.

"Please, you drank deeper draughts the night I found you than any woman I've ever laid eyes on."

Before she could respond again, it was tilted up to her, and the fiery drink swept silkily across her tongue. He brought it back down quickly, and she rolled her lips together to capture any last drops. She felt a roaring blush rise to her cheeks. They always reddened easily with drink, but what was happening now wasn't *that*. She didn't try to turn away from him or hide her risen color. Instead, she locked eyes with him recklessly, drinking him in with more enthusiasm than she'd shown to the liquor. He was the first to break their stare as he returned his attention to the knots.

She leaned forward as he worked on her wrists. Wisps of cold air had been slipping like fingers under the edges of her torn collar ever since she arrived, and Rhys' warm breath behind her was a remedy.

"There," he said.

Beth drew her creaky arms in front of her and stretched her

wrists and fingers.

He passed her the flask and, shoulder-to-shoulder, they leaned against the rotten wallpaper, exchanging sips. She succumbed to the conviviality of the moment. The only witness was the marble nymph, who would never tell anyone how a gentleman's daughter was consorting with her own kidnapper.

She snorted as she thought of something, and then the thought came tumbling quickly from her mouth—

"You are very good with knots, Rhys. I wonder if you're *knot* a sailor?" She combusted into giggles from her own joke and enjoyed it all the more when Rhys didn't laugh.

"And *I* wonder that I once called you clever." He smiled. "Besides, I think it is very clear to both of us that I am, in fact, *not* very good with knots."

Rhys set himself about the more delicate task of her bandage. Here was something that she could tell he was good at.

"Who have you stitched up before me?"

"You're the first woman, I'll say that much."

"And what do you think of your handiwork?"

The final layer of gauze was coming off. He sighed as he laid eyes on it. "If I could have completely erased it, I would have."

How did he manage to always do this? Say these things that wrung her to her core?

"For my part, I was rather too gallant that day. And foolish."

Rhys delicately cleaned the injury. "Foolish? I don't know, I rather admired you for it."

He pushed her hair aside before leaning in and running his finger along the stitches. "Tender?" he asked.

"Only a little."

She placed a hand lightly over his. It wasn't because it hurt. It wasn't to stop him. It was just *because*.

The gentle snaps of the fire were the only sound. Her chest rose and fell deeply with every breath. Their hands rose and fell together. She was leaning into him. He was leaning into her. About to lock necks like two swans in a caress.

He inhaled sharply and rose to help her stand up.

But once she was upright, he dropped himself back down to the pallet. Their sudden distance, gaping.

"So it's time for my evening constitutional, then?"

He nodded, looking up at her with a dreamy expression. She'd never seen him so relaxed in this way. It wasn't a cocky nonchalance but a certain satedness.

The door was completely unguarded. She looked down at him, apparently with a look that exposed her puzzlement.

"Can I trust you?" he asked. "Not to run down the road, or fling yourself into the forest, or threaten my throat with a hot poker?"

She nodded and began her dull commute around the small and bedless bed chamber. Her turns about the room felt awkward without Harry's light chatter filling up the space.

The door wasn't even locked. Rhys could stop her if she tried anything, even if he seemed a lazy sentry at present. Yet his trust left a strange feeling in her, and now her strongest instincts had become like two dogs pulling at either end of a rope.

"Wouldn't your men be upset at your lack of vigilance tonight?"

He shrugged. "I'm not certain I care anymore."

"Do you still care about getting money from me?"

He nodded gravely as she stepped over his legs to take another slow lap around the room.

"Why?"

"Because there's a family I have to feed."

Her step faltered.

"Oh."

"Not *my* family but people that I must protect as though they were. Until I die. I owe a great debt."

The knot that formed in her stomach upon hearing the word *family* was not unraveled quickly by the clarification that it wasn't *his* family. There was still so much about him she didn't know. She stopped walking and offered him the hand of her good arm. "Please. It feels strange to walk alone."

His immense hand tensed around hers. He actually allowed her to take some of his weight and it nearly pulled her into him before he was completely upright.

"The activity of walking already seems silly in such a small space. Makes me feel like a mouse trapped in a clock." She put her arm through his and they began to walk.

"I thought that's what ladies of your gentility do—walk around rooms."

"It's certainly an interest that some would have preferred for me."

"But you have a certain proclivity toward the out of doors?"

"I do. I like to ride. I like space and fresh air. How men don't go insane on ships, I'll never know."

"Some men *do* go insane on ships."

"Like your ship?"

He stepped in front of her abruptly, his boots striking so firmly on the floorboards that she felt an admonishment *en route*. Instead, he just stood before her, his eyes traveling across her neck and face without ever meeting her gaze. She'd had enough.

"You keep divulging all of these ominous clues to your past and then grow upset when I express my natural curiosity. A curiosity that you claim we share."

Uncomfortable though the moment was, she felt an incredible tolerance for standing in it with him. They faced one another, sharing nothing but breath. Finally, he placed a light hand where her neck met her shoulder, not far from her injury.

"I'm not upset. Not with you." He took a step closer and supported her neck as she looked up at him. "What hurts is that it would be very easy to tell you all of these things. I can tell that you're a safe place for secrets, but it's not your burden to carry mine. I'm burdening you enough. So sometimes I start to speak before realizing that it's unfair of me."

He cast his eyes to the floor and his thumb began to absently stroke the back of her neck. A charge of warmth and alertness traveled down her spine. She placed a hand on the arm that held her, steadying herself.

Rhys' subtle smile broke through the melancholy air. "Perhaps *you're* here to spy on *me*, trying to manipulate *me* out of *my* fortunes." He shook her playfully.

"Yes, that's it. Why, I may be tied up all day and at the complete mercy of a band of criminals, but I've got you exactly where I want you. I'm going to steal this pristine lodge right out from under your noses, bury you all in the garden, and live like a queen on your stolen goods."

"Does your sarcasm mock this house? I know it's half fallen down, but I'm oddly offended on its behalf."

Beth sighed, eyeing the door's ornate molding from over his shoulder. "No, I'll admit to some enchantment with it. It has some corners where, well, you can look and imagine what it once was."

"Sometimes . . ." He raised his eyes back up with a detectable flash of courage. "Sometimes, it's easy to imagine it differently. It's easy to imagine the folly as beautiful as it was in its first spring. And it's easy to imagine that those cads aren't downstairs. And to imagine that you don't have this."

His knuckles grazed her scabbing wound. "It's easy to imagine talking to you then and telling you everything. In a world where I'm not responsible for what's happening to you."

She had imagined it too. And it *was* easy. But she couldn't say so. Because he was right, he was responsible for all of this. She couldn't ever forget it, even if he sent her away on a horse right that moment.

He raised another hand to her neck.

"I didn't realize your neck was so cold," he said. He wandered to where his coat lay near the fire and pulled something out of the pocket.

Beth was about to speak to his abrupt change of subject when the pendant dropped in front of her eyes, from between his fingers. She pulled away, wary of a cruel trick. But he brushed her hair to the side and reached around her, tying the new, forest-colored ribbon behind her neck.

She lifted her hand to caress the pendant. Her fingers, her neck, her whole body sagged in relief. The cool weight of the pendant against her skin was the comforting echo of family and home.

"I don't know that this will keep my neck warm, but I accept."

"I'm getting to that part." Rhys leaned down to his bag and withdrew a scarf—tatty and loosely woven in the color of faded moss. "We need to hide your treasure anyway. Keep it safe." He bundled it around her, and she watched him in awe.

In silence, the two walked back to the pallet, where he sat and re-bandaged her shoulder. After tying it off, his hand slid down her arm to her wrist. His thumb pressed gently against her pulse. She waited for him to pick up the ropes, but instead he stood.

"I'll get Harry to bring up some food for you and help you with the rest."

"I'm not hungry. I won't need anything yet for another couple of hours."

"I'll have him come up anyway."

Rhys made hastily for the door. Beth couldn't make sense of him until—cruel wonderment solidified into realization—*the coward.*

"You don't want to be the one to tie me back up."

He turned slowly. Not denying it.

Beth was swiftly on her feet and moving toward him. His words cut her off before she reached him. "Of course I don't."

"So you're making that sweet young man do it for you? If you don't want to do it, then just let me go."

The man in front of her didn't say a word to that and it infuriated her. He did so much for her, but never that. Never just letting her go.

It was worse than that. In the time she'd spent away from him, cooped up in the little bedroom, she was increasingly ready to leave. But now, a moment spent joking by his side had twisted her senses. It had reawakened her to every dangerous sensation she'd felt the first morning. Feelings of curiosity and affection. *Nearness.* And that sensation—too rare for her—where her whole body's awareness siphons down to that spot between her legs, as though a drawstring were tightened there.

These feelings were what anchored her heels to the folly's floor, making the words *let me go* heavier and heavier every time she uttered them. If she didn't force herself to say it now, she might never.

"I'll give you two thousand pounds if you just let me go. It's the most that's possible to offer quickly, and I'll make sure it's done."

Of all the expressions she'd thought might cross his face, a confused one was not what she expected. He raised a finger to his lips to suggest her silence. She might bristle at such a gesture, but she was too focused on what any of it meant.

Wordlessly, he opened the door and called for Harry. A door somewhere in the hallway opened and shut with a bang. Soon it was Harry who stood in the doorway—Rhys having absconded like the thief he was.

9

"Evening, Miss Clarke. How may I—" Harry's gentle voice ceased to be heard as soon as the door to Beth's room was shut.

As Rhys pulled himself back down the hall, every fall of his boot soles on the carpetless floor made a heavy sound. *Lies.* He'd just told Beth so many lies. But he had to play the villain for one final night. He couldn't chance Lion or Sol overhearing that he'd acquired what he sought in the village. He'd already told the men on his way inside that he had learned nothing.

But now he knew where Greenthorne was. He was going to take her there. And he was going to accept *nothing* in return.

The idea hadn't become a certainty until returning to the folly. He'd taken the steps of the large staircase in bounds, knowing that one glimpse of her would bring an axe down on his indecision. And it did.

His abrupt entry had woken her, but in that sliver of time

before she'd jolted to consciousness, his decision was made. Seeing her—this brilliant person—leashed up on a shabby pallet, the answer was as bright and obvious to him as the sun. He'd get her the hell out of there.

Rhys closed his door with the necessary slam and crossed to the bed. The room felt cold, dead . . . empty. It wasn't for the lack of a fire, but for the lack of *her*.

Beth was right. He'd tried to ignore her plight and his part in it. When he'd made his vow to her at the bottom of the ravine, he'd only promised her safety. But tacitly, there had existed many more promises he wished to keep—ones he never uttered aloud because he knew that Lionel would be a thorn. He'd broken almost all such promises.

Women of her ilk had wounded him before, and he'd not forgotten it. They'd breathed the weighty whispers that saw him, and the others, thrown in prison. They'd attested to the honor of a madman, while Rhys' friend Dewey, a man of real honor, had dangled at the scaffold.

But Beth was not them. She wore their clothes, and she knew their language, but the core of her was made of something else entirely—of running water that adapted itself to the curves of life. She slid into one situation as easily as the next, and only rarely did he catch a hesitation or see her shake. She seemed almost more habituated to her situation than he was—ready to laugh at a moment's notice even as she was heaped upon with myriad discomforts. More than once he'd read her laughter as trust, and it had gutted him that it was so misplaced. Now he would make good on whatever she had seen in him.

Rooting around in his saddlebag, he found a piece of parchment and tore off a scrap. He'd been worried before about influencing

Harry's loyalty in any way as the group splintered, but the care that Harry had shown to Beth had made clear enough what sort of man the boy had become. Rhys wanted Harry at his side.

He pulled Beth's little pencil from his pocket. It had detached from the ties of her lost notebook. Regret over its loss swelled in him once more, but he forced it aside. He had to focus.

At midnight, Rhys returned to her room. This time he slipped in quietly, even though he'd hoped she might be awake. She was not.

Her face was mostly veiled by tangled brown waves, yet he could see where her lashes rested against her cheek. She seemed contemplative, even in dreaming. Did her curious mind ever sleep?

He smiled down at her, but a shadowed feeling was creeping up on him.

"I will be happy when you are happy," he whispered, as though hearing himself say it aloud might push the forceful specter away. Instead, the feeling only coiled tighter around his stomach.

It would be his greatest relief to see her away from this place. He'd be cut free too—from Lionel, from Sol. He'd spent enough years hiding from his ruined name in the purgatory of a criminal livelihood. They'd both be free. They'd both be—

Ah, that was it, wasn't it? He'd never see her again.

She was the only person who had spared a thought for his plight, even when she didn't know what it was and even in spite of her own. Her hand in his arm would never again transport him to some other life. It was all fantasy.

Rhys tilted his head to look at the stony maenad that lay across from Beth. The nymph smiled faintly, sympathetically. He placed a hand on the statue. "I already miss her."

He sighed.

Everything was in place. He'd passed off his note, and Harry knew what to do. They'd talk in the woods early, before the lazy cads rose.

Rhys resisted brushing the hair from Beth's cheek. There would be no more of that either. It was time to tell her the rest of his promises, even if she couldn't hear them.

Beth's strange and turbulent sleep blossomed into a curious morning.

The less cultured among the troop of thieves tended to sleep until noon, yet Beth could hear their muffled jabbering floating up from somewhere outside.

Harry hadn't come to wake her. Nor had Rhys.

What time it was, she could not quite tell, but the light still seemed gray around the curtains. The men's voices died down, and Beth concentrated on a different sound. A song thrush's whistles and trills pierced through the stillness—it was indeed early.

She shifted to make her shoulder more comfortable. Sleep had been fitful. There had first been a nightmare of Lionel and his quiet accomplice, Sol, chasing her through the forest. They'd sounded like animals, like predators behind her. Yet when she would fearfully check over her shoulder, prepared to see a real lion leaping for her throat, it would be Lionel's smudged and twisted maw instead.

She'd dreamed also of riding her horse, Cutter, over the moorlands, but then the dream had changed. She found herself sitting at the edge of Greenthorne's pond, staring into it and hearing Rhys' voice, as distant as the stars. He apologized to her. Made promises to her. And at last she was transported to the folly, where the maenad was a real woman and Beth wept into her lovely arms.

Now she looked into the nymph's familiar face, which was always eye-to-eye with her when she awoke. "I only want to daydream with you all day and purge all of the conflicts in me."

Rhys' manner had been so strange the night before—his urgency, his confusing honesty, the look on his face when she'd made her offer, an offer that seemed not to matter at all. Then he'd silenced her with one finger to his lips, and she still didn't know why.

The pendant gently bumped against her neck as she shifted again. Rhys' scent wafted from the yarns of the scarf he'd wrapped her neck in. She inhaled it deeply, then stopped herself.

"I thought last night that he might kiss me." She bit her lip against the guilt of the next part of her confession.

Her confessor, the maenad, awaited the rest. *And?*

"Don't make me say it, friend."

Beth imagined that kiss. She idealized it as part of some spell this place had cast on her. With that kiss, the wall sconces illuminated. Their flickering candles revealed gilt swirls on the walls and floors so gleaming that one's shoes reflected in it as though walking on a pond. Rhys was illuminated too and that was when the fantasy fell apart.

Her mind started over.

She stripped those fairytale layers away to find Rhys alone in that imagined kiss. Just as he was and nothing more. The wintery scents that clung to his great coat. The sweat that formed on his temples beneath his hat. Rough skin mismatched to his gentle touch. *His warmth.* There he was. And with all the brilliant trappings stripped away, she still desired that kiss.

It had been so long since she'd been touched, and now—

She shut her eyes hard against the truth.

"I confess—"

But her intimate confession was stolen as the door burst open. Lionel stood there. "Talkin' to yer friend again?" He laughed wildly as he sauntered in with his hands on his belt.

Beth squirmed upright. A barb was ready on her tongue, but something didn't feel right. There was something altogether too confident in Lionel's expression. Something . . .

Beth opened her mouth and screamed, *"Rhyyyyys!"*

Lionel winced at the sound she made but otherwise looked down pitifully at her. Her voice was still ringing in her ears. She swayed as her stomach turned over with fear.

"Where's Rhys? Harry?"

"Wish I knew." The man shrugged. "My guess is that they're off pissin' in the woods somewhere, readyin' to betray me. I'm not so dumb as they think, though." He nudged her roughly with his toe. "No matter. It's time to get ready for yer big day!"

Solomon trundled into the room behind him.

"Get 'er up, Sol. We need to clean this gentlewoman off so she can fetch a good price. You *did* want to go home, didn't you?"

Sol knelt to untie her hands.

"You don't know where my home *is*."

Lionel's horrific grin was sharp enough to slide right through her soul. "Oh darlin', we're about to."

Sol jostled her up to her feet, but she fought him, thrashing and dropping her weight. She fought with such blind and terrible rage that she hardly noticed when she'd been dragged outside.

Sol stopped at a horse trough at the side of the lodge. He shoved her toward it contemptuously, seemingly glad to be rid of her writhing body—all sharp elbows and fingernails. Stale, green water shimmered up at Beth, a thin layer of ice on its surface. Lionel set himself down on a milking stool with his pistol trained squarely at her.

Beth examined the edge of the forest, looking for any sign of Rhys, of Harry, of hope.

"No, girl. You look over here at *me*."

She pushed herself through a fog of loathing to do as she was bidden.

"Tell me where yer pa lives."

Beth's eyes drifted down briefly to the murky surface of ice. She understood what this was. Her heart pounded with violent strokes that made her teeter and sway, even as her alertness blossomed. Where were Rhys and Harry? Gone? *Dead?*

"No," she said.

"Well then," said Lionel, "why don't you make yerself pretty?" He gestured to the trough with his weapon.

"Let's clean that stench off of ye," added Sol.

A smashing force brought Beth down from behind. Her cheek broke the thin pane of ice, and she inhaled a gulp of sharp, foul water. It froze her from within, and she choked. Somewhere beyond the darkness that her head was submerged in, she felt her limbs lash out against Sol. But underwater, all was still. She was no match for the hand that held her down.

Then the sky reared up before her eyes as she gasped inwardly on a ball of water and air, unable to spit it out and with no time to take a breath before she was back under.

Air. Her whole soul concentrated on air, but there was little to be had as Sol's hand brought her up and down again.

Her body no longer fought for her, even though she willed it to. Her heels just skidded helplessly for traction in the mud, angling for leverage against the great vise that held her down.

Her face and senses were numbing when a tremendous blow knocked her to the ground and back to the spinning world. She gasped and gulped on her stomach like a beached fish. Two arms wrapped around her and pumped her body roughly upwards. Ice water gushed from her lips, and her eyes filled with tears as she finally gasped a breath that succeeded in real exhalation. She was gently lowered to the ground to breathe deeply and recover herself. It was Harry's legs that walked away from her toward a tussle she could hear but not yet make out through her bleary vision.

The ground held her like a cradle, seducing her to sleep for days, but the shouts nearby grew louder. She pushed herself up onto her hands and saw more clearly.

"I'll gut you for what you've done!"

Rhys and Lionel rolled on the ground near the trough, exchanging blows and jockeying for control of the pistol. Solomon lumbered behind Harry as they looked on.

Rhys got the better of Lionel and stood up, having won the pistol. But Sol's hands caught Beth's eye. He was reaching for something—

"Harry!" she croaked, just loud enough to be heard. Harry spun to attention, but it was too late. He was grabbed roughly by Sol, who pressed the end of a knife into his side.

An eerie calm fell over the group as they accepted the standoff. Lionel got to his feet, but Rhys didn't lower his weapon.

"You're going to die for all of this," said Rhys.

"Look Captain, I'm not so stupid as you take me for. You and dear Harry was plannin' to take her by yerselves and keep all the coin. You know where she's from and yer not sharin'. So I thought we'd do the interrogatin' that you was too soft to do before."

"You could have killed her."

"Just how would that serve us? She's better alive after this much trouble." Lionel looked in her direction and sliced his tongue between his lips. "'Haps I'll follow the gray man's lead and just wed the shrew—get the whole estate instead of just a li'l piece."

Rhys took a reckless step forward, growling his words through his teeth. "Did you touch her?"

"Whether I wed her or sell her, she's better off with her honor intact." Lionel put a hand to his heart in mock tenderness. "Even I have standards. I wouldn't take a ruined woman to wife even if I'd been the one to ruin 'er. 'Sides, fathers pay up for their daughters' reputations, not their daughters' lives."

Honor. Reputation. Ruin. This was too much. A fire was starting within Beth, and the shuddering of laughter began to ripple up through her limp body. She struck a hand to the ground and hefted herself up on it. *These bleeding fools.*

Rhys wanted to go to her as she rose up, but even if there'd been no standoff, he recognized the danger of approach. Beth staggered around, hunched and bedraggled. All of the men's attentions were drawn by it, this marsh creature that pointed at them and laughed.

Her beautiful face was lit with cold-eyed humor. "You are ransoming me on my *reputation*? How droll. Oh, you poor, *stupid* things. You have chosen very badly."

She straightened up as if gaining power from her amusement. Rhys hung on her every unhinged word—

"You think I have a *reputation* and *honor*? A boy I grew up with has my *honor*. I gave it to him freely, lovingly as a teenaged girl. If you want my honor, it's no longer mine. Go seek him out."

She laughed again, but the terrifying sound died out as her eyes met Rhys'.

"And ruin? I know it very well. Society made certain of that. *This*—" Beth gestured at all of them, making Rhys acutely aware of their absurdity. "This won't stain me at all. For what stain can show up on a garment already dyed black?"

Rhys felt every bit the fool that she was calling him—calling all of them. He'd reminded himself so ardently of their differences—she was a toff, a gentlewoman, a silk-stocking who would sooner spit on him—even as her true colors had been waved in his face. Even as every other thing he learned of her had drawn him in like some perfume on the air. She was brave. She was kind. She understood betrayal long before he brought her here.

The men had been suspended in place, agog, while she railed, but of course it was Lionel who recovered first.

"What a waste that we didn't all take a turn with ye then."

Rhys re-leveled his pistol at Lionel's face and stepped toward him.

"Don't you care about your man Harry?" asked Lionel. "After all, you care so damn much, don't you? For the quartermaster's family, for *her*." He directed his eyes at Beth.

"I cared about where you ended up too, Lionel. It's why we've done all of this."

"And it was good in the beginnin'. But we're far from the gallows now, and I want more."

"So do I, Lionel."

"Then let's get her looking spruce and ride off." Lionel's eyes opened up in desperation and he bounced in his knees, pleading. Some unexpected trace of loyalty was still there. Rhys didn't respond. He couldn't.

Lionel's face relaxed into a scowl at Rhys' silence. He snapped his fingers toward Solomon who pressed the tip of the knife more firmly at Harry's ribs.

"You betrayed me, and now I'll take her back for the ransom myself."

"You still don't know where."

"And how do you know she didn't tell us between her dips in the bath and beg us to take her there?"

Rhys fought the twitch in his lip. He was wrong about many things, but one thing he knew. "She simply wouldn't."

"Then tell me or I'll rut her and leave the lot of you dead!" Lionel screamed himself into a purple hue. A nasty spray spewed from Lion's lips as he roared. "Sol, grab her too." Lionel pointed to where Beth had been standing, but she wasn't there.

Lionel's eyes were darting around when they all heard the rumble. Only a second's warning before—

Rhys' saddled chestnut came bursting around the corner of the house, throwing the whole scene into chaos as Beth rode right through them. Rhys' heart leapt at the sight of it, even as he rolled out of her warpath. *Go. Get far away from here.*

Harry took his chance to dive away from Sol. Rhys saw Sol lunging for Harry, dagger still in hand, and turned his pistol.

CRACK

Solomon's leg instantly gave way beneath him and he clutched his hip where the ball struck.

"You bastard!" Lionel came for Rhys now that his shot was spent. Rhys' back slammed into the icy mud as two crooked thumbs pressed into his throat. Rhys shoved the heel of his hand up into Lionel's jaw, pushing, pushing—making use of his advantage in arm span—yet Lionel's grip would not relent. Rhys coughed.

A dull and heavy thud sent Lionel flying sideways off him as Harry and his helpful boot replaced Rhys' view overhead. Harry pulled his sword on the squirming man. Rhys swiftly stood and drew his own.

He glared at the pathetic man in the mud.

"Run away," he said.

Lionel pulled himself up. With a sour expression, he began a trudge toward the horses. Rhys barred him with the length of his blade.

"You know better than that how this works."

The wretched man raised an oily eyebrow and then pivoted grudgingly. He was marched to the forest's edge with Rhys and Harry's swords brushing his back.

Solomon's groans sounded like those of a man being dragged straight to hell. Lionel turned and looked over Rhys' shoulder at his injured ally. Rhys shoved away a pang of guilt and was grateful when Lionel didn't speak. Their lives were not supposed to end up this way.

Rhys and Harry both watched as Lion disappeared onto the same trail that they'd arrived on.

Rhys walked over to Solomon who breathed deeply while clamping down on his hip. "You were on the wrong side, but I wish I hadn't had to do it," said Rhys.

Solomon nodded, biting his lip.

The dark mud made it hard to see how much blood had been spilled, but Solomon's face was far whiter than it should have been.

"Did it strike the bone?"

"Dunno."

"Do you want me to look at it?"

"Nay."

"Do you want me to—"

"What? To put me out of my misery, Captain? I'll stay where I am. The cold can take me soft enough."

Rhys turned to Harry, who stood at his side, looking down at Sol with a concerned expression. "Do you have any drink in your saddlebag, Harry?" Harry nodded, and Rhys didn't have to instruct him further.

Harry soon returned with a flask and passed it down into Solomon's bloodied hand.

"Farewell, old man."

Turning his back on Sol, Rhys felt like every step away brought him ever downward, closer to hell. It was true what Lionel had said. Rhys cared, and it made it damned difficult to do the things he had to do.

They went to the remaining horses. They were all fully tacked, having been readied for their now-abandoned plan. Beth had done well to take Rhys' horse—the best of the lot.

"I'll take Lionel's," said Rhys. He took the leads of the spare hackney horse and Solomon's nag and put them in Harry's hand. "You should take these two and sell them."

"Do you want me to come with you, Captain?"

Harry said *Captain* with so much reverence in his tone. Rhys couldn't stand it any longer.

"I'm no one's captain, Harry. Least of all yours. Please, just sell the horses. Take everything that's been stashed in the folly and find a way to make ends meet." Rhys rationed out the contents of Solomon's saddlebags as they spoke.

"Where will we meet up again, Rhys?"

Rhys swung his leg up over Lionel's black horse. "You'll have a better life if you don't know me. You're too skilled and capable to suffer all of this." He gestured to the crumbling folly and its muddy side yard.

Harry tossed the sandy hair from his eyes. "Good luck, Rhys."

"Same to you, Harry." Rhys reached a hand down, laying it warmly on Harry's shoulder. It was difficult to pull away.

Rhys guided his horse toward the trees that had swallowed Beth's escape. Somewhere beyond them, she ran, and he would do what he could to ease her path.

10

Twigs snapped on Beth's arms as she wove Rhys' horse through the dense growth. She held in her mind the image of smoke rising in the distance—the view she'd caught from the window the day before. When she'd made her disappearance into the woods, she'd done so with purpose and direction. But now, boulders, embankments, and even the trees themselves conspired to throw her off her bearings.

She slowed down to think. The low morning sun was stretching its long fingers through the forest, warming her back as she rode. When she'd surveyed the area from her window, the morning sun hadn't been a part of the view. So it seemed possible she was still on the right path . . . roughly.

Unfortunately, slowing down allowed other thoughts to catch up to her too. The fog of self-preservation was lifting, unwrapping recent memories . . .

The snap of a pistol's shot.
Birds scattering upwards.
The impossibility of looking back.
The horror of not knowing.

Beth gave Rhys' horse a gentle kick before the feelings overwhelmed her. A trickle of icy trough water dribbled down her neck from where her wet hair clung to her. Bringing a hand up, she discovered that Rhys' scarf had been lost, but the pendant—it was still there. She gave her head a fierce shake, loosening the sopping tresses that might benefit from the sun at her back. An entire day stretched before her. This time, her survival would not be a fool's errand.

The sun had passed overhead, and it was well into the afternoon when Beth hopped down to rifle through Rhys' bags for food. Only by focusing on the task at hand could she seem to preserve herself from wondering what happened back at the folly.

And another concern brewed. When Rhys had ridden to town, the entire errand had taken up barely more than half the day. It meant that she was straying off course, perhaps badly.

Her search in his saddlebag yielded a familiar bundle. It was the one Rhys had pulled their little rations from when they'd eaten together that first morning. Even more familiar was the flask of gin. She fumbled it as though it burned her. Seizing it before it hit the dirt, she clutched it to her breast. Fear blossomed from where she held it.

Had Rhys been—is he all right?

A tingling ache surged to her cheeks as tears began to pool, but they were held back. Firming her jaw, she swallowed hard and lowered herself to the ground to eat. A hunting knife was bundled with some small pieces of cured meat. The mysterious voices of the forest—the caws and snaps and rustles—told her she'd do well to keep it close. When the knife's duty as a utensil was complete, she slipped it behind the front laces of her stays.

A cold breeze whisked up her spine as she packed up the remains of her repast. The thicket was all still, but the sounds of its hidden denizens were becoming more insistent. She had but a couple more hours until sunset.

Rising up too quickly, she struck her head on a low branch and let out a sickened hiss.

She turned fiercely, as though she might strike out at the cruel branch, but instead she found herself inspired by its lowness. So she climbed it.

Beth hadn't been up a tree since her youth and certainly never one so intimidating as this. She wrapped herself tight to the trunk, feeling much too breakable as a fully-grown woman. But after steadying herself, she teetered her way up a few more branches until she could see just enough of the sky—

To have her hopes completely dashed.

There was no smoke ahead. No sign at all of a town. She turned her head as far around as it could go, straining for an owl's view of things.

Far behind her was the distant, dying wisp of the folly's chimney. Then she saw it, off to the east, a whole set of cheerful puffs. She'd not been entirely off, but her direction was poor enough that she'd passed the village and was now very far out of its way.

At least it was there, proving its existence and her remaining sanity. Glumly, she climbed back down. She found it only too fitting when she slipped on the same malicious branch that had injured her before.

On her back in the damp loam, her cheeks prickled again, and this time, she allowed herself the tears. Over and over, she struck her chest with her fist as though to knock the emotion out of her. The stays, which she'd not removed for days, deadened her own strikes, so she struck harder. She kept doing so even as her knuckles dinged against the hard handle of the knife that she'd stowed there.

She gasped until she coughed, and at last her hand flopped to her side.

Her chest rose and fell deeply. Purposefully. Until her concentrated breathing brought the tears to heel.

She stood then, remembering to evade the cursed branch this time. "I've learned," she said to it—to no one.

Pulling herself up in the stirrup, she caught a glimpse of some familiar fabric rolled into a bundle on the horse's rump. She touched it. Rhys' cloak.

Soon it was around her shoulders and hanging down well past her feet in the stirrups. She pressed her nose to her shoulder, finding and inhaling that soothing trace of pine. Of winter. Of him. Memories danced toward her. Memories of his chin rested against her in the rain, of being pressed against his warm body . . .

She turned the horse in the direction of the village, but her resolve to focus had been irreparably weakened by disappointment in herself.

The canopy above was oppressive and dark—feeling ever lower—like the branches might push her down, down, right into the earth. Then their roots would knit themselves over the ground and conceal that she ever existed at all. No one would find her.

She could no longer fix her mind on the present. It was growing far too frightening. She did not think it any wiser to surrender to the past, yet it kept seducing her with its whispers of warmth and hope.

So she stopped struggling and laid herself bare to memories.

She imagined herself sinking into Rhys' cape as though it were a pool of ink. And just as she felt enveloped by the wool, so she felt enveloped by his arms. To even think of him helped her to stay upright in her seat. Her spine was a solid pillar so long as she could lean against the ghost of Rhys. The mere fantasy of his body heat was enough to warm her through.

Her lip curled wistfully as she recalled his expression when she'd had a hot fire iron to his throat. He'd not been afraid but had certainly been *surprised*. That had been enough to please her.

This morning she'd surprised them all. Find another society lady who would openly declare the state of her virtue to four men at once, and Beth would show you a unicorn. What could Beth care about her boldness when half of the shire knew the breadth of her improprieties from a network of whispers that never died? None of it mattered.

And none of it was regretted.

The boy she'd spoken of was Dyckson. The Sumner's middle son, he lived less than half a mile from Greenthorne. They'd been tutored alongside one another from the age of six. Being out in the country, they'd had few opportunities for other friendships to form, and so they were joined at the hip.

A decade of beautiful friendship passed.

Beth closed her eyes to better remember his face—the sandy hair that curled whenever it got longer than his ears, a nose that was always golden from the sun. He was a few months older than her and constantly emboldened by it. In his confident way, he'd dragged her into almost every childhood misadventure she'd ever had, whether it was nearly drowning in the pond or stepping on a snake that he'd brought to their most recent fortress.

Beth smiled. When she'd last climbed a tree prior to her present crisis, it had most certainly been with him.

He was her accomplice in almost everything fun that ever happened at Greenthorne, just as Dahlia had been at Ashecote.

Then one day, when Beth was sixteen, she fell off her horse when they were riding together. The bump to her head was bad enough that she was told she couldn't be roused for more than a minute. When she opened her eyes, Dyckson was right over her, shaking her gently, begging her to wake. She would never forget how his young eyes swam with terror.

Her instinct upon waking was to comfort him, and she did, and they'd held one another, there in the grass, for a long time. As they walked their horses back to Greenthorne that evening, something felt different.

The particulars of the day that it finally happened were now partly obscured by time, but Beth could recall how they both stood holding hands over the blanket they'd brought to an overgrown area. She could still picture his boyish face over hers, eyes twinkling from the nearby lantern. Every feeling of being there on that blanket was amplified by their daringness to sneak out at night.

It must have started awkwardly, but she could only remember their deep, indulgent kissing and the slow and novel pleasures of undressing one another, of *seeing* one another. The feeling of a summer night's air on her breasts was the most singular thing. Something experienced far too rarely.

Completely unforgotten was the moment that her eyes slid down to fix her gaze on a young man's anatomy for the first time. She'd found it very different from all the statues she'd seen. Yet her mind got over this fascination quickly, and in the next moment, his nakedness seemed as natural as the night sky.

Beth's breath caught in her throat, reliving the very instant when she pulled him down to her. There was no one in the world she'd ever trusted more. She opened herself up to him completely, and her faith in him delivered on every promise.

As they locked themselves together that night, it would be the first of many intimate embraces scattered across the next year and a half.

Even before they were caught, she was aware it could not go on forever. He was destined to have a living in Scotland, and a young lady up there had been vaguely promised to him. Beth was at peace with the fact. It was instead her greatest fear that such antics might somehow degrade their original friendship. But away from their blankets in the grass, their friendship remained as it had been—warm and adventurous and confidential.

And then one day, a gossip-loving goatherd saw them leaving a shed together on the Sumner's land. He wasn't a particularly reliable witness, but as it is with families—particularly those with daughters—there was a strong reaction.

For the next several months, that seed of salaciousness grew into the tree that would uproot her pleasant life. It was amazing to watch how her father's family and friends could talk so abundantly around it without saying *it* at all.

Her father, for his part, gave a lecture on how grave it would be were she to end up with child. But not knowing any better, Beth had already been just as reckless as he was warning about—and so many times too. It seemed clear to her that her body was not cooperative with such a state.

Dyckson went largely untarnished by the affair. His only punishment was to be sent to settle in Scotland earlier than planned. To curb his adventurous appetites beyond that would have been *a crime against his manhood,* or so they'd said. His awkward, naked-chinned, not-yet-of-eighteen years, *manhood.* And just like that, her best friend was gone.

Beth had never forgotten Dyckson. Not his adventure, not his safety, not his dark young eyes that sparkled with curiosity—eyes that were not unlike those of Rhys.

Her reveries came to a cliff, and she was alone with the sounds of her horse's steps, plodding on the soft earth.

Even that steady sound began to fade. Her eyes blinked slow and heavy. The sun suddenly seemed so low.

She drifted, then straightened. Then drifted again.

But a sound brought her upright with a start—

AAAaaarooOOOOooooo

11

The lamenting chorus of howls was near enough to raise the hairs on Beth's arms. But in a forest full of echoes, it seemed they might be anywhere.

This wasn't what it sounded like when the hunting hounds outside of Greenthorne bayed. It was like no sound heard in the whole of England. Instead, it called to mind the sort of sounds she'd read about in fairytales from the Continent.

Rhys' horse chewed on the bit and huffed. Beth eyed her surroundings—attention jerking sharply toward any little sound. A bristling in the dead undergrowth. Plops of snowmelt striking the mud . . .

She'd urged the horse forward when another echo stopped her. Again, she waited—her heart balanced on a pin.

The howls went up again and then faded. Blessedly, faded. Beth released a breath she'd long been holding and nudged the gelding back into step.

Her relief splintered as a nightmarish blur emerged at her right—already surging upward—already—

Beth landed in the mud with a sickening slap as her horse kicked and reared above her. Scrambling to her feet, she found Rhys' knife at her breast and readied it in front of her. Another shadow passed low in her periphery. Too quick to catch a sight—

WHOOSH

A long, dark-bodied thing cut through the air and slammed into the horse's neck. The horse reared again, nearly falling on top of Beth before gaining purchase on the slick ground and running away. The beast gave chase to the chestnut, as did another shape that emerged from nowhere. Beth could not believe what she was seeing.

Wolves. Unheard of.

The vicious pounding of her heart threatened her efforts to keep still. Surely the horse would lure the wolves far away. But her body did not yet yield to such hopeful thoughts, and the knife in her hand ticked upward with every shaking breath.

There. A faint rustle behind her.

Beth thought—hoped—she had only imagined it, but she knew her luck better than that. She turned.

Another wolf—a sickly, starved-looking thing—stood not a handful of paces away and growled lowly.

Beth's knuckles whitened on the knife's handle as she brought it in front of her.

Anticipating the lunge, she was able to dodge it, but she wasn't so quick the second time and was brought down. The predator twisted back around to her with that quickness that only wild animals possess. It fastened its glistening teeth into her skirt and tore viciously. Fruitlessly. Then its citrine eyes locked into hers, realizing where the real meal was. The creature's mouth fell open, and it lowered itself.

Beth raised the knife.

The wolf sprung for her neck, and her eyes were wide open as the horribly stretched jaws—lined with death—flew toward her. But her knife was there, waiting, and she thrust it upward to meet the beast.

The animal collapsed against her, heavy as a man. Its body slid down the blade to meet her hand. Warm rivulets traced paths down her wrist. The creature suddenly awoke to its own pain and its hind legs scraped at her mercilessly as it writhed. Its jaws snapped open and closed aimlessly beside her face, extracting screams from her that were as much an expulsion of fear as they were a battle cry.

Her blade had struck just to the inside of the wolf's powerful shoulder and would not loosen itself. Beth fought to extract it, to get herself away from the wolf in its dangerous throes of agony. At last, the flesh relented to her possession of the knife, and she scrambled out from beneath the unfortunate thing.

Standing up, she watched it struggle to do the same. Pathetic as the poor creature seemed now, she wouldn't dare turn her back on it. It steadied itself, but its gemstone eyes no longer contained the focus of a hunter. It was not keen on more trouble.

For one blessed moment of insanity, Beth felt triumphant. She craned her neck to thank the darkening sky.

But then came the yips and yelps behind her—the disturbance of the leaves—as the wolf's two kin returned.

The knife faltered in her hand, slippery with blood. She tightened her grip until her nails dug into the flesh of her palm.

The wolves circled around her to join their injured brother.

Her knife hand suddenly steadied.

She'd die here.

"I'm sorry, Papa." The whisper was almost too soft to reach her own ears.

The bleeding wolf growled again, as though to signal his mates that it was time.

She couldn't say which one lunged first, only that a pair of jaws narrowly missed her as she swung her knife hand. The weight of the beast knocked the knife's edge back into her own ribs, nicking against her stays. Rhys' cloak was grabbed by the other wild dog, and one yank of it brought her back to the cold ground. She struck out wildly with her heel, connecting with nothing but air.

CRACK

The wolves went still.

The echo of a gunshot was still clapping through the air as Beth pushed herself up. The ground rumbled beneath her fingers. The steady rhythm of a gallop.

The wolves split to either side as a horse barreled into the small clearing.

The yips of the small pack were as sharp as screams, but they were no longer near her. The figure on the horse wielded a blazing torch and swung it down again and again at the frantic, bloodthirsty pair. Briefly, they would break away in a panic, only to return to their harassment of the horseman. But he harassed them back.

At last, with enough rearing and trampling and swings of the torch, the two wolves were dispersed.

Beth stood up, frozen. Sick with how fiercely her blood was pumping. She couldn't cry out to him in her relief. Couldn't yet acknowledge the man that she knew had saved her.

Rhys dismounted, stabbed his torch into the mud and stared at Beth as the forest settled. One last wolf, so still as to go unnoticed by him, collapsed suddenly—dead between them. A casualty that was no doubt the result of the blood he saw dripping over the knife in her hand. *His* knife.

In the whole of his life, he'd never seen such a sight and he felt oddly blessed to bear witness—not just to see her safe, but—*all of it.*

Her.

Panting in a gloomy little clearing, in the dwindling light. Long hair clinging to the sweat of her face and tangling down past her breast. Like some medieval witch, with blood dripping off her. An artist of survival that amazed him at every turn. A woman unlike any—

"I am as a magnet to peril."

"If that's so, you bear your calling very admirably." He gestured to the expired wolf.

Finally, he crossed the gulf between them. He hadn't realized he'd opened his arms wide for her until she collapsed into them, letting the knife fall from her limp hand.

She spoke into his chest. "You're alive."

"*I'm* alive?" He pushed her to arm's length to check her for injuries.

"Yes, I heard a shot."

He'd already forgotten. Of course she hadn't seen how that played out. He pushed a long tendril of hair from her face, as he'd always found himself wishing to do. "I'm fine, Beth."

"And Harry?"

Rhys smiled for how fond they both were of Harry. "Also fine."

"Your horse is gone."

"I know. It came dashing past me. That's how I knew where to find you. There was no time to catch it."

Beth leaned into him. Her muscles seemed to go softer and softer, unhinging themselves after battle. He wanted this warrior to sleep against his chest for days. He wanted them to each take off their armor and be soft together.

Pushing one lock of hair from her eyes had been a temptation so great that he now found himself stroking every wayward strand from that divine face. And even when her eyes were clear of it, he caressed her hair still.

"Let me help you," he said, softly as he could.

She drew back, and he ached at feeling her step away.

She picked up the knife, wiped it with her skirts, and tucked it in at her breast.

"Tell me, was I very far off from a village?"

"You weren't, at least not as the crow flies, but the terrain is very poor on your chosen route."

She nodded, her eyes examining the trees.

"I think you would have made it this time."

She broke from her contemplation and smiled tiredly. "Do you?"

"Well, if not for the wolves, maybe, but even there you surprise me." He looked again at the carcass. "I don't think your gallantry was misplaced at all this time. You had a very real shot and you took it. Let me pay you my respects by helping you get home."

"I've not forgotten, Rhys, that you have obligations and debts. You still need what I have."

He sighed and leaned against Lionel's horse, gathering his thoughts. "My debts aren't from gambling or loans, Beth. They're of a guilty nature. I owe somebody because I hurt them. And now I've hurt you, and I owe a debt there too."

"You told me that you hadn't learned where Greenthorne was.

Was that a lie?"

"Yes."

"Why were you in the woods with Harry? Was Lionel right? Were you going to betray the others and ransom me? Is that why you wanted me to stay quiet the night before? So that they wouldn't hear the price—"

"No!"

"Then why were you in the woods? Where *were* you when they attacked me? I needed you." Her voice faltered. The sound of it nearly killed him "The one thing you promised was—"

"That I'd keep you safe from them. I know. Believe me I know. I'm so sorry."

She wore a strange expression. Her eyes were searching for something that couldn't be seen. "Last night, you—did you . . ." But she shook off whatever she was thinking and left her question hanging in the air, incomplete.

He stepped toward her again, and she didn't move away. Gently, he took her shoulders and turned her a few degrees.

"Look," he said. "That's southwest. It'll take an hour and a half back to the road. That road will loop you around east to the village of Cobton Dale. You can take this horse and there should be a compass in Lionel's pack. You can have the torch." He turned her around to him. His cape was twisted around her from her melee with the wolves. He set it to rights and brushed off her shoulders. "And this. You should keep it. As it looks so very good on you."

Another weak smile played on her lips as she pulled the cloak more tightly around her.

He stepped back. "You have everything you need, particularly courage, to make it to that small town where good people can help you home. But—"

All the words he'd said felt right, yet still, he could not bear the uncertainty of it. He trusted her. Trusted the sheer force of her impressive will, yet he hoped—

"Please help me," she said. "I don't want to be alone out here again."

He took her in his arms, and her whole body quivered.

"Then I have a different proposal."

"Which is?"

"Your home is off of a different road. With two of us on a horse, it's half a day away. I suggest we rest where we are and go in the morning."

She unburied her face from his chest to look up at him, her brown eyes round with alarm.

"But we have no shelter. We'll be frozen." This tinge of panic seemed so uncommon to her.

"We won't, I promise. We'll find a good spot, and I'll make us a fire." She said no more but still looked up at him with unique worry pulling at her brow. "Truly," he said, and she sank back into him.

"Do you have enough left in you that you can help make a camp before we lose the last of our light?"

Beth nodded and smiled gamely through her exhaustion. This woman, who had just killed a wolf.

Beth stepped back to admire their work. Apparently, all the men's horses carried some effects necessary for encampment. Rhys complained about the inferiority of Lionel's supplies, but Beth thought them fortunate to have at least one waxed piece of canvas to work with.

They'd settled on a low rocky overhang as their shelter, and Rhys had made a fire right in front of it. The tarpaulin was stretched across one side to block sharp winds from getting sucked over their bodies as they slept.

As they worked, he filled her in on what had happened back at the folly.

Poor Solomon. She had no love for the man, of course, but loathed that any bloodshed had come of this affair. She even felt for the wolf, a beast thought to be extinct on the isle for a century. She was certain it was the only creature larger than a spider that she'd ever extinguished.

Rhys walked past her, carrying the saddlebags from where he'd hitched Lionel's horse, and threw them into their little shelter.

"Not sure what all is in these yet. As you can imagine, Lion isn't a responsible or organized sort. There will be food though."

Beth stared into the fire, not really hearing him. She wasn't aware he had come close until he took her hand. She looked down at where their palms were joined and wondered if he, too, felt this clutching sensation beneath his ribs when they touched. The glow of the fire danced on Rhys' high cheekbone. The creases of a smile were at the corner of his eye as he drew her toward their shelter.

"After you."

She crouched down to duck under the overhang, careful not to drag the excess of Rhys' cape right through the fire. She smiled as she crept into the glowing space. Rhys, crawling in behind her, must have noticed.

"What is it?" His eyes danced with their familiar curiosity.

"This is not the first time I've been outside late at night, but it *is* the first time that I don't have to sneak back to my bed before morning. None of my female relations have ever slept outside. It will be a distinction all my own."

"So will being kidnapped. *Twice.* You could boast about that one in just about any company."

They both laughed. The mirth didn't leave Rhys' eyes as he began to sort out some food. Beth returned her eyes to the flames as though she might see her reflection there.

"I'll have many adventures to gloat about, but absolutely not a soul to tell."

"Why in heavens not?" Rhys passed her a piece of hard cheese.

"I don't have any friends."

Rhys leaned against the wall of rock, and she watched his face change as this information was digested.

"Because of what you said back at the folly? When you spoke of ruin?"

"Yes. Mostly. A lot of people turned their backs on me, and, I suppose, once that began to subside, I turned my back on them as well. It changed me. Made me quiet and small."

"Which is exactly what everyone wanted you to be."

Yes. Beth hadn't thought of that before—of just how effective their methods were. The tittering old society ladies had gotten exactly what they demanded—her *shame*. Yet they never offered any forgiveness. Her ostracism had been so deviously orchestrated that Beth had confined herself, imagining it to be her own choice.

Rhys' hand on her knee broke her from the revelation.

"I've never met this Beth, quiet and small. The only one I've ever met is a legend." Rhys said it with a confident, almost cocky expression as he brought a crumb of Cheshire cheese to his lips, but there was no trace of mocking.

A legend. Beth remembered sitting in Dyckson's fortress as a girl, clutching her stick sword. She had felt like a legend then. The way she felt now, under Rhys' gaze and the night sky, felt as similar as she would ever come again.

"When you return home, you'll be able to tell anyone you meet about this because it will all be too legendary to be believed."

Beth smiled. Perhaps that was so. She picked up some bread and inched herself until his shoulder was behind her. Something stopped her from leaning back.

"I know ruin too," said Rhys.

"How? A man may have congress with every woman in the county and not be ruined."

Rhys laughed—a loud, rich sound—the most unrestrained thing she'd ever heard from him. "I don't mean it in that way."

She knew that, but she was happy to see him laugh anyway, and she joined him in it. His brow suddenly crinkled, and he looked at her very seriously, gripping her knee more tightly. "And just to be clear, Beth, that is *not* a thing that I've done." She looked deep into his eyes, knowing he was communicating something serious to her, but also wondering who was going to collapse back into laughter first. She could see it on his lips. It would be him. "I've only slept with *half* the women in the—" He couldn't finish. Laughter had taken them both.

An arm was wrapped beneath Beth's ribs as Rhys pulled her to lean back into his shoulder. It was the invitation she'd been longing for. With it came a thick silence.

"Rhys?"

"Yes?" His breath caressed her ear, making her want to abandon her question and wrap herself around every part of him. But the desperation to know his story was somehow even stronger.

"I interrupted you. Tell me how you were ruined."

His arm around her tightened as he sighed into her hair.

"Well, Beth. You were right all along. I was a sailor. We all were. But I was far from being a captain."

An onslaught of questions was surging to Beth's lips, but she bit them back. Rhys' eyes were far away and glistened with the mist of tides that only he could see.

He would share what he was able.

"We were all on a merchant contract to Newfoundland. When we reached the Labrador Sea, our captain ordered us north. Captain Sir Ralph Cloudesley. Second son of an earl. The master and the captain's mates were all of his ilk. They put on their indiscernible, high-born expressions and followed Captain's orders to the letter. The captain was old, hadn't sailed in near a decade, and he kept ranting about an important mission on behalf of The Crown. All of those officers believed enough in their own importance that they got their heads wrapped round his delusions.

"The rest of us had never seen enough shillings in our whole lives to give a whiff about praise from The Crown, imagined or not. We just wanted to come back home with our skins intact. Going where he wanted us to go, we'd have been sunk by ice, or gotten trapped in it and starved.

"I was only the carpenter. My closest friend was Heathcote Dewey, the quartermaster."

Rhys' speech tightened around his friend's name, and he paused. Beth slipped a hand under his and his fingers responded with a grip almost too tight to bear. He kept his eyes on the fire.

"Dewey and I had heard more of the captain's delusions than some of the other crew. Harry, who was my mate, and Lion, and Sol, who were sailors—they strongly favored our concerns. So we organized a mutiny."

Rhys always had sweat beading at his temple when near a fire, but the moisture that streaked over his cheek now wasn't that.

"I believed so ardently in justice," he said. "We kept careful records of all that happened. Most of the crew sided with us. We locked up the captain and his mates and sailed back to Bristol, but the first mate perished in the brig. That was the first time I began to wonder if we'd been right to do it."

Beth stroked Rhys' hand with her thumb, as much for her comfort as his. Her heart felt fragile against his sorrow.

"On arrival, the five of us were shipped off to Bristol Newgate to await our day in court. An entire sea of nobility washed into the city to defend the captain's reputation. The officers' wives, daughters of peerage, came into the prison to titter and gawp at us. They promised us that with one flick of their tongues or one letter from their fathers, they would see us all hanged. Their words worried Dewey . . .

"He was the first to go before the judges, and unbeknownst to us all, he took full responsibility. Went so far as to tell the court that he'd murdered the perished officer. By the time we learned we were free, he'd already been hanged."

Beth squeezed his hand. It seemed time to speak.

"It's his family you take care of, isn't it?"

Rhys nodded. "I was the first one to dare speak of mutiny. I felt responsible for everything and for the way our lives were after. We'd just sailed for months with no pay. We were blackballed from contracts and banished from Bristol. The four of us walked away from the city together, not knowing where we'd go."

He looked into Beth's eyes darkly. "That night on the road, we came upon the post, with a broken wheel—"

"—and it was like a lame deer to a hungry beast?"

"Yes," he said, ruefully. "So that's how it began. And now you know all of my secrets."

"I'll keep them as safe as the marble nymph kept mine."

The fire cracked and an owl heralded the beginning of night.

"What secrets do I get to learn of you?"

Beth rolled her head in mock frustration. "Oh? Was it not enough to announce to the whole world that I'm lacking in purity?"

"I don't think you're lacking in anything," he said.

12

Periodically, Rhys would feel Beth shiver against him. No matter how tightly he held her, it took minutes for her body to still. If she were sleeping any closer to the fire, she'd be choking on its smoke, yet she could not keep warm.

He tucked his cheek against hers, hoping he might stem the chills that gripped her neck like the very hand of winter. The edge of his unshaven jaw dragged roughly against her silken skin. He prayed it wouldn't wake her.

Beneath his forearm, her ribs gently rose and fell. In spite of the fits of shivering, her slumber seemed heavy and distant.

Rhys took a deep breath. Emotions were climbing up his ribcage like a ladder, but he wouldn't know how to expel them should they ever reach his lips. Here she was, at last, in his arms again. Only days had passed since she'd been curled against him on their way to his thieves' den, but that day now felt distant and antiquated—changed incrementally through the act of remembering.

When they'd been alone at the bottom of the ravine that first day, he'd learned who she really was. His first assumptions were picked up by the fist of truth and smashed upon the ground. She'd stared him down, threatening to fling herself once more down that horrible slope—it was in that moment that her animal eyes dragged his rakish heart to its knees in respect for her.

Tonight, that respect had blossomed into borderline worship as he'd come upon her standing over the carcass of a wolf. That the only wolves on the isle even found her—wasn't that some omen? But was it the sort of omen meant to lure or the sort meant to warn away? His lip curled against her cheek. The thought that there existed some intrinsic danger to her made a thrill course through his veins.

He'd imagined the criminal life as one of permanent solitude, isolated forever from women of caliber. Not caliber measured in wealth or stature or the classical "accomplishedness" of ladies but of *this*. Whatever *this* was. Be it her buoyancy, her ferocity, or her appreciation for his eccentric outpost in the woods.

Her wealth and stature could not simply be cast aside though. They were the very things that he'd been prowling for on the road. Now they loomed as the specters that would keep the crossing of their paths temporary. Could she not just have been a horse groom's daughter? Even if he'd never taken up such illegitimate business as highway robbery, he'd have still only been a ship's carpenter. By no judge in the land was he deemed worthy enough to set foot on the lawns of her dear Greenthorne.

Another fit of gentle shaking moved up Beth's spine where her back was fitted to his chest. In an instant, his concern reignited. He pushed his face into her hair. The tangled umber waves smelled of the fire, yet felt as cold as the ground they both lay on. The gentle shivering turned into a spasm that roused her.

"Beth," he whispered. He rolled her beneath him so they might see one another. "What can I do?"

Beth's eyes opened to find Rhys almost at her nose. His eyes were round and desperate. She did her best to quell another spasm. She couldn't bear to encourage the worry that was writ on his face.

"I'm fine," she whispered as though they might wake someone. "I just shudder easily."

His leg was atop hers. The warmth of it felt so nice. She reached around his ribs and guided him to cover more of her. Then she tucked her bare hands up between their chests, seeking the sheltered heat there.

Unbidden, her chest began to rise and fall with more urgent depth.

Propped on an elbow, Rhys reached his other hand between them and smothered both her hands in his. She could feel her own heartbeat and imagined that he could feel it too.

A drop of sweat fell from his cheek onto her face. If only she could perspire in such cold.

"I'm not too heavy for you?" He shifted atop her, and their foreheads touched.

She responded only by hooking one of her fingers tightly around one of his. He understood and stayed.

Beth closed her eyes and wondered when he might be near enough to feel the flutter of her lashes.

His exhalations spread across her lips warmly.

He was so close.

Yet not enough.

She craned her neck to close the very small gap between them.

She brushed her lips on his, finally feeling what they were like. She found them as warm as the rest of him, but they didn't move against hers. The longer she hovered there, the more she worried she'd been wrong—

And then he came down on her.

Drawing her lips against his, he fought her for possession of the kiss. He covered her, and the cape at her back pressed deeply into the damp cushion of leaves and moss. Yet she rose so hard against him that had he not been there to pin her down she might have floated off into the night sky.

Her insides vibrated fiercely as an unholy swarm of passions tried to escape her. She commanded her heart to be calm but found her mind had no more authority over her than a dormouse.

Fevered, she moved to press her lips to his hard jaw, his brow, everything in reach, and he buried his face in her neck, inhaling deeply against it and leaving the marks of his ardor.

He pulled away to swallow a great gasp of air and smiled down at her. That smile—it threw the firelight at her. Beads of sweat sparkled as they peeled across the creases at his eyes.

He had a hand buried in her tangles as he observed her, but although she smiled back, she could see the specter of melancholy trying to overtake his features.

She frowned. *This moment was theirs—the past could not have it.*

Grasping his collar, she pulled him lower and locked into his eyes with all the seriousness of casting a spell. Her fingers began to work free the large buttons of his greatcoat. He helped. Soon he was sliding back down atop her, his coat open, sheltering them both. In the night's cold, it was as close as they could come to undress, but it was so much easier to feel the heat of him with only a few layers of linen and her stays between them.

He pressed her with another kiss as his hand explored her. Her neck. Her chest. A tender brush against the raised stitches in her skin.

His touch grew hungrier. Squeezing her arm. Tugging the cloth of her dress. The rip at the top of her habit had days ago left the top of her stays exposed. His hands ran helplessly over the boning of the garment—almost clawing—making her acutely aware of his desperation to feel more of her. As she felt his knee drop and tense between her legs, she grasped furiously for her skirts, tugging upward at them, consumed with the same desperation she saw in him. He completed her thought and abetted her in the act.

Having wrestled the petticoats up between their flattened bodies, she now discovered another sign of his need—one that pressed against her hip. It sobered her, made everything more real— made her even more ready to have him.

His stubbled cheek drew against hers, scraping it pleasantly. Her breath caught as she felt his hand against the inside of her knee. His heat against her coolness was enough to startle, but as his fingers spread out wide, her skin met his warmth and borrowed it.

He stroked her leg before catching the back of her thigh in a decisive grip and tugging her nearer to him. Her insides tugged downward too, and a sigh transformed into a moan as it rolled out from her body.

She pressed against his lips as he kissed her temple. As his hot, rasping breath swirled in and out of her ear—

"Beth."

Her hips responded to the name.

His hand slid along her thigh—up, up until there was no more leg to climb. The side of a warm finger slid up against her sex, and she pushed down against it on impulse, feeling her lips part slightly and weep in anticipation.

Rhys' hand squeezed that last edge of her thigh in a pleasant farewell, and then he began to stroke her teasingly with the back of his hand. Sensation unraveled her as she soaked in the foretaste of what was to come.

The wetness he teased from her was the warmest thing for miles. Beth's eyelids lolled drunkenly as she savored her own arousal.

Rhys began to swirl his fingers, lovingly, against her. Each little circle brought her more awake than the last as her own folds massaged that tender apex that she knew so well. But Rhys' hand—it was so intoxicatingly different from her own touch. There was all of this pressure inside her that made her feel powerful and vulnerable at once. Perhaps it was the strangeness of the past few days. Perhaps it was the tension of survival. But perhaps . . . perhaps it was just *him*.

Beth counted the seconds away, dying for the moment that Rhys would give her more. Then, at last, his fingertips traced the rim of her entrance, pressing her and taunting her. It took all of her summoned patience not to—*and then he stole inside.*

She gasped, pushing herself down to his knuckle and grasping at the wrist of the hand that was going to bring her such pleasure.

He lowered himself to cover her neck once more in sensuous kisses and tastes. Rhys' hold on her was certain. He had control of her from her most secret and defenseless place, and she threw herself into trusting surrender. His middle fingers hooked inside her. His palm pressed onto her mound and circled there, almost imperceptibly, and the pressure of it made her feel insane—made her feel like she had a thousand new confessions for the maenad.

Their lips met, and she breathed him in, tugged at his lip with her teeth, a plea for him to be infinitely closer—until he was a part of her.

The claws of arousal clamped down on her belly and she was

lost to it. Her hips lurched into his hand where he held her—where he *possessed* her. A gasping shriek escaped her throat as she clutched his dark hair by the fistful and crushed his face into her shoulder. His low growl settled pleasantly on her ears as the last bursts of heat spread and flared within her before settling warm and heavy in her tingling limbs.

Her chest heaved, and she felt the rumbling movement of his smothered laughter against her. She smiled at him, panting.

"Pleased . . . are you . . . with your work?"

Words came between uneven breaths.

Rhys nodded mischievously before rubbing his nose against her cheek. "I am but a humble craftsman. I suspect you're the real artist here."

His fathomless pupils danced in the firelight.

For Beth, it wasn't enough.

She reached down between them and found where his own need swelled tightly against his breeches. She stroked the taut weave before her fingers began to search keenly for the buttons.

"I need more of you."

Rhys' mirthful expression softened into one of seriousness and meaning. His fingers wrapped gently around her wrist to stay her hand. "Are you certain, Beth?"

In the morning there would be many, many things to reckon with, but now—

"Yes, Rhys. *Please.*"

She could hear the ache in her own voice. She knew he heard it too.

Soon it was not his finger that pressed at her entry but the silky tip of his cock, thick and exciting. She was ready to feel all of him.

Rhys brushed the hair from her cheek, and she suddenly

noticed that the endearing gesture had become a habit of his, even when she had no strands in her eyes.

Wrapping a strong arm behind her hips, Rhys raised her gently off the cloak, aligning the both of them for pleasure.

Slowly he pushed into her and her flesh stretched to accept him, to invite him in. Bearing down around the fullness of him, she thought her soul might part. And even when it hurt, it was bliss. She twined her legs around his hips—encouraged him to root himself fully in her depths.

When their bodies met completely, they each let out their own rasping sounds and began, gradually, to move as one.

To feel him inside of her was somehow both rapturous and peaceful at once. Yet, in the first moments, Beth struggled to not want more. More of her skin against his. More undress. More sunshine. More time. Rhys stole these thoughts away with a torrid kiss as he heaved into her again.

After that, all that Beth felt and knew was of the moment. The feel of her body drawing him into her. The way that his every thrust struck some unknown mark within. The cold was cast out completely. Beth's skin became dewy with the warm exertion of their ardor. They would *not* freeze in the wilderness tonight.

Then the pace of his kisses and gentle bites were slowed. He breathed more heavily and she with him.

She caught him studying her from above. His eyelids tightened in concentration with the depth of every thrust—thrusts that pushed delicate, pleading sounds out of her on every breath.

Never leave.

She reached up and held his face squarely in her hands, her nails curling into the skin behind his ears. He now fairly growled with every fervid stroke. His cock twitched deep inside her. He began to pull away, but she didn't let him go. Looking him deep in the eyes, she assented.

And he pushed so firmly against her body as he shuddered that she thought her little bed of earth might swallow her. Unbearably attached to the heat between her thighs, she wrapped every limb around him. And slowly every muscle atop her went slack as Rhys' last aching gasps were expelled. His breath shook, ragged, against her shoulder. She stroked her fingers through his dampened hair.

The air around them no longer smelled of smoke or of decaying leaves. It smelled of wet wool, and sweat, and seed. It smelled of *them*.

She ached at his withdrawal from her.

Rhys did a languid roll, taking Beth with him and leaving her on top. The cape she wore—his own—now trapped the heat between them. She rested her head against his heart, and their breathing steadied—matched. Spent, they were each at the edge of sleep.

A contented smile drew across Beth's face. Her body was filled with dreamy desert sands. Perfectly warmed.

But as she drifted off, a slender finger of the cold wind wrapped around her ankle, whispering—

It's over.

Beth's eyes opened to face a squirrel but a few feet in front of her, digging through the leaves for its cached nuts. She followed it with her bleary morning vision, its routine bringing a smile to her lips. The dewiness of the morning had gone right into her bones but at least there was no frost. The fire was now an ashen heap with just one thin tendril of smoke rising from its center.

She felt a stirring at her back. The squirrel froze, alert.

"Who's this little voyeur?" asked Rhys—the end of his query falling off into a yawn.

"Our breakfast guest."

"Well I didn't invite anyone."

"He's here at my invitation, and we should show him the greatest courtesy here at . . . hmm . . ."

"Camp Wolvesden."

"Oh, that's rather apt. Better than I would have come up with."

Rhys put his arm around Beth's waist and the squirrel took its nut and ran.

Beth rolled to face him. She sought his warmth but could feel that the morning dampness had suffused his clothes just as badly as her own. Still, she curled into him, her eyes as heavy as a bear's in winter.

"We shouldn't linger long," he said and kissed her above her closed eyes. She lazily opened them, mostly to take him in. His sable hair was chaos, hardly a strand left in his queue. The waves of it were in his eyes, and when he leaned close enough, they were pleasantly in her eyes too. She blew gently on one of the locks that clung to his face and searched his features. He held her hand at her chest and smiled down at her.

This. If life could just be more like this. All the time. With him, it felt like every aspect of her could be seen and embraced.

He kissed her eyebrow again and stroked her cheek with his thumb. But that hesitant melancholy that she'd caught on his face so briefly the night before seemed to be returning. His gaze pierced her deeply. "I see it in your eyes," he said. "Don't try to figure out how it can work."

The words bit. But their bite came innocently enough from their truth. She had already accepted their separation as fact, even as they'd been in the throes of intercourse.

The exciting strangeness of their time together would have to hold her over for the rest of her days. In the last week, she'd had so many revelations regarding her own strengths that it was difficult now to picture how she'd sit alone with that knowledge. Forever. She saw it before her—decades of descent into old age with a poorly embroidered sampler in her lap.

She wished for a life where she might instead wring every drop from her potential. Where she could be out of doors and active. For most of her adult life, she'd gone to sleep and woken with a terrible itching and crawling in her legs. An urge she could never satisfy. But this morning that was absent. She had used her body—to many ends—in the past day and it was wholly content to be useful.

Days ago, in the threatening shadows of Lionel and Solomon, she wanted nothing more than to be home, but now the thought brought her equal measures of longing and dread.

Now it would end.

She was being ridiculous. If she didn't take a stance against her own naiveté, it might run away with her. Not only did they have to part, but she had to accept that he could still be full-well lying to her. Nothing besides his own conscience could stop him from demanding payment for her safe return. She was quite confident that he had such a conscience, but she'd made a guarded point to be reconciled with all possibilities.

Slipping from under Rhys' arm, she left their little alcove. Standing, her limbs felt weighted by a lack of sleep. She would never take back the experience of sleeping and rutting in the woods, but surely she wouldn't mind trying it in summertime. She smothered the fire and began to collect their things.

Rhys felt the absence of her body acutely. He had to get up, but daydreams of the night before were already inundating him like an army of ghosts. His hands flexed at the memory of taking fistfuls of her thighs and backside. His eyes clamped shut as he imagined the way she'd looked under him, surrounded by fabric and leaves and her own furiously messy hair—how she'd looked when he pushed into her for the very first stroke. How she'd wrapped around him . . . drawn him deeper . . .

He shuddered and felt his groin knot up. *No more of this.*

In silence, he helped her pack up. But his thoughts were unstoppable. He lingered no longer on her body, but his mind would not release him from other, more troubling thoughts.

He'd told her not to search for ways to make it work, but the advice was just as much for himself. Never again would he lay eyes on a woman standing over the predator she'd just killed by hand. He'd place a bet with the gods on that front. But even putting aside the sweeping dramatics of the past few days—where would he ever meet another such as her? A woman who finds humor in the face of uncertainty. A fearless woman. One who loves the outdoors, not solely in a "follows the hunting party with refreshments" sort of way but in a "leaves in her hair, after a night of rutting" sort of way.

Had he even known what he wanted before he met her? That he could want such companionship at all?

He swallowed the thoughts, and they went down as easily as a peach pit.

Approaching her as she loaded the bags, he plucked one of the aforementioned leaves from her hair. A mere excuse to touch her.

She didn't turn to him.

"I'll take down the canvas," he said. He was helpless to say more.

But even as he tore down their little encampment, he was punished by wistful thoughts. He tried to remember every detail of what happened there between them. The memories of the last few days would have to last his lifetime. It was a future that, now stretching out before him, felt bereft of happiness.

She brought the horse over to him, and together they rolled up the canvas in silence and packed it.

Taking her hand, he helped her up into the saddle. Her fingers were cool and clammy.

He slid into the seat behind her, and forceful memories about their last ride together rolled over him in violent waves. His arousal was difficult to contain, but something wasn't quite right.

She felt much warmer than usual against him.

He bent to put his cheek to hers.

"Are you comfortable?"

"Mhmm." She nodded, drowsily.

But her cheek was hot against his.

"Are you feeling well?"

"I'm well enough. I'm just tired and cold. Forever, cold." She rested back against him.

Despite her reassurance, a dull panic was floating, directionless, through Rhys' chest. He turned their horse and began to head for the sunrise. He tried to keep his voice calm—

"How is your injury today?"

"I think it's fine," she mumbled. "Doesn't hurt."

He pulled back the cape anyway. "Let me have a look at it. Lean into me."

Pushing the fabric away, he looked down over her shoulder. The skin was calm and pink. *Thank God.*

He put the cape back into place and wrapped an arm around her. The intermittent shivers were the same as they'd been the night before.

Just how long had she been sick for?

13

Much of the ride had been quiet. In the absence of Beth's lovely voice, Rhys turned an ear to the countryside, but even the birds disappointed him. The winter morning was open and lonely.

Beth slept against his chest, cocooned in the fabric of his cloak. Her body shrank and expanded, bellows-like, against him. He pulled the hair back from her shining face. Her perspiration tugged at his worries.

What if the whole terrible affair had somehow doomed her? *What if—?*

To imagine a life where she was distant and untouchable was one thing. Imagining her spirit extinguished from the world was quite another. Agony swept down upon him. Thoughts of irreparable harm—

No. She's just caught cold. He tried to hold in mind the incredible constitution that he'd come to know her for. She wasn't some thin-leafed thing that wilted readily at the first lapse of attention. She was an Athena who had been stealthily concealed in drawing rooms for much of her life. Still, it took all his concentration to keep thoughts of more dire outcomes at his back.

Getting her home was the only priority.

Rhys turned them onto a narrower road, one less welcoming to carts, with the hope that they'd cross fewer travelers. They'd long since left the woodlands for the leas.

He'd groomed the rest of the forest out of her chestnut hair as she slept. The small refinement helped but did not exactly render her presentable. Even with her destroyed traveling gown concealed beneath his cape, they still made for a questionable sight. Anyone in the county might know her or might have heard tavern whispers of a local missing woman. The likelihood—and danger—of this only grew the nearer they got to her dear, familiar Greenthorne.

Rhys had been pulling off the road whenever he spotted someone in the distance, but now that forests had become fields, hiding was nigh on impossible.

Beth stirred against his chest as they crested another roll of the shallow hills.

"Beth?"

She didn't wake. Rhys looked up from his chosen spot on the horizon. The sun was lonely in a cloudless sky. The weather had broken to a more tolerable chill. Rays of light were pushing the winter away, warming up the wool on his shoulders.

He lowered his gaze.

A horse was approaching. Rhys squinted. The rider sat tall, sprucely dressed. There was no shrubbery to conceal them along the trail. Pulling off the road here would only look more suspicious. The last few travelers had left them alone, so why not this one? Rhys straightened his cap and wrapped an arm around Beth.

The gentleman approached. Rhys nodded to him.

The man nodded back. "Good day."

There was a tinge of caution in the greeting. The stranger's raised eyebrow did not go unnoticed as the two men's horses briefly aligned on the path. Rhys forced a swallow through his dry throat and tightened his grip on the reins. Yet the man passed by and the trot of his horse was already fading behind them.

Rhys began to soften with relief.

Then the trotting stopped.

"Pardon me, sir."

Rhys stilled and looked steadily over his shoulder, trying his best to bring a cheerful light to his eyes. The nob, in his long blue coat, came riding back toward them.

"Apologies, but I would be remiss if I failed to ask if you need assistance. Is she quite all right?" His look of suspicion turned to utter concern—or even, disgust?—as his eyes fell on Beth.

"Indeed, my wife is unwell. I'm taking her straight away to a nearby relation, but I pray it's just a cold." Rhys caught the man's eye again and held his gaze relentlessly, not shying away from the lie.

"Ah," said the man, his eyebrow still arcing sharply for his hairline. "Yes, I hope it's no more than that."

"Bless you for your concern—"

"Have you been traveling long? Forgive me, but she looks— well, if I may be frank—filthy. What in heaven's name has she been through?"

Rhys' lips dropped grimly. Her filth was a fact, but he bristled at someone pointing it out. "She fell off of her horse when it spooked. She's an excellent rider, but her malady has exhausted her, and she couldn't hold on. Unfortunately, the horse ran. Getting her to a bed is my only priority now." His last words were acutely true, and he longed to be rid of this inconvenient fool.

His hand stroked Beth where he held her. "We had best get moving." Rhys turned back to the road, but the blue blood aligned himself again.

"Forgive any impertinence but—"

"I'm not sure I have it in me to forgive any more impertinence." A cutting rasp painted Rhys' words as a threat.

The bothersome stranger was briefly taken aback but undeterred. He straightened himself in his seat and set his jaw. "I must have confidence in this woman's well-being before I ride off!"

"What's this now?" asked Beth. Rhys hadn't noticed her stir.

The stranger's jaw went slack, seemingly horrified that he'd woken her. He pulled his hat down to his heart.

"Forgive me, Madam. It's abhorrent of me to disrupt your slumber. I merely sought to ensure that all was well here—that no assistance be necessary. Once I have that assurance from you, I'll be on my way."

Rhys' heart pounded. Beth looked up at him sweetly.

"I'm sure my husband has things well in hand." The dreamy quality of her voice momentarily plucked Rhys from the conversation and left a strange ache traversing his skin.

The man blushed and swallowed hard. "And is there any way in which I might offer my assistance?"

"*My*, what a *lovely* stranger you are. Are they *all* so generous as you in this shire? I'll be quite well, I assure you. We are so *deeply* appreciative of your cares and concern."

Rhys bit his lip, straining not to laugh at the overly airy lilt she was putting on to gratify the nob. The man and Rhys exchanged the curtest of nods before nudging their respective mounts in opposing directions.

"Thank you for coming to my rescue back there."

"Well, anything for my *husband*." Her eyes twinkled as she looked over her shoulder at him. "Are you sure you know where you're taking me?"

"Does the country around us not look familiar?" he asked.

"It's familiar enough." Her voice dropped to a more somber tone. "How did you find out where Greenthorne was?"

Dread tugged at Rhys' throat. "I overheard people speaking of it when I was in town. News of your disappearance had spread. You must be very well-missed." She didn't respond.

A small flock of birds near the roadside scattered as they rode past. Rhys watched them launch themselves, chaotic, into the sky before falling into harmonious order and disappearing.

"Greenthorne," she said, finally, as though to no one in particular.

"What's it like there, Beth?"

"The lane will be marked with a sign, and oaks will shade the way. You'll know it by the wide gravel yard in front. The home faces north and the carriage house is right across." Her voice was marked by a certain wistfulness that wrung his heart.

"I'm sure I'll find it just fine." She was quiet again. He couldn't bear another hour of quiet. "What's it like there for you? What do you love most about it?"

"The stables."

"Really? The stables?"

Her laugh puffed out weakly. "You wouldn't be so surprised if you saw them. It's where my horse, Cutter, is kept."

"And is there a pond?"

"There is." She didn't turn to show her face to him, but there was smiling in her words.

"Tell me about it."

"It's overrun with antagonistic geese. Approaching it safely calls for a measure of stealth. Should you be so unfortunate as to meet them, you have to open your arms up wide and make strange noises to prove your superiority."

He laughed. "Sounds adventurous."

"It felt that way when I was young, but now that I'm bigger than them, it feels more like a nuisance."

"Is there no adventure for you when you're home?"

Her back fell against him as she sighed deeply.

"It was easier to find trouble when I was younger." She patted his thigh and left her hand there. "Now trouble must find me."

Her offhand affection threw him off guard. Never had it occurred to him that she might have gained more from all of this than just a strange bedfellow. There was tenderness when she spoke of trouble—had she gained something of herself? Wouldn't anyone, who had fought their way through such a thing?

No. Only her.

She squeezed his thigh.

Something was different. Some difficult tangle had come undone in the bond between them. The weavers of fate had reworked the thread they shared into a taut, direct strand—one that could be plucked to render some exquisite note belonging solely to them. He could feel half of that note starting to ring out inside himself, unfamiliar and frightening. The vibrations sent a sickness through him at the thought of their parting.

He squeezed her close, inadvertently pushing a weak cough from her. She wasn't well. His own shirt clung to him with sweat from where her fiery body lay against him. He reached for the water bladder that dangled from his saddle and passed it to her.

"Here, you should drink more."

She took it and drank deeply.

He brushed his lips against her tropical neck. The bow of her necklace's ribbon caressed his chin.

"Thank you," she said.

"For the kiss?"

"For the necklace. For returning it."

"A man shouldn't be thanked for returning something he'd taken wrongly. What does it depict?"

"My Aunt's home. As much a home to me as Greenthorne. I was traveling from there when you—when we met."

"If it's been painted with any accuracy, then it must be a very beautiful place."

"My aunt painted it herself actually. And very well." Beth toyed with the pendant. "She did many things, and she taught me all of it. Painting, riding . . . *poetry*. That little notebook I had—it—it had some of my—"

Rhys' hand tightened on the rein as Beth haltingly closed in on the topic he most wished to avoid.

"Some of the poems I wrote in my last days with Aunt Dahlia and—"

"I don't have it, Beth. It was lost and I'm so very sorry for it."

Beth nodded against his shoulder and fell quiet. Not just quiet, but still.

Rhys returned to lamenting the silence—bitter that it should sail in on the tide of one of his many mistakes.

The sun rose high and the shadows of the clouds slid over the moorlands while Beth drifted off. Rhys pulled his hat low as a farmer passed.

He was looking ahead on the road when Beth's slackened body

abruptly jerked in his arms, the way a child might lurch from a nightmare. She twisted, as best she could, to see him.

"You can't leave me without a proper goodbye." Her dark irises quivered with intensity as she clutched at his lapel. He hadn't seen her eyes like that since she'd threatened to throw herself down into the gully. He stopped their horse.

"Beth, what do you mean?" His gentle tone was helpless to soothe her.

"We're getting close, and I can barely stay upright. I need you to promise me that you'll wake me to say goodbye. We *have* to say goodbye. Promise me!"

"Beth," he said, putting a gloved hand to her cheek. Her eyes widened with heartbreak, making clear that his apologetic inflection had been understood.

"I don't care if you think it's right or helpful. I want you to do it. I want you to—because of the forest and our folly—the maenad told me—said that she would keep it secret . . ." Beth's head lolled and Rhys' hand was there to catch it. The nape of her neck sent heat right through the leather of his glove. His Beth, ever cold and shivering was now burning up.

"Just promise me—promise—" The power of her voice kept waxing and waning. "Because we were—we are . . ."

He leaned over to press a lingering kiss to her forehead. He stroked her back slowly, firmly, until her frenzied gasping settled. When he pulled away, her eyes still swam with pain.

She moved her lips again. *Promise me.*

"I promise," he said. "We'll have our goodbye."

The words freed her limbs from their rigidity. She nodded. He would swear he saw a clarity of mind reenter her expression, but she fell against him, exhausted.

They rode on.

Rhys wanted to hear more about her geese and her home. He wanted to know what her father was like and if she had other family. He wanted the two of them to think hard and remember her poems together, but of course he hadn't even let her know he'd read them.

As they neared Bartswell, she didn't wake once. He tried to rouse her to take some water but she wouldn't fully come back to him. Shaking her elicited naught but groans, each more pathetic and mousy than the last. Helplessness bore down on him, making his neckcloth tight and unbearable. He'd seen sailors this sick before. Most now rested below the water.

It no longer mattered who they passed or shocked. He *had* to get her home. He urged the horse to run as often as the beast could manage, and even that brutal gait could not stir her now.

The horse was spent a demi-hour before they arrived. The slowness of the final mile was akin to torture as Rhys watched Beth fall away from the world before his eyes.

And some of the last words they might ever exchange were about his having lost her dear book. He searched his mind for her lovely words. Something about the bravery of flowers . . .

The courage of a flower
When a storm beats down . . .
When beaten, No. *Pummeled—*
Fuck.

He looked down at Beth. A rosy blush bridged over her fine nose, stark against her pallor. He'd never thought of flowers as bold, but perhaps they might be. Perhaps showing their brilliant colors and standing up to hard weather was more than most could do. Even when a petal could be torn off by one malicious pinch, that was no fault of the flower.

Selfishly, he prayed for one last smile to part on. One more pat on his leg as she joked. One word—anything.

And then there it was. The happy sign, pointing the way to Greenthorne. Taking her away from him forever.

There was the lane of oaks, as promised.

Riding up the row seemed a curious combination of a march to the gallows and a walk down a cathedral's nave. The dappled sun passed through the branches overhead, painting them in a cheerful light, which their situation did not deserve.

The lane opened into the vast gravel yard, as promised. The stone carriage house to the right. The residence to the left. It was two stories. Stone masonry. Not even twice as large as his folly. He scoffed at himself—at the visions of splendor that had once poisoned him into thinking to rob her. This was it. Her Greenthorne. Its only real value was that it was *hers*.

There was a sudden paralysis at the thought of riding forward.

He looked down at Beth where she breathed peacefully against his chest. Cradling her against him, he pushed the sweat-slicked hair from her face. Her eyelashes fluttered against his palm, and he hoped he might be looked at by those deep, dark pools one last time.

Disappointment instead.

He bent his head over her.

"Beth," he whispered. "We have to say our goodbyes, remember?"

He squeezed her shoulder. Making it end would be his responsibility alone, and he didn't know how to do it. Their final moments would be left like blank pages at the end of a book.

He kissed her cheek and straightened in his seat. The ghostly hands of doubt that held him back released him to ride onward.

Rhys didn't have to reach the door before he heard shouts muffled behind an upstairs window.

"Oh it's her! It's her! Bless the Lord, it's her!"

The commotion compounded rapidly, and soon the door burst open so forcefully that the woman who flung it open near tumbled. She screamed over her shoulder, "Mr. Clarke!"

Rhys hoped he was ready for this.

The aproned woman straightened and covered her mouth in astonishment before bursting into tears. A few other household servants congregated hesitantly by the door. Rhys shifted in the seat as they all studied him. He didn't know what to say to urge them forward.

A tall old gentleman pushed his way out past the servants. The tails of his banyan flew out behind him as he strode quickly, but unevenly, to the horse. He looked not to Rhys at all but collapsed against Beth's knee where she sat, and wept into her leg.

Rhys stayed perfectly still, allowing the reunion to unfold without his disruption. At last the man lifted his head, seemingly grabbed by a thorn of panic.

"Does she—is she breathing?" He looked into Rhys' eyes for answers, horrified.

"Yes, but she's been in and out of consciousness. She needs to be abed immediately." Rhys called over the man's shoulder to where the servants had piled up by the door. "Help me get her down." Attendants rushed to his side, eager to be of use.

There was no time yet for explanations, and Mr. Clarke did not yet seek any. The old man's eyes were fretfully affixed to his daughter.

Rhys helped to pass her down from the saddle. He held her neck steady as a footman and a boy from the carriage house guided her down. His thumb brushed against her damp neck one last time and then she was taken from him. He had no excuse, no reason to ever be near to her again.

Even in the commotion, she didn't stir.

Rhys slid off the horse and watched remotely as the whole pack of people carried her carefully to the door. The sight arrested him—she was very loved.

It's done. Leave it.

He was about to step back into his stirrup when Mr. Clarke turned and hurried back to him. The man took Rhys' hand in both of his.

"Thank you, oh thank you. Did you see our bid for help in the journal in Hull? Please come in. How can I repay you?"

He returned Mr. Clarke's warmth by grasping his arm. The old man's nervous tremors threatened to shake him to the ground. Rhys took the man by the elbow to support him as they walked to the door.

Beth's father put a hand over his heart while he collected himself. "I'm Mr. Clarke."

Rhys swallowed hard. "Osbourne Booker. And there's nothing required. I am glad to see your daughter safe."

"Are you a thief-taker, Mr. Booker? A constable? Or just a kind citizen?"

"None. I happened, thankfully, upon her by pure serendipity." Then a strange thought came into Rhys' mind as if whispered by a spirit. "But I was on my way to London to take a position at the Home Office."

Rhys stopped at the house's threshold. If he crossed it, he'd have to answer a great many more questions. How long before an answer came out wrong?

"Please. Forget about me and go be with your daughter. She's been through a great deal."

Mr. Clarke looked over his shoulder at the frantic servants who ran up and down the stairs behind him. Then he looked back to Rhys. The anxiety rending the man between two places seemed great, and Rhys wanted nothing more than to relieve him of the burden.

"Only tell me first, what happened to her?"

Rhys inhaled sharply in discomfort. It was difficult to look into the earnest concern of Mr. Clarke's eyes and tell untruths.

"To my understanding, a traveling companion betrayed her. Had aims to elope."

Mr. Clarke's eyes widened, only briefly, before his lips drew flat and he nodded.

Rhys looked down, calculating how much to omit to make the rest as truthful as possible.

"She escaped from a horrible captivity, and I found her, and helped her here. But please, Mr. Clarke. She hasn't been very well since then."

The man's wrinkled face twisted up in anguish—the upstairs room still clearly calling to him.

"Have you ridden far? We can offer refreshments, at least."

"I only wish that I could see Miss Clarke restored to health." Rhys tipped his head. "Go to her."

Rhys extracted himself from Mr. Clarke's kind grip and retreated toward his horse, whose reins were held dutifully by a stablehand.

Rhys placed a hand on the saddle and paused. Beth's warmth still radiated from the front of the seat. "Actually . . ."

Mr. Clarke eagerly turned at his word.

"There is one thing I'd like to do."

"Yes?" The man's voice was all hope.

"Let me ride for a doctor."

Mr. Clarke's bleak eyes alit at the suggestion. "Oh yes, please.

There's a man, Wrifflewall, down the lane away from Bartswell. I will send a man out with further directions immediately."

Rhys nodded. "Thank you. *Go.*"

The man disappeared.

Rhys swung himself into the saddle and looked up. The room at the upstairs corner now glowed even brighter with a fire. Shadows crossed back and forth, but the activity was less frantic now.

She would be well cared for. She would lead a happy life.

Goodbye, Beth.

What a grace it was to have an errand. To somehow serve her still.

Rhys rode like the devil, cutting across the countryside to find the physician's home a few miles off. It was a way to keep the pain at his back for just a moment longer. He couldn't bear to anticipate the feelings that might overtake him once his usefulness ran out. Couldn't imagine what he'd do after sending the doctor off. Who he'd be. This was his final tie to her, and it would shortly be severed.

His memories twisted around her without control or direction. Her laughter with a flask of gin at her lips. Her hand on his thigh. His hand on hers . . .

What if he'd gotten her with child? What if he'd secured for her a new era of ruin? What if she didn't survive? Rhys shook his head violently but couldn't keep the terrible thoughts from sticking to him like nettles.

As he rode across the fields, the icy wind cut his face like glass.

It made it hard to tell—was it sweat or something else that streaked back from his eyes?

14

Beth leaned against Rhys and patted his leg. They burst out of the forest, galloping together into a beautiful lea. It rained steadily from a cloudless sky. Nothing made a sound. Not the rain, nor the hooves of their steed tearing across the heather. She turned to look up at him—at his stubble-framed lips parting around the gleaming crescent of his smile. Laughter and joy pulled blissfully at her eyes. Still no sound. She reached out as if she could somehow find his laughter suspended in the air. He leaned down, and his smiling lips moved with words that never reached her . . .

Beth inhaled and caught something familiar in the scent—rose water? She slid her legs back and forth between the soft, crisp surfaces, swimming in them. Was she swimming? No. There was no water. There was fire though. She could hear the little snaps of it. She smelled pine. No. There was no pine. None. Her body jerked. Her eyes popped open. Her heart raced.

She was ready to fight. To fight people. To fight wolves.

But she was only in her room.

In Greenthorne.

Alone.

With that snapping fire.

"Papa?" Her voice hardly croaked the word out.

She squinted at the wintery sunlight that slanted between her curtains. Her shift clung to her unpleasantly. Something began to grip her from within. Something she couldn't quite reach yet through the fog.

Something—

Rhys.

Her body surged from the bed, and she remained upright even as her knees buckled. She tore open the curtains. There was no sign of him down in the yard.

She staggered from the room, barefooted.

Somewhere in a distant part of the house, she heard Mrs. Brimble's voice. "Mr. Clarke, I think—come quick."

A small chorus of footsteps went up around the house, but Beth did not stop moving. She steadied herself on the hallway wall and pushed forward toward the stairs. At the bottom of them, she near collapsed into her father's arms.

"Where? Where is he?"

"Darling." Her father kissed her head and embraced her with what little support he could offer. "You should not be out of bed."

"Where—?"

Her father's expression halted her. His brows were drawn together in concern and confusion. The room spun a little, then everything stilled as she sobered from her fright. Clutching him, she realized that she must choose her next words more carefully.

"I'm sorry, Papa. I don't know what I'm saying."

"Here. Let's get you back to bed, and we can talk." She nodded and allowed him and Mrs. Brimble to help her back up the stairs.

As soon as she laid eyes on the bed again, she knew she didn't want to be in it.

"No. Please. Anywhere but there."

"A wise choice," said Mrs. Brimble. The housekeeper went to fluff a cushion for Beth on the little divan at the end of her well-trimmed room. "There wasn't enough rose water in the world to keep that bed from smelling stale. I'll send Lily up later to change all the linens."

"Thank you."

Mrs. Brimble took the words as her dismissal but paused in the doorway.

"'Tis good to have you back, Miss."

Mrs. Brimble's dour appearance was ever mismatched to how kind she was. Beth smiled as the older woman closed the door.

Then she was alone with her father, whose eyes were glassy with the need to hear his daughter speak. His chin trembled as he pressed his lips into a taut smile, trying to control something there. Was it just her or had he aged years in the mere months she'd been off to care for Dahlia?

Her arm felt heavy and uncooperative as she stretched out a hand to place on his knee.

"I'm all right."

"Seeing you on your feet was a welcome sight indeed, but you're not in any condition yet—"

"I will be soon."

Papa pressed the back of his hand to her cheek. "I think you're right. How do you feel?"

"Just weak."

He looked guiltily away and cleared his throat. "I don't want to distress you, but whenever you're ready," he looked back to her, all hope in his eyes, "do you think you'd be able to share who did this? They should be brought to justice, even if—"

"Desmarais."

She expected him to pull away in shock. Instead, he nodded solemnly.

"Yes. I suspected."

"Why even ask?"

Her father's eyes probed hers curiously.

"He sent a note. Said you'd all been accosted by highwaymen and split apart. Claimed he was too ashamed of losing you to show his face here." Her father scoffed out a bitter laugh. "Even swore on his mother's grave that he'd investigate and return you to me. I knew it was all rubbish."

Beth let out the breath she'd been holding, as she was spared from lying. *Yes. All rubbish.* That was what it would have to be. She could never tell anyone.

Her father placed a hand on hers. "We'll find him, Beth. He'll see justice. Now then, do you need anything?"

Yes. Many things.

But she shook her head and squeezed his hand. His head dropped into a hand propped at his knee, his silver hair flopping forward. He looked a mess, like he'd been living in his banyan and hadn't donned a proper waistcoat for days. *Days.*

"Papa?"

"Yes, darling?"

"How long have I been home?"

The moment he squeezed her hand back, she knew that she would not like the answer. "Five days."

There it was. Rhys was five yawning days away from her. He could be anywhere on the isle. Worse, he might even be sailing away from it.

"Beth?" She hardly heard him. "Perhaps you should lie down again." In a daze, she let her father gently lower her back onto the cushion.

Five days. A century. He hadn't even said goodbye.

Beth needed to know what others knew. "How did I get back to Greenthorne?"

"A very kind stranger, a Mr. Osbourne Booker, brought you home. We're all very grateful to him. Do you remember him?"

Booker?

Her father continued. "Tall chap, dark hair, black horse."

She looked into her father's eyes and nodded gently.

"A little."

"Is he the one who patched you up?"

Beth searched her memories, trying to catch up to what her father spoke of when she realized he was pointing to her shoulder. She raised a hand to the wound, which peeked out from the scooped neck of her shift. It felt flatter. The stitches were still there. It didn't cry out at her touch.

"Perhaps," she said.

The warmth of Rhys rushed back to her—as he leaned on her, breathed on her, concentrated on the stitches. As he rolled away from her with the relief that his gruesome little task was over. As he rolled away not knowing that some wicked instinct deep within her wished him to stay near.

"You remember nothing else?"

She shook her head against the lush pillow.

"I'm sorry. It's all very strange and hazy. It feels like a dream, and I can't quite remember."

That last part, at least, was fast feeling very true. It *did* feel like a dream. She couldn't reach out and touch any of it. She couldn't confirm it. The days of fever had robbed her of something. Her mind felt centered on Rhys, yet his features, his voice, all felt like they were disappearing at the borders of her consciousness, like a great swell of fog was already swallowing him up.

Beth could tell that many questions yet lingered in her father. He would open his mouth to speak and then his lips would settle back together into a weak smile. A pitying smile. He didn't want to bother her. She must have looked as tired as she felt.

"I'll leave you, dear. Lily will bring up some broth when she comes to take the sheets." Her father pulled a knit blanket over her feet and departed.

Beth curled herself into a ball. Shutting her eyes, her mind chased the memory of Rhys. She would catch up to him, hold his face before her and remember. But then his features would fade even as she looked at him. She wished her mind were lined with thorns to ensnare him. To hold him put.

Why had he not waked me? Said goodbye?

For days, she'd felt underwater. Little memories of the surface were only just hitting her now. A teacup pressed to her lips. Lily changing her shift. Tiptoeing shoes that hit her aching head like thunder while she slept. Perhaps, somewhere before all that, Rhys *had* said goodbye. But she would never know. What else wouldn't she know?

In the days that followed, Beth found her physical strength quickly. She got back into her dresses, came down for breakfasts with her father, and returned to her soul-saving routine of morning rides on Cutter.

Then the guests began to arrive.

She was all too familiar with this custom from her first ruination. There would be distant cousins whose names she did not know. There would be mere acquaintances who claimed the rights of age-old friends. They would all come to gawp at the kidnapped woman, just as they had once come to see the impure waif who had stroked her friend in a shed. With their curiosity thoroughly sated, they might then launch into lectures and make a great show of their departure. Through their abandonment of the Clarkes, they could signal their righteous moral purity to all.

She was braced for it, and yet it passed differently this time. Her father delivered swift dismissal to the majority who showed up on their stoop. Slamming the door on the gossip-hungry hopes of these cretins, he would throw up his arms and complain of their pitying facades. Beth was heartened to realize he had not forgotten her pain from before—that he was even changed by it.

And then Lady Weldon arrived. Beth's aunt on her mother's side, and a countess, Lucinda Weldon could not simply be turned away. Perhaps more well-meaning than the rest, any indignation would be in earnest, not merely for show. She would not play the Clarkes for gossip, but still, she'd abandoned Beth all those years ago, just like the rest.

She brought her daughter with her, Beth's cousin Lady Allison who, at nineteen years, was looking forward to her second season— that exciting part of life that had been wholly skipped over for Beth when she'd stained herself at seventeen.

One day at tea, apparently bored by her mother's prattling about their plans for London, Allison leaned in confidentially. "Tell me, Beth. When you were taken, did anything—hmm, how shall I put it? Were you harmed in any . . . you know . . . way that a lady might be? No one will tell me."

Beth admired the impropriety of it. It was on every woman's mind, but Allison had been the only one to come out with it.

"No, Allison, I was not."

"What a relief to hear it." Allison's green eyes glittered with earnest concern as she sighed. "They said you were returned by a man, and I just didn't know what that might mean for you. Everyone acts as though someone must have taken you abed."

Beth felt a pleasant twitch at the corner of her lip for the first time in days—if the girl only knew.

Beth hadn't seen Allison Weldon since she was a toddling imp balancing with the aide of a basket. Her hair, now a shiny straw blonde, had been like white cobwebs at that age. While Beth could do without endless talk of the season, she suddenly wondered if Allison might be an interesting companion when not sharing the same space as her mother.

Early the next morning, Allison accosted Beth on the staircase, nearly sending her tumbling down the last few steps.

"I'm so sorry!" blurted the girl.

"No harm." Beth straightened the jacket of her redingote and continued down the steps. "I'm just not used to seeing any but the scullery maid about at this hour."

Allison looked her up and down. "Off to ride so early?"

"Every day."

"So soon after your illness, though, and so cold out."

Beth's father didn't like it either.

"I enjoy it just fine." Indeed, it was the only thing keeping her mind intact. It rescued her daily from the melancholy that hovered overhead, always ready to drop on her like a weighted net.

"Of course." The girl lowered her head. "It's probably very nice to be outside, and you certainly seem the most self-assured woman of any I have ever known."

Beth paused in her step, warily assessing whether it was meant as an insult. Most women would sling it as such. *Self-assured* was not what women should be. It was Allison's downturned head that told Beth she needn't worry.

"Thank you, Allison. What has you up so early then?"

"Anxiety."

Beth cocked her body against the wall and began to lazily play with her whip. "Oh goodness, what for?"

"I was very sorry to have asked you such an inappropriate question yesterday afternoon. It plagued me all night."

Beth waved a hand between them. "Oh please, no. Don't be anxious on my behalf. I thought it was brave of you to ask and . . . well . . . we're friends, aren't we?" Beth shrugged as if it were that obvious. But of course, it wasn't, even to herself. Banishment was no time to try making friends, but something about Allison put Beth at ease.

Allison's eyebrows crept all the way up her forehead, drawing up the corners of her smile in unison. "Yes. I believe we are."

"Would you like to ride with me?"

Allison's cautious eyes looked ready to form excuses, but with a glance to the door, the expression was exchanged for one of eagerness. "I believe I would."

On their ride, Allison didn't complain once about the cold, even though the goose pimples between her gloves and her cuffs gave her away. Instead of calling herself cold, she said things like, "Isn't it bracing?" and smiled into the sunrise. Instead of complaints about her numb, red nose she pointed out with a laugh that they were both afflicted. For their time together, outside, Beth forgot about her sadness.

They returned to the house before breakfast. They clung to one another for balance as they swayed in the foyer, swapping their muddied shoes for clean ones.

"It is too bad that you don't know more about that Mr. Booker."

The name still caught Beth off guard when in reference to the man she had only ever known as *Rhys*.

"Your father seemed so very fond of him."

At this, Beth fell off her heel, pinching her ankle sharply and taking her companion briefly off balance. Allison helped her steady herself.

"Fond of him? Of who? Are we still talking about Mr. Booker?"

Allison nodded, unsure.

"Just how long was Mr. Booker here for?"

"I'm sorry, I don't know. I don't think it was long. Your father just said something of being grateful and called the man upstanding."

Beth was still taking this in when Mrs. Brimble entered, fracturing her line of inquiry.

"Good morning, ladies. Breakfast is just going on the table. May I take your cloak, Lady Allison?" Allison untied it and handed it to the housekeeper.

Beth put an arm around her cousin. "I hope you'll come on more rides with me, Allison."

Allison responded, but Beth failed to hear her words. Something had caught her eye over the girl's shoulder. Mrs. Brimble held open a coat cupboard that Beth had scarcely ever used and saw a long, dark, woolen thing hanging there. Her heart slammed against her ribs.

Rhys' cape. The cupboard was shut almost as soon as she recognized it. Cheerful Allison had already grabbed Beth by the wrist and now led her, dazed, toward the dining room.

A floorboard creaked as Beth placed a foot beyond her bedchamber door. The hallway was quiet. Her father's room was at the end of the corridor, and the Weldons had been put up in a room down the opposite hall. She hoped she was far enough from everyone for the sound to go unnoticed.

A chill in the air bit straight through her chemise, but she'd not been able to find her robe in the dark. No matter, what she sought would keep her warm.

She carefully descended the staircase that had been expertly navigated on so many nights of her youth when she'd slipped out for rendezvous with Dyckson. A pleasant shiver ran up her spine—the small thrill of reliving rebellion.

There it was, the inconspicuous cupboard near the fireplace, bathed in moonlight from the front windows. She hurried across to it.

The unhooked latch thudded against the wood and she cringed. She eased the door open.

It was certainly his. It was what had made him so large and menacing that first night, and it was what had kept her warm and dry when they'd lain together in the woods. Overlong for the cupboard, its abundant fabric rested in folds below.

She dragged it up to her face, inhaling.

There he was. The pine, the earth, the wool. And at last, she could see his face again. She could feel his rough cheek on hers. The scent was a tonic, clearing her mind of all her fretting about remembering. It made reminiscence as easy as taking a breath.

She lugged it the rest of the way out, and her arms sagged with its formidable heft. Wrapping herself up in it, she returned to her room.

Cocooning herself in it in her bed, she was suffused with comfort and . . . *trust.* But it was easy to feel such things from a distance, was it not? Her memory could now mold him into whatever she wished him to be. Yet a new memory was rising against her better judgment. She sifted through the confusing visions of her final, fitful night at the folly. Reached out past all the nightmares—

Rhys had entered her room. He had apologized. He had sworn to get her safely home.

Beth would have to lay such thoughts to rest. She would wrap them up with the cape into a tidy bundle and put it all into a box. If she did not, she might never get on with her own life.

But for now.

His warmth. His scent.

One last time.

Three years later . . .

15

April 1786

"Goodness! You love Lenten pie? What do you know but that so do I? It's my very favorite. There—just another thing we have in common."

Everyone in this shire loves Lenten pie. Beth smiled politely at Captain Hamilton Eadwald before pointing her nose away from him to obscure an eye-roll that could not be further postponed.

Hamm went on, "Add that to horseback rides, and sips of gin, and uh . . ."

"Don't forget warm weather and comfortable homes, Hamm."

"Yes! See, aren't we a pair?" He pulled up alongside her. "And to top it off, you're the only one on God's green earth permitted to call me *Hamm.*"

He flashed her a handsome, if barmy, smile. *Poor chap.* He was very good-looking, but he should go find some other girl. Somewhere there's a woman out there for him, or very likely, many. Someone who is just as blandly fine-looking, who enjoys savory pies and nice weather as much as everybody else in the bloody country. Someone who likes those things and little else.

This was Hamilton's second round of courting her, and it wasn't making much more sense than the first. He'd attempted it long ago, when she'd been just barely twenty. She'd been flattered at first, particularly as he'd come sniffing around in spite of the rumors that surrounded her.

But she couldn't tolerate him well. He always referred to her in terms of awe—*magnificent, curious, provocative, stimulating, mysterious—*

"I find you so exotic." *Yes. Just like that.*

"Oh, do you? It seems odd that I should be exotic when I've never left the isle." This one was new. Her hands tightened on the reins.

"I just, I don't know. You're just so *different* from any of the women I've ever met."

"You're only saying that because none of the other women you've met have ever been kidnapped." She bristled when others mentioned it, so she frequently opted to steal the pleasure from them.

"I'm *not*. I found you very effervescent and intriguing even before all that. You remember. I loved you and offered for you." He stopped his horse.

The tone had gone serious. Taxingly so. She knew she was being rude, but she didn't wait up for him. Hamm trotted past and cut her off.

She met his eyes with her scowl, but now he looked too tragic to turn away from. A twinge of guilt began to tug at her. She didn't have the stomach for guilt today.

"I just thought—well, you're so creative. So smart. You do and try a lot of interesting things. You just seem so special."

The compliments that were pouring forth were less opaque than his usual. Traits like "creative" and "smart" were the kinds of things she longed to be seen for, and yet—

What was it that bothered her? It had to be the incongruity between them. That for all he spoke of their similarities, he himself was clearly aware of the differences and was savoring them as trophies instead of recognizing them for what they were—sheer incompatibilities. To him, she was the temptation of another world, someone to live vicariously through.

The irony was that were they ever to be together, she knew he would never raise himself to her level of curiosity but instead seek to lower her to his.

His awe often reeked of some covert jealousy. It revealed that he would trap her on the mantelpiece as his saucy knick-knack. One with a past that made him look more interesting and daring via his possession of her.

A twice-ruined woman was shunned. A man with a twice-ruined woman was a fascinating rogue—a storyteller and a conqueror. He just wanted a wild horse to break.

"Hamm—" She reached between their mounts to place a hand on his elbow. "Nothing has changed."

"*Everything* has changed. I've been a captain for two years now. I could be *your* captain." Indignation simmered on his wide eyes.

Not my captain.

When he'd asked for her long ago, he'd had nothing to offer but perhaps his looks. His own name—and fortune—had been spoiled by a family of gamblers. In hindsight, she could see that he hadn't overlooked her reputation back then at all. Instead, he was taking advantage of her vulnerable position, fancying himself the rescuing sort, even though it was *her* dowry that might have rescued *him* from destitution.

But it was true, he'd spent the last decade in the navy—on a commission from a rich uncle—and had developed a very satisfactory living. He now had the respect of the aristocracy, the whole vacuous lot of them.

"That I would even ask after a girl over thirty—"

"Woman."

"Sorry?"

"That you would even ask after a *woman* over thirty. Please, go on."

His face scrunched unpleasantly.

"It's time I should be getting back. I have business to attend to."

With a knowing raise of her brows, and little else in the way of a goodbye, Beth let him depart.

A deep exhale escaped her once he was gone and she let her shoulders slump. *Exhausting.* She gave Cutter a congenial pat on the neck as though rewarding him for suffering alongside her.

She was grateful that she could return to the house without that man on her heels. *The nerve of him.*

Not my captain. Never my captain.

Fewer things brought Rhys to mind these years since, but whenever something did spark a memory, it took her over like a mischievous spirit bent on possession.

Hamm didn't have the foggiest idea of Rhys' existence, and yet it felt like he had maliciously trespassed where only Rhys should go—*Captain.*

Beth looked at the ground and hardly saw her horse's shadow. She'd been the one of them with *real* business to attend to and Hamm had nearly kept her from her noon appointment.

* * *

Beth elbowed her way through the doors of her father's study while removing her dirty riding gloves.

"All my apologies, Mr. Bunce, for both my tardiness and my appearance." She came to a stop in front of the stout man and puffed a lock of hair from her face. Mr. Edgar Bunce's rosy cheeks pushed his spectacles upward.

"You think I haven't grown accustomed to both?"

"Well, you will just have to grow accustomed to my apologies, too, then because I'm afraid I cannot stop myself." They shared a smile as Beth moved around to the business side of her father's desk and took a seat.

Beth sighed and moved her hands across the oak surface, reacquainting herself with the feel of it. She waited patiently as Mr. Bunce settled in and began to withdraw various ledgers from his satchel.

The unassuming solicitor had proven himself indispensable to her in the past few years. He had, in a sense, given her all of the freedoms she'd once longed for. It was by his hand that everything from Dahlia's estate had been settled. He provided Beth with sound advisement but adhered to her decisions without waver. This trait seemed, to Beth, the rarest thing when even the dressmakers tried to tell her her own mind.

He had not even questioned her decision to let Ashecote House to a family. In fact, he'd found the idea very smart with so many country houses languishing, idle. With every asset signed over to her, she felt more emboldened. Ideas—daring and indecent—began to take shape.

She'd been certain one day that she'd finally found the thing that would raise Mr. Bunce's eyebrow. And she'd been right.

"Just to be certain I'm hearing you correctly, you wish me to retrieve the hanging records at Bristol Newgate from 1780 to 1782?" he'd asked.

And she'd confirmed it with all the indifference of asking for a glass of water. His eyebrow then lowered, and he'd gotten to work. *Good man.* With that, he'd secured her trust forever.

Indeed he'd found those records. After hours of poring over them together, she'd found the name she was looking for. *Heathcote Dewey.* The unjustly hanged quartermaster. Rhys' friend.

They discovered Dewey's family in Cardiff and sent a representative to discover their needs and wishes, and to fulfill every one of them. Mr. Bunce had only ever asked once, "What is your connection to the widow?"

And Beth had told him, "Truthfully, I have none."

During that business, Mr. Bunce had brought several archived copies of Bristol's *Weekly Intelligencer* to her desk—each one splashed with stories of the Labrador mutiny. And there was a name, *his* name, not just *Rhys* but—

Rhys Bowen.

Her highwayman, her captain, had a name.

Now it was a different gazette that Bunce dropped onto the oak surface. Beth reached for it, but Bunce put a warning hand over it.

"I regret to inform you that it looks like another dead end. Germain David Desmarais is not our man."

Well, wasn't that just the perfect news to complete her morning? Beth snatched up the copy of *The Chelmsford Chronicle.* There it was, circled at the bottom of the back-page obituaries. It described Germain D. Desmarais as a family man of six-and-thirty, the son of a baronet.

Beth's vision blurred as she stared right through the document.

For nearly a year after she was taken from Ashecote, her father had tried to track down Desmarais. He'd occupied his worried mind by entertaining investigators and thief-takers in his study, until one day, one of his hired men got word that Desmarais had died on the Continent. A supposed acquaintance of his had said he'd expired pathetically in a debtor's prison. While Beth thought that might be an apt exit for such a man, there was no evidence. Debtor's prisons around Paris had no record of him, and the acquaintance soon disappeared.

Her father was prepared to believe it was over, but Beth didn't trust it. It would have been too easy for that simpering fraud to slither out of his identity. Indeed, they'd discovered that he'd likely done it at least once. Most had only ever known him by his surname. He'd been a servant long before he'd managed the lands, and he'd let himself be called Desmarais since boyhood. But after his disappearance, they'd found documents of his bearing many names: Germain, Didier, Jules, Gregoire, Edmund. They had even discovered an alternate surname of Janssen.

Beth had once been happily resigned to not owing that man a single further thought. But there was no way he was dead, and her need to prove herself correct—to not be caught out by that swindler again—became an obsession.

"I'm very sorry, Miss Clarke."

Beth relaxed against the back of her chair. "Me too, Mr. Bunce."

That night, Beth had Lily pour a bath to soak up her disappointments.

"Careful Miss, 'tis still quite hot." Then Lily closed the bedchamber door.

Beth stepped into the bath right away, forcing herself to bear the still-too-hot water. The sensation as she sank into it made her heart pound. Life had once again become unutterably dull and this slight, heating pain seemed as good as it got. And then even that sensation was gone.

Taking up her father's obsession with Desmarais was a hobby that was losing its legs. She looked to where she'd dropped *The Chelmsford Chronicle* on her bedside table. *Useless endeavor.* There was no new information, but it wasn't really about that anymore, was it? It was about her renewed boredom. It was about how her love for Greenthorne and her sense of suffocation at Greenthorne were battling within her, and no occupation could stave it off for long.

Life was better when Allison was around. Beth lifted the goat's milk soap from its tray and lathered her hands. Just one more night and the Weldons would be back from their tour on the Continent. Better than that, they'd be moving into a new home, much closer to Greenthorne.

Years on, her misadventure was now referred to in whispers as *The Ordeal* and her time since *The Ordeal* was now passing very much the same as her time before it, only now she was awake to aspects of herself that she'd hardly known before. The thrill of opening an atlas now paled in comparison to seeing the whole of the county quiet and still before sunrise. No country home could make her forget the ostentatious curvatures of the folly's plaster. No man's touch could make her forget . . .

Her hand was already on her thigh below the water, as a dark and beautiful feeling glided through her. Her hand slid up just as his had. Mimicked the edge of his finger finding and parting her . . .

Beth glanced darkly toward the door and pressed her lips together to strangle off the purring sighs as they rose.

Across from her bath, at the foot of her bed, was the chest that she'd long ago buried Rhys' cape in. Since the night that she'd taken it from the downstairs cupboard, it remained in that chest. It had called out to her ever since, but she'd resisted touching it again, even in those early days when the howls of temptation were furiously loud.

Beth sank lower in the water, as if to be nearer to the sensation that was emanating from her lap as she stroked. She did not take her eyes off the wooden chest.

She felt herself called by it less and less these days. Rhys was distant. Blurred. She could hear his voice but not quite see his features. She was forgetting, and it felt disappointingly similar to healing.

But the way he touched her was the one thing that could not be shaken, and she could hardly touch herself without borrowing from his memory. He was still the coal that fueled her breathless ardor in moments like this. For this, she allowed him passage into her, past all the barriers of shame.

Beth's lips dipped into the water, and she exhaled slowly, trying to draw out the grip of pleasure that was pressing her into the bottom of the basin. She slowed the swirls of her fingers, breathed deeply, tried not to—*not yet*—

A knock at the bedroom's door loosened Beth's control and she flew—too soon—over the precipice of bliss. She splashed like a netted fish, struggling to get herself upright as Lily entered. A spasm clapped Beth's thighs together, sending up one last ribbon of water.

Lily's expression exposed to Beth exactly what sort of a scene she'd caused. The young woman blushed. "I just brought—" Lily distractedly bustled to the bed, ignoring the flushed panting of her mistress. "I forgot to leave ye with some towels." A short stack of linens was set on the counterpane.

"Thank you, Lily. Would you mind?" Beth reached out an arm and Lily hurried to place a towel in her hand. The girl fiddled with her apron and did her best to look elsewhere but at Beth.

"Anything else, Miss?"

"That's it for the night, thank you."

The door closed behind the girl. Beth still quivered in blissful recovery. A cheeky smile took over her face as her body relaxed. She didn't so much mind being caught. Sometimes there were advantages to having one's reputation in the gutter.

16

Forks clinked gaily at the table that night. Candelabras cast their dancing light on half a dozen smiling faces. The Weldons' footmen stepped in and out of the fray with deliveries of silver salvers, piled high with all manner of colorful delights. Peals of laughter bounced off the walls of Tallyside's intimidatingly grand, yet sparsely furnished dining room. Glasses were fumbled and broken. Wine was spilled.

Allison chattered brightly in the middle of the long table, looking like a ray of sunshine in a crisp yellow caraco, frothy with lace and no doubt acquired in Paris. Her nose and cheeks had picked up a Mediterranean gold. Lady Weldon's stern gray eyes could not conceal a glint of pride as her daughter gushed to their nearest family about ruins in Rome, icons in Tuscany, and the dangers brewing in Paris.

Allison cast the majority of her animated storytelling toward her father, Lord Weldon, who sat at the table's head. The Earl Weldon had been dabbling in the textile trade for years but had recently abandoned the project to spend more time with his family at their new home.

The Weldon's adopted son, Stefano, was among the happy party, seated next to Lord Weldon. Unable to inherit his father's title, Stefano had taken the trade business rather more seriously. Now it was all but handed over to him, and he would soon return to Greece to run it. Allison had never said much of him. He'd been taken in by the family as a young boy back when the Weldon's believed they could not conceive. Allison had come along over a decade later. A welcomed surprise.

Beth eyed the swarthy man with curiosity. His short beard was quite a novel thing to see in England and only strengthened his mystery. He looked a touch older than his four-and-thirty, for the seaside sun had rid him of the softness of youth. Beth sipped her wine as she assessed his unique features—they didn't put her off. Her eyes grazed further down his build to where his buckskins went taut around his thigh—

Oh Lord. She was completely foxed, wasn't she? She'd be caught gawking if she did not rein it in. She looked around. Her own father swayed in his seat, his cheeks shining like persimmons. At least she was no more cup-shot than anyone else at the table. She politely brought a green bean to her mouth and missed, poking her lips with the fork's tines. From the corner of her flitting eye, she caught the twinkle in another—Stefano had seen that. He smiled, playfully poking his lip with his own fork. Beth didn't turn away at his notice but instead allowed an unstoppable smile to take her over.

Everyone else was too merry to catch them. Their little moment would be held in confidence. The thrill of such a fleeting flirt left her all the more keenly aware of just how dull things had been. She placed a hand against her embroidered stomacher, enjoying the rush she felt behind it.

The messy merry-making went late. The night had been an intimate prelude to the grand fête that was yet a few nights off. This sort of small party was much more to Beth's liking, and she couldn't stop her smiling as she watched everyone stagger off to the bedrooms of the large manor, laughter fading down every corridor. Even the staid Lady Weldon had had her long, straight back turned to jelly by the wine.

Beth linked arms with Allison. "I've never seen your mother like that."

"Like what?"

"Well . . . *laughing.*"

"Ah yes, she's not always so strict as you imagine. I believe our tour did her some good. She had not been to the Continent since she was my age. I suspect she relived a few good memories. She's gentler on me anyhow, and she's very pleased that Papa is back with us." Allison tightened her grip on Beth's arm, swaying somewhat. "Funny that you should even notice her."

"Why do you say that?"

"Because it was not *her* that you exchanged smiles with all night."

Beth still felt the buzz of the evening as she lay awake in her shift. The full moon had disappeared from her window, climbing too high to see. The feeling that had started behind her stomacher now consumed her entire body. Her skin tingled and crawled, leaving her helpless to sleep.

She sat up, fixing her eyes on the door that adjoined her guest room to Allison's. She crept over to it and creaked it open.

"What?" The whisper from the darkness was sharp and annoyed. "Are you awake?"

"Does it not sound like I'm awake? I'm dreading the morning headache too much to fall asleep. I fear I'll be losing my stomach 'til next supper."

Beth smiled at the words that emerged from the shadows. She'd no doubt be spending tomorrow in much the same fashion. Beth put her arms out ahead of her and felt her way around until she could tell she was at the bedside. The faint moonlight bounced off Allison's smile and the whites of her eyes.

"What do you need, Beth?" There was a rustling as Allison threw the covers open. "Did you have a nightmare? Do you want to get in with me and comfort yourself?"

Beth stifled a snort at the teasing and Allison squeaked a giggle.

Then Beth got serious.

"Sneak out with me."

"What?"

"Sneak out with me. It's a nice night and a full moon."

Allison was quiet for a very long time. Then the rustling started again. Beth could hear the mattress shift.

"It's going to be hard to find my mantle in the dark."

Beth smiled. "I'll help you."

The Allison of a year ago would have never acceded to such a suggestion, but here was a new woman, one who had seen Europe and tasted her independence. Beth was eager to seize on these new proclivities and drag her cousin into a bit of rebellion. What sort of disreputable sister-figure would she be if she neglected her opportunity to corrupt the impressionable?

The two of them fumbled for minutes, seeking out various wraps and slippers in the dark. But soon enough they were hand in hand, crossing the dewy west lawn toward a grove of trees near a garden rotunda on the hill.

They threw a wool blanket onto the driest patch of grass they could find and lay down.

Allison sighed peacefully.

"I don't think I've ever seen it like this before," she said, looking up at the stars.

"I have."

"You say that like you've seen it more than once."

In fact, Beth hadn't realized she'd *said* anything at all. She'd meant to keep that in her head, locked up with her other secrets. It was possible that she was still loosened by the wine. Her body tightened with control.

"I missed you, Allison."

"I missed you too." Allison rolled to her side to cradle her friend's cheek. "My adventure changed me. I feel a little less frightened of everything now."

"I can tell." Beth looked into her friend's glittering eyes. "I'm very proud of you."

"Tell me, did your adventure change you too?"

Adventure. Goodness, that sounded so much nicer than *The Ordeal.*

"It did," said Beth. "I'm also much less afraid."

Allison rolled away. "*Psh.* You were *never* afraid of anything. I don't believe it."

"You didn't really even know me before my adventure."

"No, it's clear you've always had it. Is that not why we've snuck out? You're seasoned at this, aren't you? Is this what you did all the time at my age?"

Allison reached a hand over and tickled Beth's ribs to make her talk.

"Stop!" shrieked Beth, muscling her cousin's slender but surprisingly strong wrist away from her.

"I will not believe you if you tell me it was all born of the events of a few measly days spent outside of society's purview, three years ago." Allison lunged again.

"Fine. Fine!" Beth blocked the quick girl as best she could. Then Allison's hands found an extra sinister location at her side.

Beth hushed Allison for her giggles, even as her own protestations came out in shrill reports—"Stop! I confess! I confess! I have always been a troublemaker."

Their giggling died off as Allison's agile fingers paused their torture. Then she sat up with her fingers dancing in the air above Beth like talons ready to swoop down.

"Interrogator's next question—"

"Oh, God help me."

"Were you not flirting with Stefano tonight?"

Before the girl could come down on her, Beth lunged instead, unleashing her fingers on Allison like a clutter of spiders.

"Mercy! Mercy! I plead mercy!"

Giggles tapered off into exhaustion. A truce. The two rolled apart to recover, each on their respective sides of the blanket.

"But *were* you flirting?" asked Allison.

"A bit, probably."

"Do you like him?" Allison fiddled with a long piece of grass that she'd plucked. "He's going back to Greece, you know."

"I don't really *know* him, but I know I liked smiling at him."

The two grinned and exhaled in unison.

Beth knew exactly what Stefano's smile had felt like. It had felt like a drop of water in the desert. It had raised the small hairs on her arms for the first time in three years, the first time since . . .

"Allison?"

"Yes?"

"May I tell you a secret?"

"You can tell me anything." Allison leaned on an elbow and put a reassuring hand on Beth's arm. "I know I'm young and often silly, but anything you tell me will be kept safe as a jewel in my heart."

Beth's arm shook beneath her cousin's gentle touch. Was it the wine? The full moon? Could she really do this? Allison's green eyes were wide. Reassuring. Welcoming.

"The man who brought me back to Greenthorne . . . was the same one who kept me from it." Beth waited for a gasp of shock, but none came. So she turned her gaze upward and trusted the stars. "And I did not want to be parted from him."

Then came the rest.

The whole clew of messy truths that Beth had nurtured within herself came unraveled. The night on the road. The forest. The folly. The maenad. Good Harry. Quiet Sol. Filthy, wretched Lionel and his stinking maw.

To unburden herself of the story was to liberate herself from the rubble of a building crumbled atop her, brick by brick. Beth's chest lifted higher with each detail expelled. The escape. The wolves. The encampment.

Rhys.

The pact they'd made in the ravine. How she'd been compelled to trust him, even as the spirits of the woods called her to keep running, likely to her end. How his hand gripped hers so hard once she agreed to go with him. The relief she sensed in him that she'd not die in the woods. The relief she felt herself. The innate knowledge that he wouldn't let go.

Then there was the feeling of being escorted up the stairs of that ruin for the very first time. The distraction of Rhys' body against hers as a needle pierced in and out of her skin at his hand. Threatening him with a hot poker. The long dull hours going mad with the maenad. Spilling confessions that she could now spill to the living eyes across from her—Allison's eyes—glowing with reverent attention.

Beth's tale traveled back to the forest encampment, and she thought the reliving of it might split her open. She tried to put into words for Allison what it was like to feel such rapturous desperation for another person. Being touched, being—she held back from saying it aloud—*being loved.*

Allison drew nearer, spellbound by how this highwayman had taken Beth right there in the cold and rotting leaves.

"And your very first time too," she whispered breathlessly.

Beth flung a mischievous smile meaningfully at her friend. The girl darted upright with both hands to her mouth, breathing a disbelieving *no* between her fingers.

Beth went yet further back in time, to share the sweet tale of Dyckson and the ensuing scandal that followed her for years. A scandal that Allison had been too young to know of.

At last, the stories ran out.

"Do you think I've been stupid?" Beth sought honesty yet dreaded it all the same.

Allison took her hand and pulled it into her lap before stroking Beth's hair. "You've described your story with not a drip of regret in your voice. Your eyes were dancing the whole time. You needn't have any permission of mine to feel in love."

Beth opened her mouth to protest—she'd never said a thing about love—but her voice was choked off by some mysterious hand that knew better.

Beth tightened her eyes. "We didn't have our goodbyes and I don't know where he is now."

The only thing that kept her from crumbling was the feeling of Allison's hands rubbing her arms and sides and the tenderness that the girl's voice possessed so naturally. "Well," she said softly, "didn't your father say you were unconscious when Rhys returned with you?"

Beth knew it. It didn't lessen the depths of the loss in her chest.

"I thought foolishly, and for a long time, that he might return."

"I understand why it hurts."

Beth sucked in her breath and rolled away. Allison didn't let go of her hand.

"He's fading now. I didn't want him to for a long time, but he is, and it's for the better. I scarcely know his face now." She closed her eyes as if to test her words. She sniffed against the threat of tears and exhaled. "It's the rest of it that's hard now. It's the fact that I know what I'm capable of, and I feel so wasted at Greenthorne. Boredom is killing me, dear cousin."

"Is that why you envied my tour?"

"How did you guess that?"

"Oh come, there was a reason you didn't engage with my stories at dinner."

"Yes, and we established that that *reason* was the presence of your fair-looking brother." Allison's expression remained serious, in spite of Beth's evasions. "Fine. Yes. I am bored and jealous."

"Which is ridiculous Beth, because I tell you, that as a novel, your tale would sell many more copies."

"It most truly would." Beth laughed, then sobered. "I want to be clear that it's not a resentment of any sort. Your tour just made my longing the most potent it's been since—"

"What was that?"

The hissing tone of Allison's voice brought Beth upright. Allison's hand tightened on hers. The moon was higher. The night, darker.

"What?" Beth whispered.

Allison put a finger to her lips. Beth listened. A light wind whistled through the nearby hedges. Then Beth heard it too—

tap tap tap

Allison pulled Beth up to her feet before she herself had any real purchase on the ground. The two of them tripped and staggered, leaving the blanket behind on the slick grass. They broke into a blind run.

As they fled down the hill, Beth looked over her shoulder and could swear she saw an upright shadow stalk from one column of the rotunda to another.

Keep moving.

Soon the two were back on the steps of the manor, panting and casting wary glances up the hill that they'd just fled down.

Beth's eyes and ears were still attuned to the threat. Yet Allison seemed to be trying to laugh through her gasps of air. Allison put a hand on Beth's shoulder as she recovered. "You know . . ." Allison still could not get her gulps of air quite under control. ". . . one time, I was at the seaside at night with my family. We'd all been putting our feet in the water. It was so dark that you could not see where the water met the sky. You could only see its frothy white edges. I watched it for too long . . ."

Beth only wished to go inside, but Allison slumped against the door to continue her story.

"My fear turned those shapes into a sea beast, and I bolted from the water. Just the sight of me sent a half a dozen others running too.

When people asked what I saw, I had to own that it was nothing." Allison flopped a hand onto Beth's shoulder with a grin. "Beth, I am certain that I have just now done the same thing."

Beth offered her cousin a wan smile but cast another worried glance up the hill. Perhaps Allison was right, perhaps the night had gotten the better of their senses.

Allison took Beth's hands in hers.

"At least I had a wolf-killer to protect me." She was teasing. She'd not particularly accepted that part of the story. She was too educated to believe that wolves could still be anywhere in England.

Beth's fear dissipated enough to think back on their conversation. "Allison, I think I'm going to go somewhere. Like you did. It's been long enough."

Allison's lips spread into a wide smile.

"I support that with ever fiber of my being."

Beth reached for the door, but Allison stopped her to add—

"You could always stop in Greece to see a certain someone."

Beth's eyebrows flicked mischievously in response.

The two carefully opened the heavy door together and snuck back inside. Allison, claiming hunger from their little scare, crept off to seek a morsel.

Beth whisked up the staircase, feeling reseated as the ruler of her own kingdom. A new future lay before her—adventures of her own creation. She couldn't wait to set it all in motion.

As she danced and spun down the hallway, her mantle whirled out wide and caught the dustsheet covering some decoration. It slipped off and she was confronted, mid-twirl, by the statue of a nymph in her path.

Upright and pitcher-less, but not unlike the maenad, her stony eyes took stock of Beth.

Don't look at me like that. It's over.

"Perhaps the wolves escaped from some rich fool's illicit menagerie," offered Allison.

"Are you still caught up on that?"

"It's just that I *want* to believe you."

Beth nudged Allison's side playfully, and their parasols tapped overhead. Lady Weldon invited her to shop with them in Bartswell, and Beth had seized on it. It was the perfect opportunity to speak with Mr. Bunce. She'd set her mind on the Continent and was desperate to make the arrangements.

Allison looked back over her shoulder, realizing her parents were no longer following. Beth turned too.

Lord and Lady Weldon stood under a tree laughing together while Lord Weldon straightened a bow on his tall wife's gown.

"They look happy," said Beth.

"You know that's the real reason for my trip, don't you?"

Beth shot a glance at her, confused.

"Mama wanted to make Father miss us. Make him work less and lure him back to us."

"I daresay it worked." She admired the happy couple, wondering just how far Lord Weldon had strayed.

A cart was driving up the street beyond where the cheerful pair fussed over one another in the shade. Beth's eyes squinted. A man, dingy, large, and bald, caught her notice. She only saw his face for a moment, before the cart turned a corner, but—

Her stomach twisted. He looked like a dead man. Like *Sol.* Beth didn't notice she was swaying until Allison's arm went rigid to steady her.

"What is it, Beth?"

"Sorry, I'm fine. I only thought I saw a ghost."

Allison groaned. "See you say things like that and it makes me believe you less and less about the wolf."

"Not a *real* ghost. Oh, never mind it. It's just my mind playing tricks like ours did last night."

Lord and Lady Weldon caught up to them.

"Are you ladies ready to go try on some baubles?" asked Lady Weldon.

"Actually," Beth demurred, "I'll be parting ways for a spell. I must make some arrangements at the office of Mr. Bunce."

Lady Weldon's narrow face drew down in confusion. "I don't understand. Who is Mr. Bunce?"

"You've met him, Mama. He works for Mr. Clarke," said Allison.

"Well then, surely Mr. Clarke as your guardian can help you with . . . whatever it is." She moved her fan rapidly through the air as if shoeing flies.

Allison looked ready to step in with more assistance, but Beth had it well in hand this time.

"I am an unmarried woman in my thirties with my own wealth. If I've not yet come into my own guardianship in the eyes of others, then I never shall, but I must do as I need. I'll meet you at the haberdasher's." Beth spun on her heel.

Lady Weldon's deliberately loud whisper trailed off behind her. "What a dangerous embrace of spinsterhood."

Oh, I will not only embrace it, Aunt, I will make love to it.

17

Beth perched on the edge of the bed in her guest room at the Weldon's with a letter in her lap. As she read the note, she could hear carriages rolling into the gravel drive outside and the musicians testing out their strings somewhere downstairs. She was already pinned up into her zone-front gown, a light blue changeable silk that glittered silver when it caught the light just so. Embroidered swags of dripping wisteria adorned its voluminous skirt.

A short ruffle teased out from the edge of her daring neckline and brushed against the delicate skin where her breasts lifted against it. She was all the more aware of the strained sensation as her breath became faster. She fussed with the pendant of Aunt Dahlia's necklace as she read:

> *Miss Bethany Clarke,*
>
> *I have secured your passage on an elegant yacht destined for Belgium. Your point of entry will be Bruges.*

I will have a carriage arranged to take you to Kingston upon Hull on the 8th, May. I pray this won't seem too hasty as it's on the nearer end of your suggested departure, but I know the sailing party well and they will be delighted to have you. I am interviewing for companions to have in your employ. All will be handled. Please send any questions.

And for God's sake, tell your father so that I don't have to be the bearer of such news. Spare me that.

Yours, Most Respectfully,

Mr. Bunce, Esq.

Beth could hardly hold the paper still as excitement surged into her fingertips. It was happening. She would finally exercise all the freedom that had been pent up inside her for three steady years. She was going to leave and spread her brand of trouble among unsuspecting strangers on the Continent. She'd own any scandal that came her way, collecting dints in her reputation instead of seashells like every other dull soul.

After all she had survived, there was no fear left in her of the unknown.

Even her discomfort with the ball congregating downstairs was dissipating. She'd join it now in a much more buoyant mood. On this news, she'd be absolutely gliding through the night.

A rap on the door to Allison's adjoining room snapped away her attention. She tucked the letter under her pillow, wanting to savor it as her powerful secret for the duration of the evening.

Allison popped in before Beth could condone her entrance. Her green eyes looked bigger than ever under the pile of upswept, flaxen hair. Her gown, as she often preferred, was golden to match.

"Are you ready?" she asked eagerly.

Beth nodded and stood.

"You look so beautiful, Beth. Stefano will be tripping over the toes of his boots to dance with you."

Beth certainly hoped he would.

The dancing had only just started when Beth noticed Hamm stalking her in the crowd to secure his dance. Thankfully, the Weldons were quite well-connected and a crowd it *was*. He was easily evaded. There was no shortage of young gentlemen bent on the same thing—an emphasis on *young*. Beth lit up inside as men of Allison's age asked time and time to dance with her. She fairly glittered under their enthusiasm, enjoying that none of them realized her unlikely age of three-and-thirty. And—*lucky her*—they were all too fresh into society to know her reputation.

With every turn on the dance floor, she could see Hamm pouting at the fringes, and she flung brilliant smiles at him like weapons. He didn't quite deserve that. She was simply too drunk on her own happiness to be delicate. It was an emotion that she'd been so bereft of. Perhaps her spirits were high enough that she could spare him a dance after all. Even *he* could not drag her spirits down tonight.

After twirling about the floor with a polite viscount, she pushed through the gathering in search of some fresh air. Before reaching the French doors that lined the back of the ballroom, she was stopped by the hand of Lady Weldon. "A gentleman is looking for you."

"Thank you." Beth kept walking. Why bother to ask Lady Weldon what she already knew? Hamm would catch up to her sooner or later.

She slipped out onto the back veranda. Clumps of revelers gathered in various spaces about the garden.

A large pond stretched down the lawn, plumbed at either end with fountains that were turned on for the first time that night. The Weldons' wealth was certainly a thing to behold. Beth followed a path alongside the pool's edge. The warmth of cheerfulness was settling over her and she decided, for once, to allow it. The torches that were staked along the path cast their dancing amber into the water. *A perfect evening.*

"Wondered if I might find you out here." *Hamm.*

Beth sighed and turned to the man who shadowed her. She dipped her head.

"Hamm."

"Miss Clarke," he nodded. "Are you enjoying the evening so far?"

She tried to rein in her reaction, but it was already off like a pistol shot.

"*Immensely.*" The word fairly oozed in its giddiness. She cleared her throat. "And you?"

"Well, I only just got here, but it is very fine, yes."

Rubbish. He'd been stalking her for an hour at least. Beth had no way to conceal a roll of her eyes and felt suddenly very proud that her willpower had evolved enough to contain the impulse. "Mmm."

"I was wondering if you might like to dance with me?"

"Of course, the next dance is all yours—"

"Actually, I've already asked a young lady, Miss Coopersmith, for the next two after this, but the one after those?"

So much for charity.

"Find me when you find me." Beth debated whether she should go on and free herself from his attentions indefinitely. She didn't have to sift through her thoughts for long before she located her answer.

"I want you to know that I've decided to go away."

"What? Out of town?" he asked, taken aback.

"Out of the country."

"For the summer?"

"Indefinitely."

"Don't be ridiculous."

Beth shrugged. It was unkind to blurt it out before telling her father, but Hamm was unlikely to start a rumor.

"You can't just—"

Hamm was cut off by the jovial laughter of a group of men approaching them. Beth paid the group little mind, waiting for them to pass, until—

"Ahh, there she is!"

Beth looked around, trying to discern if *she* was her. It was confirmed when a delicate sherry glass was placed in her fingers by someone coming into the light of the nearest torch. The large hand lingered on hers. She followed the arm upward.

Her heart stopped just as the music did inside the house.

"I've been looking everywhere for you." The voice gentled, intimate and lingering.

Her eyes locked into those of a distant memory. Everyone else around them faded as though painted out of reality. His features, blurred and distant for so long, came suddenly into sharpness— looking exactly as she'd remembered them and yet not at all.

Rhys.

She swayed and he placed a hand under her forearm.

"Steady," he said, nearly a whisper.

"You two know one another?"

If Beth broke her gaze, would he even still exist? Or would he recede into the darkness, some cruel mirage?

"Bethany?" Hamm's voice reported more sharply.

"Yes." She finally looked at Hamm. "Yes, I know him."

"Well, it seems Miss Clarke is too distracted at present to facilitate proper introductions," said Hamm, and she saw his hand move across her to link with that of the ghost to her right.

"Captain Hamilton Eadwald."

"Osbourne Booker." Then Rhys gestured to the men behind him. First a gray and round gentleman, "Mr. Crofty," then a thinner man of similar age, "and Mr. Sutcliffe. My colleagues."

The names fell through Beth's ears like soft flour through a sieve. All she could think about was *him*.

"Gentlemen," Rhys went on, "I'd like to introduce you to Miss Clarke, the niece of our gracious hosts."

How did he—?

The two men pushed into the circle and dipped their heads.

"Booker, you didn't tell us how lovely your friend was," exclaimed one of the gentlemen, his voice colored by drink.

"A selfish secret, I suppose." His eyes didn't let go of Beth's. He brought the sherry to his lips, and she could see a tightness in his throat as he swallowed. The gesture reminded her suddenly of the glass in her own hand.

She took a careful drink.

"So, how exactly are the two of you acquainted?" Hamm put no effort into filtering the rudeness from his tone as he glared at Rhys.

Rhys opened his mouth to answer, but Beth stepped in, feeling it necessary that the spell finally wear off.

"Mr. Booker was my rescuer three years past."

Hamm's face took on the color of her shift, much as hers had only seconds prior.

"Was he now? Well." He arranged his posture into that of a

puffed pigeon, threatened.

"It's very good to see you again, Miss Clarke," said Rhys. He had her free hand almost to his lips by the time she'd even realized he'd taken it.

Hamm shifted on his feet impatiently, throwing his eyesight anywhere other than at them as Rhys kissed her fingers.

The pressure of his lips aligned with the dictates of polite society, but the memories that his lips inspired were not quite so aligned.

"I would very much like to have a dance with you later, if that can be arranged?"

"Of course. There's much to catch up on."

His eyes had, as yet, been so unrevealing, but now a flash of pain lit across them.

"I hear the music striking up again," she said. "Perhaps we can take to the floor right now?"

"Darling." Hamm chuckled at her as though she were loony and placed her hand roughly into the crook of his arm. "*We're* set to have a dance now, recall?"

The nerve. She'd be hanged before she'd dance with him now. She took the rest of her sherry in one swallow and handed the tiny glass back to Rhys. "*Hamm*," she said, wielding the nickname like a hatchet, "what of the young lady who holds you for the next two spots on her card? You mustn't disappoint her." Yet she found herself already being guided away. She couldn't help but throw glances over her shoulder as she was led back to the house.

Rhys receded in the distance. He stood in the throw of the torchlight, watching her go. Forlorn, like a dog left on the roadside.

When they reached the veranda, Beth thrust Hamm away from her.

"Bethany, what's gotten into you?"

Beth was about to rain hell on him. Her emotions were swirling like a storm within her, and this horse's ass would be her first victim. But before she could bring the lightning down, Hamm was rescued by serendipity. Beth's eye had caught a lovely skirt sashaying up from behind him.

Beth's face alit with frothy kindness, "Miss Coopersmith," she said, reaching past Hamm to take the girl's hand. "We were just looking for you. You have the next dance with Captain Eadwald here, don't you?"

The young woman beamed eagerly as she dipped into a flirty curtsy for Hamm. Beth went so far as to lift the girl's hand and place it into his while giving him a look that could burn holes in him.

"Bless you both."

Hamm was dragged swiftly inside by his partner. Beth peeled off her counterfeit smile as soon as she was turned from them. She examined the dark lawn but could no longer see the men by the water. Her chest tightened. Every moment Rhys was out of her sight felt like an assurance that she'd never see him again—that none of this was real.

A hand gently touched her elbow and she spun.

"*Rhys*," she breathed.

But it wasn't. It was Stefano.

"I'm sorry, did I startle you?"

"No, I'm perfectly fine Mr. Weldon."

"Please, our families are so close. When we're alone, *Stefano* will suffice." *Good.* Because it's what she'd always wanted to call him anyway.

"May I have this dance?" He tendered his arm. His smile beamed brilliantly against his olive skin and she melted at the sight. Yet when she placed her hand in his arm, it was tentatively. Her ears still rushed at the dizzying complication that Rhys was here somewhere. She had to speak with him.

Stefano placed a hand over hers as they walked together to the dance floor.

"I have been waiting for this for awhile, you know." His accent was eclectic. The Italian of his birthplace, the English from his youth, the Greek from his career. She liked to hear him speak.

"For what? This dance?"

"Of *course this* dance," he said.

They stood to the side for a moment, staking out their place in the *Allemande* that was now underway. Stefano lifted her hand and elegantly brought her onto the dance floor in perfect time.

This wasn't at all how she wanted the moment to be. She'd been waiting for this dance too, and now it was impossible to lose herself to it.

Stefano's steps were perfect. His smile, perfect. Everything, perfect, except that she kept forgetting to meet his beautiful hazel eyes. Instead, she cast low glances past him, hoping that on some turn, she'd catch a glimpse of her Captain.

"My sister tells me that you feel inspired to travel?"

Beth brought her attention back to him as best she could, but distraction still tugged at her eyes. She smiled.

"Oh, Allison told you that, did she?"

"Was she not supposed to?"

"It's perfectly fine. I just haven't told my father yet. But yes, your sister inspired me, and I've just found out I'm leaving quite soon."

A turn of the dance brought their chests very close as their arms raised overhead. "So am I," he said. A twinkle in his eye. "I hope Greece is on your itinerary?"

She only nodded, blushing too much to speak.

Then she caught sight of him.

Floating through the sea of guests, Rhys stood shoulders above most—his stiff, modern collar, upright. He looked so different without the breadth of his greatcoat or cape. Without the slush of sleet on his shoulders, or dewy hair—so different from the last time she saw him.

He was unaccompanied now and headed toward a low, wide dais at the end of the ballroom, where the Weldons sat to watch over the party with their well-heeled acquaintances from across the kingdom. Her father sat with them, along with others who deemed themselves *too creaky in the knees* for dancing.

She stared distractedly as Rhys stepped up to the dais to greet her father, and she missed a step in the dance. Stefano locked his arm to steady her, his elegance concealing her *faux pas.*

"I'm sorry," she said. "I promise I am usually a much better dance partner."

"I don't really care what kind of dance partner you are. I am sure you have many attributes that make up for one misplaced foot." He smiled, but his eyebrows knit with concern. "Are you generally so hard on yourself?"

She'd never had such a thing pointed out to her before, but the comment struck her painfully, as a well-placed arrow might. The music ended before she could answer and Stefano bowed deeply.

"I see my sister waving for me." He looked over her shoulder. "But I will find you again later." He smiled and Beth curtsied before Stefano turned to escape the dance floor. Beth looked to the dais. Rhys was no longer with her father.

A hand rested against the small of her back and she quickly pulled away. *How dare anyone be so—*

But she turned, and it was *him.*

The music was already starting up again. She didn't know what to say or do.

Rhys bent over her, inappropriately near. His brown eyes pierced into her expectantly.

"May I have this dance with you?"

She gave him her hand, wordlessly, but winced as she realized they'd be dancing *La Bagatelle*. Rhys bowed, belatedly.

The cheerful music clashed with the tensions roiling inside of her. Instead of resting her hand in his, she clutched his fingers in her fist, as though she could not stay upright without the support.

They were the top pair, the first to glide down the row of smiling, oblivious faces. These people had no idea as to the cacophony raging inside of her, yet she felt exposed beneath their gaze.

If Rhys shared any of her anxiety, he wore none of it on his exterior. Though it did not take long to conclude that her Captain was not light of foot. She couldn't take her eyes from him, while he couldn't take his eyes from the progress of the other dancers.

As they circled up with another pair to prance around like fools, she thought she might die. Faintness was taking her over, and she imagined herself as a little finch about to fall from a fence post. She linked arms with the next partner and almost forgot to release herself from Rhys as she spun away.

The man she'd been passed off to was a slender fellow, fair-faced, with a royal bearing. When he finally looked up to meet her eye, she saw recognition on his face. He scowled before snatching his arm from her. Finishing the turn, he hissed, "I do not dance with *twice-ruined* women."

The man bowed curtly and left the dance floor, throwing the symmetry of the dance into a brief chaos.

Beth looked around while the others danced past her,

rearranging themselves to salvage the group's composition. Rhys was now at the end of the longways dance, but seeing her alone, he broke from his place. She shook her head at him. *No.* It was too much.

She maneuvered back into the crowd, picking up speed as she went. Back on the veranda, she clung near to the house until she escaped around its corner. She ran up the west lawn, unlit and undecorated. She ran until she reached the rotunda that she and Allison had shared secrets by. She collapsed against a pillar to weep.

Blood roared inside of her, uncomfortably heated and rapid. The sensation had not slowed even once in the quarter hour since she'd laid eyes on Rhys. Since that moment, she'd been passed from the company of one man to another with the ease of passing a handkerchief—*Rhys, Hamm, Stefano, Rhys*—and finally she'd landed with a stranger who had learned of her past and had a vile opinion of it.

Even as she'd imagined how she might settle into a sinful reputation on the Continent, she'd still possessed some competing notion that the passing of time might cleanse her. Yet, as she'd passed the first half of the night dancing in bliss, rumors had apparently been loosened somewhere in the ballroom—a bag of snakes sent to slither and multiply.

Tears ran hot down her cheeks. They could be ascribed to no singular feeling as their origin. They all came naturally, like a river's current. There was no clarity to any of it, no words to her thoughts—just pure feeling surging through her, sickening her like a poison.

"Beth?"

The out-of-breath voice was gentle and cautious. She turned to face Rhys where he'd approached from the hill.

"How dare you!"

She shoved him hard.

Unguarded, with his back to the hill, he fell to the grass.

She loomed over him, chest heaving. He didn't move yet, but she knew he was fine. The air was still—the murmur and lilt of the ballroom, distant.

At last, he pushed himself up. Standing, he gave her more space and brushed himself off.

Her eyes flitted up and down. There he was. Alive. Intact. Handsome. Real. Different. The same.

Her tears dried and her blood cooled.

"Have you nothing to say?"

He just stood there, lost and waiting.

"You didn't say goodbye."

"Beth . . ."

That cautious voice he kept approaching her with—she hated it. It broke her heart.

"You were very, very ill when I got you back to Greenthorne. I did say goodbye and—"

"I know, but—" Her voice cracked.

"Beth, I didn't get enough at the end either. I didn't—it was very hard for me to leave."

"Then why didn't you come back?"

She saw his eyebrows raise in the moonlight. He dared to take a step toward her.

"Beth."

There it was again.

"Stop saying my name like that. Listen. I know—I *know*—the complications. You needn't brace me for any lecture on them. But to me, they didn't matter. It wasn't fair. You knew where I was, but I didn't know where *you* were. I'm not sure if I can ever be at peace with that distribution of information because it's been my torment for three years." The last few words left her shaking.

He took another step forward, and she retreated, but her back found the column.

"I'm so sorry," he said. His hands reached out uncertainly between them, as though they had a memory of what it was like to hold her. She wished to be held.

"How dare you," she said again, feebly. Her eyelids burned as fresh tears were manufactured.

"How dare—?"

"How dare you show up like this. Passing me a glass of sherry like an old friend." The tears fell. "Giving me no way to—to be near you, to be reassured that you're real, to be alone with you."

He put a hand to her cheek and the spark of his touch threatened to collapse her. His thumb smoothed away a tear. "I'm sorry, I thought you would feel threatened if I caught you alone." He bent in to place his forehead against hers. Their exhales mingled. "We're alone now."

The crisp silk of her skirt rustled between them as he pressed nearer. Her cheek pushed lightly into his hand.

"And I am real." As he said it, his hand shuddered on her face, as though to force the idea into her, but it wasn't enough.

She raised her eyes to his. "Then prove it."

Her eyes.

A fierce pulse beat under the tip of his small finger where it touched the back of her jaw.

He needed the proof just as badly.

He leaned down to her wine-stained lip and tasted her, more softly than even he expected. As he drew away, she chased his lips with hers and all resistance between them fell. He crushed her against the column—unsatisfied until he was impossibly close to her. She gasped and stood on her toes to reach him.

His skin buzzed with memories as he moved against her lips. Flashes of loosened hair and of long legs wrapped around his middle. Fragments of lust, of affection—of dread.

This time, she was wrapped in swaths of crisp and frothy fabric. The night air didn't send ceaseless chills along her limbs. She was fresh and bright, and the scent of her was masked by fresh gardenias in her hair. But as she enfolded him now, as her fingers curled into his shoulders like claws, he knew that she was still his panting, bedraggled witch. The same wild and filthy wolf-killer that had awed him in the forest. The survivor whose eyes sparkled with keenness.

The memories brought blood roaring to his loins, and he ground his hips against her. Her lips broke his to take a deep gasp of air.

"Is this too much?" he rasped against her ear.

"No. Never leave me, Rhys."

But he could hear the break in her voice, the fevered sense of overwhelm. He slowed down and took her face in his hands, to brush his lips against her temple and eyelid, then kiss her nose and jaw. His hand slid down to her neck, where it brushed against the ribbon he'd bought for her so long ago.

Her body softened.

"Is the proof satisfactory?" he asked.

She quirked a smile at him before looking grimly down. When she looked up again, she seemed . . . wary.

"Someone will come looking for me soon." She sidestepped, extracting herself from the narrow space between Rhys and the column.

She walked as though she meant to leave him. He caught her

wrist loosely.

"Strange of you to walk away when you just told me never to leave."

She looked at him squarely. "You know where I am. You've known this whole time."

He stepped around to face her again. "Then it's only fair if you know where I am too."

"So then, where are you, Mr. Booker?"

He cringed at the sound of his alias on her lips.

"I've been mostly in London."

"How's the thieves' work down there? Is it profitable?"

"Much more so, since I now work at *catching* them."

Her narrowed eyes flashed. "What do you mean?"

"I'm a Bow Street Runner."

She pulled her wrist away from him. The familiar suspicion in her eyes cut him to his core. He had as little of her trust as he'd had the night he came upon her on the road. That was clear.

"You mean that *Osbourne Booker* is a Bow Street Runner? Because Rhys is still a thief."

"Yes." He could handle the barb. "A thief. But please, Beth. I can explain all of this if you'll let me. If you doubt what I'm telling you now, you can ask Mr. Crofty. He got me the job at the Home Office."

"I need to go. I've remembered something—" Beth turned away from him and began to take long strides down the gentle slope.

"Beth, wait." His call was hissed out in a loud whisper, cautious of alerting any ball-goers that might wander near. He hurried down after her. "I'm sorry that we had no real goodbyes, but please, you're not the only one who longed for one."

"It isn't just that." She turned.

As he stepped forward, she stepped back. The woman who melted comfortably in his arms just moments ago, the woman who clawed at him to stay, was gone. A new expression crossed her face, an exasperated one that told him he was a fool for not understanding.

"I will never be caught off guard again." She said it with all of the challenging conviction that she possessed the night they met on the road. The most fortunate and misfortunate night of his life.

She proceeded toward the house. The chamber music became less muddied as Rhys followed.

"Does the name *Desmarais* not catch you off guard?"

She froze but did not turn.

"He's the reason I'm here."

She didn't answer for a long time and Rhys didn't dare press her. At last, she turned her head only enough that he might hear her better.

"So it was no accident that we met tonight?"

"No, Beth."

"And you knew that I would be at the Weldons'?"

Rhys had hoped he wouldn't have to answer for that without a chance to explain.

"I'm here at your father's invitation."

Rhys watched as her fists curled into tight balls at her sides. Then she broke back into her fast strides toward the house. Her final words were cast over her shoulder.

"Stay back, Mr. Booker. We mustn't rejoin the party at the same time."

18

By the time Rhys reached the stone steps, Beth had slipped back inside the ballroom. He caught sight of her silvery silks through the French doors. She now clung to the arm of a girl in a sap-colored gown.

Beth's expression was quite in contrast to the one she'd been wearing moments before. It was now all wild-eyed smiles and congeniality. Rhys' stomach turned over at the sight of her being anything other than herself. *God, what she must be thinking.* His hands shook and he stared down at them, willing them to steady. Seeing her again had exacted a toll.

He'd not spotted her for the entire first hour of the fête. He'd nurtured a bloom of anticipation in his gut all day, and its thin petals had quickly wilted. But then, he'd asked Lady Weldon if Beth were present, and she'd assured him Beth was there.

He'd first caught sight of her from a distance, down the length of the pond. Even by the faint torchlight—having forgotten so much and with her looking so different—he'd known instantly, it was her.

His heart had been at least three paces ahead of him as he'd strode down the path to reach her. He needed her to be real. Just the whisper of touch between them as he passed off the sherry glass was enough to fill up his once empty hopes.

But she was correct about the imbalance between them, more so than she yet knew. Because he *had* come back. Once. He had to know that she'd recovered from her illness.

It was two weeks after he left her. He came in the early morning and fussed about on the fringes of Greenthorne before leaving his mount and stalking toward the house.

No candle flickered in her upstairs window. No aproned skirts fluttered past it. He must have watched for near to an hour, concealed behind a tree and feeling more like a blackguard than ever before.

He moved back at the first sign of activity—the clunking lock of a servants' entrance as someone exited. Then his eyes could scarcely believe it—not a servant emerging, but Beth. Buttoned into a tidy redingote, she looked hale and bright.

That's it. He remembered telling himself. *You can go now.* He had his confirmation. The only thing he'd promised to allow himself.

But as he'd watched the fresh and gentle snow alight on her black-feathered hat, he'd found it almost impossible to leave. He wanted to savor the way his soul soared at seeing her well. Her cheeks were rosy, and her back was straight, yet there was, tragically, no hint of a smile on her lips.

What would have happened had he made himself known then?

To learn tonight how she'd been hurt by it—would it really have been any easier on either of them? If he'd come out from the grove of trees and whistled a signal at her. If she'd lifted her eyes—would they have lit up? Would she have come running through the untouched snowfall to embrace him? Or would she have dealt with him as a visiting specter? Nodding once before looking straight through him and going on with her life?

Tonight, he'd seen her as he never had before. Wrapped in silk. Wrists, bare yet warm. He'd stolen glances at her *décolleté*, where a white scar danced jagged against her collarbone. Some part of him had hoped that it would vanish over time, in spite of its angriness.

Rhys turned his cheerless gaze back to the windows. Between the dancers, he could still catch glimpses of Beth clinging to her friend.

"She's much older than she looks, you know."

Rhys turned. It was Beth's friend—the name escaped him—*Herbert, Hen—, Hamish—*

It didn't matter. The snobbish officer only handed him a glass of wine and kept walking. Rhys narrowed his eyes at the man's back and poured the wine into the urn of the nearest topiary.

Beth wished she were at home in Greenthorne. She needed the trunk at the foot of her bed. She needed to unwrap the cloak that had long been entombed within it. She needed to bury all of her questions in its answers.

Every moment since Rhys appeared out of the darkness had felt strangely, perfectly right. The dumbstruck awe, the dreamlike haziness, the anger, the eagerness to be embraced—and then, there on the hill, she had abruptly remembered a face—the man in town who'd had the vaguest appearance of Sol.

With that memory, a seed of doubt was planted. Looking into Rhys' eyes, she could tell how much three years had changed her. She wondered about the ways it might have changed him.

His mere touch infused her with trust, just as it had three years ago, but now her wisdom warned her against that trust. What if it *had* been Sol in town? If both Rhys and Sol had resurfaced at once, did that not warrant caution? Her thoughts congealed around a conspiracy that she did not want to acknowledge. And then he he'd uttered it:

Desmarais.

She'd been certain Desmarais was still alive. Rhys gave her the confirmation she'd awaited, yet it did nothing but break her heart.

If Rhys were to be believed, then he'd returned to Yorkshire to warn her of something. A wish buried deep within her had only half come true. He'd returned. But he hadn't returned for *her*.

She couldn't sleep. The counterpane of the luxurious guest bed was suffocating. She retreated to a bench at the window, her knees tucked up to her chin, to keep vigil over her own thoughts.

If Allison had been aware that Beth's *Rhys* was at the ball, she didn't let on. She just steadied her friend for the duration of the night, asking over and over if she'd seen a ghost. In fact, she had. The one thing she was certain of now was that he wasn't going to vanish into the ether. He'd come back for a reason, and she was certain she'd learn more of it.

It was evident from the sun's punishing angle that Beth had slept much later than she was fond of. Her legs creaked out from beneath her as she unfolded herself from the tight position she'd fallen asleep in on the bench. Laughter fluttered up from somewhere downstairs.

The door to Allison's room suddenly bumped open, and Allison came floating in like a fairy, already dressed and fresh. Her face screwed up when she caught a glimpse of Beth.

That bad?

"Good Lord, did you look even look this poorly when you were returned from the woods? I didn't realize you'd had so much wine."

"I didn't," said Beth. "I just didn't sleep." She looked Allison up and down. Her young face had returned to a portrait of joyful vigor. "And how did *you* escape the grip of the ballroom demons this morning?"

Allison shrugged. "I suppose I've just sacrificed enough hens to them lately." Beth laughed, but the laughter died sharply as her cousin threw open the drapes. Beth's eyelids clamped down against the searing light. *A friend to demons indeed.*

Beth fished beneath the bench for a robe she'd abandoned in the middle of the night. Her fingers found it and she stood tall to stretch before slipping it around her. Allison stopped her before her second arm was through the sleeve.

"Oh Beth, no. Breakfast is formal this morning *and* late because everyone else looks like you. Louisa is helping my mother with something at present, but I can help you dress."

Beth allowed it, but she wasn't feeling very formal. They compromised on a chemise gown with a soft lavender *Robe à la Turque* over top. Allison helped her with her underpinnings and then rubbed some sort of mint oil under Beth's eyes. She swore it would make Beth look as though she'd "slumbered for a thousand days."

"There," said Allison. "You've been rendered presentable. No time to do more about your hair. May we please go eat now? I am starting to smell delicious things, and I'm not sure how much longer I can wait." Beth nodded, but she didn't quite make it to the door before turning around and hurrying back to her dressing table.

Gardenia blossoms floated in a bowl of water, leftover from those she'd plucked for the ball. She lifted one and without even shaking it dry, pinned it above her ear. Nodding to herself in the looking glass, she saw a face with too many stories. Beth ran to catch up to Allison, who had abandoned her to follow the wafting scent of Chelsea buns.

The Weldons' new residence was grand and didn't yet possess the warmth of being lived-in by its new tenants. Beth's heels echoed in a lonesome way as she crossed through its high-ceilinged rooms. She neared the dining room, only to realize that it was not the origin of the breakfast aromas. A faint round of laughter went up from someplace beyond, and she turned her head to it. *The terrace.* She crossed through the ballroom, where two footmen were quietly disassembling some of the installations of the night prior.

The entire wall of French doors was opened to the outside, where a long table had been set up for near on twenty of the Weldon's acquaintances. Soft chuckling and drowsy conversation lilted through the empty ballroom. It was a beautiful scene—like a painting—to see them, all smiles and crumpled silks, backlit as they were by the morning's golden sun.

Beth recognized her father's back as she approached from inside. He sat at the middle of the table, with an empty seat next to him for her. On the other side of the table, a footman held the tray of buns in front of a happy Allison. She didn't notice Beth's approach, fixated as she was on the food laid out before her. Beth put a hand on her father's shoulder.

"Good morning, Papa." She kissed his cheek as he stood up to greet her.

"Beth, dear. Look who has joined us this morning." He gestured across her, and she turned.

The seat to her left pushed out and there was Rhys, standing and bowing his head. His hair was unkempt, partly hanging by his eyes.

"Miss Clarke," he said.

Her mouth opened in a stupor that she quickly clamped down on. She had said she wouldn't be caught off guard, after all.

"Rhys," she said, forgetting herself.

"Pardon, darling?" asked her father. "Do you not remember? I could have sworn you were re-acquainted last night? This is—"

Beth caught up suddenly.

"Mr. Osbourne Booker, yes!"

A fork from across the table came clattering down to its plate. Allison caught it before it reached her lap and held it to her chest like some memento as she stared wide-eyed and agape at Beth, then at the strapping man opposite her. A devious grin of realization stole across Allison's face.

Rhys looked to Mr. Clarke in hurried explanation. "Rhys is my middle name."

Allison gasped loudly.

Rhys' lip kicked up into a smile that seemed all too knowing as he acknowledged the awestruck girl across the table.

Beth put a palm to her forehead, bracing herself to forge through the oddest breakfast of her life. Then she gestured to Allison. "Mr. Booker, my cousin, Lady Allison Weldon."

"Pleased to make your acquaintance, Lady Allison. You look well this morning, considering the toll the festivities took on so many of us."

Yes, her cousin *did* look well. Beth couldn't say the same of herself that morning and suddenly wished that she could.

Allison straightened and blushed. "The pleasure is mine. I've heard so mu—" She looked to Beth for permission and saw none. "I mean, I am just so grateful that you brought my dear friend back safely those years ago." Allison softened back into her seat and rearmed herself with a hot bun, but her smile did not relent.

Rhys pushed in Beth's chair as she sat. When they were settled, he turned to her. "And you," he said, in a private volume, "look very awake indeed."

Beth took a fruit fork in hand. "Don't tease me. I enjoy it more when I'm less tired . . ." Beth stabbed the fork's tines viciously into the nearest tangerine. ". . . and less confused."

"Give me the chance to leave you less confused."

Beth knew what he meant but found her mind caught on the words *leave you.*

Rhys' hand briefly rested on her knee below the table. Beth's eyes flashed around the group instinctively to see if the lapse in decorum had been noticed. *What did it matter if it had? Had she not promised herself not to care?*

Rhys leaned in to whisper to her. "Can we speak privately after this?"

There was something about feeling his breath on her neck, something so painfully overwhelming. Beth did her best to ignore the question. Distractedly, she looked up and down the length of the table. It took her a moment to realize whose face she was looking for. Ignoring Rhys' question, she looked to her cousin.

"Where's your brother, Mr. Weldon, this morning? Still asleep?"

Allison's smile faltered, but Lord Weldon jumped in instead. "He went off with friends after the gathering, and I'm supposing he'll stay with them until he sets back off for Greece. Bit of a free spirit, that one." Lord Weldon said it cheerfully enough, but his face sank—the face of a father wistful for the rare company of his son.

Beth's expression fell too, and she met Allison's eyes, which were writ with apology. *No matter.* She could still write to Stefano and plan her trip to Greece.

With nowhere else to throw her attention, Beth finally turned to answer Rhys' question but was interrupted by the sharp rings of a fork against a champagne glass. Her father. Several relaxed and happy faces swiveled to attend to his signal. Beth recognized so few of them.

One eager woman, a complete stranger, silver-haired and elegant, pounced first. "What is it Mr. Clarke? Are you going to announce an engagement?" The woman's eyes flitted back and forth excitedly between Rhys and Beth. Beth froze at the shocking inquiry and found it suddenly difficult to swallow the blackberry in her mouth. She heard Rhys snort into his napkin.

Mr. Clarke waved away the woman's question with a smile. "I merely wanted to make everyone aware of a guest this morning who holds a great deal of my gratitude . . ."

Oh God, Papa . . .

Rhys stood out among the aristocrats. He looked sharp and presentable, but his waistcoats had no floral embellishments and his boots retained a patina that could not be polished away.

Her father gestured to Rhys. Beth sat up straight, feeling everyone's eyes cast their way.

"As many of you, I'm sure, are aware, my daughter experienced a terrible ordeal a few years back—"

"Kidnappings aren't polite fare for the table, Papa." Beth stroked the stem of her glass.

The silver-haired woman gasped. "A *kidnapping*?!"

"See, not everyone here knows," said Beth, taking a sip of champagne.

"Yes, Ceci—I would have avoided the indelicate term, but it is accurate."

Ceci? Now it was Beth whose eyes flitted between this woman and her father with curiosity. Her father did not typically make a habit of calling ladies by pet names.

"It doesn't matter," said her father firmly, trying to regain everyone's attentions. "What matters is that this gentleman here, Mr. Osbourne Booker, is a Bow Street Runner and was her rescuer. I was overjoyed to run into him in Bartswell and ask him to be our guest here. Things were too chaotic three years ago to give him the deserved hospitality." Mr. Clarke raised his glass. "To you, Mr. Booker."

Glasses went up around the table and so did eyebrows. Including Beth's. *Had Rhys been under the same roof all night?*

Looking around the table, Beth saw faces that were scandalized to varying degrees. Mr. Clarke, however, glowed with a father's pride. Beth sighed and dragged a finger around the rim of her glass. Her improprieties were hereditary.

The woman her father called Ceci leaned over the table conspiratorially. Her bosom was about to spill right over her lace like a waterfall. She nearly tipped over her cup of chocolate as she folded her hands in front of her. To be drunk at such an early hour—the thought was dizzying. "Who took you? How long for? What was it like?" she begged.

Beth felt her cheeks heat. "I don't remember much, honestly."

The back of Rhys' knuckles brushed against her skirts. He leaned in and spoke low to her. "You have a rapt audience, Miss Clarke. Don't squander the opportunity."

His words were an injection of sense. Beth lifted her eyes to meet Ceci's. "You see, I don't recall much because I was very sick at the end. But I do recall sleeping in the woods. We were forced to make camp."

Ceci pulled back into her chair, a shocked hand to her bosom. But her face belied her delight at the increasing scandal of the account.

Several others at the table were noticeably lending their ears but with more discerning expressions. Beth punctuated the confession with another sip of her drink.

"Tell them about the rest of it, Miss Clarke," said Rhys.

She looked at him sharply. "The rest?"

Rhys turned back to the table, his face, all seriousness. "Yes. Tell them how you killed the wolf."

Champagne sucked into her nose jarringly as she choked on her drink. The gentle murmur of the breakfast conversation died down from end to end. All eyes on her. She looked desperately to her cousin for help, but Allison clenched two fists in front of her mouth, ready to bubble over with unrestrained exhilaration.

"Darling?" her father murmured.

Beth licked her lips. "Yes. There was the wolf that I killed. The only wolves in the country found me, and I managed to make them one fewer." She put a hand on her father's arm. "I didn't want to frighten you with the story before."

No one spoke. Beth let her gaze wander shyly back to the man beside her. Rhys' eyes were almost watering with brazen approval. Perhaps he'd not changed so much.

Ceci lifted a napkin to her lips, trying to conceal a chuckle that escaped into the yawning silence anyway. The sound turned fast into throes of laughter. Ceci tried to speak, but she had to wait for the spirit that seized to tire out first. She reached across the table and put a hand, heavy with jewelry, onto Beth's wrist. With the other hand, the woman wiped a tear of mirth from her eye.

"Oh, dear thing, you're joking. You had me. I completely believed you." A couple of nervous laughs rose up around the table before bewildered guests at either end resumed their prior conversations. Her father clutched at his heart in relief, and his attention was soon pulled away by Ceci.

Beth's chest lifted against her stays, and she dared to look up at Rhys.

He mouthed the words, *meet me.*

She nodded, imperceptible to any but him. "I like to ride in the fields beyond the pond after breakfast."

Rhys raised his eyebrows and popped a grape into his mouth. "What a pleasant ritual."

19

Rhys slowed his horse. There she was at the crest of a knoll, in the shade of a tree, looking down on him from atop her dapple gray, as if from a throne. It struck him to see her sitting sidesaddle, holding her seat so expertly. He could imagine her racing through a vale, moving perfectly with the horse.

He nudged his horse up the hill until he joined her.

Now that he was near, she seemed to cast her gaze anywhere but at him. Her discomfort was plain, and he longed to draw her back into the lightness they'd eventually found at breakfast.

"Did I not once tell you that you can say absolutely anything because your story is too legendary to be believed?"

"You did," she admitted.

"I hope that I—"

"May I go first?"

Rhys withdrew his words and nodded.

Beth took a deep breath. "I wanted to make you aware that I know Sol is alive and nearby. You cannot hide it from me."

It took a moment for that to settle. It couldn't be possible, but he knew better than to think her a liar. "Why do you say that?" His gut tightened with dread curiosity.

"I saw him in the village. I didn't really believe it—dismissed it as my mind playing tricks. But then you arrived. And now I don't know what to think."

Rhys struggled to imagine that Sol had survived his injury. He'd resented having to shoot the man, but still, the unlikelihood—

"Beth, I swear on my life I know nothing of it."

"What else can you swear on?"

Three days in the woods. My own bewitching. A life, reformed. A million things.

Rhys put a hand to his heart, choosing levity over vulnerability. "May the deadly geese of Greenthorne feast on my eyeballs if I lie."

Beth raised her chin. The missed shot at her laughter made him ache.

"How do you know about the geese?"

"You told me. You told me about them as you grew more ill. I wanted to know all about Greenthorne. I wanted to distract you from your discomfort."

He watched as her eyes sorted through the air for memories. He waited patiently, enjoying the small shifts in her expression—the way her softly parted lips moved around small, unspoken words. Eventually, she began to nod.

"I wish I better remembered that," she said.

"I can fill in the rest. I can tell you everything."

"But you can't tell me if Sol is alive or nearby?"

Rhys shrugged, at a loss. "I can't. As you know, I'm here

regarding another."

Beth stiffened. "Desmarais."

Her horse sensed the tension and backed away, suddenly uncomfortable on the bit. Rhys reached a hand out for its cheekpiece to steady it, but Beth reacted with a hard grip on his wrist.

"Leave it," she said.

He did. "Can we not get down and talk awhile?"

"Perhaps I feel safer on horseback."

Safer. The word slammed into his breast like a cudgel, taking the wind from him. He wanted to be gentle, but he could no longer keep the hurt from his voice. "Do you *fear* me, Beth?"

"I've never feared fewer things in my whole life, Rhys. That doesn't mean I should not look after myself."

"No. I suppose it doesn't." He looked down at his hands. The leather of his riding gloves creaked as he made fists on the reins. "Beth, I did unforgivable things to you in the beginning—"

"Did you come to me that final night?"

"What?"

"You just said that you could fill in my missing memories, so I wish for you to try this one." Her eyes pierced into his and the breeze blew stray hairs across her gaze. Rhys tightened his grip on his reins to keep himself from brushing her hair away.

"Tell me, Rhys. That last night at the folly. Did you come back into my room and apologize? Did you promise to take me away from there? Did I dream it?"

"It was not a dream."

Her gaze cooled, but she still grit her teeth. "Then where were you and Harry when those bastards started plunging me into the trough?"

"We were in the woods, preparing the diversion that we would use to get you the hell out of there. I couldn't have known that Lionel's patience would break that morning."

"You mean you didn't expect the devil to act a fiend?"

There was enough truth in that to leave him bleeding. Her pain snapped against his heart like a bullwhip, and his anguish roared up through him. "Then why let me take you in my arms in the woods? Why kiss me? Why let me linger on your—" his neck rolled over the word as though it were too big for his throat, "—body?"

She sat completely still while her horse moved beneath her, agitated.

"*Why*, Beth? If I had disappointed you so?"

"It was a very cold night," she said.

No. That wasn't it. Don't lie. He reached again for her horse's bridle, damned if she liked it or not. Their knees brushed as Rhys drew near. "One doesn't get upset over the lack of a proper goodbye if it was just one very cold night."

"Why do *I* have to say everything? When do I get to hear how *you* feel?" Her eyes lit into him as she lowered her tone. "What was that very cold night *to you*, Rhys?" She chopped at his arm with her fist until he released his grip on her tack. Then she took off on Cutter, cantering down to the meadow.

He had wanted to see her ride, and now he had his wish. Her skirts were a flurry at her side as she drove forward. He gave chase.

It brought him back to when he'd furiously ridden for the doctor's house, tears of desperation and fear slashing at his temples. Beth had known nothing of that. She didn't know how long three years were for him too. Didn't know how his heart had twisted and choked as their separation had drawn nearer.

Dewey's death had long ago left a fear in him, that any close attachments might lead to tragedy, particularly of his own doing.

He'd already visited such adversity on Beth, yet somehow, she'd ridden away from that folly with something kind left in her heart for him. He didn't know what he'd do now if some of that affection weren't still there. He didn't deserve such care, but she deserved to know that such affection was returned all along.

Beth had accelerated to a dangerous gallop. It had been one thing to imagine her racing across a vale, but it was another thing entirely to see her take up such a powerful gait when she was not riding securely astride. Rhys' chest tightened and he slowed his own horse, hoping she might slow down, but she did not.

Her horse leapt over something as it disappeared into a thick patch of trees. He followed, leaning forward as his horse leapt over the same overgrown ditch. He slowed down as he entered the grove, but Beth was nowhere to be seen. Then her horse sidled into the path . . .

Without her on it.

It was Beth's own fault. Riding like that when so upset. Tearing off on her horse on the unfamiliar property. The hop over the ditch hadn't thrown her, but the trees' low branches had all threatened to brutally dismount her as she tried to slow Cutter down. She'd saved herself from their punishment by opting for a more urgent descent—jumping off into a bed of ivy.

Now on her back, she found herself intact enough, though her white lawn skirt might need be dyed green to salvage it. Shifting, she noticed the first sign of achiness.

She heard Rhys' horse plunge forth into the area and stop. Heavy boots thudded to the ground. Beth's stomach fluttered and she stroked it in a useless bid to soothe herself. *Three years.* All that waiting, and he hadn't come for *her.* He'd only returned to warn her of Desmarais and now she didn't even care to hear it.

She listened to the soles of Rhys' boots pivot frantically in the dirt and grass. Searching. "Beth? Beth?"

Guiltily, she couldn't bring herself to cry out in response. She was too afraid of hearing her own voice crack wistfully on his name. She heard the intake of his breath at the very moment he spotted her—

"Beth!" and his steps grew quickly louder.

He flung himself down to her in the ivy. A passing shock frisked over her on realizing she was straddled by him. He held her face in his hands, the sweat in the leather reminding her faintly of his scent in winter.

"Can you hear me?"

She hoped that the crinkle in her brow was enough of an answer. She was quite obviously awake. But still, he looked so frightened. It recalled memories of Dyckson—the fear in his eyes and how that day had changed things. She nodded, making the stems of ivy rustle around her.

The heat of Rhys' thighs sank straight through her gauzy springtime layers. Her eyes closed to take in the feeling. *Just for one breath.* She inhaled deeply. But savoring the feel of him led to the unbidden onslaught of a much more indulgent scene. *Their lips together. Her hips rising up to him. The fabric of her skirts spilling out from between his fingers. An impatient tightness arising—*

Such thoughts were infuriating in how they controlled her. Her nails clawed frustratedly into the dirt beside her, and beneath her palm, she felt a stick. Her fingers closed around it and she brought it up to Rhys' throat like a dagger.

His expression pinched in curiosity at what she'd just done. So did hers. But she gripped her little stick, fierce and unwavering.

You should have returned sooner. Three years on, Beth had a life to defend. She would leave soon. Open up her world on the Continent and come back stronger, as Allison had. She would embody her mistakes. Live in her tawdry reputation. She would see every city and dance with every Stefano. She had plans . . .

But her hand shook. The firm line of Rhys' lips twitched at the corner, outlined by the familiar shadow of emergent chin hairs. His handsome eyes were blinking against something—the infuriating man was about to laugh. As soon as she realized it, Beth had to roll her lips between her teeth to prevent the same reaction. It was helpless for them both.

He must be just as aware as she of what sort of scene they made. And just as aware of how it echoed a memory from their past. The rumbles of impending laughter quaked silently up her body until both she and Rhys erupted at once.

"Do it then, Beth. End me here and now," said Rhys, through charges of laughter.

She snorted as she pressed the stick against him. It bowed before snapping against his neck. Then they laughed harder.

"I should have taken my chance when I had a hot iron in my hand."

He collapsed against her as they worked through their joyous fits. This time, the feeling of him against her didn't bring on heat between her legs so much as it warmed a place in her chest—a lonely place.

When the laughter died out, he pushed up on his arms to gaze down at her again.

"Help me up?" she asked.

But he didn't. His eyes explored her before locking into hers.

"The sweetness of solitude," he said, "is wearing thin as gauze."

Where—? Beth searched her mind for the phrase's familiarity, and found it. The words were hers.

He continued, or tried to. "Its promises for—its promise for feasts—damn." He shook his head. He didn't have it.

Beth did, and was about to complete the phrase for him, until she remembered what it was—

The sweetness of solitude

Wearing thin as gauze

Its promise for a feast of freedoms

Now sometimes seeming flawed

She wasn't certain of whether she believed in those flaws or not. She squeezed Rhys' arm.

"You read my notebook?"

"Yes. I'm sorry."

"Why did you ever take it?"

"For information? And—I don't know. I thought I had to hate you."

"Why?"

"An expensive carriage. A bright white silk stock tied round your neck. Not a crease in your traveling habit. You reminded me every bit of the women who helped condemn my friend to death."

"And that anger, that's why you took *me* too?"

"No. I took you with us because the alternative was to leave you alone in the middle of the highroads on a frigid night, with other cads lurking nearby. I hoped that I might somehow be the lesser evil."

He lowered his head. Whatever else he was about to say, he couldn't meet her eyes.

"I didn't know what you were capable of then. You would have been fine, I know that now, but there was a selfishness that night too, Beth. Wondering about your fate if we had parted would have plagued me the rest of my days."

"Tell me more."

"It would have been just as terrible not to know what happened to you after I left you at Greenthorne."

"Which is why you've come back, years later?"

"Which is why I came back, *weeks* later."

Beth waited for Rhys to go on, feeling as though she were missing something. She repeated the words in her head and grasped what they really meant. Everything felt suddenly darker, as though a cloud had moved overhead to cancel out the dappled sunlight that seeped through the trees.

"Rhys?"

"I came back, weeks after we parted. I had to see you well."

The cold fist of betrayal, at first held back by her confusion, now slammed fully into her. She pushed him up and away from her so that she might scramble to her feet. He rose to join her.

"My father told me you were welcome back anytime. Why would either of you keep a meeting from me?"

"Because he didn't know."

"Didn't know you came back? Rhys, what did you do exactly?"

Rhys pushed a taloned hand into his hairline and exhaled.

"I did the only thing I knew how. I lurked and I spied like the felon I am."

Beth wanted to know more, but the limitations of her heart were fast being reached.

She wanted to scream or to throw something. Frustrations clawed at her insides for a violent escape, but she no longer possessed the emotional lawlessness of her youth. Perhaps that was one loss from her youth that would be for the better. She took a deep breath. Here was this broad-shouldered man, shrinking from her and avoiding her gaze. A man wounded before her. His voice was thick with shame—the sort of shame that she recognized from her youth.

"But you're not that anymore, are you? You're on the other side of the law now." She stepped toward him carefully. "So you say."

"I am."

He'd looked so meek just a moment before, so in need of reassurance. But as she drew nearer, he seemed to grow taller—to loom up over her like the dark stranger that found her on the road one January night.

He took the final steps needed to close the gap between them.

Rhys wrapped an arm around her and stroked the back of her neck, coaxing her to look up at him. There it was—that hint of pine. She caught only the barest note of it, but it was a tonic that made her heart race.

She held onto his arm, steadying herself, waiting.

"You want to know what I thought in the woods that night?" he asked.

"I do."

He leaned down until she could feel his breath as he spoke.

"I thought, what will I do without her? Without another night like this?" His embrace drew her in more deeply. "How do I continue to live on the same soil and never lay my poor eyes on her again? How do I make my mind stop wondering where she is and what she's doing at any given moment? And how ever do I cope with the notion that she may not be in the same agony over me?"

"Rhys," she said, pulling away. "Is that what would have pleased you? My shared agony?"

"I didn't wish it—"

"Well you have it."

He froze.

"I *was* in agony. I was. Same as you. But as I said last night, there's that imbalance that I find hard to reckon with. You knew where I was. You had an advantage. To write to me, to visit me . . ." A harsh laugh escaped her. "To *spy* on me."

Beth lowered her head. She'd drained many hours away in her father's study, seeking Desmarais, but never Rhys. No, she was never quite brave enough to bear herself to that sort of hope.

Yet, she trembled now, wishing that she'd not pulled away from his arms. Unheld by him, she felt suddenly prone to the whims of her distress.

"Does it ease your pain, Rhys, to know that I wept into your cloak, prayed into it for some act of fate that would crash us into one another?" The timing of his return—it was so poorly chosen, so tragic. "Does it make you feel better that you lingered with me for years? That every man I spoke to was held up against you and found wanting?"

She detected a spark in his eye. He couldn't conceal it. It *did* make him feel better. Her very soul flared like a struck match. He wanted her. He missed her. But they were at odds.

He reached again for her, but she stepped back.

"The trouble is," she said. "It all improved."

"Improved?"

"I couldn't go on unless it did. So I made it get better. Not perfect. But better. And it was only very recently that I could even see my power in that. I've healed from you, Rhys." *Mostly.*

"Beth, if you—"

"How wonderful for you, that you had the fortitude to stay away from me for three long years. How excellent you are at self-deprivation." She could taste the venom in her words, was practically burned by their sting before she flung them, yet she could not stop. "That you loved me so much and martyred yourself to our unfortunate circumstance. You *saint*."

His eyes peeled wider and she realized she'd said it—had put those words into his mouth—*that you loved me.* She suddenly felt faint. It was beyond time to depart.

She whirled and made for Cutter, stopping short at the horse's side.

Damn.

On her rare rides astride, Beth had taught herself how to mount without a groom, but now she was confronted with the sidesaddle. She considered flinging a leg over it anyway, but her habit was not particularly suited to such an alternative. *Fine.* She would lead Cutter instead.

She turned to take the reins, only to nearly trip over Rhys, who had bent down at her knee. His strong hands were stirruped for her. There was guilt in his dulcet expression. She wished she could ease it, but she was the one who had put it there. Where had all of her cruelty come from?

She allowed him to heft her inelegantly into the seat.

He passed her the whip that had been discarded in her hurried dismount. Then he pulled a letter from his pocket and passed it up to her as well.

"What's this?"

"It is my thanks."

At Greenthorne, Beth's father could be found in his study at most times of day. But during their stay with the Weldons, he'd often wandered restlessly outdoors. Beth wasn't surprised when she spotted his lone figure in a chair at the pond's edge.

Riding closer, she raised her eyebrows at the sight of a fishing pole beside him. Had he gone daft?

"Papa?"

"Hmm?" He didn't look up to her but kept his gaze intently on the water.

"You *do* know there's no fish in there?"

He lifted his chin and smiled up at her pitifully. "In fact, I did not." He pushed the pole over from where it was dug into the ground and closed a novel he'd been ignoring in his lap. "I just find myself bored to death when away from home."

Beth took her knee from the pommel and slid down from Cutter's back.

"You find your darkened study at Greenthorne more engaging than socializing here at Tallyside?" she asked.

"I do."

She crouched on the grass beside her father and looked out over the large pond, its fountains no longer pumping. He placed a hand on her wrist where it rested against his chair. His widower's wedding band caught the sun.

"Quite the breakfast conversation this morning."

Beth winced. "That Ceci certainly seemed scandalized enough by it."

"Yes, well, Ceci—uh, *Lady Blount*—feigns the appropriate response—and overly dramatically if you want my opinion. Trust me, she *knows* scandal personally."

As a woman whose pet name was flung about so comfortably, Beth did not doubt it.

"I quite enjoyed it this morning—seeing everyone's eyes go wide. Hearing the silver clink sharply to the plates."

"Is that why you brought up the kidnapping, Papa, to provoke shock?"

"You weren't going to do it alone, were you?"

Unbelievable. No, she probably wouldn't have brought it up herself. She'd been saving her scandals for Europe. She still felt too raw sometimes to own it here, where men who were up on the gossip could do things like snatch their arm away during a dance.

"I had quite the conspirator in Mr. Booker, didn't I? And I didn't even know it."

"You like him, don't you?" she asked.

"My dear, he brought my only child out of hell and placed her back in my arms. I daresay I'd die for the man. But yes, beyond that, I do also think I like him."

"You don't even know him."

"When I ran into him in town, I recognized him immediately. I dragged him to the nearest tavern to shower him with ale and gratitude."

"Ah, yes—*ran into him.* You do realize he was most likely there to find you?"

"Beth, dear, I'm not so quaint. Of course I realize it."

Beth rose to her knees to be more level with his eyes. "And you never had any suspicions of him? Of a stranger that carried me to your doorstep out of a fog of mystery?"

Papa's eyes studied her. "Should I suspect?" He huffed inwardly, as though suppressing a small chuckle. "I've known you your whole life, Beth. Studied you intently for three decades. Perhaps I even knew what I was getting into when you were but a spark of mischief in your mother's eye. Oh yes, Beth. I had suspicions and worries. But I was no more suspicious of him than of you. Do not forget that I've been tested by wild lapses of propriety before."

"A kidnapping should hardly be seen as the abducted woman's fault." Beth hastened to clarify, "And the rescue of a woman should be no scandal either."

Her father tucked his chin and gave her a look that told her she was being unfair. "You're well aware that I'm in agreement with that. But all anyone else sees is an unmarried woman in the arms of an unrelated man."

Beth knew it as well as any.

Her father put a hand on her cheek. "My overwhelming relief was that you were home. The only person you expressed ire for was Desmarais. All else was inconsequential."

"I assume Rhys told you something of Desmarais?"

Her father scowled and resettled in his low seat. "He did, yes. Has he not told you?"

As though I've given him a chance.

Her father sighed. "There isn't much information but that his name is on the register of an inn in Hull. That's all we know."

"Hull. So close by? I always said he was alive. You should have told me." A chill skimmed down Beth's spine, even in the bright sun of May Day.

He shrugged. "I've hardly known for a full day myself. But the man won't come near you, I swear it."

"You're right, Papa. He won't." It was the right time to tell him. "Because I'm going away for a while."

His white eyebrows lifted. Some of his thin hair was picked up by the breeze. She had to leave now, before he grew too old, before he needed her too much. She smiled to ease her words.

"I've been inspired by Allison, and I'm going to the Continent."

He set his lips tightly, and his finger wagged in the air while he found his words. "I knew this would happen. As soon as she left, I could see your boredom grow tenfold." He suddenly took her arm urgently. "Has Mr. Bunce been helping you? I could swear he kept something from me at our meeting."

Beth smiled. "He has indeed. But Papa, please don't—"

He waved away whatever she was about to say. "It's fine. I'm happy for you. Though I do want to know what Desmarais is about before you disappear from my sight."

He pulled a rock from his pocket and skipped it across the body of water.

"Then will we return to Greenthorne this afternoon?"

Her father rolled his eyes. "If only. I'm afraid it's one engagement after another here. Lady Weldon has her heart set on everyone going to the May fair in Bartswell this eve." He narrowed his eyes warily. "Perhaps you should stay here instead of walking to town with us—because of Desmarais."

"That's ludicrous. I'll enjoy my life, no matter where he is."

Her father smiled. "Mr. Booker said you might say that."

20

Twilight gave the horizon a golden edge as the group cut through the fields toward the road. The fair was set up on the edge of Bartswell, not two miles away, and the whole party—consisting largely of the breakfast crowd—had deemed themselves fit to walk.

Beth led the pack as she often did, with her uncommonly brisk stride. Her arm was locked with Allison's, and what the girl lacked in stride, she made up for in energy, skipping intermittently to keep up. The early evening had already cast some of its magic on Beth. Badly as she'd wanted to leave for home earlier in the day, she now found herself content.

She was aware of another fast-walker at her back. Aware that he must be restraining his determinant stroll in order to hold back with the others, to give her space. Intuition kicked at her from time to time, whispering: *He's looking. If you turn right now, he watches.* But she resisted the pull of it.

She'd read Rhys' letter before supper. In it, he'd expressed his gratitude for how she had set up Dewey's family to live so well. She'd never named herself as their benefactor in any way, but, of course, she was the only one who could have done it, and Rhys was no fool. It had been so long since she'd seen to their living that she'd almost forgotten the arrangement. But Rhys had checked in on them and realized he'd been cut free of the debt he held over himself.

In the letter, he shared the wonderful details he'd learned. That all of the children had educations and apprenticeships. That Mrs. Dewey was now the proprietress of a little shop of notions. All the hopes Beth had for the family were fulfilled.

She'd not anticipated the letter's second half. *You've freed me to pursue paths that I'd never before dreamed of,* he'd said. *For some time, I was listless, not knowing how to live without owing someone.* Then he'd listed all of those he'd owed pieces of his life to: The Marine Society, the press-gangs, long merchant contracts, a mad captain, Dewey's family, his band of thieves. The trajectory of the life of a lad from Cardiff had begun to take shape, and it had started low and rotten. That he'd ever even become a career carpenter on mercantile vessels must be some testament to his will.

"Oh Beth, it nearly killed me not to see you this afternoon." The sweet voice of Allison broke Beth from her reflections. "I begged Mama not to send me on that errand."

"What did she have you do?"

"She pleaded that I ride to her acquaintances' house with some books to loan them, but it was all a contrivance. What she *really* wanted was for me to meet a wealthy nephew that was visiting them. He wasn't even home!"

Beth hugged Allison with one arm. "That's a pity that you didn't even get your fun."

"It's fine. She showed me a portrait of him in the dining room, and between us, he was lacking."

"Lacking what exactly?"

Allison thought for a moment. "A chin?"

Beth chuckled. "So harsh, Allison."

"I did have a pleasant interaction on the way home."

"Oh?"

"My hat blew off while I rode, and a gentleman kindly grabbed it for me before my footman could."

"And is this someone you would hope to see again?"

Allison batted the air with her folded fan. "Goodness no. He was much too old, but it was flattering nonetheless."

Beth looked carefully at the young woman beside her. A woman of a nature less cynical than her own. In the flaxen-haired beauty, she saw an early wisdom but also an abundance of trust. "Allison, you deserve many things in this life. You are so above being flattered emptily by those who can't draw even a wisp of your attention in return. Conquer grandly."

Allison shrank a bit—an unintended effect.

"I just like to appreciate kind people," Allison said, looking off in the distance.

Of course. Because Allison herself was kind, even if she jabbed at the rendering of a man's chin in an oil painting.

"I think that's an admirable trait," said Beth. "It was not my intention to demean it." And because of that trait, Allison's wound swiftly evaporated. She smiled and rested her head affectionately on Beth's shoulder.

Beth's intuition kicked up again as she felt the presence of Rhys like a warm glow from behind. *Conquer grandly.* What did such a judgment even mean to her? When the man she couldn't get off of her mind was a sailor-gone-thief that once thought to ransom her? But Beth appreciated kindness too. She'd once seen Rhys' kindness like a thread of light slipping through a pinhole in the dark.

Beth wasn't like her cousin. All-loving. All-trusting. Yet she had come to trust him. It happened when he'd knelt across from her in the ravine, outstretching his hand. He'd told her that she would not survive a night in the woods. It was no manipulation—only the truth. As he'd delivered that cold news, she could see in his eyes how he hated to be the bearer of it. From then on, she had trusted him. *Even now*, she realized. The distrust that darkened her heart now was not of him but of *herself*.

"Well . . ." The expectant tone of Allison's voice was clear, but Beth wasn't certain what it was expectant *of*.

Allison added another skip to her stride to keep up with Beth. "Cousin, I shall burst inside if you do not start indulging me about what happened this morning."

Oh, that.

Beth smiled and lifted her chin smugly.

"Don't think I'll stop asking. You know I possess the stamina to harass you all night."

"You're more demanding of secrets than the maenad."

Allison's voice rose indiscreetly. "Ah yes, your imaginary friend in captivity."

"Oh, hush."

"If you won't speak, I will." Allison stole a glance over her shoulder as if the topic of their impending conversation needed pointing out. Beth stiffened her arm sharply to make her friend face forward again.

Allison leaned in. "He *is* very fine."

Beth cracked a smile.

"I nearly choked this morning when I heard his name out loud—when I realized I was beholding the subject of your grand affair. I could stab you for not telling me that your man, your *highwayman,* was at the ball. Tell me, have you properly reunited with him?"

Beth put on the sedate expression that she had perfected for card games.

Allison narrowed her eyes with intent. "Dear cousin, you look overheated." Allison *whiiicked* her fan open in front of Beth's face, catching her on the nose. Beth swatted the irritating thing away.

"It's not so easy as that." Beth's voice wavered.

Allison lowered the fan, turning serious. "How do you mean?"

"Everything feels so difficult now that it's real. A memory and a person are two different things."

"That may well be, but you've spent years wanting that memory to be real again."

"I haven't."

"Truly, Beth? Because a large cape that you took from the downstairs cupboard at Greenthorne tells otherwise."

Beth's elbow tensed on her cousin's arm. "How do you know about that?"

"I was with you the very moment you spotted it. Mrs. Brimble complained of its disappearance, and I knew a fox didn't run off with it."

Beth tried to extract her arm from Allison's, but the girl only locked Beth nearer.

"Beth, just act as yourself."

"My old self? My Dyckson self? My ruined self?"

"You can't go back and just pluck one of your ages from memory. You have to be *all* of them. Before Dyckson, after Dyckson. Before *The Ordeal* and after it. Else you will always be mourning every person you ever were."

Beth met her cousin's eyes and saw the optimism there. Had she been more like Allison, a decade ago? Had she ever possessed this sort of wisdom?

"My life has taken some interesting turns to bring me here."

"*Exactly*," said Allison eagerly. "Don't you suppose it *means* something?"

Beth's skirts swished up ahead of him, keeping time with her swift and elegant gait. Rhys regretted that the morning's conversation had been one of distress instead of all the things he'd hoped.

When he'd discovered her safe and alert in the ivy, all he'd been of a mind to do was drop down against her and drink of her health. Memories of her features had been slipping through his fingers one-by-one throughout the purgatory of their separation. He was parched for reminders.

Reminders that may never come.

She was hurt. Hurt and healing. And he was the *wound.*

Still, something had slipped in their conversation that he clung to—the suggestion that he loved her. Her words—quickly passed over in the moment—had jarred him to his core. He hung on to that word, toying with it all afternoon. *Love.* Did he love her? How could he even tell when he'd never encountered it before?

He'd hardly had enough shore leave in his whole life to utter more than a compliment before bedding a woman. Prior to his night in the woods with Beth, he'd been years without knowing a woman.

Rhys' thoughts had slowed down his walking. Yet he noticed one who was even farther behind the group. He stopped, waiting for Beth's father, Barnaby, to catch up.

"You don't have to slow down for my sake." The old man tried to wave him off, but Rhys fell into step with him.

"I wanted to thank you again for your hospitality."

"Thank the Weldons." Mr. Clarke patted Rhys' back jovially but frowned. "Tell me Mr. Booker, have you any concern that Desmarais might be nearer than Hull?"

"You mean, do I think he might be in Bartswell?" The man's worried lip was answer enough. "Of course, it's possible. Don't let it spoil the night though. Beth will be safe."

"You'll be kind enough to escort her this evening?"

Oh, that he should even ask.

"Of course, Mr. Clarke. She won't leave my sight. My associates from the Home Office stayed in town last night. I sent word ahead that they should be alert tonight."

"Bless you for your reassurance. Though I can't say that I'll ever be rid of the anxiety."

"That's natural enough. She's your only daughter."

"Almost my only family now, since my sister passed." Mr. Clarke went quiet, fiddling nervously with his watch chain.

Rhys must have realized it before, but somehow, hearing the words aloud drove them into his heart more acutely. He'd once allowed this man to fear for his only child and right after the death of his sister. It was monstrous.

Any words he'd thought of saying were now knotted in his throat. The long grass silenced their footsteps. The elder Weldons and a small clutch of their friends tripped on their silks and heels as they moved through the field. Rhys could not believe he'd once likened Beth to their sort. As if bidden, Beth's laughter trickled back from where she walked with her cousin.

"Do you think she'll be safe on the Continent?" asked Mr. Clarke.

"I'm sorry?"

"I worry about her when she leaves. If that awful man wants something. He was born in France, you know. He knows the country there. She thinks she'll be safer if she leaves, but what if he follows?"

"Mr. Clarke, forgive me, but I'm not certain that *I* follow. Does Beth have plans to travel?"

Mr. Clarke threw him a pitying gaze that made his heart sink. "Has my girl told you nothing of anything?"

Nothing of anything. Rhys cleared his throat.

"She has a right to be cautious around me." Rhys didn't know why he said it, but there it was, out in the open for interpretation. Mr. Clarke let it lie.

"She was inspired by Miss Weldon's tour."

"No, she didn't tell me."

"How can you protect her if she doesn't tell you such things?" Mr. Clarke shook his head.

"I haven't been forthright with her that protecting her is my aim, though she obviously understands it. She's no fool. I suspect she'd be offended by the prospect of outright protection."

"But she needs pro—"

"Maybe she doesn't."

Mr. Clarke's brows climbed so slowly that Rhys wondered if he'd overstepped in cutting the man off. There were an awful lot of rules among the landed folk, and he couldn't claim to have them all pinned down yet. It was true though. Beth could fend for herself like few people could. It was this enterprising bent of hers that attracted him so much.

"Yes. Maybe she doesn't," mumbled Mr. Clarke, nodding. "She's a monster sometimes."

Rhys' head snapped in alarm toward the old man. The words

had been as indifferently delivered as Rhys' invitation to the fair.

Mr. Clarke's eyes went wide at whatever expression of shock Rhys wore. "I mean it in the *fondest* possible way. I mean it as a father." A tired smile peeled across the man's lips, and Rhys matched it. A silent understanding passed between them. The understanding that Beth was as rare as a wolf in an English forest.

The group came over a gentle rise that revealed Bartswell below them. The May fair centered on a bonfire that glowed like an iris, staring up into the sky. The sight reminded Rhys of a boyhood that was robbed from him by labor. Tonight, he could indulge. The thought was wholly foreign, but he knew who would remind him to enjoy it, and he couldn't wait to be down there in the masses with her.

The daytime festivities were waning as they entered town. The maypole was already tightly wrapped in its ribbons and sat ignored. A handful of boys wove through the crowd with torches, lighting lanterns and braziers—signaling the transition to the festival's wilder, nighttime state. Kegs of ale were rolled into the town center and propped up in booths. Some patrons were already ahead in their cups. They rocked on their heels, leering at the casks, their mouths watering as they waited for the tap.

Upon entering the throngs, much of the group splintered off, including many of the nobs from breakfast that Rhys neither knew nor cared about. The core group, the Weldons and the Clarkes, remained and closed ranks against the swell of bodies.

Beth and Allison were still tightly linked. They halted abruptly as a stranger cut past them. Rhys gently tripped against Beth and put a hand to her back to keep from falling into her.

"Sorry."

She looked over her shoulder to meet his eye. He expected to see a warning there. Instead, he saw curiosity.

"I forgive you." She said it too softly to rise above the din, but he understood it on her lips.

Perhaps they could start anew.

21

How could anyone enjoy themselves amid such a crush of bodies? The street ahead of Beth was packed with all manner of tottering folk and their mugs full of belch.

"Beth, my skirt is getting stepped on. It's too much." Allison clung so tightly to her arm that Beth wondered if it might not be easier to drag a stubborn mule through the throngs. Beth was taller than Allison but even on her tiptoes, she couldn't see a good path over the crowd.

"That way."

Beth turned to the sound of the decisive voice behind her and saw Rhys pointing over the heads of the masses, down a narrow lane.

The next road over was much quieter than the raucous hub of activity near the bonfire. Here, the daytime vendors were packing up their wares, but it was something farther up the street that caught Beth's eye. Cages. A traveling menagerie.

Beth glided in a trance toward the first cage. It was large enough that it might contain their entire little party, yet was too small for its tenant—a dark and rounded mass, a bear. She recognized the beast from an oil painting over the library's mantel back at Ashecote. Only here, it looked far less menacing, as appealing as a kitten . . . yet despondent too.

A hand rested on her hip and she didn't jump at the touch the way she had at the ball. Now she knew it was only Rhys, placing a gentle hand on her before speaking. It wasn't a habit of her own ilk, but her body settled at its tenderness.

His breath warmed her ear as he leaned down from behind her. "Have you seen one before?"

Beth shook her head. "Have you?"

"I have. Regrettably, it was in a cargo hold and looked just as sorry as this fellow. Perhaps you'll see another bear someday. A wilder, happier one."

Perhaps someday soon. Perhaps on my tour. The excitement that rose in Beth at the thought of her impending voyage was quickly tempered by the awareness of Rhys' hand on her. She'd not told him yet.

She spun in his grasp.

"I'm sorry, Rhys, there's something that I—"

"Apologizing? For what, dear Beth?" He reached up to brush a stray lock from her eyelashes. It was the first time he'd done so in three years, and never was there a thing so reassuring as the brush of his knuckles against her cheek. He wasn't teasing. He truly believed she had nothing to atone for.

But he doesn't know—

Beth's guilty thoughts ebbed. Suddenly she could think of little else but the fact of their nearness.

Allison slid up beside them for a look at the bear. "Good Lord, what a thing!" As her eyes settled on the creature, her expression of gleeful shock fell into one of grief. It seemed they all shared in their pity for the poor thing. Allison recovered swiftly, as was her habit. "There's more up ahead!"

Beth took Rhys' arm, and Allison couldn't conceal her delight as he proffered his other arm to her.

They stopped at a pen that contained all manner of hoofed animals, each painted as though by a different artist and each with horns uniquely sculpted. Behind them, a small ass ate hay, looking quite plain among his brethren.

Beth looked over her shoulder. The rest of their group, the elder set, had only just reached the bear. Lady Weldon looked ready to swoon. Beth exchanged a smile with her father before feeling a tap at her shoulder.

"Uh, Beth?"

There was something ominous about the caution in Allison's voice. Beth turned to find her cousin looking elsewhere. What was it? Beth's eyes took in the bobbing heads of dozens of people, and she wondered what she was supposed to see. Her stomach clenched as she remembered why Rhys was there at all—*Desmarais?*

But no. Allison had at last been kind enough to point to a little dais across the street, where a large dog rested at the feet of a seated man. No, not a dog, a *wolf.*

Beth was so entranced that she could hardly tell if she moved toward it by her own power or if Rhys were guiding them there.

"It seems you are capable of finding all the non-existent wolves in England."

Beth nodded at Rhys' comment. She herself could not believe it.

"See," said Allison. "I told you yours must have escaped from some menagerie, and now I'm certain of it."

"So, Beth." Rhys gestured to the tame specimen before them. "Think yourself good enough to take down another one?"

The wolf's docile panting belied its wild nobility. Its keeper was dressed in gaudy yet threadbare clothes and sat on his tattered chair as though it were a throne.

The wolf held Beth's eye, shooting visions of a winter's night through her soul. She relived the quick fight, heard the yips and growls, felt them tearing viciously at her petticoat—but the memory ignited no fear, only respect and curiosity as she observed the lupine ambassador before her.

Rhys spoke up so that the man holding the wolf's lead might hear him. "How much to touch the wolf?"

"Thruppence."

The man's eyes wandered to Beth and looked her up and down. His lips curled in approval. "Or nothing at all, for the lady."

Rhys scowled at the man's leering and handed him the full price. Beth leaned over the lip of the stage and stretched her fingertips into the deep bristles of the wolf's shoulder.

"Raised him from a pup to be like this," said the man.

Beth looked up.

"Took it from its mother?"

The man's chin tucked in offense.

"Nay. Found 'im orphaned in Scandinavia. You can see the rest of our beasties for a few more coins, if you please." Beth's eyes followed his to the other row of cages that Allison had ventured toward.

"No, thank you."

"You certain? We've got a lion."

Beth ignored him, quite done with seeing caged animals.

The beast leaned into her hand, warm and seemingly pleased by the touch. The depth of its coat consumed her fingers. The wolves in the forest had been ragged and starved, standing on legs like needles. This one was hale. She leaned in as far as she thought its keeper might allow.

"I'm sorry for your brother," she whispered.

Another hand slipped into the depths of fur alongside hers.

"Ay!" The man snapped at Rhys.

"I paid the three pence, didn't I?"

The man cowed under Rhys' gaze and settled back into his seat, sniffing in displeasure.

Rhys' strong fingers found Beth's. She could feel his eyes waiting for her to look up, and when she did, she was cleaved apart by the familiarity of his gaze. The shadow of the tight shave he'd had at the ball was fast growing in, reminding her of the man she'd known before—a man who saw in her all of the strengths she thought she'd lost.

"Good heavens, Bethany, sometimes you are too much. Touching one of these beasts." Beth looked over her shoulder to find Lady Weldon fanning herself and wearing a look of disgust—a look that was growing tiresome.

Beth smiled. "Did you forget the breakfast conversation, Lady Weldon? I've touched one before, remember? When I fought it for my life . . . and won."

"It's true. She killed it. She was covered in its blood." Rhys dashed off an exaggerated look of affection at her. His playful encouragement brought her spirits even higher.

Lady Weldon scowled, even as her brows knit in suspicion. Lord Weldon, looking rather lost at her side, was suddenly brought to life. "What's this now? Killed a wolf?"

Lady Weldon waved the fan in front of his face as if to whisk away a bad smell. "Pay them no mind. It's just some gauche joke they have between them." The undisputed matriarch of her little group, Lady Weldon spun on her heels to lead them away. Yet, Beth's father lingered a moment, wary and protective. When he turned to follow the Weldons, it felt purposeful—like a little gift to Beth.

Allison had crossed the street and was now pressing coins into the gate boy's hand for admission to the rest of the menagerie. Lady Weldon was going to love that.

"Should we accompany her?" Rhys asked, nodding in Allison's direction.

Beth shook her head. "She'll hardly have a moment's peace before her mother finds her. She'll be fine."

And then they were alone.

Beth's fingers rested on Rhys' arm. There seemed a detectable sliver of trust in her affection—something he'd not felt since his return. It lit through him like a sunbeam.

Together they escaped to the fringe of the village, where the crowd was thin and the torches fewer. Behind Dulcet Street, a small stage had been set up. On it, a brightly painted woman soliloquized to a handful of patrons on the grass. *"You miss'd your fortunes when you met with her, sir . . ."*

"I know this play," said Beth, in an unobtrusive whisper. Rhys followed the gentle tug on his arm, ready to glide on a cloud to wherever his Beth led him.

"Young gentleman, that only love for beauty . . . they love not wisely . . ."

Beth's eyes fixated on the performer. "It's Thomas Middleton.

Livia's speaking." But Rhys scarcely heard her. He was stuck instead on the words spoken by the actress—*They love not wisely.*

No. They certainly do not.

Beth's eyes glittered with appreciation for the performance. Her feathery lashes flicked up and down, reminding Rhys of how they'd once flicked against his cheek like soft little paintbrushes. Her lips moved with Livia's as the actress orated downstage. "And want's the key of—"

"—*whoredom.*" The word spilled loudly from Beth's lips in unison with the performer, jarring Rhys from his contemplation.

Beth caught him watching her. It was too dark to see her blush, but Rhys knew the expression she made when she did. The apples of her cheeks rose and she looked away with tight lips. Such was her tell, and she was telling.

"Do you want to stay and watch?"

She shook her head. "No. Let's wander."

There was nothing else beyond Dulcet Street. The village abruptly ended at the canal, which cut a dark gash across the land, having nothing to reflect in its still waters. They followed it to where a different sort of revelry was taking place. A field had been overtaken by the troupes who brought their skills to the fair. Here, actors changed their costumes by candlelight, and acrobats invented new feats with their nerves shored up by wine. Tents and carts and bonfires dotted the grass.

Beth stopped at a tree and pulled away from Rhys to sit at its base. She patted the ground beside her.

Rhys looked toward the village, aware of her family so nearby. Wondering if Desmarais was about. Wondering if his own associates from the Home Office were keeping their eyes open. He hadn't told her about Harry yet. She'd be glad to learn of his life now.

Rhys allowed himself to be drawn down to the ground beside her. He remembered leaning against the wall with her in the folly. Commiserating.

"What are you thinking about?" she asked, sinking into his arm.

"The folly."

"I remember it well."

"Oh?"

"Sometimes it felt like another place but only when you were there."

This truce between them—her trust, her nearness—it all felt so fragile. Rhys hesitated to speak. "How do you mean?"

"You once told me that it was easy to imagine it differently."

"Yes."

"It was the same for me. In my lonelier hours, I would close my eyes and light all of the sconces in the house. I'd imagine them flickering against gleaming wood and wallpaper. All the fires roaring. All the carpets unrolled and bright—"

"Solomon and Lionel, on a different continent," Rhys added. The smile she gave him then was warm, but sad. He pulled her closer, wishing he'd not interrupted her beautiful thoughts. Thankfully, it did not deter her.

"And all the while, I pictured this too—"

She waved a hand across his body, but he didn't understand.

"This?"

"I mean *you*, looking like this. *You*, not covered in mud and *me* not covered in mud. I saw us ascending the stairs of the folly as we did that first morning . . ." Her pupils danced as she paused, as though her story now ran ten paces ahead of her and she could not catch up.

Rhys took her hand. "Please go on."

"I saw us as if we were leaving a grand party behind us downstairs. As if we were retreating to the bedchamber for something more delicate—more *intimate* than simply stitching up my shoulder."

Rhys tightened his hand on hers. *Simply stitching up* her shoulder had been one of the most intimate moments of his life.

But he understood her. His days and nights at the hideout had been plagued by similar obsessions. Obsessions that tangled with his guilt even as they brought a foreign lightness to his heart. Obsessions that would remain to burden him if she truly was preparing to leave England.

He could hardly see her eyes in the dim light and yet felt pulled into them. He was brimming with the desire to tell her—to share with her what sort of strange and terrible ghosts messed with his stomach whenever she was near. Yet the words evaporated before he could find them. Sighing, he raked a hand over his hair.

"What is it?" she asked.

He shook off the ghosts and smiled at her.

"You knew that Middleton play so well, perhaps you should take up acting." He nudged her. She flung her head back with laughter, her throat stretching tight as she did. Rhys resisted the urge to bend down and kiss it.

"But truly," he said, "it would make your ruination complete."

"Being alone with you among the caravans is likely enough to accomplish that."

"There are ways to make it *more* complete yet."

The words hung between them. Beth matched the tightness of his grip on her hand. The air tasted suddenly humid and thick.

Rhys' arm settled around her. Drew her in. His cheek slid against hers until his lips, hot and vital, found the corner of her jaw and pressed a kiss there—a kiss which shattered the padlock on three years of longing. She turned to join his exploring lips with her own.

Perhaps they'd be discovered. Perhaps Lady Weldon would make use of her hound-like sense for rooting out impropriety. Perhaps Beth would be shunned again. But what did it matter? Beth had her highwayman and had no shame left to give to the world.

Rhys' kiss obscured all other thoughts. With every tug of her lip between his teeth, she felt sense dissolve. Something else took its place—warmth, desire—a certain effervescence as though her body tingled with a million champagne bubbles.

Yet that still did not define it. It was as powerful and as wrenching as grief . . . yet was also quite its opposite. As she searched for the poetry to describe such a thing, Rhys' tongue swept across hers. She breathed him in.

Her last thoughts slipped through her fingers. Until there was nothing. *Nothing.* Just the midnight blue sensation of his body against hers.

A loud laugh cracked like lightning through their embrace.

They both turned shyly toward the interruption.

But it wasn't *merely* laughter that had broken their embrace. It was also an exchange of moans that ebbed and flowed from a canvas pavilion across from their tree. The sound lured Beth's attention like a sweet aroma as recognition dawned on her. A woman's sighs— loaded with her mewling voice—climbed upward in octaves as a man's faint grunts kept time.

Beth's scalp tingled as Rhys combed a hand through her hair. Neither spoke as they listened to the sounds from the tent. For Beth, it brought to mind the more subdued opera of their night in the woods together. Heat blossomed in her lap. The hand she'd rested on Rhys' thigh began to tighten—grasping for something. Back in the forest, she'd not been granted the pleasure of seeing him. What did his body look and feel like when no clothing was between them?

Her fingers slid up his hard thigh, curious to confirm the reaction that she already suspected—a solid stalk straining for egress. At her touch, Rhys let out such a telling exhale that she nearly begged for him to take her then.

But as she locked eyes with his, it was clear such begging would not be necessary. She spread her hand wide across his lap and pressed against him, exploring the heat of his rod.

He jerked beneath her touch. Then his face fell to hers and his lips took such a deep pull of her essence that she thought she might turn to dust.

The very tops of her inner thighs began to slip silkily against one another, spread as they were with her response to him.

A long and shrieking sound came from the tent then, snatching Beth and Rhys' attention once more. Dim shadows moved within as the chorus of gasps died down inside.

Beth turned to Rhys seriously. His eyes were wide and thirsty, no doubt from the hand still lingering on his groin, in torturous stillness.

"Rhys, I want—"

Just then, the amorous pair staggered from the pavilion together. First, a ruffled soldier, his regimentals wadded up in the crook of one arm. Then, a woman with dark copper curls. She paused to retie the ribbons of a colorful but shabby bodice. The soldier kissed her cheek before dashing off toward the village.

The auburn-haired beauty smoothed down her locks and looked in their direction. Beth could swear that they were winked at before the woman wandered off to a darker part of the camp.

Rhys gently removed Beth from him and stood up. A burn of

rejection swept over her until he offered his hand.

He helped her up and kissed her hand—a reassurance that eased the confusion as he led her toward the now-forsaken tent. He pulled back the entry curtain.

Beth dug a heel into the grass. "Rhys, it's not our place . . ."

He looked over his shoulder at her as he ducked to go inside. "I highly doubt it belonged to those two either."

Entering the space, she found Rhys slightly hunched beneath the low swag of the canvas, extending to her a most mischievous smile. "You enjoyed me first as a highwayman, Beth. Surely you don't wish to see me *completely* reformed?"

Her smile spread like fire. *Of course not.*

22

Two lanterns burned low near the rear canvas wall, but as Beth stood in the small space, assessing it, she seemed to Rhys to be that which lit up the space the most. White voile poufed out from the edges of her pink overdress. A wilting gardenia pinned into her hair now shed its fragrant petals into her locks. She was the very spirit of spring.

Rhys swiped a palm discretely over the tightened fabric at his crotch—seeking to extend his patience yet making it worse than ever.

"I don't know," said Beth, casting a concerned look at him. "It seems rather inside-of-doors for our tastes. Does it not?"

"A bit luxurious by our standards, certainly, but I believe it still counts as an encampment, if that makes you feel any better. Even if there are carpets." A cot was set up against one side of the canvas, but Rhys was more interested in the large cushions that were strewn about. Beth silently toed the fringe of one of the threadbare carpets.

Whatever she was ruminating about, Rhys couldn't lose her to it now.

He stepped up behind her and pulled her against him. She rested her hands on his. How soft those palms were. It was this sort of soft touch that he recalled a dying shipmate crying out for in the throes of fever: *to be held again by my sweet Anne—her hands are lighter than snow resting on ye.* Rhys began to long for such a thing himself, on the endless nights spent swaying in his hammock. Such dreams could push away the ripe stench of the ship's bowels for a spell. Now here he was with his own *sweet Anne's hands*—Beth's hands—making him feel worthy and alive. He'd be just as tormented as the dead sailor, should he never be touched by these hands again.

Beth pressed her palms against the backs of his hands, persuading him to move where she pleased. She drew his left hand upward.

His fingertips lifted with the gentle ripples of whalebone that he felt through her layers. She guided him to the top edge of her stays where hardness became softness at the gentle spilling of her bosom flesh over the lip of the garment. His fingers curled into that softness with rapt appreciation as he lowered a kiss to the side of her neck.

But his right hand was being guided lower, to the dip where her many layers of sheer skirts would sink between her legs with a gentle press. As their hands slid together into that dip, the heat he discovered there made his cock lurch.

He was certain she must have felt it, pressed as he was against the low curve of her back. She pushed against him in response and again he caught the scent of that gardenia. His body flooded with gratitude. The past two days had rivaled the last three years in his impatience for this moment.

Rhys arched his body over hers, bending her with him, giving himself the range he needed to reach a hand to her inner thigh. Pressing into the cushion of fine fabric, he drew his hand upward until the heel of his palm dragged across that wonderful dip. Beth let out the most lovely noise, like that of one struck in the gut but ten times softer. A cry of need that was thrown like a bolt into Rhys as she clutched his other hand to her breast.

He didn't know how to begin, and it seemed neither did she. He lingered at her back, rubbing his nose through the wispy hairs at the nape of her neck, taking in her dewy springtime scents. They breathed in unison in their awkward embrace.

She was the first to break from it. Taking his hand, she looked to lower them both to the ground as she had beneath the tree, but Rhys stopped her.

"Not yet." His words brought a puzzled expression to her face, but she asked no questions. His heart clenched—thrilled at this sign of her trust.

The sheer fichu around her neck had already been displaced by his caresses. With one swift motion, he discarded it to the floor.

Rhys took a step back to shirk off his coat, and Beth's eyes followed it nervously to where it landed on the corner of the cot. "Rhys?"

He traced her low neckline with a fingertip. Several frog closures of gold braid stretched across her stomacher. He toyed with the first one. A hand placed gently around his wrist gave him pause, but he looked reassuringly into her eyes. He didn't see fear there, only curiosity. "Beth, I won't have this be like the forest. It won't be desperate and cold." *It will be naked and indulgent. It will be loving.* He undid the first loop. "It will be so much better."

She looked around. The only thing protecting them from passers-by was tarpaulin. It was clear how aware she was of it—how aware she was of their trespass. Rhys lowered his head, awaiting her judgment. He could make concessions if he must, but it was unbearable how badly he wanted to be against her skin.

"I've waited three years to see you and feel you." Beth's eyes skimmed across him hungrily before meeting his, keeping him in terrible suspense. "I won't forfeit any part of it. I've wanted it for too long. The risks don't matter."

The risks of scandal, she meant, and he was glad that such ideas were fading for her. She didn't deserve to feel tainted by even a drop of shame. But he was risking something too. He risked that he might once again be sharing a night with her, only to never see her once she left for the Continent. He risked becoming that sick sailor crying out in the night.

She tightened her grip on his wrist before releasing him decisively. "I want to feel you, Rhys."

Her words sent him careening off a precipice, and together they descended to their knees as they both feverishly worked at the closures down her bodice.

He growled softly against her neck as he worked his way toward her lips with his kisses and bites. Her throat uttered another needy gasp as the sides of her robe parted, as he peeled her from it and slid the sleeves down, feeling the cool skin of her forearms against his thumbs. *Beth.*

So desperate she was to snatch the cravat from his neck that she nearly choked him and they both snorted at her fumble as his fingers came to their rescue. Her eyes lingered dangerously on him every time a new flash of skin was revealed to her, and the desire evident in those looks and in her frantic fingers made him as hard as marble for her.

His eyes lingered too. As he unpeeled her from her trappings, it seemed the forest witch from his memory was revealed, layer by beautiful layer. The increasing mess of her hair, sprinkled with gardenia petals, brought back razor-sharp visions of her staring at him from behind it, breathing hard and heavy as she did now. The place in his heart that she held residence in could surely be occupied by no other.

His lifetime of sailing on rat-infested merchant brigs, the catastrophic mutiny, the desperate days of highway robbery, they all blurred together into a singular path that led him here—at last—to something he was grateful for. One day soon, it might be taken from him, as most good things were. *Most* but not *all*. Because the crossing of their paths had long ago changed his fortunes. The mistake of taking her to the folly had revealed what sort of men he'd been protecting. It cut him free of his debts. It brought him into Cobton Dale, where the loss of her things had led him to a most respectable change of career. He owed so much to her.

Their furious and clumsy disrobing of one another came to a panting halt as they reached the final layers. Beth rocked back on her heels, kneeling before him. Nothing but her fine linen shift was left. For him, it was his breeches, the fall of them still pulled taut against his arousal.

He reached out between them and trailed a knuckle down the crumpled front of her chemise. The fabric was so fine that he could already see the shadows of her nipples, which peaked against the fabric as his touch dragged past them. Bemused, he played with a lock of her hair and rearranged it near her collarbone—only to catch sight of that angry scar, stretched and jagged. It peeked out from the edge of the fabric. He hooked the linen back and leaned in to kiss it. Then traced his lips along that slender bone, thanking the stars that Beth was here.

Her hands knit into his hair, and she cradled him against her as he worshipped the remnant of their strange past. Turning an ear to her chest, he heard the pleasant whooshes of her heartbeat, and he slid a hand up to cup her breast through the fabric.

"*Rhys.*"

To hear her moan mingled with his name nearly shattered him as he lowered her onto the pile of cushions. And then it came, the touch that he'd longed to feel as she explored him, sought to free him.

Facing one another as they reclined, she looked as serene as a summer pond. Not a drop of worry poisoned the space between her brows. The worry was his now.

Her hand teased him again before dropping to the ground.

"What is it, Rhys?"

"I was very afraid after the last time, Beth. Afraid that I'd hurt you, or ruined you."

The pillows rustled as she pulled away to look at him more acutely. Her concerning expression was not absent of judgment.

"Was it not established that very day that I was un-ruin-able? The thing already having been done?"

He didn't mean—he breathed deeply and chose his words more carefully.

"I didn't mean ruin *you*." He looked steadily at her. "What I meant was that I'd ruined your *life*. That I'd—"

"That you'd left me with child? Is that it?"

He patted her hip and looked away. "I was getting to it, but yes. That's what worried me. I shall be more careful tonight."

Her eyes flitted then and glistened as though she were trying to stay ahead of some emotion. He wished he could undo whatever he'd said to cause it.

"Allow me to allay your fears, Rhys. You see, I was quite reckless in my first dalliances as a girl. I was taught about horseback riding and geography and poetry and the Greek dramas, but I was not taught about men. I attacked my girlhood passion for a neighbor boy with oblivious abandon—no sense for the consequences."

He could see what she danced around, but would not assume.

"I don't believe I am compatible with the condition that concerns you."

Beth's gut folded in half at her own words as though she'd been doubled over by a blow. Such candor was something natural to her, but suddenly, and uncharacteristically, she wished she could take the words back. Rhys' face shifted through a whole three-act tragedy of expressions—or was that just in her head?

His face settled into something more familiar. "Perhaps it was the lad's problem?" Rhys took her hand, and she smiled.

"That's a rather novel idea, isn't it?" *But it isn't the truth.*

He needn't know that her cycle was rare or that barrenness ran like a brook through her family tree—though her lack of kin might have come to his notice. The thought of not having children had never daunted her personally—she'd anticipated spinsterhood, after all. But the notion that it *should* be daunting felt often foisted upon her by others. That shrill chorus of society types chimed in now to warn her—

You will not be loved.

Yet here was Rhys' thumb, still smoothing away the hairs that were never in her eye. And the terrible voices in her head suddenly sounded very much like liars.

She melted back into the cushion at his touch. Why should she be so upset? Some version of *forever* seemed wounded by her admission to him, but to marry him was so out of the question that—

"I love you, Beth."

Her busy thoughts fled into hiding and her eyes refocused on the man before her, now silent. Blood rushed to her cheeks. She couldn't possibly have heard—

"What?"

"I love you," he said.

Her heart felt suddenly crowded in her chest, and she wished she might free it for awhile, as a bird from a cage. Words swirled loosely in her dark skull and she felt helpless to speak. "I'd not thought of that." Foolish words. They escaped her, meager and squeaky.

Rhys smiled good-naturedly, perhaps at her turn of helplessness.

What did it change? Anything? Could she still go to the Continent, when *this* existed? He was suddenly like a story become real. He was no longer just her shocking anecdote or her *Ordeal*. He was flesh and blood. He was possibility.

He was—

He was looking at her, that boyish smile still across his lips. He propped his head up on a hand, looking utterly un-expectant of a sensical response from her.

He was—

Hers.

She pulled up against him and tasted his lips, inhaling that dash of pine that he carried even in spring. Her fingers rooted into his hair, clutched at it, in disbelief of his realness—of his *love*.

He rolled on top of her and sat up, stroking her thigh, assessing her. Had he looked at her in such a way only minutes before, she might have shrunk beneath his gaze, but now she felt as she had during her youthful liaisons. She felt safe and confident and cherished. She felt like the maenad, spilling wine and keeping secrets—being altogether herself. Her body was tingly and slack. No gin had a hand in it this time. She was drunk on something else entirely.

Rhys' neck moved with a dry swallow as he took her in. "More than I ever dreamed."

He stretched himself down over her legs. Taking her hem in hand, he nudged his face beneath it, pushing the garment upward and kissing precious places along the way. Beth's lungs lost their air as his chin brushed against her quim and he kissed her there too. It was not the same as the pecks along her thighs. It was open-mouthed. Luxurious. Consuming. The tip of his tongue burned hot paths through the soft pleats of her sex. The very awareness of his face between her thighs as he drank from her—she would sacrifice herself to the maenad's cult to feel more of it.

Beth shimmied against the cushions, wriggling until she freed herself from the chemise. All the while, she bucked gently from the fire that was rising beneath Rhys' lips as they worked over her flesh.

Then his kisses began to travel. To her belly. To her rib. He delivered an urgent but delicate bite to the underside of one breast. Her lap—now slickened and warm—was aching at the loss of his lips, until his fingers came to replace them.

She loved the sense of him taking her in hand, of being held on his fingers as they controlled her pleasure from within her. She should not have worried over the loss of his mouth, for his lips trailed their way back down to her. Found her soft dusting of curls. Lapped at her. His tongue caressed her, pulled her apart—*accessed* her. He moaned against her, and the sound pushed dizzying vibrations through her delicate skin as she bore down against his face and hand. With a curl of his knuckles inside her, her hips drew upward, greedy for the sensation.

He moaned again—that *humming*—it drilled into her tension like a corkscrew. She clawed helplessly at Rhys' deliciously naked back as he buried his face against her—giving her everything she needed, everything she—

She snapped.

Sensation spilled over her, striking her with the force of waves hitting a jetty. Her eyes clamped down against the shivers of blinding white bliss.

When she opened them again, Rhys was already sitting back on his heels. Looking down at her the way a gallery patron might admire the glowing pigments of a Fragonard.

His body was glorious. The hard chest that she'd been pulled against so many times was now bared for her, revealing its firmness in the hills and valleys that rippled when he moved. His arms were braided with muscle. It was easy to picture the sun gleaming off his sweat-slicked skin on a ship's deck.

Rhys' grin was self-satisfied as he dragged a forearm across his slick mouth. She needed every part of him against her.

The buttons on his breeches puckered and strained. She sat up to do something about it.

He sat higher on his knees as she worked his buttons and his hands stroked through her hair with tender encouragement. At last, he stood up and turned to shed that final piece. Beth had a view of his buttocks as he did. She tasted her lips as she watched his strong muscles shift with every small movement.

He turned. The lick of a grin accompanied his blush as her eyes reveled in his nakedness. He was broad. A man. He had the marks of life on him. So many small and scattered scars from his years of labor. A spray of dark hair winged out from the center of his chest and trailed down his middle to another, thicker patch. Her eyes fell soberly on the swollen evidence that he was ready to have her.

But she felt drawn to him first. She inched toward him on

her knees as he stood facing her. She reached her hands around his backside to feel those muscles and draw him nearer, so that she might plant a kiss on the underside of that powerfully upright shaft. It was warm, vital—

The sensation was too much for him.

He swept down onto her and steadied a ragged exhale as his cock twitched against her.

Her chest lifted against the weight of him. "Does it make you remember the last time?" she asked.

"It does. I still see you with leaves in your hair."

"It's much warmer now."

"It is."

He kissed her and ground his hips against her. The thick stalk parted her folds, and reminded them both of how slick she was. He resettled above her and grabbed himself, adjusting to sit against her entrance. She felt the moisture at the tip of it and longed for him to thrust. She pressed herself down, chased his cock needfully. Her flesh opened for him, wrapped around the head of him—but it wasn't enough.

And then he finally drove into her and she was lifted by it.

"*Yes.*"

Rhys would get his wish. This wouldn't be like the woods. They weren't cold and stiff, but hot and fevered. Driven mad by their eagerness, they moved with one another and drank in their freedom.

Beth felt so near to him that it threatened to undo her. He pulled her into a seated position on his lap, and her knees bent up like wings at either side of him. As he moved inside of her, it was almost too much to look him in the eyes, but nor could she look away. There was some dangerous feeling that he was looking at her in the same way.

His moans grew longer, wilder, and she could sense something was near. But he inhaled sharply and she was surprised when he pulled away from her. Words of confusion crept up her throat, but Rhys pulled her chin up, made her look deeply at him, so that she could see the reassuring lust still sparkling in those deep eyes. He shook himself as though to dispose of his own impatience—a shiver that flew down his body.

With a smile playing at his lip's corner, he knelt and guided Beth to turn around. Then he wrapped her tightly from behind—a familiar embrace—just as they'd been on that first ride to the folly. An embrace that she loved.

Her mind flew with memories of the twisted safety she'd felt when riding against him, when his hat had protected her from cold raindrops. She'd had wicked thoughts—and now such thoughts were brought to life. He guided her back onto him—hard and slick and hot—and she felt once more the adventuress, indulging in sins she saw nothing sinful about. If what she felt was a sin—the flooding of every limb with warmth and nearness and trust—then let her fall through the rings of hell now and drag Rhys with her.

His breath at her neck made every hair on her body stand at attention. His sturdy arm wrapped around her like the strap on some instrument of torture, but she was here to be tortured in exactly this way. She sweated with anticipation as his hand began to trail down her belly, within perfect reach of—

"*Rhys.*"

She shuddered as he touched her. His fingertips were slickened with only a few strokes of her folds. She reached a hand down on top of his. She wanted to feel it too. Wanted to feel herself, feel him, feel everything. Her fingertips bumped the edge of his hardness where he stroked into her from behind. The sensation of being speared there was singularly the most erotic thing she'd ever known. Her gasp of euphoric surprise was responded to with another deep thrust.

"Beth . . ." His voice was low and ragged. "You are legendary."

It was what she'd always wanted to be, and now she was going to seal her coronation as a queen, a witch, and a legend.

She rocked harder against his strokes, let his hand and staff take her places.

She clutched behind herself for a grip on him. His groans climbed ever upward, yet he seemed to fight them.

"Rhys, please . . ."

Her desperate words renewed something in him, and he became so ravenous that staying upright against him became impossible. She stretched down along the cushions for him, and he stroked her back before lying against her, kissing her back and neck, tracing her shoulders with a gentle drag of his teeth, never once leaving the place where he was nested hotly between her thighs.

His hand still reached around her as he thrust. The muscles of his abdomen worked against her skin as he pulled her into rhythm with him. Her breaths came in short gasps from the wonderful weight of him. Pleasure once more began to tighten its hold on her belly—every exhale brought it nearer.

And when it came, it triggered her lover's destruction too.

As her whole body crushed inward around flame and ecstasy, his seemed to explode outward, in roars and shudders, and another *I love you* that she would never tire of hearing, even as it scared her—or perhaps *because* it scared her.

He wilted down to her back like a rose petal in the sun—only heavier—blanket-like and comforting. He must have noticed her short breaths because he rolled to his side to relieve her lungs.

The last tendrils of euphoria were unwrapping themselves

from her limbs and releasing her womb from a vise. The air in the tent hung heavy. Her claw-like grip on a colorful cushion loosened. Reality closed in much too quickly, just as it had in the woods.

23

"We shouldn't linger." Beth drew away from him and her skin instantly cooled in the absence of his touch. "We're in a borrowed place."

He pushed the hair from her face, and she could feel how the lock had clung to her with sweat. Making herself presentable would take some doing.

"You're probably right." A sigh deflated his broad chest as he examined the mess of *their discarded apparel.*

Together, they hastily redressed. At the end of it, his waistcoat buttons were somewhat off and her stays were re-laced in a barely serviceable manner. Here was her man, deft at undressing her and completely at a loss to put her back together. He now fussed with a blob of rosy silk, trying to organize it into the proper womanly shape. She took the crumpled overdress from him with a weary smile. "You go ahead, I'll finish up and be out shortly."

He kissed her cheek. "I need to relieve myself something fierce, so if you don't see me right away, I'll have wandered somewhere to that purpose."

She nodded and was almost grateful when he slipped out beyond the tent's flap. She could work herself back into a proper condition more speedily in his absence. As she slipped the open robe on over her chemise dress, she realized that a crucial pin had flown off during their harried undressing. "Damn."

She knelt down, searching.

"Well, isn't this a sight?" The female voice made Beth's head whip over her shoulder. The copper-haired woman, whose liaison had inspired her own tryst, now stood at the curtain grinning as a small pipe lolled in the corner of her mouth.

"I'm so sorry! I'll leave immediately, I just—"

The woman put up a hand against her words. "Don't worry your head. I just came back for this." She leaned down to the cushions to pick up a paisley shawl that Beth hadn't noticed amid all the garish patterns of the carpets. The woman shrugged and winked. "'Tisn't my domain anymore than 'tis yours, but we've given it some good fun tonight, eh?" Beth tossed back her disheveled hair but suppressed an incoming denial and nodded bashfully.

"Are you after this?" The woman picked up a shiny sliver from the carpet and passed it to Beth.

"Yes, thank you—"

"Emily."

"I'm Beth."

"Are you going back out there like this?" Emily gestured to Beth with a pitying look on her face. "*Ouf.* You could use more help than just the pin. Come with me."

Beth relented and the two slipped outside to the canal's edge.

A boathouse lined with torches gave them enough light by which to arrange Beth's hair back into a shape that looked vaguely deliberate. Something about the intimacy of having the stranger's hands in her hair melted the tension from Beth's shoulders.

No smoke rose from Emily's pipe, but she gnawed on it fondly as she spoke.

"I seen plenty of folk make like animals at the fair before but few in such a bold state of undress." Emily pinched the crisp silk between her fingers. "And what a dress, that."

Beth blushed. "We had our reasons."

"I mean it to be a compliment. And compliments to that gent with you too. He seemed a simple, handsome chap."

Beth couldn't suppress a snort. *Simple.* Rhys was anything but. It dawned on Beth that she'd not spotted him as she and Emily had strolled the short distance to the boathouse.

The woman threaded a ribbon through Beth's hair, tugging as Beth frowned.

"What have you to be worried about?"

Beth hadn't realized that her expression was flaunting such worries.

"I don't know." And then she suddenly did. "I suppose I—I keep hesitating about something because my head and my heart aren't aligned.

"Pretty clear where your heart falls, judgin' by those last sounds that came caterwaulin' from the pavilion."

God, she'd heard them.

"So what's this head of yours want?" Emily tugged playfully on the ribbon, jerking Beth's head back a bit.

"Freedom."

"Lady—isn't no sign of oppression in what you just did. Seems to me you've claimed your freedom."

It was true. Beth cared more about trespassing in someone's tent than she cared about what immoral activities she and Rhys might have been caught in. Emily was right. She was free. Even if she caught up to the party with her skirt askew and her frogs undone, even if she hung off Rhys' arm while the scent of desire wafted from them, of what consequence was it now? Her father *had* never and *would* never abandon her. Lady Weldon might try to remove Allison from Beth's devilish influence, but if Beth had wielded her influence over Allison as deftly as she'd estimated, then Lady Weldon would have a hard time of keeping them apart. Who else mattered?

Beth looked down at her hands as if to confirm that there was no embroidery hoop there. No, she'd dodged those fears of dull oblivion and shaped her life into something else entirely. Instead of a man like Hamm breaking her like a horse and boasting about it, she'd discovered one who blew on her sparks of bad behavior until they became bonfires.

And it was what she wanted.

He loves me.

But fears still swirled that their paths had crossed but not aligned.

Her years of aloneness had made independence grow on her like a fine, fresh thing. She was on the cusp of her own renewal right as Rhys returned. She'd lit herself inwardly with Mediterranean promises—sleeping late in Venice, riding through *la Loire*, finding Stefano for a dance . . . yet already that name—*Stefano*—had lost its allure. Still, her Continental dreams could not be forfeited and she couldn't even bring herself to speak of them.

"'Haps your heart and your head can both have what they want."

Beth snapped out of her reverie and tried to catch up to what

Emily had said. "I don't follow."

Emily spun Beth around roughly and began to fuss about the strands of hair that framed her face. The woman's hands smelled like strawberries.

"If you talk to him, about the concerns of your head, they might line up better than you thought. The heart can be very smart." Emily slapped her on the shoulders and looked at her with pride. "You're all back put. Will you be off to find your man now?"

Beth took Emily's arm fondly. "Thank—"

But she was cut off when a small boy darted from nowhere and near skidded into them. They both instinctively reached down to steady him. His threadbare shirt was damp and dirty, and he barely rose to Beth's chest. His eyes shined with fear as he looked up at her.

"For the lady." His shaking hand passed her a sealed note.

Beth looked around again for Rhys. Suddenly the whole encampment seemed more swallowed by the dark than she'd recalled. He was nowhere.

Emily watched her, waiting and gripping the messenger's arm.

Beth flicked away the unstamped drop of wax with her thumb and read:

> *Go to the stables at the end of Partridge Street.*
> *Go alone or Allison will suffer.*
> *—Desmarais*

It was as though the skeletal hand of the reaper himself had palmed her heart to squeeze it as his plaything.

But she was already running. The letter, left somewhere on the ground behind her. Faint calls to her—Emily's voice. Words she couldn't hear.

Run. Just run.

*　　*　　*

Rhys faced the trunk of a sycamore and strained to relieve himself in spite of a cock that had come roaring back to life the moment he'd reflected on what had just happened. Such reflections were not, it seemed, a thing that he could quell.

He sighed, propping an elbow against the bark and tapping it with his fist—trying to use its roughness to erase the memories of smoothness from moments before.

The muscles of his back, the body he'd honed on ships and maintained by sawing wood—it all felt like sap now. He didn't walk or lean, he *oozed*. He reached out to the tree for support because every part of him that wasn't in his loins was limp from the exercise of love that he'd just shared with Beth.

He rebuttoned his breeches. The single-mindedness of returning to her felt essential, inborn. He *needed* to be near her. He needed to have her on his arm again. He couldn't wait to rejoin the party with an unspoken understanding humming between them.

He returned to where the carts and tents were circled. One of the plays must have ended because costumed actors were now skipping between the campfires, getting as foxed as they could before the night was up. The pavilion he fixed his eyes on looked quiet, but as he neared it, a group of performers ducked inside. He stopped and held his breath, but no noises of discovery erupted from it. Beth must have finished dressing.

Amid the many spheres of firelight, he caught no glimpse of Beth's blush frock. He rolled his lips between his teeth, trying to stave off the thread of worry that was now knitting itself into his mind.

His investigative side took over. He strode among the groups of revelers that now dotted the camp. He circled the tents. No sign of her. No trace of her voice.

His ear caught another sound instead—a raised voice in the distance. His narrowed eyes searched the dark bank of the canal. Then he spotted her, the auburn-haired woman who had enjoyed the tent just before them. She knelt next to a boy, gripping his arms and . . . admonishing him?

The woman's voice became clearer as he moved close.

"Where did he give you the note? Think, lad."

Just as Rhys wondered if he should interfere, the woman caught sight of him and waved him over desperately. The boy twisted out of her grip and ran off.

"Ay!" The boy paid no heed to her shouts.

She turned her eyes back to Rhys and pointed at him. "You're Beth's man." It felt like an accusation.

"Aye." The sailor in him came out as if to speak her language. "Where is she?"

"She was with me, then she got this note and run off."

Rhys' heart lurched into a rhythm that did not match his stillness. He didn't have to hear another word to know he should be fearful. This woman's face said it all.

"And that boy brought the note?"

She nodded.

"What does he know about it? Did he say where she went?"

"'Tis no use. He's not sayin'."

"Which way did she go?"

The woman stretched out a solid arm and pointed. "She disappeared right 'tween those buildin'."

"Thank you—"

"Emily."

He'd already backed away several paces when he turned and

broke into a furious sprint. Even at such a breakneck pace, he took in everything around him. Ribbons that decorated performer's belts. A craggy old man cursing his bottle of wine for its stuck cork. Discarded bottles. Paper caught in tree roots. Festoons that had blown away . . .

The corner of the village that he ran for was quiet and dark. Far from the frenzy. Uncertainty lurked there.

His mind retread his fleeting observations—drawing him back to something—something he'd missed. He turned so abruptly that his heel slid in the clover. *The piece of paper in the tree roots.* He returned to it and picked it up.

The words were ingested almost all at once. From the very first syllable, he knew he'd see Desmarais' name signed to it.

He'd failed her. Failed *everyone.*

Beth had taken up every drop of acreage in his imagination, and he'd not any room left for common sense. He had *allowed* this to happen. But he could linger on self-loathing later. He wadded the paper and thrust it into a pocket as he ran.

There was no one there.

Not Allison. Not Desmarais. Not even the stable boy.

The light of a few sconces lent the space an eerie flicker.

Beth was alone yet watched by a dozen sets of dark eyes. The nearest mare tossed her head anxiously. Beth reached out a hand to stroke its nose, but rather than calming the creature, the gesture seemed instead to infect Beth with the horse's unease.

She went up on her toes to peek into the inky shadow of the stall. No sign of anyone.

She wandered. At the front of the space was an alcove for smithing horseshoes. There, a glowing brazier sat unattended near an anvil.

Finally, the faint sound of metal on metal—a *click*.

Beth turned slowly, bracing herself for that ugly visage—the face of Desmarais, sunken and sallow.

The gray velveteen coat was the same, but the face—

Not the one that she expected.

Difficult to recognize clean-shaven—

Without the mane.

The Lion.

Bethany straightened up and tensed, and the shiver that went down her spine pulled every taut muscle mercilessly out of alignment. Desmarais she could have faced. He was a snake that she could step on. She had, after all, taken a wolf since last they met. But besting a wolf could not secure her chances of besting a lion. This beast was too great. Too unpredictable.

Lionel leveled his pistol at her heart.

"They told me there was a lion at the menagerie, but I didn't think it was worth my coin."

He shrugged. "Well, now you get to see me for no coin at all."

That hideous smile of his widened, revealing a new set of repulsive teeth, poorly rendered dentures, too big for him and likely stolen. She grimaced, expecting to be struck by a smell just as putrid as that of his old maw. He approached as if beckoned by her fear of catching a whiff.

"What do you want?"

"Didn't get my promised prize from before. Got nothin' but a banishment to the forest and my friend shot in the leg."

"Solomon is alive, isn't he?"

"Aye, Sol's alive. Alive and lame. But he's well enough to be drivin' yer cousin from town in the back of a cart."

Beth lunged forward as though she might strike him, but

common sense, and Lionel's warning eye, stayed her midway.

"Watch yerself." He retrained his weapon, standing only a man's height away from her.

She took a step back and nearly placed a hand in the brazier when she bumped into it.

He laughed at her. "Nearly settin' yerself afire, eh? You gonna do my revenge for me?" The shrill, giddy squeal of his laughter struck a harsh contrast against the menace of his pistol.

Beth glanced down discretely at the brazier so that she might side step it without catching her skirts on fire. But beyond it, she ran out of room to evade the wretch.

"What do you want with Allison? You can have me. I'm here."

Lion placed his free hand over his heart and painted a dramatic pout on his lips. "Don't take offense, I did come back fer you first. But you were spendin' time with this girl, this *Lady* Allison, who is fairer, younger . . ." His eyes narrowed. ". . . *richer*, I gather."

"And you wish to ransom her as you once did me?"

"Actually, after meetin' this Desmarais," Lionel fondled the lapel of Desmarais' velveteen coat. "I decided I like his way better—a li'l elopement."

Beth's body ached from the steely control that she exerted on her fear. She wouldn't let her face betray how his talk of Allison made her feel. Wouldn't let it show how dangerous she knew his answers might be when she asked, "And what of Desmarais?"

Lionel cocked an eyebrow casually. "Dead."

"I figured as much, but how?"

"How about you trust yer instinct on that front as well." He tossed a devilish grin her way.

"Did you hunt him down?"

"He *did* graze me with a ball once, if you recall." Lionel's face briefly crunched down in ire but settled back into a smug calm. "Aye. I sought 'im out. The *captain* thinks I'm stupid and *you* think I'm stupid, but I'm not stupid, and I found him."

Beth's eyes widened at his lapse of confidence.

"I sought 'im out while Sol recovered. Wanted to see if he'd pay well for aid in catchin' you again. But he couldn't pay well on account o' bein' dyin' o' the Covent Garden pox."

Beth sucked in a tight breath. Lionel's rugged dialect became more exaggerated with every outraged sputter.

"He was sickly when I found 'im but too slow to the grave fer my likin'."

"So you helped him shed his mortal coil."

The foul man nodded. "I made myself comfortable in his chairs. His accounts kept Sol and me goin' for a coupla years. Then a man came pryin' about, lookin' fer Desmarais. I offered him a drink— many drinks—and wouldn't you know it, he uttered your name as his employer." Lionel began to encroach once more, leading with the barrel of his gun.

There was no place left to go. The wall of the smithy's area was close at her back and hung with all manner of iron instruments. The forge between them lit the crags of Lionel's face to menacing perfection. Beth's knuckles bumped against something solid, and it sent a pinch of fire dancing through her slender hand. A little sound—high and embarrassing—was gasped from her lungs as she brought her hand to her chest. Lionel laughed. It had been the blacksmith's tongs, with their handles resting on the lip of the forge's dying fire. The heat had not been so bad, had only surprised her.

"You empty, clumsy girl! I can just stand here all night makin' you so nervous that you accidentally burn yerself to death."

"Why dead though? What is it that you want from me?"

"Now *that*," he wagged his weapon at her casually in a way that made her heart skip, "is a'last the right question. I didn't like the troubles it wrought when you fell on our crew, but my anger wasn't at you—now my lust, perhaps—" He grabbed his bollocks coarsely and Beth cast her eyes back down to the coals. "But not my ire. 'Tis Rhys who ruined my life and couldn't fix it. And that's why you matter. 'Cause I recently heard you tell a story to yer pretty cousin, 'bout how in love you was with a highwayman."

That clandestine night on the hill.

The shadow in the rotunda.

Not their imaginations—

"When Allison and I ran that night. It was *you*."

"I been spreadin' rumors of Desmarais for months. Knew it would send my Captain runnin'. He's weak fer you, ya see."

Beth drew her spine up.

"How sad of you to think that what he has for me is a weakness."

"He took my livelihood!" Lionel spat past his awful dentures and gestured wildly with the weapon again. "He was a young fella and a leader, and I thought he'd be fit to tie my interests to—but my trust was misplaced—"

Beth's eyes lifted to his. "He did everything he could for you." There was no response but Lionel's shrug and the snapping of the coals.

Beth put every fiber of herself into the look she gave him. She bore deeper and deeper with her gaze until she saw the brazier's glow reflected in his dry, dead eyes. Until she saw that glow become clouded by his fear. Then she held him there—a prisoner of her cursed stare, he wouldn't notice her reaching for the tongs—

Coal blasted through the space between them as she batted a flurry of coals from the forge's pedestal. The volley of hellfire struck him face on, pocking his stolen coat with black and amber. His pistol clacked to the floor as he batted fiery bits from his face and sleeves.

Beth got her own share of hot pebbles and ash but barely felt the searing hail as she lunged for him with the heated tongs aching in her hand.

The lion was still recovering. Breathing heavy. Hunched.

Beth lunged for him, raising the tongs high in the hopes that they would come down hard on her stronger foe. But as she brought the weight of them down, her strike was blocked by the handle of a smithing hammer that the lion had found. Her arms rang with the vibrations of her halted blow and she staggered backward, caught a heel in her skirt, and went down.

She heard Lionel picking himself up off the floor behind her. *The pistol. Where was the pistol?* The floor revealed nothing but ash and coal. As Beth stood up, she could feel him rushing behind her, but she couldn't raise the tongs soon enough.

She expelled a harrowing gasp as the blow slammed her against a stall. A loud *snap* at her side marked the fracture of a piece of whalebone in her stays. The planks that held her upright rumbled with the distress of the horse within.

Lionel was swinging back for another blow. His warped face seemed frozen in time, even as she dodged him with a limp roll against the wall.

She caught up to the breath that she'd been choking on since his blow, and she reached out to glance his filthy chin with the tip of the still-hot tongs. He hissed but otherwise did not flinch as he drew his hammer back again. She drew back her weapon too—against hope, arms shaking—and she was faintly aware of another figure approaching as she let the blow fly—

*   *   *

It was like the wolves. It was like riding up to Beth as the beasts mercilessly tugged at her. Not yet knowing what damage was done. It was just like that, only worse, because Rhys knew that men were far more dangerous.

The pair's struggle was framed perfectly by the carriage doors at the stable's other end. Beth was doubled over. She had a tool high in hand, but so did he.

Rhys' feet ran ahead of his mind, wishing to do anything to keep that hammer from coming down on her. But time was measured in hairs' breadths and everything was already in motion, without him.

A terrible, meaty crunch deadened the air, but it was Beth's assailant who was falling, after she struck a blow so fast and heavy that it spun her. Rhys dodged the falling man and reached for Beth.

Before his arms could wrap around her, he was met with a harsh pain cracking across the ridge of his cheekbone.

The iron tongs clanged noisily to the floor.

"Rhys!"

He pushed Beth away, thinking her still in danger, but looked down and saw that she'd felled the man completely. *The man.* Rhys swayed on his heels—the pain in his face was one thing, but the shock of seeing the other man's face was quite another. *Lionel. How?*

Beth still stood where he'd pushed her. She panted. She hunched. The frothy voile of her skirts was marred by a spray of singes. Her features, smudged with ash.

Every bit his witch.

He must have smiled.

"Rhys, that's very unnerving."

"What is?"

"Your smile. Did I hit you very hard?"

She approached him, one hand already lifting tentatively to his cheek. "God, what have I done? I thought you were some awful henchman, I thought—"

"It's fine," he said, not really sure how fine it was. He'd not been hit hard, but he didn't know how bad the burn might be. "I'm reminded of having a fire iron at my throat. You've a fondness for fiery, improvised armaments, don't you?" He made a strange expression to test the pain in his cheek.

"I could have blinded you—"

"But you didn't."

"I could have killed you—"

"But you *didn't.*" Rhys looked down at Lionel, still not really believing his eyes. "I'm not even sure you've killed him, thankfully. You don't want that on your conscience."

Something in what he said seemed to make her eyes go distant. It was a cold expression. It reminded him too much of the night before, when she'd broken from their embrace at the ball and left him wondering.

This time he pulled her into his arms and said nothing.

For one brief, sweet moment, she sank into him before pulling away. Her eyes were unlit. Darkened. Full of purpose.

"We're not yet finished."

24

"I know." Rhys wanted nothing more than to return to a certain pavilion with her and demonstrate his gratefulness that she was alive. But she was right. The night would not be over until Allison was safe. "I saw the note. Do you know where she is?"

Beth was already moving away from him, stepping over the stinking lump of man on the floor and moving from stall to stall . . . searching for something.

"She's with Sol. He *is* alive. He's taken her in a cart." Beth pulled a bridle down from its hook and let herself into the nearest stall.

Rhys followed, curious. "We shouldn't waste any time."

"Then let's get on with it." She waved him closer and Rhys angled himself to see what she was doing. She couldn't possibly mean to—

"You can't just steal a horse, Beth."

"Says the once-horse-thief. Besides, I stole yours that time, did

I not?"

"And I never saw it again."

"This will be different, we'll *return* these."

"Says the woman who was over-nervous to trespass in a tent."

Beth cocked her head at him seriously. "Allison's life is more crucial a thing than us getting our loins licked, Rhys."

Touché.

Beth pointed to a stall that she had a good view into. "That one. Try him."

But before Rhys took to horseback, there was something else that needed being done. Taking a length of rope from a hook, he walked to Lionel. The man had begun to moan and snarl in his skull-bruised sleep. Rhys wrapped the goblin tightly before dragging him to a spike in the blacksmithing area that he could be secured to.

Looking now at Lionel's wretched face—which reflected the quality of his soul in every measure—Rhys couldn't remember what had once possessed him to protect such a man. He patted him on the shoulder. "You're under arrest." Another moan. That would have to suffice for now.

When Rhys joined Beth outside, she was facing down the road that ran alongside the village. He turned his horse in the other direction, where the road stretched to the horizon. "This way," he said. "No wise person would drive a captive back through town."

"Are we counting Sol a wise person?"

Rhys sighed. Sol wasn't like Lionel. He'd once been a better man, a *smarter* man, but he'd never quite recovered from the sour lifestyle of prison. "He may be quiet, but he was never a simpleton."

Beth resettled herself, her skirts riding nearly to her knees while astride. "Well Rhys, we've a cart to catch up to. It seems time that you show me how to be a proper highwayman."

*   *   *

Beth's stomach twisted at the reality that her dear cousin, practically a sister, was out of sight. A victim to the swirling unknown.

She stole a glance at her riding partner. Eyes forward. Mouth firm. Stray hairs whipping at his cheek. A paragon of intent. Was this how Rhys had looked when riding toward her carriage three years ago?

The long, rolling strides of her horse brought with them the small thrills of times past. Memories of youth. Memories of Rhys. Memories of every time that she'd ever done something secret or bold.

Guilt reached out for her, to scold her for the fond feelings that suffused her furiously rushing blood in such a dire time. But it was just such feelings that were her armor against fear. *Guilt and fear—dash them both to hell.* Her horse surged into a faster run, as if it, too, felt freshly unburdened.

The road grew rougher. The leas opened up before them, bleeding indiscernibly into a nighttime sky that cloaked the stars in clouds. Allison was out here somewhere, in what suddenly seemed a very dark and large world. But Beth had been out there once too, and had found her way home.

"We'll find her."

Beth turned at Rhys' voice. He'd read her thoughts and now she had a glimpse into his. His eyes were shadowed, but she knew that he held her gaze there, before looking back to the road.

"Ho!" He brought his horse up, nearly sliding to a stop.

Beth pulled up ahead of him, her heart pounding. *Why stop? There isn't time to stop.* But she tried to trust him as he studied the dark road silently. Then she saw what he saw, the hint of a fork in the road.

She walked her horse up to his, to get a closer look at the split from the main road. An overgrown trail. Nothing but muddy ruts separated by the width of an axle—a dark mass of weeds and wildflowers flourishing between.

"I see it. Do you suppose—"

A gentle hand on her wrist stopped her speech. Rhys raised a finger to his lips. He craned his neck, lending an ear to the darkness.

Beth did the same, holding her breath to hear the air—the skitter of some vermin in the gravel, the resettling of her horse's weight on its hooves, a light whistle of wind, and—

There.

The distant jangle of a cart's wheels on uneven terrain.

The two of them flew off of the main road without any discussion. *We're coming, Allison.*

The clouds shifted to bless their mission with more moonlight. The creaking complaints of the old rig grew louder until they spotted its boxy rear. A canvas sheet in the back glowed in the gray night.

A bald head looked over a hunched shoulder, and the cart lurched to gain speed. Its back end began to dance like a devil on coals, unable to withstand the old road.

Beth pulled ahead until the bed of the cart was just beside her knee. Allison was under that sheet. She had to be.

"Beth, don't!" Rhys called out to her—the call of a man that now seemed to know her thoughts before she did. A man that probably knew she was going to jump anyway—

Beth fell against the canvas and was mostly met by the plank beneath it. But to her side, a squirming mass of bony elbows struck out at her. Like a kitten beneath a counterpane. *Allison.*

The rough ride rattled Beth's every bone as her fingers searched for a corner of the canvas. Whipping it aside, she was met with

Allison's saucer eyes. Beth tore a cloth from her cousin's mouth.

"Oh, Beth—" Allison's features crumpled as she rolled into Beth's arms.

Beth spotted Rhys over the lip of the cart. He was reaching out for Sol's collar. The men painted the night with curses that they flung at one another over the din of the wheels.

The planks beneath Beth suddenly bucked, and a groan turned into a *CRACK*—the cart's reckoning was at hand. The whole thing jerked from the road, and Beth hugged Allison to her chest, wrapping every limb around the tied girl.

Another fierce sound—and then an eternity spent in motion after everything else stopped hard . . .

Rhys stared into his old shipmate's gray eye.

Sol swatted at him and missed. "Off me! Ya cursed bastard—"

"It's over. Lionel is done!"

Sol's features went slack. For a fleeting moment, Rhys felt the harsh weave of Sol's collar, but his fingers never had a chance to close around it—

CRACK.

The cart bucked harshly and peeled away, out of control, off the road.

Beth.

Every moment seemed to happen on top of the last, and Rhys felt as though he were miles away when the cart struck a tree and tipped halfway into it, surely ejecting its contents, one and all. The ground felt as molasses as he rode to catch up, as his eyes searched the scene ahead for the spills of silk and voile that he prayed would still be rippling with movement and breath.

Sol be damned, wherever he'd landed.

Rhys frantically dismounted. The cart was empty. He looked in every direction, and there, beyond the tree, caught sight of it. Pink and white and yellow, hair both dark and blonde, tangled together. Beth was curled around her precious cousin like a seedpod.

As he knelt beside them, Allison's eyes flickered open. Rhys stretched a trembling hand toward Beth's shoulder. Would it rise and fall with her breath? He squeezed it, unsure. He couldn't sense anything past the miserable, pounding swell of his own pulse.

Allison's eyes flitted between his concerned gaze and Beth's sealed lashes.

"Beth?" she squeaked. She rocked in her cousin's arms, as though to rouse her, but her arms were still bound. Rhys freed her hands from their ties. The girl looked over her shoulder at him, and he knew her question would be unbearable, "Is she . . . ?"

Rhys had no response. He didn't know.

Allison held her cousin's face. "Beth?"

Rhys squeezed Beth's arm again, more tightly. The sliver of her old scar gleamed silver in the moonlight. The sight of it usually made him guilt-ridden and ill, but now it was a different sort of reminder—

You're too strong for this, Beth. Too legendary.

A cool wind whisked past them all. The early quakes of sobs began to work their way up Allison's body. When the first whimpers of those sobs broke into the air, they dragged Rhys into the same purgatory. The wound on his cheek burned as a salty bead slipped past it.

Rhys traced the scar at Beth's collarbone, moving upward to her neck. It still felt warm and vital, but Rhys knew his mind wanted—*needed*—things to be a certain way, and he couldn't tell if it was real. Couldn't tell if—

Her neck tensed beneath his fingers, and the faint rumble of a groan travelled up her delicate throat. Then Beth tugged her cousin into an even tighter embrace, were it possible.

Rhys' relief was so blunt a force that he nearly choked on his own gasp.

"Beth!" Allison's eyes squeezed out the hovering tears as they clutched at one another.

Beth's eye caught Rhys' for a moment, a look injected with so much meaning that it dizzied him.

The women began to touch one another's faces and hands frantically, checking that they were safe and intact as tears of joy began to spill from each of them. Rhys stood, feeling like an interloper yet unable to look away from their reunion.

"You came for me, Beth," cried Allison, through her copious tears of relief.

"Of course, sister."

"Did you hit your head? We aren't sisters."

"But we are," said Beth, certainty ringing through her voice. "We are. You are as near to me as any sister."

Rhys marveled at the moment. He felt his heart being pulled toward it—pulled toward Beth and her love. He was a ship on a forbidden sea, and her love was a maelstrom that would pull him to the depths. She was his center. And there was no escape.

He wanted her, and a life, and a family that felt like this.

Somehow, he tore himself away, leaving them to their glad reunion on the grass.

Rhys spotted another mass on the ground. Old Sol. His fate required no assessment beyond the first glance. This was the sort of family Rhys was accustomed to. Cold and wicked and deserving of such ends.

The tarpaulin that had concealed Allison in the cart was still crumpled nearby. Rhys dragged it over Sol.

"I'm sorry that our mutiny has ended here."

A hand slipped into the crook of his elbow.

"You aren't responsible for the choices he's made." Beth looked up at him from her place at his side. Her hair was tangled and littered with nature, just as he liked it. "He chose everything that led him here. It isn't your fault. And he wasn't yours to save."

Some part of him knew it, but the fates of the other men had been his only excuse when he'd turned to highway robbery. His excuse for stopping Beth's carriage that night, for haunting her—stripped of such excuses, what sort of blackguard was he?

With a warm palm against his sore cheek, all of his thoughts stilled at once.

"Everything happened as it had to."

And he believed her.

He faced her, his hands traveling up and down her arms and shoulders, checking.

"Are you hurt?"

"Yes. My ribs could not sufficiently cage a bird right now, but I'll be fine."

She said it with as little gravity as tossing forth an offer of afternoon tea. He knew it might risk a painfully deep breath against those aching ribs, but—

He lowered his lips to hers and she floated up to meet him. To *accept* him.

The pain was nothing. Nothing at all compared to how it felt be alive and in his arms. Nothing compared to knowing Allison was safe—safe and still very much herself.

"Well, I suppose I must write off this new caraco as a loss." Beth turned to see her dearest friend fruitlessly dusting her yellow frock. Allison looked up, too, and cocked her head fondly at their embrace. "You see, this is what I'd like someday. A man like this."

Beth put her face in her palm, as proud of Allison's boldness as she was wincing at it. Yet the man she leaned on began to tremble with laughter.

"If you secure a man like this," said Beth, "you'll have to make yourself more accustomed to the constant ruin of your wardrobe." Allison gazed at Rhys almost reverently, and it sent a spark of pride through Beth as she leaned into the man beside her.

Allison suddenly gasped. "You really *did* kill a wolf, then, didn't you?"

"She did," said Rhys.

"I didn't always believe it, but you came to my rescue and I'll never doubt another word you say for so long as I live." Allison caught a glimpse then of the substantial lump beneath the canvas. "My God! You didn't also—"

"No. She *did not*," said Rhys.

"Your abductor didn't fair as well in our accident, Allison." Beth stroked a hair from her cousin's face. "Did he hurt you at all?"

Allison shook her head, and her voice fell, weary. "May we go back now?"

Beth decided it best that they walk the horses back to town. She may have cast her reputation to the four winds, but perhaps some shred of Allison's good name could still be spared, provided they not ride into town astride, with Allison in one of their laps.

Allison walked lightly ahead, seemingly unbruised from the massive toss they'd experienced. The benefits of being a decade younger, perhaps. Beth bit her lip as another inhale pressed against her battered ribs.

Rhys walked ahead too, only occasionally throwing a look over his shoulder to pull Beth along with his eyes.

If any other man left any other lady behind him on the road like this, he might expect to find himself swatted by a fan. For Beth, it was perfect. He didn't fuss over her simply for the sake of her sex. They were instead like two children. Equals in fort building and footraces. Like she and Dyckson once were, before the realities of adulthood had intruded.

And reality would intrude here too, wouldn't it? After all, there was a dead man in the brush.

Rhys cut a tempting figure from behind. Beth wished to pull herself toward him, to join him at his side, yet the more she desired it, the more her footfalls seemed to drag. Why did he always feel so distant, even when right there?

He looked over his shoulder again. This time he stopped and waited for her.

"Are you certain you're well?" He extended a hand to her as she inched his way. She nodded and her loosened hair flopped in front of her face. He brushed it aside for her.

"Rhys?"

He waited. Eyes full of unbearable patience.

She recognized what she felt now, and it felt hardly any different from fear—

She loved him.

"I haven't told you yet." She swallowed and placed a hand on his arm.

"Told me what?"

That I love you. "That I'm leaving."

He tipped his head regretfully but without surprise. He cupped her cheek.

"I know," he said.

Had he not heard her? "For a long time, I think."

His hand slid from her face and he clucked to make the horse join him as he started walking again.

"I know."

"Did my father say something?"

"He did."

Beth followed quietly at his side, a riot of thoughts coursing through her mind. She plucked one such thought from the swarm. "You've risked your heart, then, by saying that you love me?"

He looked down into her eyes again. The faintest reflection of light was there.

"I know."

It was utterly mystifying. She stopped again.

Just be that rash girl running on the lawns of Ashecote and tupping in the greenhouses of Greenthorne. Be once again that girl that didn't have her soul on a leash or her heart in a cage. Just be—

"Then I wish to risk something too, even if—even if it hurts us both."

They were almost to town. It might be the last chance before chaos.

Rhys stepped close. The edges of his worn coat brushed against her.

"It doesn't seem fair," she started, "that your heart should be out in the cold air and mine should not join it when I feel very much the same as you." A smile began to twitch at Rhys' lip, and she'd have done anything to see it overtake him. "I love you, Rhys. I don't know what anything means beyond that, but I love you."

She'd imagined him kissing her then. Scooping her into him so suddenly and deeply that she would be turned into a part of him.

She imagined embarrassing Allison again, if such a delighted voyeur might ever truly be called embarrassed.

But he didn't.

He touched her face fondly, regretfully. She could swear that he mouthed the words *Thank you* in the low light.

Soon the dirt turned back into stone and the stables were ahead.

25

The stables were much more crowded than when they'd left them.

The women at Rhys' side were covered in dirt and grass. With a wince, he realized that Allison had a harmless trickle of blood down her cheek. The two looked more like frisky dairy maidens than gentlewomen.

The Weldon girl's parents were there and Lady Weldon would be full of words for them. But it was the presence of Beth's father that struck real pain into his heart. Because Desmarais hadn't been the threat at all. Lionel had. And Lionel was an extension of Rhys—an artifact of his past that he had once again brought, most unwelcomely, to the doorstep of the Clarkes.

Beth and Allison linked hands as they approached the center of the barn.

The three of them halted, leaving a narrow aisle between

themselves and the ranks of their morose welcome party. The space between them contained one groaning Lionel, laid on his side and, wisely, still bound.

Lady Weldon stepped forward to snatch Allison and drag her to the other side.

"Mother!"

Apart from the Weldons and Mr. Clarke, there were two unknown men that rivaled Rhys in height—a gruff fellow of middle age and a lanky lad, quite likely his own son.

Now Allison stood there too, a hostage to the other side. Her mother's eyes glowed brighter than the forge in the corner. "Well?!" she commanded.

Before Rhys could open his mouth to speak up, she stepped into the space between them and cracked an open palm across his face, right where the scorching tongs had nicked him. Beth gasped and wrapped her hands protectively around his arm. But as the sting settled on his cheek, he bowed his head to Lady Weldon. He deserved her ire.

But then she focused on a different target, one that Rhys could not so readily accept.

"Bethany Kathryn Clarke. After all of these years, I brought you and your father back into my family, thinking you a renewed woman. Now you would thank me for my charity by corrupting my only daughter?"

Rhys could not stay silent. "Beth *rescued* your only daughter from a scoundrel." Just then, Lionel groaned and Rhys amended, "Two scoundrels, actually."

The Weldon matron retreated to her side of the stables, but her poisonous looks did not relent.

One of the large strangers piped in. "Is this true?"

"Of course it isn't true," said Lady Weldon. "They have this fool's jest between them that she's some sort of hero who strikes down wolves and knocks out scoundrels, and God knows what else." She waved a crinkled kerchief at them dismissively, but her eyes fell on Beth, full of noxious pity.

At that, Lady Weldon excused herself to the back of the group, ostensibly to conceal her incoming tears.

The tall stranger who'd spoken up before stepped forward. He pointed at Lionel. "Did you do this?"

"Tie him up? Yes. Subdue him? No." Rhys looked down at Beth. "That was her doing."

"Trying to put a crime on a lady isn't a pretty look."

Before either of them could respond, Allison stirred to their defense, stepping into the space and nearly tripping over Lionel.

"These two just saved my life. If this cad on the floor and his dead henchman in the forest hadn't been stopped by them—"

"*Dead* henchman, eh?" The stranger's eyebrows raised, almost in amusement, as he turned back to them. "So there's been a murder too?"

Allison shrank.

Mr. Clarke put a hand to his head and uttered an "Oh, heaven help us."

Lord Weldon pulled his daughter back into line in the absence of his sobbing wife.

Rhys straightened. "Introductions are in order."

"Terrence Mills. Constable."

Rhys tightened his jaw. "Osbourne Booker. Bow Street Runner."

"Bow Street what? Horse thief, more like."

"We brought them back!" Beth's ridiculous interruption elicited a dry snort from Mr. Mills.

"The way I see it, I should arrest both you and this fellow on the floor until we get sorted."

Mr. Clarke stepped forward. "I wish to reiterate something I said before they returned—"

Mr. Mills put up a hand to shush him. "I know, I know, this man rescued your daughter once."

"Rescued—" spat a coarse voice. They all looked to the writhing creature on the floor. "Rescued?" Lionel began to shake, wracked with a chuckle. "This arse took 'er in the first place!"

A fine time for a toothless Lion to come to his senses.

Rhys caught the exchange of a tight look between Beth and her father. He took a deep breath. "If you'll let me explain, Mr. Mills."

"You can explain behind bars." He whistled over his shoulder to his boy. "Jacob, find something to tie Mr. Booker with."

"Please Mr. Mills, if you'll just wait." But Mr. Clarke's plea fell on deaf ears.

Rhys held himself steady as Mills' young man pulled rope from a hook and came toward him.

So this was where his choices got him. He'd almost escaped his mistakes, almost started a new life . . .

Beth's hand slid down his arm to knit her fingers tightly with his. He was too afraid to look at her. He had to feel her instead, as best he could.

Allison broke away from her father for another round with the constable. Her skirts, still seeming sunny in spite of their raggedness, whirled around her as she planted herself before him.

"You're not listening. Two men absconded with me, and my *friends*—one of them, a Bow Street Runner—came and found me. Where were you then?"

Mr. Mills set his jaw and looked over her head, nodding to

his boy to proceed. "I was asleep in bed. A place I'd soon return to, young lady."

Young Jacob politely asked that Rhys put his hands behind him. Rhys should have put a ball between Lion's eyes when he'd had the chance, but he hadn't. Now the Lion's roars might see him sent to the gallows.

"Please, just—" Beth's reassuring touch on his arm abandoned him then. She went forth to make her own pleas. There was no touch now but for the rough drag of sisal against his wrists.

Such cold, avoidant eyes. Beth knew that her pleas might fall wasted on a man such as Mr. Mills, but she had to try.

"This man on the ground, he can't be trusted. He wears a dead man's clothes and pretends to be someone he's not. He's a dangerous, ruthless man, who tried to kill me not an hour ago—"

"He stalked me on the road earlier today," added Allison. "Pretending at being some gentleman."

Beth's head snapped up. Painful realizations unfolded in the gaze she shared with Allison. "He's stalked us both, for some time."

She returned her eyes to the constable who was, predictably, unmoved. He stood still as a statue while his boy tied Rhys' hands.

Beth felt a heavy hand on her shoulder. Her father's. "Mr. Mills, surely it's not necessary to tie him. He'll go as a gentleman and we'll all happily follow to the jailhouse."

"'Tis late and the jail is brimming with drunkards from the fair." The man, who suddenly seemed more weary than evil, pinched the bridge of his nose. "It'll all have to wait 'til tomorrow."

Fruitless.

Papa patted her shoulder, defeat in his eyes.

"And what of the dead man in the woods?" asked Beth.

Lionel writhed again and moaned out Sol's name.

"He can wait too. I'll send someone out before the critters get to him."

Lazy brute.

Beth dared to look at Rhys even as she sensed that he did not want to be seen.

It was unbelievable to see him standing there, being bound. So stoic. Perhaps they were not so invincible a pair after all. Everything that had just begun to feel surmountable . . . was not. The rope was tightened on his wrists with finality, and Jacob led him to Mr. Mills.

It was too much. "Rhys has done *nothing* wrong!"

"Who's Rhys?" asked Mr. Mills.

Beth set her teeth, flushing at her mistake, but not giving in. "It is his middle name, and beside the point. This man has done a great service tonight, as he did years ago—"

"When he saved my daughter's life," said Mr. Clarke.

"As he helped to save me tonight," added Allison.

The voices began to overlap in their pleas to the harried constable of Bartswell. Even the horses began to nicker, agitated by the swell of voices.

whhhhhh-CRACK

Everyone was immediately silenced. Looking around. Scouring for danger. Had a shot gone off?

But Beth saw him first.

Harry.

Her chest inhaled a bit of hope.

He stood in the broad carriage doorway. Bullwhip in hand. With the other hand, he grasped a boy's collar. Poor Harry looked as nervous as any of them as he gingerly replaced the whip on a hook by the doorway and cleared his throat.

"I believe I might elucidate a few things."

Rhys spoke up then. "Mr. Mills, allow me to introduce my deputy, Mr. Harry Plymouth."

Harry nudged the boy forward. "This lad—Paul, did you say?" The sulky adolescent nodded. "Paul was keeping the stables when that man on the floor there—whose name happens to be Lionel Dilswitch—paid him out of his duties for the night. But Paul stayed nearby, outside." Harry looked to Rhys, then to Beth. "And he heard a *lot* in the last hour."

Paul crossed his hands politely and looked down. "He gave my l'il brother a note and had him run off with it. Don't know where he is now."

"I believe your brother is somewhere safe." Rhys' voice was soft. To hear him gentle his voice to reassure another when he himself was in such straits—it unwound her.

Mr. Mills approached Harry and the boy. "Paul. The Evans' boy, right? I know you. Tell us what you heard."

And the boy did.

The stable boy's testimony corroborated what everyone had been saying. Of course, Lionel had things to say about it, but flapped his maw so much that Mr. Mills had his son shove a ball of linen in the Lion's mouth to cease his grousing.

By the end of Paul's recounting, Mills was swaying in his boots, half-asleep. Harry wisely seized on his impairment. "Mr. Mills, if you would just release my associate, we can all walk to the inn where Mr. Crofty, an administrator from the Home Office, is staying. He can further attest to Mr. Booker's purpose here."

The constable was nodding mutely, as though he might accept anything that was said to him in that late hour. But then he put a rough hand up in protest and shook his head as violently as a dog might shake off water. "No." He pinched his nose again. "No. It can wait 'til morning."

Beth looked past the carriage doors. The sky was grayer. The town quieter. There was a dewy chill in the air and Beth knelt by her tired father who had set himself on an upturned pail. It already *was* morning.

But Beth's exhausted heart lifted when Mills directed Jacob to untie Rhys. Mr. Mills followed, wearily dragging his feet before drawing up to his full height in front of Rhys. "If you're not at that inn later with this Mr. Crofty, I'll see that every thief-taker in the land has your head on their docket."

Then Mills toed the squirming Lionel. "Jacob, help me with this one." And the two men took Lionel out of sight and, Beth hoped, out of their lives.

Her half-lidded eyes met Rhys' gaze. They both flinched to move toward one another, when Harry stepped between them to help her up.

"Dear Harry. I've wondered about you." Beth placed a fond hand on his arm, looking him over. Three years had certainly made a difference in the breadth of his shoulders.

"I've been quite well in Rhys' employ, Miss Clarke."

"Why didn't you tell me he was with you?" she asked Rhys.

"I needed him as an extra set of eyes. One that kept more to the shadows, while we investigated the possibility of Desmarais."

"Well, that arrangement certainly turned out to be useful tonight," said Beth.

Mr. Clarke planted his cane and stood at the sound of Desmarais' name. "And it's true that Desmarais is dead all this time?"

"*Nearly* all this time," she said.

From Beth's side came the delicate clearing of a throat. "Cousin, you've not introduced me."

Beth turned to face Allison, but all she saw was a girl caught up in a flagrant assessment of Harry's fine features. Beth smiled. Allison—whom she'd openly encouraged to find trouble—was blazing straight ahead in that pursuit.

Beth gestured toward Harry. "Harry—"

He leaned in. "*Mr. Plymouth*, will do."

Beth cleared her throat to restart. "Mr. Plymouth, may I introduce to you my dear cousin and friend, Lady Allison Weldon." He bowed overly-deeply and lit up in that positively Harry way.

"A pleasure, Lady Allison. I'm very heartened to see you safe and sound."

Allison's guileless smile was wide enough to span the Thames. "Mr. Plymouth, the pleasure is mine. If you like, I can share with you all of the details of the ordeal?"

Harry raked a hand through his tawny hair. "Well, the hour is late and the stable lad already—"

"Wouldn't you *like* to hear about it?" Her question was rephrased with the cadence of a command.

"Yes. Yes, I would." He proffered his arm, and the two wandered to the stables' opposite end to chat.

Poor man. Doesn't stand a chance.

At their departure, Beth felt another figure arrive at her side, and she leaned into him instinctively. Rhys stretched a long arm around her shoulder as she lifted his hand to inspect it. His wrist was still wrapped with the pink irritations of the ropes he'd just been freed from. *If he'd been taken away from her tonight—*

Beth halted the thought before it went too far and comforted herself by looking up at him.

"See!" A shrill voice cut through Beth's thoughts. Lady Weldon swept up in front of them. "Mystery swarms around these two like bees. Not all of this scandal can be buried by morning, but something has to be done about these two."

Lady Weldon was so preoccupied with them, it seemed, that she was altogether ignorant of her daughter flirting with another handsome lawman from London.

"Mr. Clarke," Lady Weldon pouted as she spun to catch Beth's poor father off guard. "If you don't rein this in, well—I'm not sure if I can weather another scandal at your side."

"You didn't *weather* the first one, Auntie Lu, you *left*." Beth had certainly taken chances by flinging a moniker that she hadn't used for her aunt since childhood.

"I came *back*." Lady Weldon hesitated. "Eventually."

Papa looked ready to topple from exhaustion. "What do you propose they do?"

Lady Weldon sputtered out a dramatic, exasperated sound, before delivering a sharply raised eyebrow to Beth and Rhys.

"Marry." When no one jumped on Mrs. Weldon's statement with their agreement, she continued. "Have you ever seen two unwed people touch each other so much in polite society in your lives?"

Beth looked around at *polite society*. Lord Weldon leaning against a post, snoring. An earl's daughter flirting shamelessly with a once-footpad. Mr. Clarke with his ever-wild tufts of white hair. The path in the hay where a filthy madman had been dragged away. The aftermath of a rowdy town fair and an abduction.

She went on. "Have you ever even seen *wed* people touch one another so much?"

"I've not." *Ahh, so Lord Weldon was not asleep.* He joined his wife.

"You all exhaust me," she said, before leaning in to tower over Beth. "And you will not be seeing my daughter until we understand the repercussions of this eve."

"To my understanding, such repercussions rely a great deal on what story the highest-ranking people here will tell. The story *you* will tell."

Beth's aunt straightened, but she had no retort. With a sleepy husband in tow, she went off to collect her daughter.

Mr. Clarke kissed Beth softly on the cheek and nodded to Rhys. There was a lot in that nod—a whole male communication there that she could only vaguely sense. And then her father walked away too.

"You know," Rhys took Beth's hand. "I always imagined that even if all else between us were to be sorted, we'd never have the blessing to marry. Never had I imagined it would be outright demanded."

"Oh sir, clearly you are unacquainted with the absurdity of the ton."

"So . . ."

"Yes?"

His pause struck her in the chest like a little pebble.

He took her hand. "Are the other things still there? Does the barrier to spending my days with you still contain so many bricks?"

She looked down at his thumb where it rubbed along the back of her hand as he held it. Could she pull her hand away even if she tried? Or had the Fates already woven them together?

She thought back to Emily's words: *'Haps your heart and your head can both have what they want.*

One stolen glance into his eyes felt like a journey into the future. There she saw love and loyalty, freedom and laughter. There was anxiety there too, as he hung on this moment.

Beth shook her head. "No, Rhys. I am certain the wall has fallen."

He inhaled through a smile that looked ready to split his face in two. She knew that he was going to kiss her, but she put a hand to his chest and whispered to him as he bent over her.

"Come to the Continent with me."

He nodded against her nose. He might have assented to anything in that moment, so happy he seemed, but she knew that he would *want* to go. For all her fears that he might spoil her autonomy, she felt her heart falling into a new realization—that he was a party to her independence. In him, she exercised her freedom to love.

She pulled away from his lips to make certain that he knew it.

"I love you, Rhys. The trust I have in you—it is a vivid and frightening thing."

Rhys wished there were a way to taste a dream in the air because he feared he might be in one. Yet the longer the moment stretched on, the more convincingly real it became.

It stretched on through their walk from the stables. It stretched on as they held hands, white-knuckled, waiting for the hired hack that would temporarily part them. It stretched on in their dramatically long goodbye at the inn.

Rhys passed Beth up into the conveyance in a daze. A slap on his shoulder finally drew his attention elsewhere from the woman who would be his forever—

"Well, she has flattened her reputation, and I've no doubt that it pleases her," said Mr. Clarke.

Rhys tried to smother his pleasure at that, particularly because the man before him had grown suddenly sullen. "After your tour together, will you be taking her away from me to London?"

"Mr. Clarke, I will not dare take her so far if she does not wish it."

The old man nodded. Rhys took his cane and helped him up into the hack that would see them the short distance back to the Weldons' manse.

No. I won't take her far.

Epilogue

Every tree was increasingly familiar. Every bird sang a song of the past. Beth was no fool. She knew precisely where they were riding to, and her heart kicked up a beat every minute they drew nearer.

Husband. *That word.* She was still rolling it on her tongue, getting used to it. Never had she seen *that* in her future. Rhys rode alongside her, occasionally pulling his horse ahead as though boyish excitement were getting the better of him.

She liked how the back of his coat splayed out on the horse's backside. Liked how Rhys looked in the sunshine.

They were staying at an inn on their way to set sail for the Continent. An inn of his choosing, a *strategic* choice, no doubt, for a day trip insisted upon just as strategically.

Toying with him, she'd feigned drowsiness in the bed that morning.

"I don't feel like riding." She *always* felt like riding.

"You rode just fine last night," he winked.

Wicked man. Then he pushed his face into her naked side, using his days-unshaven chin to make her squirm. "Perhaps we should do some more indoor riding if you're not feeling fond of the out-of-doors today."

"I find that agreeable." She awed at his tossed hair in the morning. How the waves of deep brown spilled into his eyes. Having him in a bed, a bed with sheets, no less! How novel for them. Lovely as he must have found her suggestion, it didn't satisfy him to play into her bluff. He sat on his heels seriously and pulled the cover from her.

"No, we must ride. You need air."

She laughed, knowing full well what her lack of cooperation was doing to him. To his surprise.

And so they rode.

And she thought she would *pretend* to be surprised.

Then she laid eyes on it, and no performance was required.

The folly.

Their folly.

Just as she'd expected, yet . . . not.

It rose up before her, somehow grand and quaint, at once. But something had changed. The menace and mystery it once was cloaked with had changed. The place seemed somehow recast, and it wasn't simply for a lack of fog.

She rode forward to investigate. Lumber dotted the yard, which had otherwise been landscaped in a simple fashion. Exploring the side of the house, her jaw went slack.

"It's . . . intact?"

She threw the look of astonishment over her shoulder. Then looked back to the once-missing wall of the downstairs.

"It's yours. If you wish to return to it after our tour."

"But your job is in London."

He seemed unbothered. "I am in discussions for a new position. We won't be able to be here the whole year, but trust me that it will work out."

She scrambled from her saddle and ran for him as he dropped much more elegantly from his own seat. She collided with him fully, and a puff of air escaped them both before he laughed and buried his pine-smelling face in her hair.

She examined the yard again from his embrace. The lumber, the plantings . . .

"Rhys, how long have you been working at this?"

"Three years. Any time I could escape London."

Three years.

The entire—

Beth looked up at him, knowing that her eyes glistened, ready to spill over. She didn't care.

"Rhys," she whispered.

"Yes, love?"

"Might we ascend those stairs again, right now, and be happier this time? Like we imagined."

He pushed a hair from her eye, one that he'd just displaced.

"We can."

He placed her hand in his arm and together they walked to the door—intact and grand but still surrounded with lush ivy. Nothing could steal the magic from such a place.

Her heart lifted, ready to leap through the doors as they opened. The floors were still water-stained but the ruined furniture gone. And there at the base of the staircase was someone to greet them home . . .

The marble maenad, holding their long-kept secrets and spilling her wine in honor of their union.

Acknowledgments

Almost as soon as I committed to writing this book, my mom was there at my side (as much as one can be from 500 miles away). Thank you for all of our little plotting conferences, for being my first reader, and most of all, for coming up with the perfect name for this book!

I was fortunate to grow up with another writer in the family—my dad. His poetry helped instill a love of writing in me from my earliest memory. Thanks for all of your inspiration and encouragement.

It's atypical of me to conclude that anything in life is a sign, but meeting my amazing critique group sure felt like one and I don't know if I could have done this without them. Thank you Genevieve Kersten, Brianne Gillen, Amanda Pereira, and Jillian Graves for all of the ways that you helped shape these pages. And thank you to The Ripped Bodice for bringing us all together.

Julie Ganis, I already love talking about ice skating with you, but then I find out you love romance? It's almost too much. Thank you endlessly for your friendship and all of your advice.

Thank you, Lauren Smith, for your generosity with publishing pointers. I will gladly indulge in shoptalk anytime.

Romayne Putna, our "research" day may have devolved mostly into wine-drinking and laughter, but it relieved so much anxiety. Thanks.

To my editor, Melanie Cossey, thank you for all of your hard work and great communication.

Lastly, I was already aware that I have some amazing friends, but this summer just made it really sink in how warm, unique and supportive you all are. I'm so fortunate to have you as my chosen family. Thank you.

Bio

Daria Vernon grew up in the Southwest in houses brimming with antiques. Playing dress-up in old clothes, reading old books . . . is it any wonder she developed a passion for the historical?

Graduating into a recession and a writer's strike with a screenwriting degree didn't get her too far, but it led to the slew of odd jobs that would fuel her imagination for a lifetime, and for that she is grateful.

She writes from her well-nested (but woefully cat-less) introvert's cocoon, emerging mostly to twirl around at the local ice rink.

www.dariavernon.com
daria.vernon.romance
AuthorDariaV

For updates and excerpts from the next book in

The Rewards of Ruin series,

The Rogue's Last Letter

go to:

www.DariaVernon.com

Thanks for reading!

—Daria

www.ingramcontent.com/pod-product-compliance
Lightning Source LLC
Chambersburg PA
CBHW050902130726
47900CB00015B/1894